Night Navigation

A *New York Times Book Review* Editors' Choice

•

Winner of the 2009 National Alliance on Mental
Illness of New York State Media Award

PRAISE FOR

Night Navigation

"A needle-sharp look into the life of a mentally ill drug addict
... Howard's writing showcases the beauty that exists in the
mundane, if we only open our eyes to see it." — Shelf Life

"Pitch-perfect . . . This is a book that will leave the reader re-
flecting on the life and death struggle of one family, only one
among many." — CurledUp.com

"Fine writing." — *Morning News*

"What makes this novel shine is the writer's seemingly effortless
ability to bring to the page living, breathing characters, each
deeply flawed but trying . . . The story unfolds easily, though it
is anything but an easy story. Yet in the abundance of evident
pathology there is never a cheap shot: There's no attempt at
tear-jerking, no poor-me-look-what-I've-been-through attitude
underlying Howard's spare prose, which makes the telling all
the more powerful." — *Chronogram*

"A powerful and singular work." — WSKG.org

"Howard is a graceful, spare, and fluid writer, and her somber
and bleak novel has the power to lift and inspire."
— *Publishers Weekly*

Night Navigation

Ginnah Howard

Mariner Books
Houghton Mifflin Harcourt
BOSTON · NEW YORK

First Mariner Books edition 2010
Copyright © 2009 by Ginnah Howard
ALL RIGHTS RESERVED

www.hmhbooks.com

Library of Congress Cataloging-in-Publication Data
Howard, Ginnah.
Night navigation / Ginnah Howard. — 1st ed.
p. cm.
relationship between a mother and her 37-year-old
heroin-addicted son as they try to find their way after
the suicide of two family members.
ISBN 978-0-15-101432-3
1. Mothers and sons — Fiction. 2. Drug addiction — Fiction.
3. Suicide victims — Family relationships — Fiction. I. Title.
PS3608.O922N54 2009   813'.63 — dc22   2008029347
ISBN 978-0-547-33597-1 (pbk.)

Printed in the United States of America

Book design by Robert Overholtzer

DOM 10 9 8 7 6 5 4 3 2 1

Part I

MARCH

That's the way the dope chase goes. Hardly any time between good and bad.

— GEORGE VELTRI, *Nice Boy*

The mother sang a lullaby. She made it up, a song of comfort, mentioning all the child's favorite toys.

—ANNE MICHAELS, *Fugitive Pieces*

1 : Home

THE HOUSE IS COLD. He doesn't look at her, just sits hunched at the kitchen table, with the hood of his sweatshirt up: under cover. Her son. He is even thinner than when she left.

The stink of cigarettes. Something rotting in the dark of a cupboard, and the sink is right to the top with dirty dishes, hardened strings of spaghetti, grease congealed in a pan. A still life. She could paint it on a wall of canvas: moldy glasses big as barrels, their funhouse faces wavering beyond. Welcome Home.

The wood box is empty. She knows, without even going in there, what the bottom of the tub looks like. One whole end of the pole barn will be stacked high with trash, a month's worth of garbage, leaking random pools on the floor. And all of it is pretty much how she thought it would be given what he was up to when she left.

"I'm too sick to do anything," he says. His hands pull at the sides of his hood.

"I can see that." Close the shutters. Goodbye.

"Luke took off running with the Bensons' dogs just before you came up the road."

When Luke didn't come rushing to greet her, she'd hoped it was only this. How she's missed that dog.

"Some woman from your painters' group called. It's on the machine."

He finally looks her way. "If you can drive me up to Carla's to get enough to where I can function for the next few days, I'll be able to make the calls to line up a bed at a detox. I'll get some wood in, clean up around here. Make me almost normal."

Through the window she watches the plastic tarp smack the uprights, most of the last few cords exposed: a lot of the logs will be wet. "All right," she says.

If you agree not to contaminate this space, she had told him — two years ago — you may stay until you become more stable. This, after she said he could not come home when he called desperate from Oregon. After she had refused to send him bus fare. After she had changed her phone number to unlisted. A week later she'd found him crashed in his drum-room down in the barn, the heat turned to eighty. A cigarette burn as big as a nickel between his fingers where he had passed out without even feeling it there.

The path from the house to the wood is a slick of ice. It's so March she almost laughs. Everything gray. Dank. Sleet finds its way down the back of her neck as she shifts the wood around, looking for a few small, semi-dry splits to start a fire. Hard to believe that only forty-eight hours ago she was kayaking on the Gulf toward a small island, ahead of her an egret, still, waiting: a shock of white in all that green. That's what she'd like to put on the canvas: the shock of white on green. Or the light and dark of flesh. The life drawing group will be getting together again in Marna's studio now that the hard cold is past.

She hears barking, scans the hillside toward the Bensons' for a dash of brown. Need to deal with the Bensons' dogs on the loose. It's the only time Luke leaves their land. Soon the Bensons' hill will disappear. Once the leaves are on, no one would know anyone lives over here. Only another six weeks or so. The buds are already making their move.

The stove is so full of ashes, they spill out as she opens the door. Above her in the loft she can hear Mark on the phone, putting together some arrangement that will yield him some of Carla's morphine, what he needs to bring him to "almost normal."

She taps the stovepipe to hear how much buildup. Chunks of

creosote crunch around the edges of the clean-out door when she starts to ease that open. Probably a lot of low smoky fires all of February. The stove was always Aaron's job, something he took on when he was in sixth grade, the winter they moved into the stone house, the year after their father . . . after Lee's death.

There's no newspaper. She needs something to get the fire going. She hates to risk the refrigerator. Any Buddha-calm she's got left, or denial, may drop away. She reaches in, without really looking, and grabs what she knows will be a mostly empty, sour carton of milk. She rinses out the stink, shakes it good and crushes it under her heel. That, with a couple of ripped cereal boxes, has a fifty-fifty chance if the right amount of air goes between the splits.

She hears Mark say he'll get the whole two hundred he owes to Smithy when his money comes. Smithy, Carla's *boy*friend. Smithy's got to be at least fifty, the same age as Carla. Ten years or so younger than she is. Drug accounting is complicated: food stamps, benzoid-meds, transport to buy, homegrown, miscellaneous. What equals what is open to interpretation. Anyway Mark may be gone by the time his disability check gets deposited. Tucked away in detox.

Do not grasp the detox plan. It may happen; it may not.

No kitchen matches. The book matches jar is empty as well. These will all have been used to cook up in a flare and now dozens of them will be out in the March muck, tossed from the loft window, still aflame, she supposes. Though it's always painful to come upon these burnt offerings, she appreciates their honesty: This is what I'm doing — this week. She's never actually seen Mark, any of them, in the act. Her first hypodermic encounters — something banging in the dryer, something dropping from a pocket in a stack of clothes getting bagged to go to the Salvation Army during one of Mark's cross-country-bus times — produced a case of the shakes, left her breathless. Now when she stumbles on something, a blackened spoon behind a paint can in the barn, it may make her cry, but it's no longer as if someone kicked her in the chest. She reaches back into the cupboard behind the flour. Kitchen matches, cached for just such occasions.

But he's been straight with her. Mostly. Her being his rep-payee for his disability money is critical. Gas to drive him to Mental Health when he's going to Mental Health, when he's taking his meds — his license suspended two years ago for not paying a speeding ticket. Food, heat, phone, DirecTV NBA pass, socks. Whatever it costs for him to be here comes right off the top. And he never tries to con any of that. What's left is his. Usually about two hundred dollars. And it's all gone in a couple of days. Running out of cigarettes caused hassles for the first couple of months. Him, needy and wanting an advance for just one more pack. The nine-mile trips to the Quickway in Stanton. The looming possibility that if he didn't get a Camel, she'd end up having to drive him to Crisis on a night when freezing rain would increase her anxiety by times ten. She started buying six cans of tobacco, plus rolling papers, right out of his grocery fund. When his cigarette money is blown, he has the wherewithal to make his own. Which he hates doing. Please, may she never hear another whine for nicotine in any of her future lives.

She tilts the top log at a good angle and opens the front vents all the way. She loves this big old stove, but it's a bitch to start.

"Definitely. If I end up getting a bed somewhere, then I'll wire the money."

There are long pauses. She knows Carla is giving him full scenes of the latest: He said this, then I said that. Her arms doing flamenco accompaniment, her eyes . . . Her eyes. Back when she and Carla were marijuana-smokers together, back when she was Carla's friend. There in Carla's kitchen, fascinated by it all. The motorcycles parked in the yard, the stories of Harley Rendezvous. The family album of Pagan arrests. Way back. Twelve, thirteen years ago. Five years before Aaron's death. Back before Carla's surgery, before Carla got into pain medication. Before Carla's son Rudy, before Mark, became junkies.

This fire's not going to work. She rummages around in the bottom of the kindling box for shreds of bark and pushes them under the top log to rest on the milk carton.

"Yeah, I called Rudy up and threatened to tell. He owed me fifty for the food stamps. I wanted my money." Mark doesn't lower his voice. She's on the truth-side of the operation.

Drug dramas. And manic-depression. Hard to know which roller coaster you're riding. In the two years Mark's been back from Portland, off and on crashing with her, she's never consciously tracked the sequence of events, but each month unfolds almost exactly like the last: everybody's got money so there's a frenzy — cars in and out down at the barn, the lights burning late, the rumble of Mark's drums, the throb of guitars; the money's gone and everybody's starting to get sick; despair and isolation; somebody hocks something, another flurry; treading dark water until the beginning of the next month when everybody's got money . . . All of it punctuated by variations of fall-out: car wrecks and arrests — not Mark, he never goes to that edge, thank the gods, or he's just lucky. And, yes, the occasional plunge toward sanity: the Navy, a halfway house in Arizona.

She's a reluctant witness. She turns off the ringers, turns down the answering machine. Closes as many doors between her and it as she can. How many years, how many years has Mark been her main concern? And every time she comes to that question, she always has to add it up again. Since she and Lee separated the first time, when Aaron was two and Mark was four? Since Mark was fourteen, right after Lee's death? In utero? At least twenty years that any call in the night registers ten on her adrenaline Richter. When things heat up beyond her tolerance, she plans flight: a one-room apartment with no return address. She wakes in the night, a rock of anxiety jammed under her sternum, and she starts mind-listing her options: he goes, she goes and all the permutations of that. Or, in what she thinks of as Tarbaby Time, say when he's got another knot of infection swelling his arm that's red-lining its way toward his heart and she's driving him to Emergency again, she wishes he'd just go ahead and kill himself and put them all out of their misery.

But she knows he's getting somewhere. A lot of the time she's sure this is the best place for him to be. His father's, his brother's ashes buried up on their hill. They're all here together: working on it.

"For sure. If I go, it'll be at the Great American before noon . . . Yeah, she's going to bring me up in about fifteen minutes."

She is preferable to *Mom* when you're thirty-seven.

His long legs appear, make their way down the loft-ladder.

"Approaching Wellsville," he says.

"What?"

"It's all set. I could take your car."

"I'll drive you." Up the dirt road to Carla's. But she cannot, she will not, out on winter highways drive him anywhere else.

She touches the match to the waxy edges of the raisin bran wrap and closes the stove. Within seconds, there's that reassuring roar.

2 : Carpet

He PUSHES THE ENVELOPE with the remaining tablets under the microwave. Welcome to Wellsville. Got enough to extend the visit until tomorrow night. Maybe.

Get the fuck out of here. Detox. Rehab. Some halfway house on another planet. A different sun. Jesus Christ, thirty-seven years old. The. Fuck. Out. Of. Here.

Luke leans into him.

"Right, Luke, for the next twenty-four, we've got to focus. You know how hard that is: One thing at a time, right, buddy?"

Detox. Somewhere, somewhere, somewhere, there's a bitty piece of paper with the name of the detox, the number. A methadone detox. More than the Tylenol and TLC around here. Thirty, twenty, ten milligrams of methadone, touch down easy, taxi to the gate in three days.

Luke follows him up the first four steps toward the loft. "Better not come any further. No way I can carry your hundred-pound ass down."

He actually had to do that once when Luke made it up all the way. What they'd assumed impossible given the width of the tread, the angle of the ladder. First thing he knew: Luke, licking him in the ear. He'd been sick, sick as a dog, up there in the dark for god knows how many days and Luke makes a house call.

The name of the hospital? Begins with a *B*. Begins with a *C*. North. Way north. Up near the Canadian border. Six, seven hours from here. Pass by Syracuse. Begins with a *B*. He rummages through the piles under his weight bench. He goes through some pockets. He could call Carla. She had helped navigate the time he took Rudy there. That time he'd made dozens of phone calls, spent half a morning on the web, locating a methadone detox for Rudy. Amazing. That trip probably they were all wasted. They were all wasted. No, he's not calling Carla. He's made his last call to that house. Rudy's ass is in jail. Good.

Rozmer won't know. These trips during amnesia-time. His connection to his NA sponsor so off, off, on, off again these past four years, hard to believe Rozmer is still saying, You can count on me, man, to get you there. His mom would be able to locate the name and the number: she's a machine of cope and find. He's given her plenty of practice. Begins with a *C*. He could call her at Richard's. He could wait for her to come back later tonight. Thirty-seven years old and he can't find the fucking name of the hospital. Time. Time. Wellsville time's ticking. He drums it on his leg: tickatime, tickatime, timatick, tick.

He pulls the high stool over and sits under Aaron's world map, slanting up the low slope of the loft, the one thing he salvaged from Aaron's cabin. The one time he could bear to go in. After. He loosens a couple of the pushpins and flattens the center-sag, smoothes the world all the way to the edge. It starts with a *B*, north beyond Syracuse. Aaron would have known right off.

Stay with me, Mark. Wood is safe. Stone is dangerous.

He can't go there. Can't go there, Aar. Won't make it the fuck out of here if he does.

What's this? Two circles not far from the Canadian border. Brookfield and Camden. A line leading out to the blank blue of the Atlantic, from which dangles 3155647222. He does not remember doing any of this, but he knows it's the number.

He stretches out on the bed. Lights a *real* cigarette, a gift from his mom. Finds the phone card she has fronted him until his next money comes — a phone card necessary to dial long distance, a block having been placed on their phone in a supreme-cope moment by his mom when he had been on such a long manic-jag he'd run up a bill that, added to his pay-per-view charges, soon blocked as well, scarfed up one whole month's SSD. Survivor's benefits. He laughs. He begins dialing the numbers, certainly a test in itself. He knows all he has to do to get admitted to Crisis is to say he's suicidal. He knows to get admitted to detox all he has to do is tell the truth.

Yes, he's got Medicare *and* Medicaid. He last used thirty minutes ago. Morphine. No, he prefers not to mention his pharmaceutical source. He's just got enough to keep him functional until maybe tomorrow evening. His drug of choice is heroin. About two bags a day for as long as he's got money. Yes, he uses cocaine, too. Uses Xanax to come down. No, he does not smoke crack. No, he does not do meth crystals. He's been using since he was maybe thirteen: LSD, marijuana. Lots of LSD. Heroin, off and on since he was maybe in his late twenties. Alcohol? Only enough to quiet things down. He's dual diagnosis. Bipolar disorder. Onset probably about thirteen, his original psychiatrist thought. Just after his father's death. Just after his father killed himself. Though all was not well long before that, he's sure. His present meds, which he's been mostly noncompliant with for a while: one Zyprexa five milligrams before bed, two Neurontin three hundred milligrams two times a day, one Celexa fifty milligrams. They switch him to Gregorian chants. Then an all-business woman back in his ear. He's *on* the waiting list. Call at seven tomorrow morning, see if they've got a bed.

Sounds of violent shaking below. He looks down over the loft railing. Luke is at the far end of the living room, his mouth locked in a death grip on one of the pillows. Since he moved his drum set up from the barn during his mother's month away, that corner is Luke's favorite barricade. "Luke. Drop it. Or you're going to be in big trouble with your moms."

For a second he scans the living room through his mother's eyes. Her careful pencil drawings of hands mounted at eye level. The bedlam below. "Luke! We've got to begin where we are."

Luke sinks into a get-ready position. I want attention and I want it now. "Look, buddy, I'm busy. Time's ticking." Luke cocks his head to the side.

Rozmer. He gets Rozmer's machine: " 'Every moment and place says, Put this design in your carpet.' "

"It's me. Mark. I'm waiting for a detox bed in . . . up around Brookfield . . . Camden. I'll give you a call a little after seven to-morrow morning if I don't get hold of you later tonight. I'm hop-ing it's still on for you to take me. Thanks."

Rozmer always has on his machine some wild-ass thought for the day that half the time makes no sense to him whatsoever. Rozmer, half the time, makes no sense to him whatsoever. Is that me, Rozmer, or you? You, man, it's you. About his sponsees, Rozmer always says, Send the crazies to me. No shit, he says this. Rozmer's just what he needs. Someone who's a tad de-rockered himself. Rozmer's been clean for twenty-three years. A speed freak. No rehab for Rozmer. Just after he gets out of the Marines, one day, Rozmer's sitting at some bar on Houston Street, bar-tender shuts him down. That's it, Rozmer says, I'm done. Never took another hit of anything.

Wood. Nasty stuff coming out of the sky. The wood is wet. His negligence. Againgingin. Mostly only big logs left. Whoever sold her wood last year, one split was it, when two were required. Nothing to say, of course, he couldn't have given the go-devil a go himself. Ahh, but the junkie's busy elsewhere. Busybusybuzzzz. Luke races back and forth between the wheels and the door. "Watch it, buddy. You make me upend this load, your ass is grass."

He is able to bounce the barrow into the house over the low sill, jockey it right up to the stove, fill one of the wood boxes to the top. Three more loads should do it.

Dishes. He may have been high, he may have been just about comatose, but he did remember almost always to put enough water in each dirty pot, glass, and bowl to keep it from being hopeless. He brings all the dirty shit down from the loft and washes that too. Plus bags and bags of trash. He slides his fingers beneath the microwave again. Ten pills. His getaway depends on these. He should have conned more.

Laundry. Luke joins him and begins rooting around in the chaos. His choice of plunder: underwear. "Luke, come back here with that."

A dog? No, she said. He'd be the main caretaker. Up early with a puppy every morning? He promised. That's why she finally gave in. A puppy was to be the instrument of getting his ass out of bed before noon. Behavior modification. Of course that plan had circled the drain of all similar rescues. Her, out there in the dark on January mornings, freezing, saying, Pee, Luke. Her, pissed. *But.* Luke. He cracked them up. He cracked them open. Luke, their buoy out on the black sea.

A couple of big comforters. Sheets. Stinking from the night-sweats. Every towel. Just about everything he owns, swelling in piles almost level with the dryer. He grabs the top layer and shoves it in the machine. It all goes in together: dark, light, towels, sweaters. But doesn't it get a little gray, she sometimes asks. Yes, but he's into gloom. Glooooooom. Ahhh, the clothes he's lost. It's always get out of town before sunset, so he boards the Greyhound unencumbered: his army jacket in Austin, his slit-drum in San Francisco, his mountain bike in Key West, his four-track in Portland. Owhereowhereo underwearo. Approaching worn-out-your-welcome, it all gets jettisoned. By that time his bass long gone for dope. His real bass long-long. Three cheapos since he came back upstate. Sold for seventy apiece. Then no bass and he's so down; she fronts him another one and he pays her back in installments. Last time, the absolute last time, she tells him. Of course, he's bassless now.

He's awake by six, commotion zinging his extremities. He starts the coffee. Okay, he's got enough left for three more hits. All the edges nicely dim. Better land himself a bed today or . . . To con more. He does not want to do that. He still hasn't made contact with Rozmer. He tries him again. Gets his machine. Same carpet message. "It's me, Mark. Yo, Rozmer, if you're there, pick up the phone. I'm getting a little concerned . . . I'll try you again right after I get word from the hospital." What the fuck? He smokes and waits. Coffee, so strong, so sweet — no spoons, of course, so you have to pour in the sugar — it's a hot weight he hefts up the ladder.

Seven A.M. He punches down the new numbers, one rubber finger at a time. "Detox unit? Mark Merrick. Just checking in to see if you've got a bed today." They do. Bring just the empty vials for his meds. Only a few clothes. Can he be there by four? He can. Just has to get hold of his sponsor and make the final arrangements for a ride.

Four. This is good. He should still be in Wellsville, with hours to spare. He figures it on his fingers. Nine hours. Say it's six hours to get there from here. That's three hours to: Get hold of Rozmer. Get his shit together. Get his drums down and stowed. She'll have to pack up the computer. Hide that someplace safe. Maybe Richard's. When Smithy doesn't get a wire, who knows? Conceivable someone could bust in and steal the G4. More than conceivable.

He dials Rozmer again. Carpet. Have to wait a million beeps. "Rozmer, I've got a detox bed. It's a little after seven now. It's about, maybe, six hours there. Need to leave here by . . . Well, you figure, you're the genius with time. Call me. Thanks." Thanks for nothing. You can count on me, man, to get you there. Where are you, Rozmer?

What day is it? Somewhere, somewhere he's got a calendar his mom gave him. But he's got no point to work from — the last time he knew what day it was. She even gave him one of those watches, you press the little top right button and it tells you the date. Hey, but where's that? As a kid, he could read Dickens, but he didn't know what month came after March. His mom will know, of course. Year, month, day, hour, minute. And every appointment into perpetuity. Rozmer can't be at work already. Rozmer's Construction. Can't work much today anyway. The sky is falling.

He opens the heavy door between the living room and the extension, what he thinks of as the dividing line between his part of the house and hers: her studio, her bedroom. She's wood; he's stone. Richard built the extension when his mother insisted they move back to the land, that the land was not haunted. The summer Aaron broke his arm when he fell from Sawyer's Bridge. Sixth grade. Her part of the house, all windows. Richard's house all windows, too. His mother and Richard are into light. He goes to the foot of the stairs that lead up to his mother's room. "Mom, I think you may want to get up. This is going to be my last morning here. They've got a bed. I have to be there by four."

He jams in another load and carries a bunch of clean clothes to the loft. He hears Luke's dry food clatter into his dog bowl. This is the first thing she does every weekday after yoga. Weekends she stays at Richard's and he can stay under, buried in the dark until Luke's restlessness below forces him to surface. He hears Luke's tags jingle on the edge of the bowl. Luke will now go sit by the door, wait for her to finish her cereal so they can go for a walk up to the falls. If she takes longer than he can tolerate, Luke goes after his tail. In the loft if he's in the depths, it's about now he rushes down and pushes Luke out in a fit of irritation. Then he stomps back to bed. Ahhh, but today, he's up and going, going, soon gone.

She's salvaged the kitchen. On her return from Richard's last night, she spent the whole evening scrubbing, singing "Goodnight, Irene," over and over. He hears her get down the frying pan. She'll ask him if he'd like some breakfast next. He calls down, "What day is it?"

"Saturday, March 2nd." See — right there in the front of her brain. "Your money's probably been deposited since the third's on a Sunday."

Money. Money. And for the first time in forever, he's not on his way to get high. He can buy a carton of cigarettes, pay for Rozmer's gas. Be a grownup with some green.

She calls up, cheery, "How about some breakfast?" From her voice, he knows she's in whatever-I-can-do mode. "Two eggs, fried potatoes?" she says.

"Yeah, that'd be good." A blast of protein and carbs. Got a lot to do. He knows, like him, she's circling. That she wants to tell him, Don't forget your toothbrush . . . She wants to ask a whole string of where, when, what. But mostly, Deargod, do you have a ride?

She's a frightened driver. If she ever has to go somewhere she's never been, she worries for days. Cities, she flat-out won't do. He remembers when she used to have to drive him to Lawrence when he'd tried going to high school in Massachusetts, living with his cousins. The night before, she'd write out the directions — every fucking turn, when she had to change lanes. She told him "getting over" was her biggest fear, followed by having to make a left across two lanes, without an arrow. She'd write the directions in black marker and fasten the sheet to the dashboard. She always insisted on leaving at some godforsaken time so she could miss the rush hours around Albany and Boston. Already he was having trouble sleeping by then. Having her drag him out in the dark put him in a state of fury. Her perched at the wheel, on the verge of asking him some bummer question. He always felt like smashing something. And she's no easy rider either. It's good Rozmer's promised to transport him because already she's down there shredding potatoes, breathing, letting her questions fly out the top of her head. Fucking worry-birds.

He brings down the last bag of trash and joins her at the table. He knows she registers this. It's rare he faces her across that space. More often he takes the occasional meals she fixes up to the loft. Taketaketake. She hands him a bagel to butter.

"I still haven't gotten Rozmer — but don't worry — last time I talked to him, he said he'd take me *whenever*. Worse comes to worst, somebody else from program can drive." The eggs are perfect. He mixes them into the home fries and loads on the salt.

"Where is it?"

He hesitates. Camden or Brookfield? He realizes he doesn't know for sure. "Brookfield. It's way north. Just before Camden." Unknown driving territory for her.

"After you finish eating, why don't you get the road atlas from the car? Check about how far it is, what's the best route."

She's got the two worry lines between the eyes. His mother is not a big woman, but when she's anxious . . . one hundred and twenty pounds of nervous coming at you. He does not want to get pulled into this energy. He needs to stay easy. Eeeeeezzzzzze. "Rozmer will know how to get there." He watches her check the outside thermometer.

"It's right on the border between rain and ice," she says.

He scrapes what's left into Luke's bowl. He hears Luke lumber off his bed. He needs . . . he needs to get the fuck out of here.

11:00. Already he probably can't make the hospital by four. One hit left.

He's left a message at Charlie's, but he doesn't think that's a real alternative. Charlie's schizophrenic. Five years in recovery, but a six-hour drive up, a six-hour drive back . . . It's a job for someone like Rozmer. Besides, he's been counting on Rozmer's counsel. Shit, he does not want to have to give up this bed, to have to wait and try again tomorrow morning. To go in there sick. Sick he won't go in at all. Or to have to go to Carla again. And she's down there rustling the pages of the road map, her panic seeping up through the floor.

He dials the detox number. "This is Mark Merrick again. I haven't yet been able to connect with my sponsor for a ride." Sweat running down his back. "But I'm still counting on getting there today . . . I'll check in right before I'm ready to leave . . . Thanks."

She's back from the Quickway. She's gotten him a carton of Camels and a phone card, money from the ATM. "It's pouring rain, and it feels like the temperature's dropping."

Fucking heebie-jeebies wheeling his way.

He's packed. The loft's as good as he's going to get it. Probably she'll take down the sheets he's got pushpinned to close his space off; she'll take down the towels over his window. Once a year, at least, she recounts how when he was thirteen he woke up one summer morning, yelling, I *hate* the sun. Like — there it is. She doesn't mention how hot it was, the glare, the flies buzzing the corners of his mouth.

She's back with the map again. "Looks to me like it's about three hundred miles. Six or seven hours. How long did it take you when you drove Rudy?"

"About that," he tells her, but he doesn't really remember.

He unscrews the cymbals. The hundreds of times he's taken down these drums. "Can you stow the computer at Richard's? It isn't safe here." This machine he still hasn't learned to use to record his own music, edit. He's wanted it for years, and just before she left for Florida — hoping to make him happy — she'd said, Let's buy it together. You pay me for half, a little each month. It'll be part mine. She meant, Don't ever sell this for drugs.

"Luke and I are going for a walk. Be back before Rozmer gets here," she says.

"Just me again, hoping," he tells Rozmer's machine. No response from Charlie.

There is Richard. A trip to detox with his mother and Richard — not his choice scenario. Not that he dislikes Richard. There's no bullshit with Richard. He respects that. Back at the beginning Richard tried to line him up with jobs: helping him roof, split wood to sell. Richard's counsel: Keep it simple. But he'd always fucked it up: not met Richard on time, not showed up at all. No doubt Richard has his own demons, but, well ... he and Richard ... never the twain. Still, Richard is *the* long-distance driver, commuting to the city all those years. No, she'd say, I can't live here on my own all week and then turn to Richard when it's handy. Besides he knows Richard believes she should drive into her fear. When bucked, get on that horse and ride.

4:00. His nose is starting to run. He's going to have to do the last hit. How much well-time after that? Maybe . . . probably . . . all depends.

"Feel like taking me over to Rozmer's in Otego? I want to try that last thing." He puts a message on their machine. "Rozmer, I'm on my way to your house. If you're not there, I'll be back here by five."

They lock all the doors. The rain, coming down loud, and even through that, the cold roar of the brook rising. They're silent all the way to Otego.

"Maybe his wife is home now and she'll know where he is."

"Nope. She's gone." Took the kid. Gone.

Rozmer's truck is not parked in his driveway. The garage is empty. He bangs on the door. Looks in a few windows from the porch. Rozmer's gone too. You can count on me, man, to get you there. He watches her from the steps. Leaning forward, tense, her hands gripping the wheel like she's about to lift up the car. He gets back in. Soaking. For a few minutes they just sit there. The rain so hard, the whole world blurs.

"Well," she says, still looking straight ahead.

"Yeah."

"Well," she says again, turning the key in the ignition, "looks like you and I are going to have to do this by ourselves."

3 : Ice

U<small>TICA 35 MILES</small>

Already it's starting to get dark. The sky leaden, the constant din of rain. Heading north, so the temperature's bound to drop. The wipers keep time with her jitters. Almost no traffic since they left Marwick. If only they could get there on two-lane routes, if time wasn't a factor. She glances at Mark. His hood's down. He looks okay.

"Tell me again what we're going to do when we get to Utica."

He turns a little her way. "We'll start to see signs I'll recognize. Then I'll know where we're going next."

Knowing the way as they get to it is not the way she wants to go. When he'd said he basically knew, she hadn't wanted to undermine him by calling the hospital to get directions. He told them he'd be there by nine. Nine. That had never been a possible time. It's six now. It's going to take longer than three hours. "Did the hospital say anything about not being able to admit you after a certain time?"

Mark switches on the radio. The music is too loud. He lights a cigarette from the one he's smoking now. He opens the window a few more inches. More cold air. In her haste to leave, she forgot her gloves. She defiantly packed them away with most of her winter clothes before she left for Florida. "Why don't you see if you can find a weather report."

Mark presses the seek button. Loud, loud blasts by. "There,"

she says. "NPR, the news, after that, they'll give a local report."
She turns the sound down.

Dan Burns, a news voice she trusts, says, "U.S. and Afghan
troops target remaining Al Qaeda and Taliban fighters in a mission dubbed Operation Anaconda."

"Operation Anaconda. What a load of crap. Bunch of fat PR
guys sitting in safety making up product names to cover collat-
eral damage. 'Dubbed.' They got that right." Mark switches back
to music. "Get the weather later. Got to stop. I need to find a pay
phone to try Rozmer again. I have to eat. You can look at the
map then."

Mark is not a map reader, but then neither is she. Only in the
last few years has she started to decipher road maps: the black
arrows, the tiny red numbers between exits, where to find how
many miles between Danford and Crystal Key. And only under
pressure from Richard: If you won't share in the driving, at least
you can navigate. It was Aaron who was their map reader. He
would know how to get there. The green leather-bound atlas her
mother gave him for Christmas, the best present he ever got, he
told them. Second grade. The year he did the report on Japan.
Need to know where anything is in Japan, he said, just ask me.

"Mark, could you check to see if we've even got the map?"

"It's on the back seat," he says, without looking.

What will she do if Mark gets too sick to tell her where to go
next? She'd tried to get directions from Richard, but all she got
was his machine. She smiles to think of his terse announcement:
not one syllable beyond the necessary in a tone that said, Be brief.
She was. She was driving Mark to detox in Brookfield. Would he
come down and give Luke a bathroom run? She'd be in touch
tomorrow. Even if Richard had answered, the text of her message wouldn't have changed much. Richard would have given her
all the routes, but he wouldn't have offered sympathy or opti-
mism. We'll see, his terra firma. Actions, not words. Words: Get
to the point. But this is the point, Richard, I need to blather on.
In the twenty-plus years she and Richard have been together, on
and off, they've never chatted on the phone. Even those long-ago

calls. True, his tone was warmer then: Can you meet me? And in a few minutes she'd be on her way.

The traffic is starting to increase. "Uh-oh."

Mark leans forward. "What?"

"Three lanes coming up."

"Relax," he tells her. He turns down the volume.

The road widens. She stays to the right. Cars seem to be traveling at their normal speeds, but the ice on the windshield tells the truth. She gives Mark a quick check. You look tired . . . you seem . . . In a support group meeting someone once said, Don't keep taking their emotional temperatures. She's gotten better, but here she is again feeling if she doesn't press on his chest, he won't be able to breathe. The umbilical SOS.

"You need to get over. Think the exit we want is coming up."

She checks the blind spot. "I can't get over. There's no room."

"Put your signal on, and I'll tell you when it's safe . . . Go . . . go."

But she can't. The SUV behind her is going to ram her rear.

NEW YORK THRUWAY

"That's it. That's it. That's where we need to . . ." Mark turns to check the right lane.

But it's too late. Too many cars. Her timing too slow.

RT. 5 SYRACUSE

A big arrow sweeps left. She signals. "I can't handle highway driving now. This will take us in the right direction. As soon as we see a place to eat and a phone, I'll figure out how to get us headed toward Watertown." He doesn't say anything. "Maybe we should think about you doing the highway driving. I can't go at those speeds in this weather."

Again he is silent. There are only a few cars on 5. One of them has turned off the radio. She looks over at Mark. His hood is up. "Got to get some matches," he says. In the rush, his fire has gone out.

"You can close the window now and put the fan on high for a few minutes. I'm cold." Maybe he didn't hear her. "Mark?"

"I'm starting to feel sick."

"All the more reason to close the window and turn up the fan."
He does.

MICHELANGELO'S RISTORANTE

"There," he says. "We can eat here."

She slows. "It doesn't look fast-service."

"I have to get matches. I have to eat. I have to get hold of Rozmer."

Soft lights, low jazz. The smell of garlic and cheese. A long bar full of Saturday-evening people making merry. People dressed up for a night out. She and Mark, immigrants. They wait to be seated. Ashtrays. Essential or she knows Mark will be out, standing on the entry porch, smoking, two or three times before they get through the meal. Mark puts his hood down. He looks exhausted.

As soon as they're seated, he goes to the men's room. It would have been better if he had waited until they'd ordered. She already knows what she'll have: a cup of soup, a small salad. Her stomach's so knotted, even this seems unlikely. She opens the atlas to *New York (north)*. Even with her reading glasses, she still can't see the finer print. It always takes her an age to locate where she *is*. She tries tipping the shade of the table lamp up, with the map tilted toward it, but still it's too dim. People come here for dim, not to find out where they are.

A smiling waitress appears. "Nasty night out there," she says.

Tears. Even such routine commiseration. She's that close to giving way.

"The other person should be right back. Could we have two coffees? And would you be able to locate a flashlight and, maybe, a marker?"

"Sure. No night to be traveling though."

Finally Mark returns with matches, lights up. "No pay phone."

The sweet waitress with the long black hair appears with coffee, a small flashlight, an indelible pen. Mark aims his what-now look across the table. He orders spaghetti; she orders minestrone, a salad. This shouldn't take too long.

"Food," Mark says, while they wait. "I didn't get much sleep.

That's it as much as anything. If I could just talk to Rozmer, get some flash that'll remind me why I'm here."

She knows his "here" does not refer to Route 5. She leans toward him. "As soon as we eat, we can find a phone. Rozmer must be home by now. Who'd be out on a night like this?"

"Fools," he says. "Fools and moms."

She turns the placemat over, the perfect size to list the directions. Then she moves the little light along 5, in the direction of Syracuse. "Here we are: Vernon." Vernon, Canastota, Chittenango. She resists saying, Canastota, where you were born in the little five-bed hospital. Mentioning his birth, too risky. Once years ago, when she was still teaching, he called her long distance during her ninth-grade art class. He told the school secretary it was an emergency. "Why did you ever have me?" he'd screamed. "It's always been too much bother." This, his enraged response to finding a fifty-gallon barrel gone from the barn on an unexpected return after a move to the city. A barrel he'd planned for his noise-making system. This attack, as she stood in a room full of students. Could she call him back later? She couldn't discuss it right then. "My point exactly," he'd said. Then the accusing dial tone. She had to face the curious eyes of those fourteen-year-olds, sure they'd heard the screams. "Let's continue from this point of perspective, shall we?" But she is not, forever, going to detour around every moment of their past.

"We're going right through Chittenango, where we lived until you were about one." Their first apartment. A jerry-rigged second floor of an old house, with an open stairwell, no doors to close them off from the entry to the two apartments downstairs. Their early-marriage silence available to all.

Mark makes no response. Several times the last few years she's started to tell him baby stories: how when he was only nine months old, he hauled himself up and edged around until he reached the record player where, with his legs planted wide, he jounced up and down to "All You Need Is Love." But just as she'd begin these stories, he'd put up his hand: Don't tell me that stuff, he'd say. And true, part of her impulse is to offer these memories as evidence: See, sometimes I was *completely* there.

The waitress brings the bread, her salad. Though her jaw no longer feels wired shut, still, under her ribs, a clenched fist. Food seems impossible. Mark is managing hunks of bread, soaking them in the little pool of oil. He seems more okay. Thin as he is now, he looks like Lee those last months. Both of them graying early. Lee, thirty-nine, only two years older than Mark was when he died.

He catches her staring at him. "Better eat," he says.

Don't cry. Not now.

Rain, steady and cold, but no ice covers the windshield. She hands the list of directions to Mark and starts the car. The steering wheel is clammy, the interior airless, rank with smoke, sweat, the odor of burning plastic. He switches on the overhead and tips the paper down so she can see it too. "Things may begin to look familiar somewhere along that way. Say . . . ninety miles from here?" he says.

"Right. Then we should be able to pick up Route 11 to Brookfield. That looks to be about fifty miles."

"Okay . . . one hundred and forty."

"It's seven thirty now. Don't you think you better call the hospital after you get hold of Rozmer?" Maybe they won't admit after a certain hour, maybe they'll give that bed to someone else, maybe the roads north of here will be a glare of ice and we'll be stuck in a ditch . . .

They're buckled up, the heat and defroster on. He gives her a reassuring look. "Once we get to the highway, I'll drive unless I'm in the throes. You're good this way," he says, motioning her back onto the road.

Risky to have Mark drive without a license, but there's no way she can go sixty-five in this kind of weather. They pass into darkness. The only light the green numbers on the dashboard, that steady revision of now: 7:51 . . . 7:52. Killing time: how she's always hated that expression. "Killing time" and "keeping busy." When she first retired — more like graduated — people who were still working used to say, Are you finding ways to keep busy? She wanted to say, I'm finding ways to do nothing. Twenty-seven years of good, but scary, work, hauling herself out of bed at five thirty, to bump down in the midst of one hundred and twenty-five oscillating adolescents. Fear of all that random motion compelling her to overprepare: every minute planned. Minimal is what she longs for: a white room, a few pencils, good paper, the limb of the old maple leaning low and away through the open window. Following the edge of that twig, the curl of that leaf. Nobody needing her.

CHITTENANGO 5 MILES

"Surely there'll be a pay phone in Chittenango. I remember Route 5 became a commercial strip even thirty-five years ago."

"If I didn't have to find a bathroom, I'd say fuck it. Rozmer isn't going to be there. I can't stand to hear that carpet message one more time."

Route 5 Chittenango is one grubby little business after another. Much worse than she recalls.

Mark turns up the fan. "Be ready to signal on short notice. There's got to be a gas station along here. There, up ahead on the right. The Mobil sign." Mark starts preparing to disembark.

"I'll get gas while you call." She sticks the nozzle in the tank and manages to figure out what to press to hear that reassuring hum vibrating through the hose. Raining hard, but her hiking boots are proving to be truly waterproof, no dampness in her socks. At least her feet are ready for whatever happens farther north.

The glare of the lights, the racks of junk food bring on a sudden nausea. Edward Hopper emptiness. Back outside Mark leans into a phone-cubbyhole, his back to her. She can't tell if he's connected down the wire to Rozmer. His sponsor. An alternate lifeline. Always she is grateful for the times when she is not the *only one*. Any other link that feels safe, loosens the umbilical. Sammi, Mark's longtime girlfriend, is only a telephone support now. For self-preservation, she had to distance. But those first few years after

Aaron died, Sammi's presence may have been what kept Mark alive. Sammi, the one who'd called the police that first time he overdosed on a fistful of Klonopin, wedged himself against the door, told Sammi, I am done with being *here*.

If Mark has gotten hold of Rozmer, a blast of new energy will fuel the drive north; if not . . . Please let him say he's called the hospital, that whenever he gets there, they'll let him in. She waits in the car. 8:10.

He gets in. Lights a cigarette. Puts away his phone card. Fastens his seat belt. He cranks his hand for her to get rolling. She pulls back onto Route 5. She could reassure him with the news that a man inside said DeWitt was only ten miles away, that I-81 is an easy connection. Or the less assuring news, that it was no night to be heading north. But goddammit, she is not going to say anything. She is not going to ask him any questions whatsoever. Fuck it, as he so often says.

Then through the blur of rain she sees the house. A light in the upstairs hall window where she so often pressed her forehead against the glass to see if Lee was coming home. The Coors sign still blinks in the bar across the street next to the all-night Laundromat where all their sheets, all the diapers, Lee's shirts were stolen wet from a machine when she'd run over to check on Mark asleep in his crib. "Mark, there it is. Where we lived." Where you said your first words. Where Aaron was conceived. She weaves a little toward it.

Mark turns the wheel back into her lane. "Rozmer's line was busy. This may mean he's still of this world. And, no, I didn't call the hospital. I didn't have the strength."

DeWitt. Everything gets faster, more. Her heart ups its bang against her chest. Her hands, more clammy on the wheel. She sits up a little closer. "Eighty-one North can't be far."

"Pull in at the Red Barrel coming up and I'll take the wheel. Going to try Rozmer one more time."

While he goes to the phone, she looks for the restroom. Takes advantage of every opportunity. He's in the driver's seat with the engine running when she comes out. Classical music turned low. The smells of Juicy Fruit gum and oranges. He's smiling. She slides in and fastens her belt. "Well?" she says.

"No Rozmer. But he's been there and left me a message: Call him when I get to detox."

She squeezes his knee. "I'm so glad."

"How about this one?" He deepens his voice and sweeps his hand toward the windshield. "'This being human is a guesthouse. Every morning a new arrival.'"

"What?"

"Rozmer's new message for the day." He laughs. "Especially comforting for us paranoids." He backs, adjusts his mirror, checks his blind spots, signals, pulls into traffic, makes the left turn across two lanes — without an arrow — all in a flow. Mark has that confidence in space that Lee had. What Lee called great peripheral vision.

She's relieved to not have to drive into the speed, the rush of cars entering, passing, but it's still hard to let go. "Don't go too fast," she says.

I-81 NORTH WATERTOWN

Mark swings the car around the curve of the ramp and moves into four-lane traffic. She lets go of the door, breathes, and glances at the speedometer: sixty-five. Too fast for her. Especially in this weather, but she sees everybody's going that fast. Even faster. "Hard to see?"

"I'm seeing all right." He lights a cigarette. "I'll keep it to sixty-five, but if you get too nervous, say so."

She closes her eyes. That's much better.

"How many miles to Watertown?" he says.

She checks the directions. "Seventy. It's eight forty-five. We should get to Watertown by around ten."

"Then fifty to Brookfield, right? Say eleven o'clock we should be there."

She closes her eyes again as Mark passes the car in front of him. "If we don't hit freezing conditions," she says.

"Don't go there," he warns her.

But she must ask this: "How are you feeling?"

"Not too bad. Sweaty. Nothing acute."

With her eyes closed, she feels the car swing back into the center lane.

"We'll see how we're doing when we get to Watertown. If it's getting too late, I'll call the hospital. Tell them I'm on my way."

They are quiet. The radio's off and she's glad. One less thing coming in. He drives; she breathes. The gods willing, a couple of hours and they'll be there. Mark will go away, she will clean and draw. In the fall maybe the artist residency in the Adirondacks will come through. Owl Lake. Not that far from here really, but a much easier drive from home. Home. For the first time she thinks about the return trip. Of course she will find a motel. No way that she'll drive back alone in the dark, in this rain or worse. If no motels are open that late, well ... she can sleep in the hospital lobby. Cars are slowing down. Mark turns up the defrost fan.

"Freezing rain?" she says. Mark has slowed to fifty. Still a few fools speeding by.

"Looks like it."

And then it happens. Cars all over the road. "Hold on," he tells her.

Dear Jesus. She squeezes her eyes tight and grips the door. She feels the car slide, but no impact, no impact, and then they roll to a stop.

"A fucking miracle," Mark says. For a few seconds they sit and are grateful.

Mark opens his door a little, checks where they are. "We should be okay if no one slides into us."

She pulls off her coat and places it on her knees. A possible cushion against something head-on. They are parked as close to the guardrail as you can get. Several cars are off on the median. Everybody's creeping now. "Black ice?"

"I guess." He taxis along the shoulder until he can ease out into the lane, slowly accelerates to thirty, finally forty — what the rest of the traffic is doing. Then there are a couple more cars off on the median, red flares, again the cars slow to a crawl.

She rolls down the window enough to feel the icy rain on her palm. "Mark, I think you should get off onto 11 at this exit and not wait until Watertown. I don't want to be this scared for another forty miles." The cars start to move again. Mark signals as they approach the exit.

9:45. They're the only car on the road. Mark edges up from thirty to forty-five. She's not going to press him with any more anxious pleas. He's a good driver; he'll let the feel of the road guide him. The rain has changed to snow, a vortex of white, them tunneling in. Mannsville. Pierrepont Manor. Adams. Route 11 is even less traveled than 5. No traffic lights, the towns, just main street–deep, often only the blue glow of TVs from otherwise dark houses or a single light in an upstairs room. No stores. No motels. Every now and then a beat-up gas station–garage, but of course these are closed, maybe no longer in business. A pay phone? Not likely.

No snow, no rain for the last few miles. Maybe they're through the worst of it. She stretches forward and tries to relieve the tightness in her back. Turns her head from side to side.

Mark taps a new pack of Camels against the dash. It's a sound she's often heard in her dreams. Mark, sleepless in the loft, in the middle of the night, but with the comfort of a new pack. Cigarettes: one of the strangest of habits. What had been its satisfactions? She knows she's always got to quell the righteousness of one who's quit. Every night for years, before he went to bed, Lee threw the last of his Luckies in the trash. Often the first sounds of the morning were him digging them out. Habits. Her quitting pot. The spring she planted her potatoes by the moon, took what was left of an ounce and dumped it into the rushing waters of the brook.

Mark turns down the defrost. The quiet after the constant shoosh of the wipers. "You're going to be getting a lot of phone calls. Shit I'm leaving behind."

Does she have to know this? "Like what?"

"Smithy's going to call about the two hundred. Put the polite 'Your son' on you."

"Nobody's going to try to break in the house when I'm there, right?"

"You're Aaron's mother. No. Anyway they don't do things when people are around."

"And when I'm not around?"

"Just lock up and take the Mac to Richard's. Rudy's going to call collect from jail. It's a long jail recording to see if you'll accept the charges."

"This has nothing to do with me. I probably won't even answer the phone. Just let the machine monitor my calls."

"Yeah. That's the best way. Carla's going to figure out where I am right off. But I'll be able to refuse any calls I want to at detox. Smithy, Carla, Rudy — they're not going to mess with me much because if they do, I'm going to really fuck their shit over. Totally." He laughs and bangs on the wheel. That laugh that isn't a laugh.

"Mark." She knows he took his medication. The anti-psychotic, Zyprexa. Neurontin, the mood stabilizer. But she feels the manic edge. She should be driving.

"Totally." He laughs again. "These people, they even steal from each other. Nooley's got forty thousand dollars stashed from his marijuana harvest. Somebody breaks into his garage and steals it all. He calls me up, crying: the money for his mortgage, his taxes, his kid's braces."

10:15. Please. Only about sixty miles to go. She rolls down the window, puts her hand out to gauge the temperature.

"See, that's the point: I know. And if they fuck with me: 'Hello, guess what?' But here's the best part, I've fucked my own shit over. My deal's done. Finito. I've burned all my connections." Again that laugh. "Because I can never live there again. That house: Aaron's everywhere. Danford. All my junkie friends. I'm not even coming back to the house for a night if it turns out there's a gap between rehab and halfway. Rozmer'll put me up."

Route 11 takes them through what must have been the old part of Watertown: nothing is open. No people anywhere and only an occasional car. They come to a fork. No route sign.

"Which way?" Mark says.

She leans forward. "How can they not put a sign at a place like this?"

Mark bears to the right. They go for four or five blocks. Still no signs for 11.

"Why don't you pull over. I'll drive. We've only got fifty miles to go. I don't mind these two-lane roads. You can watch for the signs." He stops the car abruptly. No resistance. They switch. She adjusts the seat, the mirrors. Mark puts his hood up and lowers the seat back as far as it will go.

She pulls out. "How are you doing?"

"I am not doing well."

"One hour," she says. "Just one more hour. Hang on."

ROUTE 11 NORTH

An arrow straight ahead and within minutes they're out on the open road again. 10:45. Dark and the steady mist of rain, so hard to see. And constantly she must turn the wipers on, but after a minute, the squeaking is so grating, she must turn them off again. Still almost no cars.

Mark's head is back. His arms are across his chest. Maybe he will fall asleep. Leaning forward, her right hand tight on the wheel, when she turns the wipers off and on, that spot at the base of her neck is on fire. Once, she had been saying something about Lee in such a rage that her anger grabbed hold of the muscles in the back of her neck, a spasm so severe it has never completely relaxed. Twenty-five years ago. Right after Lee's death. August 10, 1977. She and the kids had been living in town for a couple of months. She'd packed up a car full of stuff and moved them as soon as school was out, left Lee, his silence, his strange looks, to live by himself in the pole barn, the stone house still just a shell. He'd told her he was sorry he'd taken her best years. Deargod, old at thirty-seven. And deargod, for a while she'd believed that. Their third separation and this time she said she was never going back. He would never reject her again. So many years before she understood it wasn't about her. Sitting in a chair in that little town kitchen — him dead only a few days — her scorned, damning him forever, she was seized by the neck. She presses her fingers on the burning vertebra. She's sixty-two years old. How could she have believed that, at thirty-seven, her best years were over? Then up from her belly comes a laugh so loud, Mark bolts upright.

"What?" he says.

"Sorry. I didn't mean to alarm you. We're getting there. Try to sleep."

Mark has twisted onto his side. She reaches over and touches his back. His sweatshirt is damp. "Cramps," he says.

BROOKFIELD 5 MILES

"Only five more miles." He sits up, puts his hood down. "Is the hospital right in town?"

"Yeah, we'll start to see signs soon after we get there."

11:30. They'll go right to the Emergency entrance. Emergency is always open. They'll see what shape he's in. Surely they'll take him even if they no longer have a bed in detox. They move through the outskirts of Brookfield.

"Should be seeing signs soon," he says. "I hope they're going to give me the first thirty milligrams right after I walk in the door. Not have to go through a bunch of paperwork."

"I'm not seeing any signs. Are you sure they're on the main route through town?" And then they are leaving Brookfield. "Somehow we missed it. I can't believe it. You'll have to help me find a good place to turn around; it's so dark."

Mark is looking back. His voice in the darkness is low. "I think the hospital may be in Camden."

"Camden? My god, Mark. How can it be in Camden all of a sudden? All along you've been saying Brookfield. Why would you have thought it was in Brookfield if it wasn't?"

"Now it's coming to me that it's in Camden. I'm pretty sure it's in Camden."

"What if we go all the way to Camden and it turns out it was in Brookfield?"

Mark turns his back, curls up again. The fetal position. How fitting. "Mark."

"Go back. Turn around if you think that's right. But I'm telling you, I think it's in Camden."

She slows down. Still the squeaking wipers. "How far to Camden, do you think?"

"I don't think it's too far. Must be the next town."

She hears his teeth chattering. He's a dark mound beside her, but she can't reach in and save him. "Luke's blanket is on the floor in back. Put it over you. Okay, I think you're right."

It's raining harder. "At least the fucking wipers have stopped squeaking," he says.

CAMDEN

Right away there's a blue hospital sign. "Thank you, thank you," she says.

Mark sits up, kind of shakes himself the way Luke does. "Bluuuuuh." Another sign. He rolls down the window and leans his head into the rain.

She slows. "Are you all right?"

"Oxygen." He wipes his face with his hood and points. "I think, just beyond the Burger King, you're going to turn right." An arrow. And here it is: Camden-Brookfield Hospital Emergency Entrance. "Well, I wasn't totally wrong," Mark says. He reaches over the seat and wrestles his backpack to the front.

The car in park, the ignition off. She does not ask, Are you sure you've got everything?

"Ready?" he says.

They push out of the car and rush toward the light. Just inside the portico they halt, smooth themselves. Breathe. Foreign shores. They pass through the invisible beam, the door opens and they march in. Three people behind the desk: a young woman with a pierced eyebrow; a lean, older woman, busy at a computer; and a large black man, tipped back in a chair, wearing a dark shirt and a security badge. She steps off to the side. Suppresses her instinct to take charge, her longing to hover.

Mark goes to the desk. All three turn a little his way. "My name's Mark Merrick." His voice is weary. "I was supposed to be admitted to detox around nine thirty. Bad roads."

The older woman scans her computer. "Here you are. Mark L. Merrick. Birthday: November 13, 1964. Medicare and Medicaid." Mark shakes his head yes, yes, yes. "I'll just need to have your insurance cards to make copies. We'll call the floor and someone will be down to get you, but it may be a few minutes. They'll do the admission once you get up there. After you sign a release, after they've made you more comfortable." She smiles.

Mark digs out his cards. "Is there a bathroom?"

"Right over there." The guard points down the hall. Just as Mark starts that way, he says, "But leave your bag here."

A clear imperative, but said in a friendly way. So far so good for the Camden-Brookfield Hospital. She finds the ladies' room. There's the smell of vomit beneath the antiseptic spray. The yellow walls make her skin appear jaundiced. Looks like she could use thirty milligrams of something. The woman staring back at her is her mother: this never stops being a surprise. Especially now with this very short haircut she'd thought very beachy in Crystal Key, but now, flattened from the rain, it's got a female-inmate slant to it.

Back in the lobby and no Mark. "He went to try the pay phone," the guard tells her. "Then he said he might step out for a cigarette. They'll be down to get him in a few minutes."

"Thank you. We're so glad to finally arrive."

"I'll bet," he says and his entire face smiles, like he's looked down the road they've come on and he's glad they made it too.

"Is there some sort of smoking room in detox?" It just comes out. One blink and a jumpy question escapes.

"Oh, sure," the guard says. "Twenty-four-seven. One thing at a time, right?"

Even though she doesn't completely follow this, she's reassured. The first time Mark was hospitalized, after taking one hundred Klonopin, when they refused to allow him to go out with the aide during the smoking break, he had crashed one of the chairs through the sunroom window and escaped. The Marwick police, out searching for hours. In a call to Sammi, he'd included his whereabouts in his colorful tale, so that she could inform the police. Once again she's glad it was Sammi who did the dirty work. They pepper-sprayed him. Back at the hospital, they stripped him and put him in a straitjacket. Shot him full of Thorazine. She somehow felt responsible, but his psychiatrist said, Maybe he's paid off some of his guilt about his brother. She leans into the counter; she is that exhausted. "I was wondering if one of you might know of a motel in the area."

The young girl glances at the clock. 12:20. "There's the Gateway Inn. Where a lot of the parents stay when they come for something at the college. Very expensive. There's the Fairmont, more reasonable."

"I just need a single. As long as it's clean. Reasonable's good. If you could just give me the numbers or a phone book."

"Oh, I'll call for you," the young woman says.

The other woman looks up from her printouts. "Why don't you have a seat. You're a long way from home."

"Yes," she says. "Yes, I am." She feels her body let down. She can just catch bits of the girl's words.

"The Fairmont's full," the girl tells her.

"Why don't you give Parson's a call," the guard says. "Under new management. The new owners may be using the same number."

Again she nods. She watches the girl's expressions. She sees her nodding. "They need your name."

"Del Merrick."

"I told her you'd be over in the next half hour. It's their last room. I'll write out the directions. Just off 11. Big neon sign out front says Nomad Motel."

Nomad Motel. How right that is. Relief. Tomorrow she'll find her way home. Richard. Luke. But don't think about any of that now. Maybe she *will* go searching for Mark. Where could he be for so long? Then there's that surge of fear: Mark has taken off. She gropes in her bag for her keys. Down the hall, a man in hospital greens steps off the elevator. She's about to offer some defense for Mark's absence when Mark comes around the corner.

"Mark Merrick?" the man says.

Mark nods, shifts his backpack. Then he turns her way. "Just had a good talk with Rozmer," he says. "I'll give you a call." He leans over and hugs her.

"Yes," she says. "Call." Call. But don't come home. Don't come to live with me again.

She watches him walk away, this tall, thin boy-man with the graying hair. How grateful she was when she saw that the Canastota hospital nursery was almost dark — no shock of antiseptic bright — only one dim light far from his crib; just visible, the crown of his small head, covered by a thicket of black hair.

The elevator door starts to close, a gray sleeve appears. He waves.

4 : ID

HE DOES NOT READ what he's giving them permission to do to him, just signs the release. The tremor in his hand when he squeezes the pen ekes out its own message. His nose is running and he is cold, an ache that spreads from the bones of his feet, his wrists, the sockets of his hips. Diarrhea and puking to follow, he knows. Terrible dreams. Someone places a warm something around him, hands him a wad of tissues. Just need to check your vitals. The pump of the blood pressure cuff tightening makes him clamp his clicking teeth: he's tying off, the end of his belt clenched in his mouth. He wants to moan. Maybe he does. Then someone in white reaches over and hands him a paper cup, pink liquid, glowing inside. Thirty milligrams. In half an hour, you're going to start to feel better. Tomorrow, twenty. Monday, ten. By Tuesday or Wednesday your system will be clean.

He follows the pink glow down, flashing into the rush of his blood, washing up along his edges. There's a plastic band snapped to his wrist. His ID bracelet: Mark Merrick. In case he forgets who he is. In case when they check his vitals there aren't any there. His vitals. If he had the strength, he knows he could do a riff on that one. Why don't I walk you to the smoking room, she says. It's open twenty-four hours, every day. She shows him the safety-lighter in the wall. Just like the one at New Vistas. Yes, he nods, he's used these before. Soon you may feel like a shower, clean clothes before you get into bed, she says. Just push this button if you need anything or come on out to the nurses' station when you're ready.

He lights a Camel, takes the smoke all the way down. The comforting hiss of the radiator: radiating, radiating. He reaches over and opens the refrigerator. Shelves of water, juices. Ginger ale. Cold cuts. Withdrawal heaven.

They say it only takes seventy-two hours to kick. Seventy-two hours for all the opiate to leave the body. Kicking on your own: seventy-two hours of being inside the torture cage, up to your nose in black water — cold, and the dope-snakes biting you all over. But with methadone you pay the piper less. That's why he's here. He is sick of being dope-sick. He's heard there's an even quicker fix: they knock you out, drain your kidneys, your liver, few hours later you're all better. Follow-up pill-a-day, keeps the cravings away. Even if you take a hit, you can't get high.

The main thing: put the dope-demon out on the street; double lock the door. He remembers the time some junkies robbed the guy in the apartment right below where he and Sammi were staying, blowtorched the center panel right out of the door. That's the way the junkie-joker operates. Extreme measures always up his sleeve.

The shower is hot, pulses of heat prick the muscles of his neck. Under these lights his skin over his bony ribs has that shocking hue of things long under rocks: colorless, see-through.

The sheets are hospital-clean. There's someone in the bed just beyond the divider: a compadre of the depths. A quiet breather, and the methadone is in charge, not a high, just a steady patrolling of the perimeters.

How did he get here?

He doesn't have a real ugly habit. Usually keeps it under control. Shoots only two or three times a week. Takes it easy going through a bundle. Usually holds back a little to come down slow. Takes a few weeks off before he shoots again. Not like Rudy. A real superduper dope fiend. Picking and scratching. Got the junkie-itch. Sores all over his body. Keeps ripping off the scabs.

Nasty. If Smithy and Rudy hadn't had all that money, he wouldn't have gotten so fucking wasted. Every breaker blown.

Only the shadow of hall-light through the half-open door.

Dark. Bring it on. He's got a lot he needs *not* to think about. Aaron.

You knew he was delusional, but you left him up there in his cabin all alone. Getting weird messages from Dad. Our father, who . . . Father? Where was he? Blew himself to kingdom gone.

And what about you? The Wizard who beakered up your chemistry fucked the formula for sure. Eight years old and already a monster. Misfire. Misfire.

Stay with me, Mark. Wood is safe. Stone is dangerous.

5 : Leave a Message

ALMOST HOME. Blue sky, the icy rain over at last —
only five hours from the Nomad to here. Even the ruts in their
road are sweet. There's a twist of gray beyond the trees: chimney
smoke. Richard has been here this morning. Just as the car lifts
over the rise, she sees Luke's eyes looking out from the kitchen.
Del rolls down her window to the rush of the brook, the smell
of March mud. Soon the geese will return.

She loves this long view of the stone house. Once the drive
curves past the pole barn, the lawn stretching to the woods in
back, broken only by a few trees: the big maple, some of its low-
reaching branches almost touching her studio windows; the two
old thorn apples, their gnarled silhouettes reminding her of Mings.
And by itself across from the barn, the Japanese cherry Kyle,
Aaron's music school friend, planted after the memorial service.
She and Mark, many of the people closest to Aaron, in a circle,
each holding a small candle, while Kyle placed the tiny tree in
the ground.

Rather than going for a view and wind, she and Lee had chosen to nestle the house between the brook, with its line of poplars,
and a hill of sumac and hemlocks. Close enough for her to haul
most of the stones for the house walls from the brook bed to be
piled by the site. Hundreds and hundreds. Her job, while Lee dug
the footer trenches by hand.

Luke has both paws up on the sill, his nose pressed to the glass. As soon as she opens the car door, she hears his bark. The yard in front is littered with bits of trash: cigarette butts, Luke's sodden stuffed animals, Mark's basketball tucked under the lilac bush. November and March, the world exposed.

What to do first? Maybe enough calm to begin to work on the drawings from Crystal Key. Five days of detox. Then, please, rehab: twenty-eight days. Then a year or two in halfway. He's said himself he mustn't come back here. But, no matter what, the chances are more than good she's got five low-worry days to be here *all by herself*. A bubble of joy expands in her chest. Luke bursts out as she unlocks the door. Del wraps her arms around his neck, breathes in his dog-breath.

"I'm thrilled too," she says. "But what to do with you weekends?" Luke will not be welcome at Richard's. She'd tried that a few times. Then Luke chewed up Richard's reading glasses.

The house is toasty. The gauge on the stovepipe registers in the yellow zone. Perfect: no creosote buildup and no danger of flashing out of control. Richard is the great fire builder. Willing to load the stove to the top, the front vents opened just enough. Fires that burn through the night. Luke's water bowl is brimming. Richard hasn't been gone long. He must have gotten her message from Watertown. What did people do before answering machines? Talked to each other.

For a few minutes she's not going near where their machine sits. Luke leans against her. She knuckles his ears and scratches just below his chin. When she gets up, he's still fastened to her leg. "I'm not going anywhere." It's likely Richard took Luke for a run while he surveyed the needs of the property: what trees should be thinned, how much the bank has eroded along the drive, how the roof he did for her a few years ago is holding up. The inventory habit. Richard likes to intone deeply, You don't own the land; the land owns you. And Richard is owned by one hundred acres in the hills on the other side of Danford, only fifteen minutes away by the Back River Road. One hundred acres of deep woods and a beaver pond and fields. Richard is a hunter and a lover of machinery. Whenever the world is too much with him, he brush hogs: mows and mows and mows.

"I hope you were at your best, Lu." She and Mark consider Luke to be high-spirited. Unruly, Richard says. First, she's got to call Richard. And then: order. She relocks the front door. Even when she's home. That's how it's going to be.

The light on the machine signals: warning, warning, warning. Five blinks. She takes a deep breath and listens. Two of them jail-computer calls: Rudy. Three hang-ups. She clears the machine and presses the Announcement button. She's got a *new* message: "Mark no longer lives here. If you're calling me, Del, please leave your number." Then she turns the volume as low as it will go.

The two phone cradles are empty. She goes up into the loft. The reek of cigarettes is even worse up here. The once white walls and ceiling overcast by a film of gray. Give me a smog report, she used to call up to Mark in the haze. If it was a day he was talking, he'd say, Breathing's not recommended.

First Del removes the pushpins from the Indian tapestries Mark put up to curtain his space from downstairs; then she unfastens the towels from the window. The living room brightens. Though the place needs a vigorous vacuuming, Mark's done a good job of clearing away, even stripped his bed. But the burns not so easily dealt with. On the foam mattress, a brown hole as big as her fist; the comforter's navy flannel covering, dotted through to its white batting. Black strips mark the window ledge, the chest, the floor. Amazing that they've never had a house fire.

The phones? She wants to silence their ringers, be in control of all incoming. Delude on. Mark's books cascade from the ledge by his bed. Noam Chomsky, *The Portable Jung, Soul on Ice, A Beautiful Mind,* Aaron's old copy of the Bhagavad Gita, the cover attached with a strip of duct tape. Mark was a reader, but between the manic-depression, the medication, the drugs, he's said, he lost his focus. Maybe he'll want her to send him some books in rehab. She can't resist reaching over to straighten the disarray, and there, underneath, are the phones.

Downstairs again, she sets them to charging and goes into her studio. Aaron's room. Her studio. She feels like a fraud calling it that; it's been so long since she's done any work in here. Still she did at least do some drawings in Crystal Key. She pulls these out of the portfolio case and spreads them on the day bed: the best ones are the conté on brown paper, with just bits of chalk highlights done while they drifted in one of the inlets of a little island nearby. The play of light and shade is what does it. Especially this one of Richard at rest in the back of the jon boat, his knees jutting up, with his fingers splayed over them, the knuckles foreshortened. Richard has large graceful hands that know what they're doing. Because she chose to sit low in the boat, her back resting against the front seat, beyond Richard's knees there's just a patch of shirt, the roll of his soft collar and then his profile, the bony ridge of his brow, his jaw toward the sky. A glint of green in his eye. For once she managed to get the warmth of Richard, rather than the fierceness that usually takes over most of her studies of him. They had lolled there on that little stream for several hours, her drawing, Richard watching an eagle on its nest in the top of a live oak. They'd had a good month, a stilling of much of their usual tension — all that distance from Mark's troubles.

Del gathers up the drawings and slides them back into the case. Once she's gotten the house straightened out, maybe she'll have the quiet to get going on something. Something that will build to a project for an artist residency next fall. Spare. Lots of white, something carefully rendered off to the side. *Her* peripheral vision. When Marna returns, they'll get together at Marna's studio again, draw their grandly fat model — Betty Dawes, with all that lovely flesh slumping down. It will be good to see Marna, Betty, Leddy, Lynne.

As she dials Richard's number, she rehearses the story of the detox journey, what to highlight, what to leave out. Richard had tried to make a connection with Mark and Aaron early on, but they had proved unreliable. Of course he wished them well, but the way they lived, their choices, the music they played all seemed so negative to him. The three of them were never easy together. Polite, but not easy. For years she'd tried to get him to understand she was not looking for advice concerning her children, she just needed to fill him in. Now her summaries of Mark's current storms are usually greeted with silence. Did you hear me? she sometimes says. I did, his answer.

Richard's machine comes on after only five rings and she's relieved, but a few seconds into, "It's me. I'm back . . . ," Richard picks up the phone. "Oh, you're there."

"I'm putting linoleum on the landing."

"I see you were down this morning. Thanks for the warm house."

"I took Luke up on the hill. Found your missing boundary stakes."

"Even the one down by the gravel bank? Probably that's where you were when I called from Watertown. It was a terrible trip up. Black ice. We got lost in Utica. We missed I-90. Ended up on 5."

"Route 5? That's the worst way to go."

"It took us forever. I spent the night at a place called the Nomad Motel. That about says it all. It was strange because . . ." Suddenly it feels as if there's no one on the line. "Richard?"

"What?"

"Well, anyway, Mark's there, the detox at Camden-Brookfield Hospital. He'll be there about five days and then on to a month of rehab and he says he's going to a halfway house in another state, that he is not coming back here." Silence. But she will keep on until she gets to the end. "In fact, he said if there's a gap between places, he'll stay with his NA sponsor, rather than come back here for even a day or two. Richard?"

"Yes."

"How are you?"

"I'm all right."

"Well, it's good to be back. I need to take the next few days to get sorted out here at . . ." She stops before she gets to *home*. "Are you working in Ithaca this week?"

"Tuesday and Wednesday."

Richard's trying a couple of days a week of carpentry work for a friend. Transitioning into the free fall of his retirement from the city.

"Why don't you come down here for dinner Thursday, maybe spend the night? I should be out from under by then. We can have the house to ourselves."

"Don't plan on that."

"All right, then I'll see you Friday about four."

He hangs up; she hangs up. He's unhappy: Why is his home not hers? She switches the ringer off.

Even from the hall she hears the machine going through the click and whir it makes as it rewinds a new message. Right away, her heart. She could bury the machine under pillows, put electrical tape over the blinker. Pull the connections altogether, but that would make her even more anxious. On her way by the side door she passes her hand over the knob to make sure the lock is turned to horizontal.

Del crosses the living room, heads for the refrigerator, Luke right by her side. He will miss Mark. The milk, orange juice and half-and-half cartons lined up on the left; the cheese and butter in their little dairy compartments. The grapes, the Granny Smith apples, their plastic bags peeled back and ready on the bottom shelf. The refrigerator is done. All right, now the machine. She slides the volume up enough to catch the voice: "Mrs. Merrick, this is Wayne Smith, your son promised . . ." Smithy. She erases the message.

First, where to take Mark's computer? She doesn't want to ask Richard. Boxed, it will take up half of somebody's guest room. May I stash my son's computer in your home. We're afraid his drug associates might break in here. Please let me slide a little of this darkness and paranoia into your space. On her front door she could hang a sign like the one they have on the glass at Stop & Go warning that late at night there's very little in the till: MARK'S VALUABLES ARE GONE TOO.

The answering machine clicks on again. She breathes, goes over and presses Play: a hang-up. She lifts a heavy afghan her mother-in-law made for her and wraps it, triple-thickness, around the machine. If she were being observed, the guys in white coats would be on their way. A couple of times a day, when she feels up to it, she'll check the messages.

A pyramid of empty boxes is in the corner: for the monitor, the computer, the printer, the speakers, the four-track. Taller than she is. Save the original packing, she told Mark before she left for Florida at the end of January. Without the original packing, you'll have trouble if you ever want to ship it. A ridiculous caution and she knew this.

She puts Luke behind the gate in the hall, so he won't be in the way. Maybe she's going to have to take the computer to Richard's after all. She unplugs, unscrews, unclamps all of the cords and connections, careful to keep things that go together, together. Such a tangle, this crossing over, under, through, around, that, by the time she's finished diving beneath the table, snaking wires about, her motivation to get this damn thing out of the house has tipped toward "I must be out of my mind."

Luke barks. Scares her so, she almost knocks the boxes over. Someone is coming. She doesn't know whether to go to the window or to rush to a part of the house where she can't be seen. Luke charges back and forth between the hall door and the gate.

She moves to the edge of the window and peers down the road. An old truck, the front grille gone. The driver invisible. The truck pulls around beside her car and stops, but no one gets out. Barking, barking. Her throat so dry she can't swallow. Finally the door on the driver's side opens. Wild gray hair. A long red sweater. A woman, thank god. She's coming right up the walk.

A loud rap on the window and above the barking, a voice, "Mark. Mark, I've got to talk to you."

Carla. She has not seen her since the night they planted Aaron's cherry tree. Seven years ago and now Carla has come to her house.

Luke stops. She slides back the bolt and opens the door partway. "Mark isn't here."

"Del." Carla's face is shocking.

Del pushes the door a few more inches toward closing. That's all she has to say. She does not want to hear about Smithy, the money.

"Rudy was just released from jail. Somebody picked him up. Not me. But he called me from somewhere. In a crazy rage because he thinks Mark ratted him out. Insanity: how he's going to burn down your barn. I've been trying to get Mark on the phone."

"Mark's gone away and isn't coming back. I don't want anything to do with this."

Carla's eyes. Carla's eyes begin to cry. "Could I use your phone?" Carla moves forward.

Del backs away and as she does the door opens a bit more. "Phone?"

Carla's crying eyes glance up at the loft. Maybe she thinks Mark is still here.

"I want to call the jail. Maybe they'll pick him up."

Del tries to process the sentence: Rudy is going to burn down the barn. "I'll get you a phone." She must let go of the door.

"And would you have a tissue?"

Del hands Carla a paper towel and then retrieves the phone by the computer rather than lead Carla's eyes to the afghan bundle. She means to have Carla make the call from outside, but as she turns back, Carla steps in. She takes in the room.

"Some movers are coming soon to get Mark's stuff. It's all going into locked storage." This tidy lie rises up whole, Express. She pulls a phone card from her pocket. "You'll have to use this to get the jail. You need a phone book?"

"I know the number by heart," Carla says, patting her chest. "I know it all by heart." Carla leans against the counter with the card before her, dials like one experienced with the use of dozens of numbers to reach the outside world.

The Sophia Loren look is gone. She's junkie-thin. The gray of a heavy smoker.

"This is Carla Morletti, Rudy Morletti's mother. He was released sometime this morning . . . That's right, Rudolph Mor-letti . . . Yes, I know you can't give me any information. I want to give *you* some information. Rudy called me about an hour ago and he started making threats." Carla shifts in her direction. Motions, does she want to make this a three-way conversation?

No. No, she does not. *Her* heart is blocking *her* throat and she can barely breathe.

"Well, not threats to me personally. But he's talking about burning down a neighbor's barn. Can you pick him back up for that?"

Luke responds to Carla's voice by slumping to the hall floor, his paws almost touching the gate.

Carla listens a long time, shakes her head. She tucks the phone between her ear and shoulder, throws up her hands. On both wrists, braces. Carpal tunnel braces. Surgery that, Mark said, went very wrong. The braces are a surprise, but hands flung to the heavens, such a familiar gesture. Carla's "Can you believe it?" On the wall just beyond Carla's head there's a drawing of these flying hands. Long ago this woman was her friend.

"Right. Right, 911. Yeah, I'll tell her." Carla hangs up and hands her back the phone and the card. "He said if Rudy shows up here and behaves in a menacing manner, that's what he said, a menacing manner, full of poetry this guy, he said then you should call 911. That'll bring out the troopers. But they can't respond to indirect phone threats unless you get an order of protection against Rudy."

Del feels the phone clamped hard against her chest.

"You want to know how to get an order of protection? You won't believe this. First thing you have to go to the town justice. Guess who the town justice is?"

Does she need to know this?

"Hoop Dawes. Hoop, the town justice. Needless to say I never have to give too much of the background in my dealings with him. His son Tommy was Tess's first boyfriend. Tess. At least she's well out of this."

Tess. Carla's daughter. Twenty-seven, twenty-eight by now. According to Mark, traveling with a girl-band in Texas.

"To say nothing of the fact that Hoop is almost certainly the grandfather of what is Rudy's kid. For sure. Got our eyes. You know Hoop's youngest daughter, Katie, the one who always wore the black lipstick, has a bat tattooed on her neck. Mind if I smoke?"

Del pushes a chipped saucer along the counter, one of the many located all over to prevent the house burning down. "No, I don't mind." And she doesn't.

Carla surveys the place again, directs her dark eyes toward the round stained-glass window high on the wall at the end of the living room. The broken window, two of the sections missing. "Always thought it was such a shame about that. Bet you just bawled."

She did. When she opened the door and saw the jagged hole. Aaron was thirteen. He said he'd been playing the tongue drum. The SuperBall drumstick had flipped out of his hand, ricocheted from the loft, across the space above the living room. Del sank down and cried. And she never quite believed that was the way it happened. She borrowed a tall ladder and Aaron carefully pulled out the shards. Now, through the outside Plexiglas, you can see the corner of her room, the branches of a hemlock beyond.

"And look at you, Luke. Bigger than ever."

Luke rises, wags his tail. Del knows Carla has been here when she wasn't home.

"Well, got to go," and Carla turns toward the door. "About Rudy. Don't hold back on 911, but there's a chance he's over it. That a lot of it went out with the screams."

"Thank you."

Just as Carla opens the door, she stops and looks back at Del. Those eyes sad again. "A lot's happened since then, hasn't it?" The door closes.

Yes. Through her own blur, Del watches Carla go down the stone walk, the walk Aaron built the summer he was eighteen.

For a second there's a flash of him there: a bandanna tied around his head to keep the sweat back, him lifting the big flat stones he'd dragged from the brook, setting them down in the loose gravel bed he'd made inside the wooden forms. So determined to stay with it, get it right.

Del watches the truck zigzag down to turn at the barn. She watches until it is gone.

6 : Living Trust

ALONG THE SMOKING room wall, above the microwave, the TV, is a row of hand-printed signs: IT DOESN'T HAPPEN OVERNIGHT. GOAL: SANITY. WE STOOD AT THE TURNING POINT.

Mark smokes and reads them left to right and back again. One voice telling him, Hold the bromide; while another says, Shut up. Last little cup of methadone doing its final good deed. If somebody asks him, What day is it? He's got it ready to go: Monday, March 4, 2002. Pull him in for a head-check, he could probably do the Rolling Stone Gathers No Moss test. A stitch in time is better than two bush-birds.

Out this side of the hospital, big trees line the road. Sap buckets. It's been a long time since he's seen trees. Taken in that much distance. Sap. He and Aaron, racing to the big, old maples, seeing who could get the most. Grandpa Merrick poking along the edge of Cobb's Corners Road in his truck. Lift the buckets off their hooks, get rid of any ice chunks, pour what's left into their pails and back to the open tailgate, without spilling. Aaron Cobb Merrick. Mark Lane Merrick. He'd always wished he'd gotten the Cobb. Cobb's Corners Road. It even appears on some maps. A long line: there's the missionary, his son that built the model ship on their return from India, his grandmother's father, his grandmother, his father. Him. Six generations of blood on that land. Blood. When the stone house ends up being his, probably one day he'll just sell the place. Too many ghosts. Spend the money to set up a recording studio. Buy a decent car. Travel. Some payment for all the shit that's happened to him.

Right, or put it all in your arm.

He hears his name down the hall and steps to the door. His social worker, Ms. Lund, heading his way, smiling. About the same age as his mother, but without the two lines between her eyes — none of these guys are going home with *her.* The detox staff has got the compassionate thing down. Detox — better than working in a rehab. Only six beds. The clientele earning the big E's for effort. Especially in a methadone place. Forgive my sins and lay the wafer on me. And gone in five days. Before Mr. Fiend knocketyknocks, starts running his usual numbers. Before Hyde tracks Jekyll down.

When Ms. Lund gets in range, she mimes the phone at her ear, whisper-calls, "A woman. Says it's a friend. Says it's important."

"No calls for me here will be from friends," he says. It's Carla. His mom won't call unless he leaves her a "Call me" message.

She nods. "You're unavailable." Seems to make sense to her. "Tomorrow after group, you ready to start looking for a rehab bed?"

He gives her the thumbs-up. "Thanks," he says. He's trying to remember the thank yous. Rozmer's big on thank yous.

Tuesday, March 5, 2002, third day here. They're waiting on his mental health clinic to fax some records. Right now seems like New Vistas is the way to go. It's a place he knows. It's got a MICA section. That's him: a mentally ill chemical abuser. MICA Mark. Dual diagnosis. Brochures say 70 percent of people with severe mental illness abuse something. You are not alone. And at New Vistas he can have a bass. If he's a good boy and follows the rules. Got to *get* a bass. Time to call his mom. Call her collect. Keep the pay phone from eating up his card. Save that for Rozmer-minutes. A bass and Puma sneakers.

He waves to the people at the nurses' station on his way by. Phone booth cave painting — not your usual WANT A BLOW JOB subterranea.

RIGOROUS HONESTY   FILLING THE VOID
HITTING BOTTOM

He dials home using zero. He hears his mom pick up. That's a surprise. "Collect call from . . . 'Mark' . . . say yes if you'll accept the charges."

"Yes," she says. Scared voice.

"Nothing's wrong. Just didn't want to use up my card. Thought I better save that for calls to Rozmer."

"How are you doing?"

"I'm doing good. Had my last dose of methadone yesterday. That's all gone okay. It's a good place."

"I'm glad."

The relief sigh. Ask her about her trip home. "How did the drive back go?"

"Well, I had a strange night, a weird night at the Nomad Motel, but the trip home was easy. I made it in five hours."

"How's Luke?"

"He's fine. Luke and I just came back from the falls."

"I'm surprised you answered the phone. People calling for me?"

That flicker of hesitation: censor-filter to On. "Wayne Smith left a message on the machine about the money you owe him. A few computer calls from the jail. I had everything turned off, but then I decided it was easier just to listen to who it was and pick up if I needed to."

"I just refused a call from Carla."

"Oh."

Her "Oh" means she doesn't want to know any more. "How about the computer?"

She laughs. "Well, I had a dilly of a time getting it all boxed. Richard came down yesterday and took it up there in the truck."

Thank-you time. "I appreciated you giving me the ride. I know how hard that was for you." Pause. He sits down on the little seat. One of those old wooden phone booths. You think about it. A phone booth has a lot of metaphorical potential.

"It was the right thing to do," she says.

He hears the tears in her voice. "Sorry about the hassle, the phone calls. Should cool down the longer I'm gone. One of the reasons I'm going away so all this . . . chaos doesn't have to be in your . . . environment."

"Yes," she says. "Flat. I'm ready for flat."

"The social worker's helping me line up a rehab. I'm thinking New Vistas. Though I don't want to go through all that psychodrama stuff again with John."

"Will Rozmer be able to give you a ride?"

"Don't worry. I'm sure we'll work something out." He shouldn't have mentioned a topic that involved transport, zoned her into anxiety before bringing up the bass. Too late now. "I'm wondering if you can express me the Musician's Friend catalog? It's on the shelf in the loft. Could you possibly help me get a bass? I feel like being able to play bass while I'm at rehab, when I go to halfway is critical. I must have some money left from this month."

A long breath. Possibly gathering "just say no" energy. "You're going to need cigarettes, phone cards, maybe bus fare. There's your part of the computer payment. I don't have the figures right here, but I did list it all out."

He has got to have the bass. And sneakers. But don't get into the Pumas now. "Well, if you could just send me the catalog. I don't need anything really expensive." He can feel her thinking. Main thing: for him not to end up back there.

"How much longer do you think you're going to be at the hospital? I'll send you the catalog express, but it probably won't get there until Thursday."

"Oh, it'll get here in time."

"Well, let me know how much the bass will cost and we'll see."

"Thank you." She will go for it. He knows she will. "Once I get through all this, I'm going to be able to get a job. I'm planning to pay you back." This is a tired line, but he means it.

"I'll give you a call as soon as New Vistas is all set." He lets her hang up first. Right by the return coin slot, an inch-high scrawl:

HAVING FUN YET?

A few inches below that he writes:

WEIRD NIGHT IN THE NOMAD MOTEL

New Vistas is full up. They're having trouble finding beds for everybody, not just him. March must be a bottom month. At least he's got the insurance, the disability shit in place already. Most everybody else here, sitting around filling out the forms. He's actually been helping people. Pages and pages. All the places you ever lived, your jobs, your hospitalizations. When-to-whens. If you're actually able to fill in all these blanks, remember all that past shit, prima facie evidence, you aren't eligible. His mom did most of his forms, him sitting beside her, having delusions. Social Security interviewer grilling him for an hour on the phone. Only interview you don't want to do too well on. Incoherent is good. Final clincher, his mom's therapy records. Those records helped prove he was out-there-wacko before he was twenty-two. How he got the survivor's benefits on his dad's Social Security. Got to prove you're sick to qualify as a survivor. 'Course in his more lucid moments — like now — he wonders if it's a scam. Is it his head or the drugs? His head and the drugs? Or maybe just an everyday character disorder?

His roommate says, "What day is it?" Kid from Brooklyn. Crack. Nasty rattle. The guy's third time here.

"Wednesday, March 6th, 2002." Nothing to it.

From the hall: "Phone call for Mark Merrick." He pokes his head out. "Your mom. Said to tell you she's got bus schedules."

Bus schedules — definitely his mom. The phone booth as sarcophagus, as space capsule, as sentry box, as womb.

"Mark?"

"What's up?" he says.

"Well, I just thought, in case Rozmer isn't able to take you to New Vistas, I'd better do some bus and train checks. I know no matter what, there's no way I could get back from the White Plains area, even if you do the driving there."

Got to face it: Rozmer getting him there is looking less of a go. If he doesn't get in today and it's three o'clock now . . . "Shoot," he tells her.

"First of all. You cannot get from Camden to White Plains by bus. The only connection is a one-day layover in Syracuse."

Right away, she's coming at him. He needs a cigarette. "Somebody's got to use the phone. I'll call you back in the next half hour. I'll have a piece of paper so I can get it down."

Two cigarettes later, paper and a pencil, he's as ready as he's going to get. Still no word from New Vistas. His mom picks the phone up first half-a-ring. "Lay it on me," he says.

"Well, there's no bus from Camden or Watertown to Marwick either. Same deal. A two-day trip. So if Rozmer can't take you, as long as it's daytime, I can pick you up at the hospital. There's a bus from Marwick to White Plains at seven fifteen A.M. every day. That's the only connection. Then you can take the train from White Plains to Ridgeway. They run every hour. If the bus is on time and you make a dash — it's just across the street — you can catch the one thirty to Ridgeway. Be in Ridgeway by two fifteen. I talked to the dispatcher of a Ridgeway taxi and if we call ahead, they'll be at the train waiting for you. Get you to New Vistas by two forty-five."

All this on one blast of breath. "Mark? Are you still there?"

"Yepo."

"Taxi's ten dollars, plus a tip. You think you can stay at Rozmer's since there's going to be a gap of a day to make the connections?"

On the paper before him he has drawn a grotesque picture of a man plastered up against the door of a phone booth, looking out, terror-eyes. An empty bubble ballooning from his mouth. "You know, Mom, I may not even get a bed at New Vistas."

"I know, but as soon as I began to feel like Rozmer might not be able to give you a ride, then the only way I could deal with that was to make all these phone calls, get on the internet. Write it all down on paper. Call you with the information. As soon as I figured out there was a way, then I could calm down."

In the bubble he writes THANK YOU. "I'm probably going to know something definite about New Vistas by five. I'll call you around six."

Someone's added:

CAMEL BELLS, THE INCESSANT SOUGH OF SAND

Countdown and he's on his last pack: 5:15 and no Ms. Lund. He goes to her office, knocks.

"Just coming to get you. They've got a bed. They want to know can you be there tomorrow?"

"Tell them I can," he says.

Somebody is on the pay phone. Mark signals the guy it's a 911. Rozmer, live. Amazing. "It's Mark. New Vistas has a bed. If you can pick me up tonight, I can get a bus from Marwick to White Plains tomorrow morning."

"I'm on my way," Rozmer says. "Be there by, say . . . eleven. Get you to your mom's by, maybe . . . four A.M."

"My mom's?" The call box is cold on his forehead. She is not going to like that. "Yeah, right. She can take me to the bus. Stuff I need to get. Yeah, thanks."

He uses his card. The machine comes on. "It's me, Mark, pick up." Where the fuck can she be?

"Hello?" Lots of static. "Mark? Wait, I'm outside raking leaves. I'm going in. Luke, get out of the way." The static stops. "Luke is always right where I'm going. Mark?"

"Rozmer's on his way here."

"You got a bed?" Relief you could cut with a knife.

"I have to be at New Vistas by tomorrow afternoon. I'll get

home about four A.M. Got to do some laundry, get stuff together. You can take me to the bus in the morning."

"You're coming here?"

"Don't worry. Three hours. I think I can handle it." He hears his voice. Hyde, right there, ready. "Maybe we'll have time to order a bass." See how he makes her pay. "See you around four," he says, and hangs up.

He sits in that little corner. After a few minutes, on the wall, close to the receiver, he draws the terror-man's mouth, then the balloon. Small, in the center, just a whisper, SORRY.

11:00. Discharge completed. He's done all the thank yous. If there's a Junkie-Detox website, this place gets five stars. New sign between the windows: TRUST.

Last cigarette. No matter. No smoking in Rozmer's space. Chances are good his mom will have gone out and gotten him a couple of cartons of Camels, phone cards, a superpack of Trident. For the teeth grinding.

Soft knock on the door frame. Ms. Dybek, the night supervisor. Everybody calls her Little Nurse because she's about five feet tall and sweet, the opposite of Kesey's Ratched. "Mark, your ride's here. They just said 'Rozmer.' He's in the lobby."

"I'll be right there." He gathers his stuff — his backpack, the hospital folder. On the way out he stops at the table, selects a fat green marker, makes the letters so large they almost fill the page and then tapes the paper in the center of the door.

TREES

"Good luck," Ms. Dybek says at the elevator, and she shakes his hand.

In the lobby — no Rozmer. The security guard, Joe, points toward the lounge. Over in the corner, Rozmer, all two hundred fifty pounds, feet up in one of those big La-Z-Boys, zonked. Rozmer is an instant sleeper. You're talking, you look over, Rozmer's in shut-eye mode. Catch as catch can, he calls it. But if you call him in the middle of the night, he can come awake in an instant. He shakes Rozmer's boot. Rozmer's eyes open. "Yo," he says.

Rozmer's got the Buddha-on-his-lotus smile. He lowers the footrest, big tower rising up to Mark's eye level. "So, how are you doing? Red ghoulies gone?"

"Good. I'm doing good. Watching the world."

Outside, Rozmer steers him toward a big old station wagon. A bumper sticker that says, DON'T CROWD ME; I'M PARANOID. "Where's your truck?"

"I borrowed Charlie's car. I've got to be in Ellenville by seven in the morning. You okay to drive?"

"Drive? What about the suspended license?"

"Don't get stopped." Rozmer gives him a hug. "I love you, man," he says, and crawls into the back.

The keys are in the ignition. "Am I going to know the way?" he says to the dark mountain in the rearview.

"Yes," the mountain tells him.

Before Mark makes the turn at Burger King, Rozmer's in dreamland.

7 : Free Dog

THE MINUTE SHE PUTS her electric toothbrush in its case, Luke goes and sits by the door. "You have to stay, Luke." He's not buying it.

She unplugs the floor lamp and pushes it into a corner. The Bensons' three dogs nosing around when Luke is shut up for long stretches on weekends, tormenting him with their freedom, while he tears from window to window, knocking over things: she should deal with that. Driving down from Richard's twice a day to give him a run isn't going to stop his longing to play when his friends drop by. This is the trade-off for having Mark gone.

She rechecks the front lock: Rudy, on the loose. Her pole barn's still standing, though she dreamed of its charred remains rising up in the fog. No weird calls on the machine for several days. She hadn't mentioned any of that to Mark on his brief entry and exit early this morning. He did some laundry while she ordered the bass and the sneakers, an hour of sleep, and then the successful arrival at Trailways in Marwick in time for him to be off to New Vistas.

She packs her portfolio case. Somehow she must fit in time to draw at Richard's. She wants to work on the natural world, clean edges, white space. Not these dark images that surge up. As soon as Marna returns, the group will get together again to work from a model. That'll be a boost. Luke rejects the marrow bone she offers to placate as she steps out the door. "I know, but that's the way it is."

Cold rain and a whiff of manure. At the end of her road, she looks into the hills. If it weren't for the stand of pines, she's sure she could see Richard's house on the far ridge. She turns toward Danford. Pick up Richard's mail. Already there's flooding along the creek. March changing from gray to brown. When Richard gets back from Ithaca, she'll have a fire going. Instead of coming home to a cold house, there she'll be. A day early. She makes the right onto Commercial Street — commercial, still strikes her as funny. Danford, population five hundred. The Danford Block — a Tudor building, currently occupied by Onango Hardware, Valley Antiques, and JAKE'S Grocery. Upstairs, three artist studios, Marna's the biggest one, and meeting rooms for the Masons or VFW or Moose. Across the street, the small post office and on the corner, The Inn, Tudor as well, once a hotel for the wealthy, now a place for warm-weather weddings. She pulls in beside the mail truck.

"How was Florida?" Fred, the postmaster, says.

"Great," she tells him. "Better weather, for sure." She's finally forgiven the postmaster for not allowing her to tack up an open invitation to the town to attend Aaron's memorial service at the Presbyterian church. When she had shown him her neatly lettered five-by-eight card for approval, he'd said, No, only public announcements and school news permitted.

Going back to her car, she nods, smiles, greets several people she knows from coming and going to JAKE'S. One of the many good things about small towns: small talk–chitchat outside the P.O. never stumbles into inquiries like, And how are *your* kids doing? Everybody already knows.

She turns left at the monument to take the back road to Richard's. True, she can now buy her stamps without that burn of resentment. Grief. Seven years since Aaron's death, but she's never completely forgotten the energy it took to stand up against people urging her that it was time to get on with her life. She went to a few Compassionate Friends meetings. Sitting in a circle with all those parents who had lost a child, one of the biggest struggles they all shared was that people in their lives kept telling them they needed to move on. I'll move on, goddammit, when I'm able to move on. They'd all agreed that's what they wanted to say.

After the first terrible days for her, for Mark, a surge of adrenal energy had filled her: she must arrange the memorial service. She had to get permission to use the church sanctuary. No, please don't light the big cross behind the altar, she told the puzzled church secretary. All of Aaron's friends from music school must be called, his friends from high school in Lawrence. She needed to choose the hymns. The words for "May the Circle Be Unbroken," a song Carla said Aaron loved, must be tracked down. Then she had to find someone to play the piano, to arrange for Marna to make programs with a section from the Bhagavad Gita she knew Aaron would have accepted, that Mark would find right. Especially she needed the part that said, "I am always with all beings; I abandon no one. And however great your inner darkness, you are never separate from me." The same words she and Mark had engraved on the plaque fastened to the big stone that Mark brought from the brook to set above Aaron's ashes up on the hill beside his father's marker.

The back road is a sluice of mud ruts, her wheels catch, and for part of the climb, it's best to let the car slip and slide as it will. Red water rushes down the ditches.

The not seeing it coming, the not reaching in . . . In the summer of 1977, news of Lee's suicide had spread through the town. When a person kills himself, herself, even distant acquaintances are struck with guilt. Shouldn't they have known this person was filled with despair, done something to help? Lee's parents could not face any ceremony at all when he died. They had waited months before Ruth and Ed, before she and Aaron and Mark marched up the hill above the stone house on a gray November day to bury Lee's ashes. All of them numb. She would, damn it, have a real memorial service for Aaron. She was in a rage of grief to have his death claimed. Several hundred people came. Her dear friends, Aaron's and Mark's, many from the town. Mostly she concentrated on keeping Mark from coming apart. He sat beside her, his face hidden by his hood. Sammi supported him on the other side. There was no spoken service, just the hymns, and a friend of Aaron's played one of Aaron's songs on his guitar. The most comforting thing anyone said to her, during all those words that people offer up: "You will never get over this." At last someone fully got it.

Through the rain, she sees Richard's house, its floor-to-roof windows. Smoke. Richard's truck. Her fantasy of pleasing him with her unexpected warm presence fades. Maybe bad weather canceled the day in Ithaca. She heads toward the back, manages the door. The warm smell of the stove, something lemony. "Hello, it's me. Where are you?" She hears the screech of metal on metal from below. Richard is in his shop, deep in some project. She goes up the stairs. Richard's living room and kitchen are in one large room. His house is even more open than hers because two sides of one end are mostly glass; the outside world is always with them, especially the big snows.

She pulls some venison cutlets from the freezer and sets them on top of a pan of hot water, then inventories the vegetables. Banging from below, again the squeal of a machine. If he were starting a new career, Richard says, he'd like to fabricate: special metal parts that solve the problem. She goes into the little bedroom where she keeps her clothes, the drafting table Richard gave her for Christmas. The tower of computer boxes is stacked in one corner. Storing Mark's computer here will work out fine for now. A couple of times a year, when Richard's son and daughter come for a visit, they need this bed; otherwise, the room is hers.

The bathroom hamper is full. She carries it downstairs, sets it by the washer, and steps into the shop. The lathe stops and Richard looks up, still bent over the piece he's working on.

"What's up?" he says. He straightens. Richard, tall and solid, hair so light, the gray doesn't show. He smiles. Richard has a lovely smile. There he is in his green corduroy shirt, sleeves rolled back, lovely forearms as well; the machine between them.

She steps in closer and leans on his workbench. "You didn't go to Ithaca?"

"Careful," he says, "that's greasy. No, too wet."

"It worked out for me to come up a day early."

"Good, I'm almost done here."

Hanging on the wall beside her: hammers, screwdrivers, wire cutters; above these, shelves for electrical tape, staples, glues.

"You've . . . put away. Everything in its place."

"March," he says.

Along the back of the bench, stacks of little drawers. Each of the other walls, floor-to-ceiling equipment and supplies. His tinkering shop, he calls it. A right tool for every job and it isn't usually a hammer. During major projects, it all jumbles again. The garage is where he keeps his automotive tools, his table saw, the air compressor, the setup for butchering deer. Sometimes she spends hours down here drawing: a wrench, the spirals that widen and tighten on the nut, the ridge of dark and light along the handle. His burnished carpenter's belt.

Richard switches his lathe back on. She sees that his hair is starting to curl over his ears. He'll want her to give him a haircut. She pulls a bag of peaches from the big freezer.

"Want to eat in about an hour?"

"What are we having?"

"Parmesan."

He nods and again bends over the lathe. She sets the peaches on the landing and turns back to the laundry. The grind of metal resumes. First the towels, then the lighter stuff, spread evenly. Her machine calls for putting the soap in first; in Richard's, it goes last, *sprinkled around the agitator.* She always has to stop and remember this. It's a tricky washer, the balance delicate, and she hates to have to come rushing back down when a load shifts, causing the machine to bang and walk away from the wall. Especially if Richard's around.

From the bank of cabinets beside the freezer, she takes a box of linguine; idly she surveys what's on hand. When Richard put in the downstairs cabinets, he took over the grocery shopping —

never a job she relished. He likes to stock up, to figure ounces to prices. Often she runs the dinner choices by him. She does better with suggestions before than with instructions during or criticism after. Most of their battles, her subsequent flights, begin in the kitchen.

Good that she brought onions from home, the few left from Richard's garden are past use. On her way up, she opens the door and tosses them over the bank. Then Richard is behind her, his hands, warm on her hips, up the next flight.

"How about giving me a haircut tomorrow?"

"All right," she says, "but the last time you told me never again."

"It's not rocket science."

Her stomach clinches. That expression would be near the top of the list of things she'd like to negotiate away if they ever went to a marriage counselor. Richard bends to inspect what's in the refrigerator. "Might as well use up the rest of this lettuce," he tells her. "It's going."

"I was about to do that," she says.

She watches his thighs while she rinses the tomatoes. On his way by, he settles his face into her neck and sets the lettuce on the counter. He slides his hands under her arms, rests them on her belly. Richard always gives off heat. She leans into him, and they sway for a minute.

The light's low, the parmesan bubbling between them, they face each other. Richard's green eyes. The morning paper is still open, close at hand, but he resists. Breakfast and lunch he reads. Meals are for eating, eating and reading the papers. Perhaps this is a result of growing up with ten other people at the table.

A strange pink glob oozes onto her salad when she tilts the bottle. She looks at the label. "What have you added to this?" Richard, the ex–science teacher. Sometimes she sticks masking tape pleas on certain bottles: NO ADULTERATION! "How's it going in Ithaca?"

"What could I have been thinking?" he says. "Two hours there, two hours back. A few days of working and I remember all the reasons why I retired." He scoops a mound of salad onto his plate, uses no dressing. "I've decided no more Ithaca work until the summer. If then."

Work. A couple of hours of chores: bringing in her wood, doing the laundry, she doesn't mind that, but Richard takes on huge projects such as stretching out on his garage floor under his truck for hours converting it from two- to four-wheel drive. How on earth did you and I get together? she sometimes says to him.

Richard waves his hand toward the dark windows, the rain blowing against them. "This weather makes a few weeks in Vegas necessary."

She feels that rush of pleasure: a stretch of alone-time ahead. Richard often goes to Vegas toward the end of winter, but he didn't plan to this year because he thought their first trial month in Florida would be enough time away. She went to Vegas with Richard once. A terrible place: all neon and cigarette pallor.

He leans toward her, gives her a full-attention look. "Don't suppose you'd want to go to Vegas? Stay with Will. A few weeks, until sun returns to this part of the world. We could do some desert exploring."

This surprises her. He knows how she dislikes Vegas. "Hummm," she says, as if she's thinking it over. Anyway what would she do with Luke? "I don't think so. I'm needing to just hole up here for a while. Draw."

"Suit yourself," he says.

She checks his jaw, the look in his eyes. He seems okay. She's ready for him to say, How are *you* doing? Twenty years and she's still not sure what his not asking is about. She passes him the garlic bread. "Mark took the bus to rehab this morning. I'm feeling a lot less anxious."

"Good," he says. "That's good."

She watches the bony ridge of his brow, his big head bent to the task of eating.

He sets his plate on the counter. "Want a toddy? New formula." He squeezes her shoulder on his way to the fridge.

She gets up. "No, I think I'll wait until I get back." She starts the hot water, so the dishes can soak while she's gone.

"Where are you off to?" Richard settles into his chair by the window, unties his boots.

"Luke. I have to go let him out." She checks the closet for her raincoat. Richard is calling something from the living room. She wants him to be saying, Hey, why not bring Luke up here? "What?"

"I said, How about 'Free Dog. Needs plenty of room to run.'"

"You know I can't do that. Mark loves that dog. I love that dog."

She's careful not to bang the door on her way out. God knows what Mark would do if she gave Luke away. From the dark driveway, she looks back at the house. A man, his shadowed profile, the glow of his reading lamp beyond, low in his chair, stocking feet up, his arms folded across his chest. A man thinking. What is he thinking about?

As she approaches her road, an old truck turns in front of her onto the highway. Carla Morletti's truck? One of the brake lights is out. She slows to see if it makes a right onto Cobb's Corners Road toward the Morlettis'. It does. She speeds up, actually checks above the pine bluff for smoke. Always, now, just before the stone house comes into view, she feels a surge of apprehension. Even when there's no mystery truck. The barn is there. The house is dark. From now on when she leaves after her midafternoon visit, she'll turn on at least one lamp and both of the outside lights. Nothing looks amiss. No barking. As soon as she unlocks and twists the knob, Luke's nose pokes out, his whole back end wagging. "I know, I know. You're lonely."

The stale smell of cigarettes. Though she has scrubbed lots of the surfaces, shampooed the rugs, the air is still foul. She makes a tour of the house, turning on lights as she goes. Two blinks on the machine. Her anxiety report to Richard, underestimated. Still a bed of coals in the stove. She stacks in about half of what the big firebox will hold and shoves in a few loose wads of paper. In a few seconds, the whisper of fire. Luke's head across her knees, she presses Play. "Del, this is Carla. Please have Mark call me. It's urgent." She scratches hard beneath Luke's collar. The final message: "It's me. Got here okay. Turns out this place isn't a rehab anymore. They just do the psychiatric thing. They're going to evaluate my meds. My social worker will start lining up a rehab in a few days. I'll be able to stay here for a few weeks while that comes together. My last call for seventy-two hours. Blackout time." Mark whistles a few bars of "You've Got a Friend," then says, "Hello, Luke." She plays the message again. Luke stands by the machine, raises his ears each time Mark whistles or says his name.

Only the back light on at Richard's, the low orange glow on the stairs when she opens the door. She switches it off. They both love sleeping in the kind of darkness that night brings. Only nine and Richard's in bed. This is not unusual.

The bathroom is warm with Richard's clean smell. Often her Richard-resentments dissolve when she breathes in this smell. Mouthwash, soap, the sweet sweat of work, the scent of trees. Whatever it is, she always takes it in with pleasure. The mornings, the same. She slips her nightgown over her head, the cotton grown soft from years of washing. The lace around the scoop neck, the cuffs. The careful flossing, electric toothbrushing, estrogen, baby aspirin, a dab of lubricant: the bathing ritual of the older woman. She smiles at that woman.

A rising moon lights the bedroom. A gibbous moon. Beneath the comforter, Richard's a white ridge, stretching from corner to corner. She lifts her gown and drops it on the floor beside the bed and crawls into the warmth of his familiar body. She lays her hand on the flat of his belly. He lifts his elbow to let her roll against him, nestle her nose into the soft hair beneath his arm, stretch along his thigh, this thigh, this hollow beneath his hip bone that she knows so well. For a while the comfort of this flesh beneath her fingers: along his shoulder blade, the silken folds below his ear, the thin, square bones of his knee. His body, still, waiting. She lifts to kneel between his legs, takes him in her mouth. He hardens. This, they still feel as a sweet gift. For a long time after the prostate surgery, though they had always found ways to have sex, Richard never hardened enough to enter her. Slowly she lifts and lowers, runs her hands along his chest, his hips. He places his hands on her head, guides her. Then he lifts her onto her back, her legs high, she places him inside her. She cannot feel him as she once did. She misses this. They move together, her legs around his back. And when he comes, she cradles him, eases down, lets go beneath his weight. Beside her again, he knows she is almost ready. He touches her, touches her, his mouth, his hands, his fingers. And as she comes, she cries; sobs, she buries in his chest. He holds her, shelters her inside his warmth.

8 : Ten-Foot Wall

Only ten more minutes of what's supposed to be Quiet Time. Mark takes up a position near the door, keeps the new roommate, Dick Goode — how apt — in his periphery. Guy's been here fifteen minutes maybe and already he's used up most of the oxygen. The room's small: fit for a monk or a solitary. Maybe two people who score high on the Sanity Test.

He watches Mister Goode drag his bed over, make the aisle even narrower. "I can't be too close to the wall," new roomie says. The first few days he'd had the room to himself. That's over. "Soooo, what was your drug of choice?" Dick Goode asks.

Mark answers this by opening the window-vent. Can't open the window itself. He taps the glass that isn't glass. Couldn't put a chair through this.

Quick-Dick, oblivious, just keeps on yakkety-yakking, unloading his L. L. Bean backpack. "I could tell you stories," Good Dick says.

He gives Dickie-boy the shut-the-fuck-up look, but this guy's so fogged in, floating around in his own little talk-bubble, nothing's getting through. Going to have to rip a hole, reach in and tape his lips. The increase in Zyprexa is giving him a strange zinging in his brain. His social worker isn't offering him much information on possible places to go from here. His new bass hasn't arrived and this latest addition to the community is wearing a black T-shirt which says in luminous letters LET THERE BE LIGHT. Trouble ahead.

"Bet this is one of those I'm-a-good-person-with-a-bad-disease programs. The judge said I have to either come here or go to some therapeutic community. Hey, call me crazy, better than having some ape in my face. Right?"

Tear a little hole; reach in with a piano wire.

Good Dick lowers his voice. "The staff isn't the most competent when it comes to ..." — he unwads a pair of socks — "searching for contraband." He waves a small brown vial. "Strictly for medicinal purposes. Percocet. Glad to share should you feel the need."

Fuck. Time to call Rozmer. The pay phone is actually free. Ring, ring, ring. No Rozmer. Going to get his machine, Rozmer's Word for the Day. Instead it's a computer voice: "Leave a message."

"What's up with the zombie greeting? Got a little situation here I want to run by you. Have a session now. I'll try to get you again after lunch." He's actually disappointed not to get a Rozmer koan. Try his mother. Four rings. He hangs up before the machine comes on. Try Richard's.

"Hello." His mother's voice, distant, nervous.

"It's me. I only have about a minute. Think you could look up some places on the web?" He finds the wad of paper in his pocket. Ding-ding: progress. "Okay. Besides rehabs, you might check for something long term." "Long term" will bring her to full attention. "Places that have been recommended by people here." He knows she has a stack of little papers, cut up and ready, a jar of pens. "My social worker's name is Lindsey Clarke. You can fax the stuff to her. The fax number is 715-367-9920. None of the social workers here have access to the internet. I forgot New Vistas is not that good at lining up 'After.'"

"Richard's leaving for Vegas soon. That's why I'm up here instead of home. I'll have some extra time."

"If you send the info, I can make the calls to the places that sound good. Ready? First, try typing in capital $S \ldots A \ldots M \ldots$

H . . . S . . . A. Don't know what that stands for, but it's supposed to get you to a list of places."

"Like go to Google and type in those letters?"

"I guess. Now these are rehabs: Smithers in New York . . . St. Mary's in Troy . . . Good Samaritan in Brooklyn." She's getting it all down. "Got to make sure they take dual diagnosis." Beatabeat, next request. "Still no sign of the bass. I was wondering if you could check UPS, see what's up. Should have been here yesterday."

"Okay."

Exit time. She's getting edgy. "All right, got to go to study hall. They give us assignments."

"I'll start right away."

He knows "right away" is just how she'll do it. He falls in with the crowd heading out for a smoke. A lot of extra poundage in the covey: one of the side effects of the anti-psychotics. No fat on him yet. Have to start tonguing the Zyprexa if that happens. Ten men, ten women in the Mentally Ill Chemical Abuse section. MICA. MICA Mouse Club. Everybody tramping out into the rain for a butt. Choke down two if you suck them up quick enough. One woman, Lorraine, young, in her early twenties, all the time giving him the look. No-contact rule. Lorraine is pretty. Porcelain. More trouble. Good Dick is talking up one of the aides.

Percocet. Jesus. Now what's he going to do about that?

Study hall. Assignment: one paragraph on your assets, one paragraph on your defects. Got to do the assets first. Ten guys arranged in various attitudes of reflection: ten junkies bent over their clipboards, trying to figure how to hustle this one.

One of my main assets is . . . I need something, I know how to get it. He's got the best study hall seat: near a window, near the door, back to the wall. Easy view of the clock. Could take the boys' room pass. Stall in the stall. But wannabe roommate's already copped it. Oh, just another rainy day at the loco motel. Assets? *American Heritage Dictionary* at your disposal. The alphabet a little wobbly like what comes after March — albatross,

ambulance, Apocalypse, April. If he was in a paranoid state —
synchronicity abounding — he'd say the dictionary was all part
of the plot.

> *asset* 1. a useful or valuable trait or thing ... possession, belong-
> ings, resource ... an item that can be turned into cash.

Hey, any asset in *his* possession that could be turned into cash,
long gone. A valuable trait: *I do not steal from my mother.*

Wannabe's back. Parents named him Dick Goode. Think of all
the wolf-pack possibilities, sixth-grade extrapolations. No wonder he wannabe bad. Whiff, whiff. Macaroni and cheese. Olfac-
tory factory in production again. Your better quality M & C —
Westchester quality. Got your better class of dual diagnosis here
as well. White on white. Mostly private insurance. New Vistas
does not accept Medicaid. *I love my dog.*

Big hand on the ten, little hand creeping toward the twelve.
Ticketytock. Almost smoke time. *My girlfriends have not been
dope fiends.* Good chance Sammi will come for a visit. Choo-
choo comes right from Grand Central. Sammi. Haven't seen her
since when? The last go-round with recovery. That first year back
from Portland. When Luke was only a few months old. That winter, that spring. Then holes in the body made further deception
impossible. Bye, Mark; bye, Sammi. Almost two years. *I loved
my brother.* Almost seven years. What day is it? Tuesday, March
12. *I know what day it is.* When did I first stick a needle in my
arm? *I do not have AIDS or hep C.* Yet.

Leon, one of the resident aides, is making getting-ready-to-
speak moves. Leon, the only person of color on staff. Their token
dreadlocks man. A recovering addict himself. Leon stands. "Okay,
guys, good focus." Joy in the ranks. Everybody tucking their clipboards under their arms, face down. "You can leave your papers
in your lockers. Both paragraphs due by your next individual
counseling session." Come on, come on. Smoke-time burning.
Rule: nobody too restless until Leon gives the Dismissed. "Com-

munity meeting, one o'clock. What's the usual reminder for on-your-own time?"

In unison: "No war stories." A regular tragic chorus.

"Any questions?" Everybody's feet ready to run. Wannabe's got a question. Dick-head knows everybody's in nicotine withdrawal. What the fuck. "Yo, Dick."

"What's on for today in Recreational Therapy?"

"Ten-foot wall." Groans. "Okay, guys, cigarette break, ten minutes. See you at lunch, twelve fifteen." Everybody quelling stampede. Without obvious hurry, he's the first one out the door.

Percocet. Jesus.

Shuffle, shuffle. People lining up for the community meeting. Got to make up his mind. Make up the beddybye he's going to lie in. Ring, ring, ring. "Leave a message."

"It's Mark; guess I'm going to have to figure this one out on my own." Going to have to deal with this. Get there in time to be somewhere in the middle. Not gold-star-first, not fuck-you-last. See Wannabe's right next to John, today's counselor-in-charge. A positive that John's the honcho heading up the session. Drop a dime, John's going to be up for damage control. Better than Lindsey or that other social worker — what's her name — that bitch.

Lorraine enters, checks the circle. Lorraine glides over. "This seat saved?"

"Guess not."

Musky perfume. A top that reveals that one crescent of pale belly. She crosses her legs so her knee is breathing onto his thigh. "How's it going?" she says.

"Up and down. How about you?"

"More down," she tells him.

The room gets quieter. Wannabe's going to do roll, clean the erasers. Roll: all part of the ritual of surrender. Everybody trying to give their own unique call of submission: here, yep, yo.

"Mark?"

"Present." May have a present for you, Good Dick.

New Vista costumes: Nike warm-ups, white stripes flash, flash as people get arranged. His costume as well, but with little melted craters from cigarette burns. John's eyes sweep the circle. He's a small man, with a round glow. John leans back — his body open. Slight shifting in the circle to mirror that. Lorraine increases the distance from his thigh. "All right, let's have a moment of silence. Get ourselves *here* for this meeting." John's checking each one of them out.

A real contact person is John. Who's looking at him, who's gray and edgy. He gives John an eye to eye, but not too intense. That'd be a giveaway that he's trying too hard. How *is* he looking? Shaky. John's big on "Listen to what your body is telling you." His body is saying, "Do not call on me."

John rests one palm in the other. Breathes. "What's one of the main things each of us has got to stay focused on as a member of this community?" He waits a few seconds, keeps them all on alert, before he picks a person he knows needs to be picked. "Jarvis?"

Jarvis is still in perpetual Don't-fuck-with-me mode. A little guy with arms too long for the rest of him. Jarvis stares at the ceiling, sighs. "Everything is your responsibility." John cocks his head like he didn't quite hear. Jarvis sighs again. "I mean, everything is *my* responsibility."

"Everybody agree to that."

"Yes." He calls it out with the rest.

"What's another important part of keeping this community healthy?" Again John waits. No guessing game here. Same two questions begin every community meeting. He knows John is going to call on him, has sniffed his fear. "Mark?"

"No secrets." Cold sweat now.

"All right, let's go around the circle. If you have anything that needs to be brought before the group, let's hear it. Start with you, Mark. Looks like you've got something on your mind."

Pass or rat? His body wants to twitch. He sets his jaw on the spasm. "Someone in this group has drugs. These drugs are a threat to my sobriety." Breathe. "He needs to tell the truth about this or I'm going to turn him in." He makes himself look at John. John doesn't say anything. Rest of the circle — eyes down. A few white stripes flail out: the run reflex. Wannabe's gone ghosty. He gives Wannabe a stare. A blast of power, no question. Finally a couple of the older guys look his way, but they're still in neutral. Nobody's saying anything. Let no shit fall on them. John's got all day.

Wannabe sits up, places both his feet flat in front of his chair. Swallows. "Probably it's me he's talking about. I've got some pain medication."

Bad confession, Wannabe. Now you're going down. "Yes?" John says.

"I've got a few doses of Percocet. For a back injury."

John waits, head cocked again. Waits some more. "Anything else you want to say, Dick?"

Dick shakes his head. John leans forward. "No," Dick says.

"All right. Let's go around the group. Let's hear what you're feeling about this. Start with you, Mark."

Truth or flim-flam? "Relieved. Percocet available in my room is a major threat." John gives him the what-else? lean. He should mention the motive thing — the plus Good Dick is a dick-head — but he's not going to.

"Anything else?" John says.

"That's it," he tells him, another eye to eye.

"All right. Lorraine, let's start it off in your direction."

"Pass," she says. "I've got to catch my breath."

"Good idea. Everybody catch your breath. You, too, Dick."

And the room becomes one big take-it-in-let-it-out. A couple of passes. He tries to keep from knotting into a shield. Then it's all coming at him from a distance. Like through a din of rain. Bullshit — pain medication — one of the old-timers finally takes it on. Glad it wasn't me had to do the duty, but it had to be done — Lorraine, a couple of the younger women. All of us are at risk — Big Jerry. Lots of Too Bad for you, Dick, but you know the rules. Sort of like a round. Some telling the truth; some just trying to cover their backs.

Only Jarvis doesn't sing the song: "Fuck this," he tells them all. A few people laugh. "Go, Jarvis."

Everything gets quiet. They all know they're down to the last licks. Wannabe will have to go first. Wannabe knows it too. He's sitting straight, looking earnest.

"Anything more you want to say to the group, Dick?" John's voice so calm. So up-to-you.

Dick's all red and blurry. Show your dick-head colors, your junkie scam. "Honestly . . ." Bullshit to follow. And it's like the whole group sinks back. ". . . my doctor gave me the meds. I felt like I needed them for the pain. I didn't realize it was such a big deal."

John waits. The group's suspended. Then they lean his way. "Anything more you want to add, Mark?" John says, reaching both hands toward him.

"I've said enough," he tells them. His clothes are so wet, he may leave tracks.

On the way out a few of the older guys give him the thumbs-up, but even so he feels a lot of the group draw away.

Smoke break, Dick Goode is among the missing. Back in his room before ten-foot-wall time, Dick Goode is gone.

9 : Password

BENEATH THE ROAR of the vacuum, Del feels a bang, bang, bang. It takes her a few seconds to register: the washing machine. On these rushes down the stairs to shut it off, she always remembers to grab the rail. If she fell and broke her neck, she'd never forgive Richard. She pushes in the dial and the machinery comes to a clunking halt, makes those metal-parts-going-the-wrong-way clangs that cause Richard to wince if he's around. Thank the gods he's not around. She looks toward the garage and sees his legs still stretching from under her car. Repairing her exhaust system. Finally she gets the heavy towels shifted so the machine will hold the spin and goes back up to shut off the vacuum. It's almost dinnertime anyway.

Richard's expecting a call about his taxes, so she mustn't tie up the phone by going online, but she's itching to find some long-term place that will take hold of Mark long enough for him to learn how to put together a day, stack one hour on top of another, on top of another, without knocking them over. How many years might that take? Once she gets off some faxes of good places, the knot beneath her sternum will loosen. Even a quick check would calm her some.

In Richard's office, with one eye on his legs, she switches on his computer and types in his password: R5555555. Half the time she screws this up, so easy to lose track of what 5 you're on. Why such a hard password? she'd asked him. That's why, he told her.

Richard will leave for Vegas in two days. An uninterrupted stretch of two weeks at her house. No abandoning Luke. Plenty of time to research rehabs on the web without worrying that she's hogging the line. Without Richard's comments on the unhealthiness of staring at a screen all day whenever he goes by. When his two kids were young, he came home one sunny summer afternoon and found them with their faces a few feet from the screen, mouths agog; he picked up the TV, walked out the door and dumped it over the bank. Makes her own web-time when he's around, edgy.

She types SAMHSA into the Google box and instantly the words "Substance Abuse Mental Health Service Administration" appear on the screen. As if it's been waiting for her to summon it. The Higher Power of cyberspace. Farther down, "Find Treatment," click on that and the site opens: happy music, photographs of people smiling, assuring you you can find help. Next she's taken to a map of the U.S. Click on NY: she's told there are 11,000 treatment centers available. Think of the tangle of umbilici connecting all those mothers to all those "treatments." "Type in your location." Marwick. "There are 286 facilities within 100 miles of your starting point." Please, please. She hears the downstairs door open, and quick as she can, she disconnects and turns off the computer, her heart banging as if she's been caught. Which indeed she has. Almost. She steps into the kitchen.

"Any calls?" Richard says as he comes up the stairs. "What's up? You look a little . . . rattled." He hooks his arm through hers and bounces against her with a two-step. Then he licks her ear. When, laughing, she tries to pull away, he holds her close and whispers, "Just your clamps had rusted."

She backs him up against the sink. "You want to eat now?"

"You know it's still not too late to change your mind about going to Vegas." He rocks her a little. "We could even drive out. Maybe go up in the mountains. Not spend so much time in the casinos. That's why you didn't have fun before."

Fun? She does not want to go anywhere. She wants to be alone. She wants to help Mark get settled in the right place. She wants to sit down and draw a branch of shadbush in first blossom. Once this rain stops, to walk with Luke up through the woods and watch spring go green. She kisses his neck. No's are hard for Richard. The first ten years she knew him, she never told him no about anything. They got along better then. She puts her arms around his warm body. He smells good, rain tinged with oil.

"I don't want to go anywhere right now. I need to stay here." She feels his body tense. He moves away from her and settles at the table. He opens the paper. "Richard."

He doesn't respond. For years she's said, Let's talk. He will not or cannot. He reads. She heats up the clam chowder, switches on the toaster-oven for the garlic bread. Adds apples to the tossed salad. She breathes and loosens her shoulders. When Lee was silent, for months at a time, her movements became robotic. She mumbled when she spoke to Mark and Aaron, her throat so locked, her jaw trembled when she opened her mouth. Sometimes when Richard refuses to speak, she can float on the edge of it, without clinching. But usually it pisses her off.

Richard lifts his chowder and sniffs it while he reads. He takes the spoon back and forth to his mouth without even looking at the bowl. When he finishes with the first section of the *Marwick Sun,* she slides it her way. She's always refused to read at the table, her small daily protest, but lately when he reads, she reads too. At first she told herself it was just a yield to reality, but now she sees it means "I'm not here either."

Bedtime and she still hasn't been able to get back on the internet. Two hundred eighty-six facilities within a hundred miles of Marwick. She'd like to find a fax place to get the information off to Mark first thing tomorrow. She knows he'll be expecting something from her by then. But it's better not to change her routine of going to bed when Richard does, especially now when he's already upset with her.

It's dark. She goes slow, not wanting to bump into the sharp corner of the footboard. There's only a heap of covers once she gets to the edge of the bed. Usually Richard sleeps from corner to corner, but tonight his body's confined to one side, *his* side. She pulls her gown off and slides in. Sometimes when they aren't speaking, when it feels as if she's lying down with a stranger, she has to keep her nightgown on, but tonight she wants the silence to end. His back is to her. She settles on her side, pushes her toes against his heel. He doesn't move away. Then she warms her always-cold hands between her legs. After a few minutes she rests a palm against his shoulder blade, feels his heat. Then she pulls her knees up to tuck into his. He's still, but not tensed. Minutes more, then he reaches back and places his hand on her thigh. She puts her hand over his, slides her fingers through his fingers, touches the warm flesh-wrinkles between, the smooth pad of his thumb.

She leans into the bathroom. Richard's got a big yellow towel wrapped around his waist; his face, lathered and close to the mirror. "Oatmeal?"

He seems to be over it. He leaves tomorrow. If she's careful, they may part in good spirits: Have a lovely time. I'll miss you. She knows in about a week this will be true. She measures the water exactly and is mindful of the number of raisins. She punctures the canned milk, just one small hole because Richard says it keeps better that way.

Richard comes through to check the temperature, still wrapped in the duck-yellow towel. His linen closet is stacked high with thick towels: lavender, pale blue, fuchsia. There was never a dry one, he told her when she asked him about the stockpile.

"Thirty-five degrees. Probably be in the seventies in Vegas." He switches on the CD player. Mario Lanza. She and Richard have joined one of those clubs where you tear out the little pictures and paste them on the little card: ten free CDs and you only have to buy three and then you can get out. Each of them got five choices. Maybe seventy-five little perforated patches, but fifty, groups you've never heard of, and maybe only two you'd even consider actually buying if you were at a store. She always rips out *New World Symphony* and *Pictures at an Exhibition,* but then remembers she's got both of those on tape somewhere. After they lick the little jagged oblongs and slap them onto the ten spaces, they comment on the other's picks: You don't even like the Rolling Stones. You think you're ready for Mahler? Usually they sleep on it and the next day agree to throw the whole lot in the trash, but this last time, Richard actually dropped the envelope in the mailbox. Mario Lanza singing "Danny Boy" made him do it, he said.

She sets the oatmeal pot on the table. "Okay," she tells him.

He turns Mario up, "Be my love . . . ," then up even louder and he joins in, his lovely arms spread wide, slowly swaying from foot to foot, raising his leg delicately into the air each time he shifts his weight. "'Just fill my arms the way you've filled my dreams . . .'"

"Richard." Richard has long, slender, very white legs. He moves toward her. She ducks under his arm and turns down the CD. He's over it. She misses him already.

He comes back to the kitchen in his jockeys and a new white T-shirt and starts to divide up the oatmeal. "You're going to eat in your underwear?"

"I am."

Another benefit of wood heat. She lets the pot slip into the soapy water as soon as he scrapes her share into her bowl. "Richard, pretty soon we're going to switch to raisin bran."

"Just as soon as we hear the first geese," he tells her. He stops eating and beams. "And this year you're not going to put sugar on yours."

"Oh."

They eat and Mario sings. She takes her vitamins, the big gray one for seniors, always a test. He clanks his spoon around the edges of his bowl to get the last of his cereal just as she's beginning hers. While she eats, he sticks things back into the refrigerator. She watches him, the rounds of his buttocks as he bends. His big, agile body.

"What time's your plane tomorrow?" She turns up the heat under the kettle. "Want tea?"

He hesitates, then says, "I think I will." This is a break from routine. Usually he's out and doing before she starts the dishes, sometimes even before she finishes eating. Out splitting logs or filling the bird feeder or hauling wood in the wheelbarrow to stack in the bins downstairs.

"What time do you have to leave here?" The kettle is making those popping sounds which mean it's about to whistle.

He sits down at the table. "Around two." He pauses. "I'd like you to drive me to the airport. The last time I left the truck in the parking lot, someone rammed into my tailgate."

Her stomach lurches. The kettle screams. For a few seconds she draws a blank on how to get it to stop. When she tips it up to pour, her hands are shaking. How quickly the body answers. She pushes each of the bags down into the cups.

"Del?"

She sets the cups on the table. Gets out the Hazelnut International Delight. But she doesn't sit down. Instead she leans against the sink and takes a deep breath. "Richard, you know how hard it is for me to do that drive."

"You've done it before. You only have to drive back. You'll have a chance to look over the route on the way down." He leans toward her, makes sure he's got her full attention. "Much easier than driving to Camden."

"Richard."

"You stay on 88 to Albany, then get on the Northway and get off at Exit 4. The airport is right there."

Her heart thuds. She'll be starting back around five o'clock. "That's going to put me returning in rush-hour traffic."

He looks at her, starts to rise.

She sits down, picks up the warm mug. "All right. I'm afraid to do this, but I guess I can. I'll just have to drop you at the airline though. You'll pull up and I'll get in the driver's seat and just swing on out. Getting back to the highway will be less confusing. The last time I got totally turned around."

"Good," he says. "We'll take your car. Every time you do it, it gets easier."

She unlocks the front door, yanks it open and steps into the icy rain, looks up at the dark sky, opens her mouth and screams. Talons release, weight lifts, flashes up and away. Back inside she walks up and down the hall. Her breathing is easier now. Certainly she does not have to invite anger up as the Buddhist monk Thich Nhat Hanh suggests. It's burst right in on its own. She dials Marna's number, gets her friendly "get back to you." "It's Del. Hope you had a good trip. I'm really just calling to vent. I'm so angry, I was finding it hard to breathe. I'll try to get hold of you tomorrow evening when I get back from the Albany airport. Maybe you could come for chili at my house Thursday . . ." and the machine clicks off. She does feel better. Venting to an answering machine. So much a minute. The weather, porn, vent: take your pick. In fact there's probably such a thing already. Good lord, why did she have to step out of the house to scream? Because Richard would have come back from the P.O., walked in and said, "I smell something burning." Like that time he was away working in the city, when she was renting her house to Mark and Aaron, living at Richard's, and she'd left water boiling, came in to find the bottom of one of her cheap pots melting, welding right to the thin outer ring and under-pan, seconds after she turned off the on-high glow. She'd rushed out and miraculously found replacements. She left the windows open, ran the fan, sprayed Lysol, but the faint chemical odor of melted metal lingered. The first thing he said when he opened the door, What's that smell? I don't know, she told him. Maybe the only time she'd out-and-out lied.

All day every time she thinks about swinging around the circle to get out of the airport, her stomach takes a dive. Now you've promised, you have to do this. She goes through the motions of being a person: putting on the mayonnaise, rinsing the lettuce. She feels too jittery to try to deal with the internet. With a knife, she removes the little screw that keeps one of the glass shower doors from sliding — a screw Richard had inserted because water had started to erode the grouting of the floor tiles in that corner the year his son had been living with them. Now, in order to get rid of the buildup, you have to take all your clothes off and stand in the tub. Unless you remove the screw to slide the door. With soft-scrub and a non-scratch pad, with methodical circles, she works her way from the top to the bottom, removing all the lime and soap residue she's been meaning to go at for weeks.

It isn't until Richard goes to sit down and she starts to set the salmon on the table that it comes to her: she is going to have to pick him up as well. She takes hold of the edge of the sink. "What time does your return plane get into Albany?"

He gives her a weary look. "I don't remember the exact time."

"About what time?" Her voice has that about-to-cry tremor.

He cuts up the salmon and puts a piece on her plate. "Around midnight."

"You mean I am going to have to drive down there late, in the dark . . ." — she points to the windows — "in possibly freezing rain?"

"Del."

"Something that is terrifying to me . . ."

"Terrifying?"

". . . so you don't have to leave your truck in the parking lot?"

He stands up. "Thanks," he says. "Wouldn't want you to put yourself out." His back is to her now.

She follows him a few steps on his way to the stairs. "You know that's not it."

From the stairway, he says, "When you want to, you can drive."

He disappears. She stands looking down into the stairwell. "Richard, you are not going to equate this with me driving Mark to detox?"

She follows him down the stairs. "You aren't going to eat?" He is sitting in his chair by the stove, the paper already before him. He doesn't answer.

"You know this is not about that I can't be bothered." He turns the page. She goes back upstairs. She would like to break something. She dumps the salmon into the garbage, bangs the rice pot on the side of the can until it breaks loose and drops in one steaming mound. She feels sick. Bastard. She starts the dishes. Then she sets the salmon pan back in the water and goes to the head of the stairs. "If you cared about me, really cared, you would not ask me to do something that you know makes me so anxious. Or if you did ask, you would know that I have the right, I have the right to say no." Silence. She rinses the glasses, the silverware, the plates. She wipes the table and dries her hands. When she gets downstairs, she pulls her chair closer to his, then sits on the edge and looks at him. He does not look at her, just turns the page. "We need to talk." Nothing. "You know if it was an emergency — say you needed to go to the hospital — I would drive you. I would drive you. But this is so you don't have to leave your vehicle in the airport parking lot. Hundreds of people leave their cars in airport parking lots." No response. "We should talk." She leans toward him.

Without looking at her, without setting the paper down, he finally says, "Nothing to talk about. Go on to your house."

"Richard, this is so unfair."

"Maybe it is. But I want you to go now. I'll call you when I get back."

Her chest is tight. Let her not sob. It is not sorrow, it's fury. She goes back upstairs. Rage. And she's supposed to bring the rage up and give it sympathy: There, there. Fuck.

She takes her coat from the back of the door and checks her purse for keys. She unplugs her toothbrush and jams the whole thing into her bag. She goes into her little room and packs up her drawings, wraps newspaper around the dried horseshoe crab she's been thinking about and tucks that deep where it won't be crushed. She is going home. She has a home to go to.

Her headlights flash on her mailbox, the iridescent numbers 541 lurch toward the highway, the metal door askew — the whole business knocked cockeyed by the plow, so that nothing lines up anymore. She pumps the brakes to check for ice and makes the turn down into B & R Roto-Rooter & Excavating. The high beams hit the mountains of gravel dumped on her right-of-way, flash on her road up the little knoll just beyond that and then she sees the outside lights, what she's left on to make her returns less anxious. No one moving about. Just the dark shape of Luke in the front window. Before she can pull the key from the lock, Luke's wiggling his way through the narrow opening. "Lucas, my pal." There's a bed of fiery coals: such a fine stove. So loyal, so true. "Right, Luke." She folds her arms around his neck, presses her cheek to the roll of stiff hair that mounds over his collar, lets him give her a wet slurp. Then she pushes him with her knee so she can get to the right logs.

Three flashes on the machine. "Del, it's Carla. Thought you'd like to know Rudy's gone to detox. Would you please have Mark call me?" Well, depending on when Rudy went to detox, there are that many days of not having to think about her barn burning down. The second call is a hang-up. Then, "It's me. Just wondering if you'd been able to find any info. Thought maybe the fax got fucked up since nothing came through today. Still no bass. I'll try you at Richard's. Or . . . you could call me. Things a little intense here, but nothing to worry about."

"Oh, right," she says. He has given her several pay phone numbers. It's only seven o'clock. She could call, but she does not want to talk to him until she's found some possible places, until she's tracked down the bass. He's got Rozmer for anything that requires real listening. Best she not talk to anyone, lest she start venting about Richard. She has taken flight so many times she now gives this disclaimer: Just roll your eyes and say, They're at it again. This after Richard's sister said to her the last time, Christ, you're both over sixty. Grow up. This, from a woman who decided to live alone long ago. No, she does not want to talk to anyone. She plays Mark's message again for Luke, then she reaches over and turns off the ringer.

"There are 286 facilities within 100 miles of your starting

point." Anywhere but here. Mark has said this many times. She's put in the wrong starting point. She types in White Plains instead of Marwick. "There are 490 facilities within 100 miles." She scrolls down nine or ten screens, scanning for the right words: Dual Diagnosis, Long Term, Accepts Medicaid. The words she wishes for: We're going to hold on to him until he's okay enough to go out into the world and take care of himself. Then she sees it, number 201: "Lazarus House, Therapeutic Community . . . non-hospital residential 24 hours . . . accepts dual diagnosis . . . Hedgebrook, NY." She goes back to the little map at the top of the screen. Red X 201. It looks as if it's not that far from New Vistas. Maybe even on the same train line. She types in the Lazarus House website address and the page opens up: "Lazarus House, Inc. Therapeutic Community." She skims for length of stay. "12 to 14 months." That flutter in her chest.

SELF DESCRIPTION:
Structured behavior modification self-help treatment facility.

TREATMENT PHILOSOPHY:
Expectation that the clients are the primary architects of their treatment under the supervision of the clinician.

One day on top of another on top of another.

APPROACH TO DUAL DIAGNOSIS:
Primarily referred to psychiatric social worker and agency psychiatrist for clinical management.

POSITION ON 12 STEP INVOLVEMENT:
All clients are actively exposed to the 12 Step program.

POSITION ON CONFRONTATION:
Used when deemed appropriate to a specific clinical issue.

She reads that several times. Mark has always said TCs are too hard core, too confrontational. Already she can feel herself pushing for this place. Twelve to fourteen months. She wishes they hadn't put in that part about confrontation — it might turn Mark off. She glances through the section marked "General":

GENERAL:
115 beds, 25% women, 20% under 25, 15% with a college education, 85% covered by Public Assistance, 67% receiving some form of psychiatric medication other than for detoxification.

FAMILY PROGRAM:
Family and significant others are integrated into the clinical process as thoroughly as possible on an encouraged voluntary basis.

"As thoroughly as possible" . . . "on an encouraged voluntary basis." Between these carefully edited phrases, this chorus: Night after night we expected to find out this person was dead. Hundreds of promises have been broken. You want us to open up, on an encouraged voluntary basis, to hope again, as thoroughly as possible to feel that pain once more.

She prints it all out, even the Lazarus House feedback on one of the link sites, testimonials from former clients: "Lazarus House saved my life." "Ten years clean and sober." "Bless you."

She prints out the other places Mark has told her to look up as well. They don't sound as good. None are long term, just your standard "fix you up in twenty-eight days" rehabs. She puts the stack on the counter, ready to go first thing in the morning when the fax place opens. The bad news is that the bass hasn't even been sent, some foul-up and now it's on back order. She's got it all explained in a note to fax with the rest. Better than having to tell him over the phone.

All the way to Sidney, her shoulders were in count-down, but when she makes the turn back into the gravel bank, she realizes they've unlocked. She looks toward the bluff and catches the slant of Aaron's roof rising up. What happens in her gut when the phone rings and whether she can look up this hill or not are the two barometers of how she's really feeling. For years, when she drove up this road, she had to look away.

She turns off the wipers. No sun, but across the road, there's a glimmer of light. She tips the rearview to check the back seat. Luke has conked, finally exhausted from leaping and barking at every passing vehicle, with her saying NO in a firm voice each time. Surely this ignored NO is better than nothing. The minute Luke gets in the house, he collapses on his bed.

"Next time I'm going to put a bag over your head," she tells him, but he isn't listening. 11:00. Most likely Mark's going to call any time now. She knows just what he'll say first, Fucking downer about the bass.

Oh, it'll be good to see Marna. Once Richard said, Seems like having a friend whose son is so messed up, the two of you talking so much about all that, well, wouldn't it be better to be with mothers whose kids are okay? Better not to dwell. You mean, she told him, mothers who are concerned about whether their children are going to go to Colgate or Brown, concerned because their son just came home with a pierced ear?

She takes the venison hamburger out of the refrigerator and her mother's heavy roaster from the bottom cupboard. The onions are sprouting green shoots in the dark of the bin. She gropes around for the hardest one, peels away the first couple of watery layers before chopping. Marna will help her calm down. Marna, you are my detachment guru. When that phone rings, think marsupial: once he gets too big for the pouch, out you go, joey. During this routine, Marna's long-boned body always assumes the Mama Kanga stance: she shortens her arms, sinks her six-foot frame into her haunches. Say it in the mirror every morning: Mama Marsupial, *not* Mama Bear. That way you can call the police if he forges one of your checks.

The onions go yellow, translucent. Their sweet sharpness burns away the last dank smell of so many days without sun. Covers the remains of cigarette smoke. She breaks up the first of the three pounds of meat, the center still a hard ball that must be pinched apart with freezing fingers. Freed from constructive guidance, she actually likes to cook, especially big pots of stuff that, lined up in jars in the freezer, give her a zap of cornucopian fullness every time she opens the door. Plus Marna loves her mother's chili recipe: light on the powder, heavy on the sugar and Tabasco for the tomatoes, and lots of onions and fresh mushrooms. Once the beans get added, it will threaten to roll over the top until it cooks down. Making chili is always like being back in one of their small apartment kitchens again, talking with her mother.

The phone. Sink into your haunches. She turns the heat low. All the systems are on, but she decides to let the machine pick up. "It's me, where are you?"

She sits down and breathes. "I'm right here. Just making chili. Marna's coming out for a late lunch. Did you get the faxes?"

"Bummer about the bass. Might have been better to still have it come here. But I guess as long as you express it to me once it gets to the house."

She keeps her voice light, tries for marsupial tones. "How about the faxes of places? Anything look promising?"

"Lindsey thinks this Lazarus House sounds good. Heavy-duty name. She got hold of somebody in their office to make sure I'd be eligible for coverage."

She breathes. "Would you be eligible?"

"You'd have to send a copy of my birth certificate."

"I can do that." She hears a faint drumming. Probably Mark rapping on something near the receiver. "I'm taking the phone to where I've got all your files." She turns the meat off.

"I don't know. Twelve months in a therapeutic community. Twelve months is a long time."

It still feels surreal to be walking along and have a voice, cordlessly, coming into your ear at the same time. "Okay, I'm in my studio. Can you hear me all right?" She pulls on the file drawer that holds all Mark's records, but it's jammed. "Are you there?"

"One whole year of 'do this, do that.'" His voice is so low she can barely hear him.

"Did it sound like they had any openings?"

"Don't worry, I'm not coming back there." His voice fades again. "That certainly has been the main thrust of the counseling here: how I need to grow up."

She hesitates a second then speaks precisely into the receiver: "I think we've both come a long way."

"Yeah, that's what I told John."

She loosens her delivery. "Both of us trying to do as little harm as possible under the circumstances."

The drumming is louder. "Under the circumstances," he says above the noise.

She gives the drawer a yank. It opens a little. There's a folder twisted up so the heavy drawer won't give another inch. She'll probably have to rip it to get in there. "Should I fax a copy of your birth certificate?"

There's a long silence. Finally his voice, without any accompaniment. "Some of it depends on if they'll let me have my bass. I'm not going any place where I can't have the bass."

"I could fax a copy from Sidney once I get the chili simmering. Before Marna comes."

Mark's voice sounds as if he's put the phone down and he's walking away. "What did you say was going on with Jason?"

Don't think cub, think joey. She doesn't want to tell him Marna's son, Jason, is in jail again. That Marna's worried they're finally going to make him do real prison time. Stop treating his shoplifting thefts as drug-related. "He's struggling. Should I go ahead and fax the birth certificate?"

Tap. Tap. Tap. Then a long sigh. "Sammi may come down later."

"Oh, I hope that works out. Is she still reading short stories for *Laser*? What is it she's called herself? Slush-pile Sammi?"

Just the sound of Mark breathing, then finally, "Yes."

She wishes she hadn't asked about Sammi's job. Another reminder of Mark's stalled life. "Well, tell her I said hello." Something metal clanks near the receiver. "Mark?"

"I'm here," he says.

One more time, then give it up. "What about the birth certificate?"

"Yeah. The weekend's coming up. Better get it to them now before it all falls through."

And he's gone. And here she is, humped against a bulging sky, pushing with all her Mama-Bear might to keep it from falling. Poking her fingers into the gap in the drawer, she grasps the wedged folder and hauls. REHAB tears away with such a rush that the drawer flies forward and almost lands her on her rear. The opened drawer is so heavy it tips the whole cabinet. It's packed solid, each section, each folder with its Magic Marker label: BENEFITS: MEDICARE, MEDICAID, SOCIAL SECURITY, SSI. What has she got his birth certificate under? She shuffles back to IMPORTANT DOCUMENTS: a sixth-grade report card, his correspondence high school diploma, a photocopy of an expired license. No birth certificate. Surely this is where she would have filed it and it isn't there. How can that be? She would never have sent the original without replacing it. She looks in front of the folder, behind it. Every other goddamned record, but not the one she needs to get *Mark* filed away. She'll have to go through the whole friggin' drawer. Maybe once she gets the chili to simmering. Of course it has to get faxed before five minutes ago. That's how it always is: dire. Urgent.

She pulls out a few of the other drawers for counter-balance. There is no drawer for Aaron. There never was. Her few anxious rushes at him had always been met with, Stay out. I'm okay. Just the one box of drawings and song lyrics and notebooks in the studio closet. Upstairs with her will, one thin folder marked with his name: his death certificate. What can ever counterweight that?

Slowly she eases Mark's drawer all the way forward. Most of what's in here, beyond the Benefits chunk, and maybe that too, could be under R for RESCUES. She thumbs through the section marked SCHOOLS. That's where his shot chart is. She leafs through, sheet by sheet, knowing that the marbled paper, with its small footprint, inked in the lower corner, will jump out at her when she gets to it. ONANGO VALLEY: Mark's transfer from Danford Central to her school, fifteen miles away. Ninth grade. LAWRENCE: sending him to live with Lee's cousin to go to high school in Massachusetts. AMERICAN SCHOOL so he could get a high school diploma after he dropped out, with Aaron doing most of his algebra correspondence lessons for, she found out later, a bag of pot. ANTIOCH, the superwoman energy she exerted in putting that together. No birth certificate in any of these.

Maybe she could just crack up and go merrily, merrily down that stream. She begins lifting out the folders, one section at a time: MONEY WIRES, KEY WEST, then AUSTIN, then PORTLAND, in each of these the lists of hotline numbers and mobile rescue units, then a bunch of files so far back they're hard to pull forward. Each stack gets placed in careful piles along the edge of the large door that forms the top of her drawing table–desk, so that the piles don't all sprawl together.

She hugs the first big bunch in her arms, checks to be sure Luke is nowhere in her path and makes it to the long counter beside the sink without dropping anything. When she lets go, the pile topples over. The purple, yellow, green labels bury themselves in the slide, her ordered headings no longer accessible. She turns the meat on again as Luke do-si-dos back and forth, his nose raised in keen interest. "I'm not free to dance at this time," she tells him. 12:00. She's got to get the currently nonexistent birth certificate materialized and faxed by two at the latest so Lindsey Clarke has time to send it to Lazarus House. Marna's due around one. The chili's got to start simmering *now*.

She places the cutting board on the table since it's the only clear surface left and scoops the mushrooms from the colander. Chops, chops. Then wipes her hands on the legs of her jeans. While she stirs the mushroom crescents into the meat, she begins to leaf through the first folder in the section marked APARTMENTS. Plus there's the salad to make, the garlic to mince for the bread, this mess to clear away. Shit. Her fingers leave greasy smears. CATHOLIC CHARITIES: the single-room-occupancy housing with counseling that he moved into his first time back from treatment. CHESTNUT: the place his intensive case manager had to have the police open up when Mark couldn't come to the door. MAIN: the one-room studio that had no windows and was at least ninety degrees the day she helped him move in. The futons they've dragged up and then down, the leases broken, the security lost. But no pale tan document with his baby foot stepping almost off the edge.

She opens four cans of stewed tomatoes and dumps them into the roaster, then liberal doses of salt, sugar, chili powder, Tabasco, pepper. Her mother's secret: keep seasoning each layer. Okay, she'll systematically go through the whole lot if necessary. The birth certificate is in one of the files. She'd put her life on that. She may have to press Marna into duty. Do a lot of marsupial mantras. Here she is once more, patching together another mission, opening her pouch. Dear Kanga-god, I swear this is my last major bailout.

1:00. The chili is thickening. Down an inch from the top. She opens three cans of kidney beans, drains them and then carefully folds them in. Tastes. More chili powder, more Tabasco. Now to be really right it should simmer for a few hours. She and Marna can munch celery. No birth certificate in the benefits folders or the money wires, any of the dozens of folders she's gone through. Only one more stack to go. And goddammit she knows any moment it's going to be there. Maybe Marna will be a bit late so she can find it and then get rid of all this incriminating rescue evidence, stuff all the folders back in the drawer.

She returns with the last batch: RECORDING COURSE, DRUM STUDIO, ADDITION PLANS, CARS. She starts going through the ESCORT folder. Why in heaven's name does she still have insurance papers for a car long gone to the crusher? As soon as Mark's settled, she going to dispose of everything but the few records that are critical. Like the birth certificate. She winces when she gets to the TEMPO folder. That and the recording studio course: the two actions that still cause her to screw up her face, that she still thinks about in terms of "How could I have been that stupid?"

Luke barks, barks and bounces against the door. Through the window she sees Marna heading up the walk in a long yellow slicker, her bush of red hair blazing. Marna: here comes the sun. She opens the door and waves. Might as well come clean.

Marna hugs her, bends down from what she refers to as her lofty view, then squats to take hold of Luke, to kiss the knob on the top of his head with a big smack. "What a hunk of masculine charm you've gotten to be," she tells him when he gives her his paw. Marna peels out of the slicker and hangs it on the back of the door. She pulls a bulky plastic bag from one of the pockets. "Brought us a little something. Next best thing to a bottle of Kahlúa. Got to stick it in your freezer." Halfway there she stops and looks around. "Mother of God, Del, are you all right?" She spreads one arm wide to note the clutter. The stovetop littered with open cans, the counter covered with folders, the sink full of dishes. The salad-makings on a chair. "I am impressed with such uncharacteristic disarray."

"I thought you might be."

"What's going on?"

"Mark *may* be going to that place I told you about on the phone — Lazarus House. He needs a copy of his birth certificate before his social worker leaves for the weekend. I told him I'd send it to him . . ." — she glances at the clock — "now."

Marna throws back her fiery head and laughs. "Sorry, but it's just so, you know, how the dance goes."

"I can't find it. I know it's here" — she points to the remaining folders — "but I've misfiled it. I've been, paper by paper, through everything but these."

"What can I do?"

"Go through the last stack while I deal with this." She swings her hand toward the mess. "Then I can make a quick run to fax a copy from Sidney. Got to get it there by two."

"These?" Marna picks up a folder.

"The certificate's tan, State of New York arced across the top and . . ." She turns the water on full. ". . . and in the right corner, there's his footprint. His heel, his baby toes."

Marna's eyes widen. "You're kidding. In case he got kidnapped. In case he got accidentally switched." Then she grins. "All along maybe you got the wrong kid."

"Oh, he's Lee's double. He's our child all right."

Marna shoves part of the stack her way. "Forget lunch. Let's both go through the folders."

"Please. You do the folders. I don't even want to see that stuff right now. Just let me get this mess cleaned up."

Marna leans over the counter, steps out of her clogs. "Should I begin with the one marked Tempo? God, I remember that."

"I'd forgotten I'd told you about the Tempo. Yeah, start there. You can put the finished ones . . ." She searches for a clear surface.

Marna's so much better at drawing the line. If her son had asked her for the title to the Tempo, Marna would have said, When you finish paying me for the car. But when Mark asked, she gave it to him, to show she trusted him, to treat him like a man. Two days later he sold an eight-thousand-dollar car for seven hundred at some chop shop in New York. She wraps the buttered loaf in foil. "Marna, why do I allow myself to get pulled in? Rescue after rescue?"

Marna stops going through the files and leans her way. "Surely some of it has to do with Aaron." Marna looks at her to see how she takes that in.

Aaron almost never asked. The few times he did that didn't feel like the right thing to do, she said No. Like the time he asked her to co-sign on his truck. I don't think that's a good idea, she told him. And look at what happened to Aaron.

"Oh, Del, how can you not be afraid for Mark if you don't help?" Marna places her hand on her heart as if she's about to say the pledge. "Every time Jason asks for something, like now, Can he tell the judge he's going to stay with me until he's put together six months of recovery, I always feel like Helen Keller at the water pump. I'm dragging a word up from the depths of my guts: Nnnnnnoooo. And afterwards, for days I feel like shit. What kind of mother am I that I won't let him come home?"

Del lets the spoon sink into the chili and disappear. "That's it. With Mark — I can't get the Nnnoooo out."

Marna opens the folder again. "I can't let him come home. I just can't do that to myself — carry around in the trunk of my car everything that might be stolen, take my VCR to work every day — I can't and I'm not going to. That gets me through." Marna throws up both hands. "I hate to tell you this, but there's nothing in Drum Studio either. That's the last folder."

Del leans against the refrigerator and breathes. "All right, just let me figure out what I need to do next." She fishes around in the chili for the wooden handle, then turns to watch Marna sink down on the rug and settle herself in the lotus position, watches her bend forward to touch her forehead on the floor.

Luke lifts his paw and places it on Marna's back while she intones, "Ommmmmm." Then in the same voice, she chants, "Luke, you are the dom-in-ant dooooooog."

Del drops the spoon back into the simmering pot and cackles. Whatever had been weighting down her chest, lifts. "Marna." She washes her hands and pulls her address book from her purse. "How's this: Mark, I haven't been able to find your birth certificate. As soon as I do, I'll fax it to your social worker. Goodbye."

"Yes," Marna says, rising back up. "I'm going to transfer the folders to the couch so I can start on the salad."

Del dials the number and clears her throat, goes over her speech while it rings and rings. "Del. Wait." Marna takes hold of her elbow and leads her to the counter. "It just fell out when I pushed the files aside."

A tiny footprint in the corner. Five small toes.

Del surveys the room. Eight quart jars of chili sit up against the window, cooling to go in the refrigerator. The dishes are done and the fire's settled into a steady glow of heat. Marna has stacked the folders in rows along one end of the couch and is now stretched out on the rug, propped on a stack of pillows, her toes resting against Luke's backside, her bowl of ice cream balanced on her belly. Probably Mark's birth certificate, all his records have arrived at Lazarus House by now. She turns the dimmer switch so the room fades into shadow, then settles with her own bowl into the rocker by the stove. "Is that enough light?"

Marna answers in a husky whisper, "Don't need to see to taste."

For a while they eat in silence.

"Chunks of German chocolate," Marna says.

Del presses the cold against the roof of her mouth and lets it slowly dissolve. "Crunched Heath Bars."

Marna smiles. "Coffee fudge ripples."

"A hint of Amaretto."

"Chocolate-covered almonds."

"Pecans and something I can't quite name," she tells Marna, huffing her breath to her nose to see if she can catch the scent.

Marna sits up and licks her lips. "Have you ever tasted anything..."

"More yummy?" Del sucks on the last chocolate chunk she's been saving and scrapes her spoon along the bottom to gather the last little bit, then runs her tongue around the edge of the bowl. "Want another scoop?"

Marna looks at the ceiling as if she's conferring with higher powers. "No, I'm good." She slips her toes under Luke. His eyes open a slit and then droop. He moans and Marna sings in her blues contralto, "Here we are, the three of us. Jason under wraps."

Del slides in with her own line, "Mark safe."

Then Marna croons, "Nick, on hold."

Under Marna's held note, Del adds, "And Richard, far away."

Marna smiles again. "Just the three of us, and we are...," then she looks over at Del and waits.

"Full," Del says. "Right down to our toes."

Marna sets her bowl aside and stretches out flat, curls her long legs up to her chest and then rolls back and forth. "I sometimes think how much Richard and I are alike: both of us longing for more. You and Nick, on little islands, making occasional trips to the mainland for supplies."

There's that warning flutter beneath her ribs. "Is that how it feels?"

"Sometimes." Marna is now cradling her foot in the crook of the opposite arm. "I'm there on Nick's mainland list. Sometimes up with the staples, sometimes under extras. Likely he's going to come ashore, but never quite knowing when."

She leans toward Marna, wanting to see her face. "Are we talking a sack of flour versus a chunk of chocolate?"

Marna stills. "I'm talking Yes, rather than Maybe."

She doesn't answer Marna right away. "I don't know if extra's quite the way I'd put it, but a lot of the time I have to be out in my own little boat, most of what I need right on board."

Marna's eyes widen. "But what if you paddle by, knock-knock, and there's nobody home?"

"You think that's what's going on with Richard? That he resents being treated like a . . . chocolate chunk?"

Marna squints at her. "Maybe that's some of it. Richard and I, two motherless lambs, wanting to get a guaranteed place to nestle — no matter what we do."

She'd like to get up and rinse the bowls, dry them, put the spoons in next to the forks. Marna waits, her head tipped to one side. "No matter what, Marna? Why does Richard feel he has the right to be angry about me not driving him to the airport?"

Marna closes her eyes, rests her hands palms up on her lotus-knees. Mama Buddha.

"Marna, it's *my* fear. Not up to Richard to say what I should do with it."

Sitting above Marna in the rocking chair, now all Del can see is the bright ring of her bowed head. Then her quiet answer, "Extraordinary measures for Mark, but not for him."

"Jesus Christ. Richard is not my . . ."

Marna looks at her, a sad look. "Motherless lambs."

"All right, maybe they are cries in the night . . . sometimes I can, but sometimes . . . I can't." Her hands are freezing. She stretches them toward the stove and fans her fingers. "Richard needs for me to range between Okay and Good. When I skid toward Poor, he gets anxious. Sometimes I think if he didn't blame the rotten potato left undetected in the bottom of the bag on me, if he didn't see that as a sure sign of my lack of interest in our relationship, I could live with him. Maybe if you *lived* with Nick, you might find it's more than you want."

"Oh, I know. Probably I'd still baaaaaa. But now that Mark's going to be settled, maybe Richard will feel like there's more room for him to snuggle in."

Del reaches over and picks up Marna's bowl, sets it on top of her own. "Maybe there will be."

Marna sits up and gives her a searching look. "But here's the thing. Why is it that the island people don't get together — paddle over when the wind's right. Why don't the mainlanders pair up?"

She takes the dishes to the sink and sets them quietly in. "That's the puzzle. The piece looks like it would go right in there, but it doesn't quite fit."

Marna has sunk into Down-Facing Dog, but she goes right on talking. "Maybe it's so the gene pool doesn't get green stuff scumming the top because there's not enough turmoil."

Marna rises and squeezes Del's shoulder, then she drifts to the CDs arranged around a little plastic tower. She pulls one out. "*Rain Dogs.* Hummm, I love Tom Waits. But look at him all nestled up on some mama's breast. Tom's a mainlander for sure." She places the CD in the tray. "We'd never get together. Not enough of a mismatch." She sings along, swings around the living room with her eyes shut, her voice buried under Tom Waits's gravel tones. Then she pulls off a woolly sock, shifts and slides off the other. "Got to be barefoot for Tom."

While Del glides each of the jars into the fridge, she dances too. How she loves to dance. Those Friday nights when she first knew Richard, when she waited at the Plymouth Mill House, hoping that he might be able to get away, that she'd look up and see him across the dance floor, smiling. Back when Aaron and Mark were just kids who were going to grow up and bring their children over for Thanksgiving. She loves to slow dance with Richard. The best of all slow dancers. You become water and he takes you wherever he wants to go. She misses Richard. His warm hands, his smell. She circles around the couch. Only the stacks of folders to return to the file drawers and then everything will be back in place. She lifts the first pile and starts toward her studio. Dodges as Marna whirls by. Tom Waits growls into a new song.

Del stops. She cradles the bulky pile of folders to her chest, dips, goes into a sliding waltz. She and Marna pass each other as they turn around the room, both of them singing, their shadows moving on the wall. Luke sleeps on, only the in and out of his big brown sides.

By the woodstove Del slows to a sway and opens the door. A bed of red coals. She spins the vents as wide as they'll go. From the stack she takes the TEMPO folder, then RECORDING STUDIO; those go in first. She watches them curl black along their edges. Flare up.

10 : Sharps

THE WEIGHT ROOM'S EMPTY. From this window Mark's got a long view of the parking lot. He'll be able to see her get out of the taxi, watch her walk his way. A warm rush swells his chest, a flutter of fear. Bomb-shelter urge coming on strong. Been a while, been a long while since he's been with anyone. Been that close. Open. His hinges have rusted.

He folds the pass so the yellow edge sticks out of his pocket — that way the body-counter won't have to give him any hassle. Free until eight P.M., says so right there in purple. Everybody else is watching a Bill W. movie. He swings his leg over an exercise bike and slowly pedals, just enough to keep his muscles from bunching up, but not enough to sweat. Still getting occasional zaps to the brain, but his hands feel steady enough to light her cigarette. Carry a cup of coffee across the room. He checks his pits — human, no junkie-stench.

You'll hardly know me, she told him over the phone, I'm getting so fat. This means she's gained maybe two ounces since he last saw her two years ago. Sammi, always slinky-slender, doing the ballet barre every week. Living on Diet Coke and granola. Oh, I'll recognize you, I'd recognize you anywhere, he'd said. He hadn't said *know*. Oh, I'll know you. The three or four years they'd been together — living at her apartment on Main when she was in grad school, those months in Austin, the millions of cigarettes they'd smoked together stretched out on some futon, staring up at a gray ceiling, talking, not talking, watching videos into the night — one thing he could never have honestly said: I know you.

Big hand on the twelve, little hand on the six. Sammi's about to pass through his current situation. Two hours. What are he and Sammi going to do for two hours? Want to smoke, have to shiver out in the courtyard. Introduce her to the MICAs in the trees. Steer away from Lorraine. Lorraine's transmissions of stalker-static. But don't be going ironic on the place, telling mocking New Vistas tales to fill in the blanks. Wad rehab into a ball of wit to chuck around in lieu of any real contact. Fuck up what recovery he's got going here. Just be yourself. And which self might that be? Main thing, stay with How Are You? Don't get on a Me soliloquy. Poor fucking me me me. One definite at least: he's looking better. Put on some weight, got some color, a good haircut. No holes in his clothes or his body. Fourteen days clean. Look, Sammi, no holes.

Leon pokes his head in the door, eyebrows up in surprise. Body-count duty.

He raises the yellow pass, but keeps pedaling. "I'm free till eight. Got a visitor coming."

Leon smiles. "I was wondering what that squeaking was." This Leon's all right.

"An old girlfriend's coming. Now what am I going to do to entertain her?"

Leon begins a slow climb on the StairMaster. "One step, then another and another," he says. Leon's a long time clean. "You could take her for a walk around the courtyard, but it's drizzling out there. You still got an ache in your heart for this woman? You still love her?"

He stops pedaling. "Love her?"

"Yeah," Leon says. "Your heart still going thomp, thomp?"

Mark gets off the bike and leans his forehead into the cold of the glass. "I burned that bridge. Fucking flames lit up the sky for days." Years.

Leon climbs down and heads for the door. "Well, you never

know. Get your life turned around. Maybe you'll see the sky's full of stars once the smoke clears." Leon sends him a look straight to the heart. "You want to talk later, I'll be here till eleven."

The drizzle has turned to hard rain and through that rain there's a yellow-and-black bird heading straight for him. Sammi's taxi. Sammi coming up the drive. No question his heart's going thomp, thomp, but it's more like panic than love. The taxi door opens and here she is. Sammi. Looking just like herself. Looking good. Hair a little longer, shaggy, a little bluer red. All in black: her favorite black leather skirt, turtleneck sweater. No raincoat. Tall shoes. Her eyes searchlight, and she finds him there behind the glass. Knew he'd be watching for her somewhere close. She smiles, waves. Hey, her red-red mouth says. His own lips say Hey back.

Awkward standing in the fluorescent light at the nurses' station while Leon goes piece by piece through Sammi's bag, the things she's brought him: a carton of Camels, a photo folder of Wolfie pictures. Wolfie sends his love, she said when she hugged him at the door. A real hug, but no kisses. Going to be a dearfriend visit. He knew this, he knew this, but still there's a sinking in his chest. Heart going down quick behind them thar hills.

Leon is not officious, but he's thorough. Going through the makeup bag, opening the lipstick tubes. Her change purse. He sets aside Sammi's lighter, her pen. No sharps allowed. "Have to hold these until you're ready to go," he says. Leon gives Sammi a clinical look-over. No pockets, no obvious bulges. This is not the way Mark would like to have started the visit.

"How about right here?" she says. She's pulled the hood of his sweatshirt so tight around her face, she's just an oval of eyes and nose and mouth. A face Kabuki-white in the courtyard light.

He's glad for the darkness. He pushes a bench back under the eaves. They're right next to the wall lighter and well out of the rain. From the windows across the courtyard there's the blue flicker of Bill W.

"Nifty," she says when he shows her how the wall lighter works.

He lights her cigarette, sucks until the tip glows red, and then does his own. They settle, close but not touching. For a minute, they just smoke, let go of the tension of arrival. Sigh.

"So?" she says, looking at him through her mascara and liner and shadow. Always it's been tricky to pass through that. Never leave home without it, she's told him. C-l-o-a-k.

"So. Like I told you on the phone. It's going okay. There's the anxiety about getting into Lazarus. The wondering if that's the best thing for me, if I need something so hard-core."

"Like how?" she says, giving her head that familiar tilt, that lead with her chin.

"Confrontation — 'when deemed appropriate for therapeutic purposes.'"

Her eyes are black in this light, but really they are the green of cat eyes. She looks away. "Dual diagnosis?"

"Seventy percent on psychotropic medication."

"Really?"

"Yep."

Still the scar below her lip: her first try on a skateboard. "What's Rozmer think?"

Beneath the smell of smoke, there's her Sammi-smell. Pepper. He could always go inside that. "Oh, you know Rozmer. 'Do this or do that, all part of what you're doing. It's all going round and round in the same washing machine.'"

She laughs. "The Laundromat School." Still the chip on her eyetooth.

"So" — he leans toward her — "how are you?"

A shift away, a flicker, but there it is: Don't come any closer. "Hummm, how am I?" She's quiet for a minute. "This story I've been working on." She pulls at the corner of the folder sticking out of her bag. "I can't find the end, a place to get out. So I'm not writing at all."

S-t-u-c-k. "That's a bad one."

"Like when you're not doing music," she says, turning toward him.

Like fucking now. "Bummer." He throws that at her head-on. Why? He knows she hates that word.

"No," she says, turning away again. "That is not what it is."

The distance between them. Diverging. "Okay, how about this? Are you depressed?"

"Depressed? It's this job. I'm sick of slogging through the slush." She shifts toward him, but then leans back against the wall. "We're getting an average of two thousand stories a month. Frank's gone. That only leaves three of us reading the over-the-transom stuff. Six or seven hundred stories each if everybody's doing their share." She does a gagging motion with her finger. "Word bulimia."

Her nails look black, with a flash of something bright on each one. He takes hold of her hand to see. Vinyl, with silver stars. She holds both hands up to the light and ripples her fingers. They flicker. A crescent moon on each thumb. "My friend Varsi does them. Nice, huh?"

"Makes it a little hard to use your fingers, doesn't it?" he says.

"Well, I can't play my cello, if that's what you mean. And I have to lift the Coke tab with a knife. Have to come at the keyboard at an angle to cause carpal tunnel, but other than that." She joins the tips of her nails. "Remember this one?"

"Two spiders shaking hands."

"A spider doing pushups on a mirror."

She intertwines her fingers, her black nails hidden inside. "How about this one?"

He studies her clinched hands, his finger to his brain. "Two elephants dressed up as spiders hiding in a refrigerator."

She ripples her hands in the light again. "They cheer me up when I'm on my six-hundredth bad story."

One more cigarette and then he's going to have to take Sammi inside for warmth. What fun thing can he find for them to do next? The lights come on in the lounge. Bill W.'s done. People start moving about. Bees in a jar. Lorraine, Gerald, Jarvis, Tom . . . Lorraine looks out. No doubt sees them there. Better fill Sammi in on Lorraine. Soon they'll all be out to smoke. No question

Lorraine's going to insinuate herself into the situation before Sammi leaves.

"One of the women here, Lorraine, has been leaning into me since I arrived. No encouragement from me."

"Oh," she says. Wary.

"I'm just telling you because if we run into her, she'll give you some weird vibes." It has got to be at least seven. Time going so fast, going so slow.

As though she's read his thoughts, she says, "Taxi's coming right at eight."

The wind's picked up. They both start to shiver. She's sending out the signals, This is as close as I want you to get. "Let's go in," he says.

It's warm inside. He tries to slip them by the lounge, but no, Lorraine turns just as he glides Sammi by. Lorraine on recon and chances are no matter where he and Sammi go, she's going to track them down. Sammi takes off his sweatshirt and ties it around her waist, rubs her starry hands together. She's right: they are cheerful. "Are you hungry," he says, moving toward the kitchen. A desperate waylay: Sammi's not into food.

"We could play Scrabble. Bring the board out here." Too déjà vu Austin. They had played a million hours of Scrabble, when he wasn't sneaking off to get high. She gives him that flicker of recognition. "You said there's a gym, right? Well, how about I challenge you to a game of H-O-R-S-E?" she says.

"Horse? Really?"

"Yeah, I've been practicing my shots after I work out. Whip your ass if you give me an H-O handicap."

When he returns from his locker with his new Spalding, she's on the foul line, barefoot, the waist of her skirt rolled up a few inches to give her a bit more clearance. Her sleeves shoved up. Legs tan, tan in March. The gym is so big and they are so small. Bright-bright — no place to duck for cover. He spins the ball on his finger, extending it toward her as it whirls, then moving it away. The hundreds of hours he spent learning how to do this. Look, Dad. See me. See me.

She feints toward him, grinning. "You trying to intimidate me, boy," she says.

He takes a hook shot from the corner. It swishes through. "Intimidate you, Sammi. I don't think so. But I am wondering how you are going to get your fingers around the ball."

"Very carefully," she says. He sets the ball into her bowled palms. She bounces it. Bounces it. Each time catching it in the heels of her hands. "Okay, now you've got to pass it to me gently. No, maybe you better just hand it to me. And, don't forget, you're starting off with an H-O already besmirching your dazzle."

He moves to the basket. "We know she can talk," he says, "but can she shoot?"

"Ready?" She spreads her legs and takes an underhand foul shot. It rolls around the rim, wobbles, and drops through. "Huh, I told you I was getting better. Now you have to do it exactly the same."

"Wobble it around the rim?"

"The Horse gods don't like hubris."

The thud of the ball as he dribbles: how he loves that sound, the smack of the leather against his palm. He spreads his legs in imitation of her stance and releases the ball. It drops through clean.

She moves into the lane. "Ready," she says. She raises her arms, focuses on the basket.

"Go," he tells her.

There's the suck of the door closing. He turns. Lorraine. His stomach tightens. This is a little more dramatic action than he needs. Lorraine in complete doll-up: a bright spot of color on each cheek, lacy shirt. Lorraine, giving Sammi the full Geiger. Lorraine coming on, coming on, big smile. Blonde on blonde. Sammi, the dark angel, moving toward the foul line.

"Lorraine," he says when she finally enters their zone. "Lorraine, this is Sammi."

Sammi wedges the ball against her hip, her lovely hip, and extends her glittering hand. "Hello," she says.

A second of fluster before Lorraine gets her hand out. "We

were wondering where you were," Lorraine says, turning toward him.

"I've got a pass," he tells her.

"You missed a good movie," she says.

Sammi hands him the ball and looks at her watch. "How about pointing me in the direction of the bathroom. Then maybe we can hang out by the entry and look at the pictures of Wolfie while I wait for the taxi. Nice to meet you," she tells Lorraine. Full face on, her most genuine smile.

"To the left of the main entrance," he tells her.

Sammi gathers her bag, slips on her shoes, swings his sweatshirt over her shoulder. Sammi, the pro. The door sucks closed behind her.

"Your girlfriend? I didn't know you had a girlfriend."

Draw a line, but don't draw blood. "She and I go way back, but I wrecked all that. We're friends now." He takes a shot from the corner. The ball hits the rim.

"Looks like she's more than a friend," Lorraine says.

"Nope. Just friends." He retrieves the ball. He turns toward the far exit. Lorraine moves along with him. He holds the door for her. "See you guys later," he tells her.

Final scene coming up. Can he leave them laughing? Sammi's waiting by the window under the light. She's pulled a chair over for him, the Wolfie pictures, her story folder in her lap. She's all set. Ten to one she won't mention Lorraine. She's going for an upbeat goodbye.

He presses his shirt against the trickle of sweat making its way down his spine.

"Does Leon have to come to let me out?" she says when he gets within range.

"No. You just can't come back once the door closes. What about your lighter?" Grab on to the ordinary, buddy, and don't let go.

"It's almost out of fluid anyway. How about if I borrow your sweatshirt though. Mail it to you at Lazarus House."

She pulls his chair a little more into the light. He sits down. Careful. Careful. "Want to look at the Wolfie pictures?"

He takes a breath, swallows the rising swell in his throat. "Sure," he says.

She pulls out the photos. "If you see any you want, you can have them." She hands him the first one. "This is my favorite."

Wolfie is sprawled on his back on the couch, all four legs in the air, his big shepherd head drooped over the side, tongue lolling. He tries to make his lips turn up in a grin. Good old Wolfie, but his mouth will not smile. Not going to be able to give her the golden goodbye. He hands the picture back to her. He stands and turns away from the light, presses his fingers against the bar that opens the door. "Sammi, I'm going to go up to my room now."

She comes toward him. He turns for her hug, takes it head-on.

Then the stairs, one step at a time. "I'll call you," he says from the landing. "Once I get where I'm going, I'll give you a call."

11 : Claws

Sun. DEL HAS TO push to free the swollen window
frame. Still a bit too chilly, but she leaves it open a crack. Maybe
Mark will call this morning to say if his records have gotten
to Lazarus House okay. Maybe the visit from Sammi cheered
him up.

She lifts the horseshoe crab from the window ledge. Just a few
preliminary studies. She knows she's not going to loosen up
enough to really get going on a project until Mark's settled, but
at least she can start drawing, get back into "seeing." The front
shell of the horseshoe crab is at least eight inches in diameter. No
question this is a mama: her size, the claws of a female. Mama
Kanga, Mama Bear, Mama Horseshoe Crab.

She turns the dried crab's body on its back, so the light will
dip into the cavity, cast shadows behind its legs. All that vulner-
ability once it gets flipped over. This crab that is not a crab, but
more of a three-hundred-million-year-old spider. She and Richard
had found it at the end of the airstrip in Crystal Key, circles of
sand where it had tried to make its way back to the tide line. She
rips the paper carefully along the straightedge. This lovely thin
paper with no grain. Right for these fragile remains. A hard pencil. She'll begin fine and build up from there.

The phone. That squeeze in her chest.

"It's me. I just had a phone interview, sort of, with the people
in the business office."

She slides the paper away and sits down. "Did you get the birth certificate?"

"Yeah. Now you have to send a rep-payee release. Can you fax that here?"

"Have you been accepted?" She keeps away from the high tones of joy.

"Sounds like it's almost a done deal once they get the release. But I don't know."

"Well . . ."

"Sammi may call you. To see about getting a recommendation. She's thinking about applying for one of those residencies. In writing."

"Sammi. How did that go?" No answer. She shouldn't have asked.

Finally his voice, tired, far away. "How could it go? Sammi's got a life. It was awkward. I almost wish she hadn't come."

The swelling in her throat, the sadness she feels for this child. "I'm sorry."

"So anyway. About this Lazarus House. One of the aides here went through the program. He says it's definitely confrontational. They give you something they call Haircuts."

She unlocks the door. Surely that was the last fax trip to Sidney. Five blinks on the phone. All of them Mark, sighs and incomplete sentences of defeat. She finds the lists of pay-phone numbers and works on calming in time to the rings. The voice that answers is Mark's. She sits down and settles all the way in. "You sound discouraged."

"I haven't been sleeping." His voice is flat. "I'm feeling irritable."

"What's going on with your medication?"

"They lowered the Zyprexa back to what it was before. I was getting a reaction. I'm on a new antidepressant."

"How long have you had trouble sleeping?"

There's a pause. She can hear him breathing.

"Since Tuesday. Today's Friday. Three nights."

"That's a good sign."

"What?"

"That you know that."

A weary laugh. "Fucking hopeless that being able to count to three is a good sign."

"You know that's not true. Sounds like you're heading into a manic episode. Maybe it's the antidepressant."

He sighs. "My psychiatrist won't be back until Monday. Weekend. Everything goes minimal around here."

"There's a psychiatrist on call. Get the nurses to have him reduce the antidepressant."

"I'll talk to them."

"Something's going to work out."

"Something better."

The horseshoe in morning light is someone else. She starts over. Maybe a cream-colored paper with more tooth. A softer pencil. Turned so the spiked tail is the nearest point. This fierce-looking tail not a weapon at all. What the horseshoe uses to balance, to flip herself upright. Her soft underbody armored again. She closes one eye, flattens the mass. The absence of any light where this connects to that. An edge rounding, into shadow . . . Ringing jolts her.

"It's me. The rep-payee release got here. They put it in Lindsey's box. I'll let you know if I'm able to connect with Lazarus House Monday. Any news on the bass?"

Patience. "Remember they said it won't be available for delivery until next week."

"Rozmer says, 'Don't think so much.' Maybe I can just whistle," he says and does a few notes.

"Right."

"Well, one thing I've been doing is making lots of contact calls. Charlie, when I want to talk to someone who understands being nuts or when I want to talk about music. Rozmer, every morning at six thirty."

"Six thirty?"

"Yep. Breakfast at seven. Nobody eats till everybody's lined up on the ramp. Let me speak to Luke."

"I've got Luke barricaded out of where I'm drawing. Otherwise he pushes my subject around. Just a minute." She extends the phone over the gate and Luke rises. She positions the receiver so he can both listen and speak. His head cocks to the side. She hears Mark doing "Just whistle a happy tune." "He knows it's you."

"Later," Mark says. He's wound; she's wound. When he's conversational, sounds normal, there's always that edge: Is it the up of mania only a few days around the bend?

There's a skin of ice on the puddles and the air smells like snow coming. After the first toss, the ball is smeared with a glaze of mud. It's too slippery to take Luke to the falls and if he doesn't get a wear-him-out run, he's too bouncy to live with. Chasing this ball: he can stay with it for longer than she's ever been willing to reciprocate. No question, the trees up the hill are brighter than they were even a week ago. No white gleams of shadbush blossoms yet, but they're only a few weeks away if the sun would bless them with a run of warmth.

"Want to go to the mailbox, Luke?" He leaps into the air. Yes, yes he does.

They come to the gravel-bank business: B & R Roto-Rooter, the big flat they must cross to get to the main highway. Several huge piles of various grades of stone rise up on both sides, sometimes cascading onto her right-of-way, so that you have to jog around, driving in and out. Richard keeps telling her she should speak to the owner about his infringement. You let him do that for a few years without registering any notice and that land becomes his. Richard.

It's good to see they've cleaned up the business some. The rusty van, stuffed full of pipe and wire, the piles of tires, no longer sprawl along the edge of the turn into the gravel bank, leaving open the rise where on bright-moon nights, hundreds of Queen Anne's lace used to shimmer. As they approach the highway, she shortens Luke's leash to heel length. His instinct to leap for cars as though they are birds makes this last stage of picking up her mail always a bit tense. She waits until she sees no cars coming in either direction and then makes a run up the last rise to her box, grabs what's inside — a package, junk mail. She heads away from the highway and back toward her house, the leash unlocked once more. The package is addressed in Richard's bold hand, with *M. Lanza* for the return. Chocolates, she already knows. Each mound flavored with a touch of liqueur: Irish cream, Amaretto, Kahlúa . . . Richard is sorry.

The horseshoe caught on an angle as though banked against a rush of sea oats with a wide view of the armored plate. She tucks a square of paper under the heel of her hand to keep the smearing down. This armored body, the horseshoe's final home. The crab molts four times each year, growing new armor beneath until it splits its too-small shell. She'd like to do a series of that metamorphosis. Even the screeching descent of the gulls on the eggs before the tides cover them. Good studies for the larger work at the Owl Lake Center in October — if she gets in.

Mark's papers have all gone to Lazarus House. Surely he'll hear something definite from Lazarus in the next few days. She blows a line of carbon into the trash.

Finally he calls. "It's me. Nothing from Lazarus House. Lindsey contacted the business office. They said the people at Lazarus House in Hansen will contact me here."

"I've been looking at the map. Hansen isn't on the rail line. New Paltz is the closest bus town. Maybe I should do some checking."

"I haven't even gotten into the place."

"I know, but I've started to worry about your transportation if you do."

Far down the road just before the corner, something strange is crossing. What in god's name can it be? A long dark creature, humping across, more and more of it emerging from the bushes

—like nothing she's ever seen. She accelerates and then she sees it is not one creature, but many, all flocked together, undulating. Wild turkeys. Twenty or more. As the car approaches, several waddle into the field, the rest manage to lift their bottom-heavy bodies to land in the low branches of a sycamore.

Just as she goes to open the door, the phone begins to ring. It's Mark and probably he's going to tell her something she doesn't want to know.

"It's me. I've screwed things up for getting into Lazarus House."

She leans back and closes her eyes. "What do you mean?"

"I wasn't going to tell you, but..." Feel free not to. "... I think maybe the reason I haven't heard from Lazarus is because of some trouble I've had here. Black mark on my record." She lifts her hand to ward off what's coming. "There's this woman. She's followed me around ever since I got here. They've got these no-contact rules at New Vistas." He's spelling it out. "I've got no problem with that. Really nothing much happened. Just occasional hugs. Support. Sort of. But it's like everywhere I go, there she is." She breathes. This doesn't sound as if it's headed toward crisis. "I don't know. Things felt so fucked up with Sammi, I just kind of let down my guard. Anyway. What happened is we got written up. Counselors said I should have come to them, laid out the situation. This was on my record that went over to Lazarus."

Her chest opens, eases. "Oh, Mark, I can't think that's going to count heavily. How's it going now?"

"She's gone. Went for some special program for anorexia. But she keeps calling me. I don't want to hurt her feelings."

"Sounds like a tough one."

"Yeah. You know I'm starting to feel like none of this is going to come together. Like maybe it'd be better if I just went down to the city. Tried for a bike-messenger job."

Do not rush over that drop-off. "Might be a good time to run it all by the therapist, by John. I think you know what's the best thing for you to do."

"It's Friday. John's gone. Everybody's gone."

"How about Rozmer?"

"He's at some workshop this weekend. I've got to go."

"All right, but if you feel like talking, I'm going to be around the next couple of days." Me and the horseshoe crab.

She sits and listens to the dial tone. She pulls the Lazarus House folder out of the drawer. How far out of line would she be? She rehearses what to say. She dials the number. On an encouraged voluntary basis she's integrating early.

"Lazarus House."

She's startled. "Oh." Her prepared speech vanishes. "Would it be possible for me to speak to . . . the director?"

"The director?"

"The person in charge of admissions?"

"Hold on." She hears a muffled exchange. "Who's calling?"

"Del Merrick. It's regarding the pending admission of my son, Mark Merrick."

"Pending admission? Just a minute." Again there's an exchange — maybe with a hand over the receiver.

"This is the director." A voice of dignity and authority. "How may I help you?"

"My son, Mark Merrick, was told by your business office that his admission was in process. His records have been forwarded to Lazarus House. He's been trying to get you himself, but . . ."

"Where is he now?"

"He's at New Vistas in Ridgeway."

"Mark Merrick?"

"Yes. I can give you his social worker's name and number." For a second she blanks on where she's got that written down. As she pulls her address book from her purse, the whole thing upends and dumps at Luke's feet. He picks up her plastic baggie of ibuprofen and Kleenex and goes to the far side of the living room. She gives the director Lindsey's name and number.

"I'll look into this, Ms. Merrick. I'm not sure why your son hasn't been contacted. He should have been. Since it's almost five on Friday, I'll have to wait until Monday to check. I'll get in touch with Ms. Clarke as soon as I talk to my staff Monday morning."

Joy, and it lifts her voice almost to song. "Oh, thank you. I know if Mark could have reached you, he would have taken care of this himself."

"Monday morning," he says again.

She dials the same pay phone that Mark answered before. A woman answers. She'll see if she can find Mark. In a few minutes she hears him moving toward the phone, talking to someone. She works on calming. How's Mark going to feel about her intervention?

"Yo," he says.

"Mark, I was able to reach Lazarus House. I got the director and it sounded to me like your admission is going to work out. He said you should have been contacted by now and he's going to deal with it first thing Monday morning, then call your social worker."

His voice is joyful, too. "You are the man," he says.

Two days of sun and temperatures in the fifties and almost all the snow's gone. Water pours from the gutters, makes pools at the end of the house. She finds the pickax in the corner of the barn and digs two trenches long enough to reach where the ground slopes away to let the water run off. Richard has put extra vents in the floor to deal with the dampness in the crawl space, but it's important not to let water stand close to the walls. One more day and things should be settled for Mark. Now only the problem of how to get him there.

As soon as Mark calls tomorrow to say his admission is settled, she'll fax him the info. Deposit $120.00 for him to withdraw from the ATM in Ridgeway. Enough for cigarettes as well.

> Ridgeway Taxi (715) 456-8888.
> Call for pickup at New Vistas 9:30 A.M. ($12.)
> Train:
> Leave Ridgeway 10:15 A.M.
> Arrive White Plains 11:00 A.M. ($9.)

Trailways:
   Leave White Plains 11:30 A.M.
   Arrive New Paltz 1:30 P.M. ($34.)
A&S Taxi (415) 433-0000.
   Call for pickup at bus station around 1:50 P.M. ($25.)
   Arrive Lazarus House in Hansen approx. 2:45 P.M.

Monday. Maybe only a few more hours of this limbo. The first geese have passed through and even without Richard, she's made the big switch. She pours raisin bran into her favorite bowl and sprinkles on some sugar. She turns her chair toward the big window to see the maple limb that drops low, with the loop of thick rope, all that's left of the old swing. The glow of spring coming on: sun and a morning frost on grass that's going green. Between getting up for her tea and returning, it happens. The backyard's full of robins. A dozen or so, little tipped wheelbarrows, pecking the mole-tunneled ground.

The phone. Too early for Mark to have heard from Lazarus. "Rise and shine."

It's Richard and she is happy to hear his voice. "I got the candy. I've been thinking about us dancing at the Plymouth Mill House. How are you?"

10:00. Mark could call any time now. As soon as Lazarus House connects with Lindsey. She places the travel information on the counter by the door, along with her purse.

She takes a few sheets from the pile of used paper and sharpens a number 2 pencil. Positions the horseshoe so it's flat, its inside fully exposed to the morning light. Contours only. Empty the mind of waiting. Get to know the underside of the armor. She moves her chair to catch another angle.

1:00. Surely Mark has heard something by now. She can't focus. Better to start taking the plastic off the windows even though it's a little early. Maybe begin washing them inside. Move about. If she's got Windex, paper towels. A good indoor job that doesn't make any noise.

She places the horseshoe crab back on the window ledge, tidies her drawing table. Once Mark is really settled, she'll set aside time each morning so she and Luke can get out to collect signs of spring coming. Maybe something from each month, each object carefully rendered. Magnified. By early April she should hear if she's been granted a residency at Owl Lake for the fall. If she has, that will give her new energy to really get going on a project. She could call him. No, she couldn't.

The phone. Marna. "Marna, I'm ready to jump out of my skin waiting to hear if Mark got into this friggin' Lazarus House."

"Just checking in to see if you'd heard anything."

"I'll call you tonight. Meanwhile I'm going to start on the windows."

"The windows?" Marna laughs. "Oh, yeah, the windows, right."

Mark still hasn't called. Something has definitely gone wrong. She presses the announcement button: "I have an errand I have to take care of. I should be back by noon at the latest." She doesn't want to mention Mark's name in case somebody like Rudy or Carla calls. Of course she could just call him and find out what's wrong. But she isn't going to. "Luke, you have to stay." She's too skittery to listen to him barking at every vehicle. She puts *Simple Things* in the car's tape deck and turns it up.

Three red flashes. "It's me. Okay, I'll call back." . . . "It's me. I guess you aren't back yet." . . . "It's me again. There's been some trouble here. I shoved a guy during the AA meeting yesterday and ended up being put in isolation. I gave my seventy-two hours' notice to leave, but I withdrew that this morning after a session with John and Lindsey. Sounds like the Lazarus House thing is fucked anyway. Call me here around one. Don't worry."

If Lazarus House isn't going to work out, maybe she should have some alternatives ready when she calls Mark at one. Google. She types in "therapeutic communities." Over the top of the LAZARUS HOUSE label, she folds down a new one: THERAPEUTIC COMMUNITIES. She places the folder by the phone.

"MICA Unit." A woman's voice. Older.

"Yes, this is Del Merrick calling, Mark Merrick's mother. He asked me to call him at one, but two of the pay-phone numbers have been busy for the last hour and no one's answering the other one. I wondered if you might be able to arrange for me to speak to him briefly on this phone or you could let him know I'm trying to get him and he can call me as soon as a pay phone's free."

"Just a moment, Ms. Merrick," the woman says.

She sits down, scratches hard beneath Luke's collar. Another long speech, rehearsed and delivered up in a rush.

"Hello. Ms. Merrick? This is John Burns, one of Mark's counselors. It's break time. I'll track him down and one way or another he'll give you a call." John Burns knows all about her supermom exploits.

She is not going to do anything. Just sit here by this phone and scratch Luke's backside and breathe until the goddamned thing rings and tells her the story. She sees she's pulled the cushion over to rest on her knees. The pillow to shield against a head-on.

"It's me. First of all — things have settled down here. Maybe even a good thing I blew up. This guy just kept bearing down on a new kid, all sorts of cross-talk shit and I don't know what happened, but at the end of the meeting, I just lost it. Gave him a shove when he got in my face."

"And they put you in isolation?"

"Yeah, and that was a good thing, too. Both John and Lindsey spent a lot of time with me. Just dealing with my anger. Though it is another black mark."

"How are you doing now?"

"I'm okay. All right, now, the other thing is that the man from Lazarus didn't call Lindsey. I tried many times to get the place, but again I just kept getting their machine."

"Oh me. The director was so definite."

"Did you get this guy's name?"

She thinks back through the conversation. "I don't know if he even gave it to me. I was so tensed up; if he did, I didn't register it."

Mark laughs. "Well, get this. Lindsey finally calls the business office again. She tells them about your conversation with this director. The woman she talks to says, Director, what director? She says she can't imagine who that would be. That the place is basically run by the clients themselves, that the main supervisor is a woman. Mom, you were talking to one of the addicts." He laughs again.

She realizes her hand is gripping her hair. "What sort of place is this? It sounded so great on the internet, this man who talked to me spoke with such authority."

"Addict authority. But don't feel bad. You were dealing with a pro."

"So, you still want to go to Lazarus House? I got some names of a few more therapeutic communities. But now I feel like you ought to have a chance to go and check them out, have an interview there." She opens the folder.

There's a pause, the sound of tapping. "Well, maybe you can fax Lindsey the stuff tomorrow morning. Definitely time for me to make a move out of here. Before I get myself in any more trouble. Got to go, got to do the ten-foot wall."

Richard will be back April 3. Five days. What she needs is to have Mark tucked away safe. Then a few days to rebalance. Days of sun and the shadbushes to finally blossom. There's the sound of a motor and then Luke's bark. The UPS truck is just backing toward the house. By the time she gets to the truck, the UPS lady is reaching out a hand to give Luke a biscuit.

"Oh, my son will be so glad to get this," she says.

"Must be going into the guitar business," the woman says with a friendly smile. "Seems like I've delivered three or four of these here since I came on this route. This bruiser was just a puppy then. What's he weigh now?"

"One hundred and three pounds — the last time we got him on the vet's scale," she says with pride. Luke, her progeny. The bass is here at last. This will give Mark a lift.

There's a message on the machine. She presses hard on Play: "It's me. Be careful what you wish for. The Lazarus van is here to pick me up. I'm in a rush to get my shit together. Send the bass when it comes. No calls for two weeks. Bye, Luke. I love you, Mom."

12 : Lazarus

THEY DROP HIM off in front. "Last chance to make a
run for it," the guy in the back tells him when he reaches in to
get his stuff. Big grin. A lot of teeth missing.

"Right," he says. Maybe the guy's name is Clifford. He's got
to do better at remembering their names.

Ricardo, the driver, his name's tattooed on his forearm, rolls
down the window, calls back, "Better have a smoke. Last chance
before they put you in the chair." The chair. What the fuck has
he gotten himself into?

"Trust the process, baby," the back-seat guy yells above the
rumble of exhaust. Piece-of-shit van. "Stick and stay. Look at us."

He hears them laughing as they pull out, make the turn down
a steep driveway. Still, they've been okay. Gave him the deal during the two-hour ride from New Vistas. Both of them six months
clean to his twenty-one days. Junkie boot camp. Going to tear
you down; then build you back up. Mortification and absolution.
You're going to want to leave; you're going to head for the door
a hundred times, but just ask yourself this: Then what?

When his legs move him along, the ground isn't quite where
it's supposed to be. Something funny going on up there. Did he
tongue the Zyprexa this morning? Yesterday? The day before that?
He can't remember. His hand's shaking when he lights up. Can't
go loony out here in the strange. The peeling sign on the iron
gate says LAZARUS HOUSE. He does a quick once-over: gray

stone, three stories, fire escapes, rusty gutters. Got the same gothic-horror feeling of Langston Psych, except there aren't any bars on the windows. Looking down at him from the portico roof, a pink plastic flamingo. It's a sign. A sign of what?

He shifts his backpack, twists a knot in the pillowcase that holds his books, his dirty clothes. Likely he's going to be one of the few white boys here. One of the few not mandated. Jail or rehab. Going to be the real thing. None of your New Vistas Let's Pretend. Big double doors. Little sign in brass. TODAY IS THE FIRST DAY OF THE REST OF YOUR LIFE. A Rozmer favorite. Through the glass he sees there's no one in the entry hall. He turns the knob. A blast of heat and the smell of wax. To the left there's a sign marked OFFICE. A poster by the office door says,

> ACT AS IF:
> YOU'RE MATURE.
> YOU'RE CONFIDENT.
> YOU FEEL GOOD.
> YOU ARE THE PERSON YOU ASPIRE TO BE.

There's somebody sitting at a computer. Shaved head. A scar as thick as his thumb below the jawbone. He gives a quick glance for breasts. Hard to say. "Excuse me. My name's Mark Merrick. I just arrived."

The person gives him a long look and then picks up the phone. He sees the name tag says *Bonita M., December 23, 2001.* Bonita. Bonita. Ricardo. And maybe Clifford.

"This is Bonita in the office. Would you let Sydney know Mark M. is here ... You want me to make the announcement?" She eases the phone back in place with two hands like it's breakable. "You're going to be in Sydney's group. He'll be down in a few minutes." She doesn't do anything friendly with her face. She turns on a small mike and taps to see if it's live. "Attention, Family." She waits a few beats. "Would you please assemble for a welcoming party for Mark, our new Brother. Thank you."

Welcoming party. Brother. Family. Sydney. Bonita. Ricardo. Maybe Clifford. My name is Mark M. He'd like to sit down, but he doesn't want to ask this woman if that's okay. He fingers the edge of the pack of Camels in his sweatshirt pocket, sucks in. At least three hours before they'll let him smoke. He sees he's left wet marks where he gripped the counter. He brushes his hands against the sides of his pants.

The lobe of Sydney's left ear is missing. He pulls his eyes away, but Sydney looks right into him. Sydney's got the glint, the burn of been-there. Not going to scam Sydney.

"First the Family's going to give you the traditional welcome. Then you'll have some time to think it over: how you got here, if this is the place for you. Sit yourself down in the reflection chair in an empty room — just you and you. We call it the Initiation Monad. See how that goes. Then we'll set you up with a Big Brother to help orient you, keep you up on the rules. Going to take it easy on you the first few days. Ricardo and Clifford ran it by you, right?"

Sydney's voice, a fuzz of echoes: what's going to happen first, what's going to happen next. Can't talk to anyone outside the house for two weeks. No letters. Not even Rozmer. Going to be given a job like dishwashing first, then can work his way up: Ramrod, Expediter, Coordinator . . . He nods like he actually follows. His feet take him along.

"Going to meet your Sisters and Brothers," Sydney tells him.

The stairs are marble, winding, worn down in the middle. Up, up, up. Twenty-eight steps. Got to remember that number. There's the heat of getting closer. Breath-heat. And then the hall's alive: they're lined up on both sides. Someone grabs his hand. "Welcome home, Mark." Smiling faces. Mouths: dark holes with teeth gone. "Welcome home, Mark." He nods, tries to raise the corners of his lips. Their palms dry, callused; his hands clammy. "Going to run your story by us soon, Mark?" One side of a woman's face, a blue-red birthmark. They pass him along: men, women, down the full length of the hall, people reaching out to grip his hand, then they pull him the other way. He makes his fish-fingers grip back. "You're home now, Brother." A lot of sad eyes. Got to be more than a hundred. Maybe ten or twelve other white boys. Clifford and Ricardo blur by. "Home, Brother." His head has a telephone inside and it's ringing, ringing. Don't freak on me now, buddy. Not here. Not now. The last man, a giant, reaches down and pats his cheek, a jiggling sign on his chest says I AM A BABY. PLEASE HELP ME GROW UP.

Rooniebingdelooniebingbalooniebing. The hall's empty; the chair's hard. Behind one of these doors, buttons banging in a dryer. All the doors closed, but breathing's coming through some of them. Twenty-eight bings. Aaron. Twenty-eight. Aaron's trying to tell him something. The sound stops. Only distant voices now. His armpits, his groin, his ass, everything itches. His thermal underwear's still damp and creeping. Not a junkie-itch. He's been clean for twenty-one days. Twenty-eight minus seven. He sneaks a look down the hall out the sides of his eyes. No one's watching. Unless there's a little hole in the door across from the chair. He rolls his pupils up to look through his lashes. That way he doesn't have to move his head. He can't find the hole in the door. He wiggles his rear, his back against the chair to scratch what he can. He's not to move, not to lift his eyes. Monad? If he can't get through it, he's out the door. Just you and you. Three hours. No way to know how much time has passed. He needs a cigarette. He needs to piss. Piss. Piss.

Now listen to me. Listen to me. You're going to come apart and run down the wall if you don't listen to me. Close your eyes. No one is watching through the door. Do the breathing. Take the air in the left nostril, down, down. Let it out the right. In right . . . down, down. Now — put yourself someplace safe and do what they tell you for now. Don't let them find out.

"Nicotine time," a voice says. He feels a hand on his shoulder. "You don't look so good, man." He pulls his lids apart, blinks to focus. He's seen this face somewhere before. "Okay, Little Brother." The hand touches his shoulder again. The face laughing. "You made it through the first big one." He can barely hear the words through the hum.

"I remember at the end of three hours, I was ready for the rubber room." The voice happy about something. It's Ricardo. Says so right there on his arm. "Arise," and Ricardo gives him a little boost up. "You know, Laz, like Lazarus. Coming out of the Monad's like coming back to alive." He does rise. "You okay?" Ricardo says. "Come on. Smoking room's just at the end of the hall there." He holds up a plastic sack. "Brought you a soda and something to eat. Everybody's at Evening Meeting right now."

"Got to take a piss," he says.

"Right through that door," Ricardo tells him. "I'll wait here."

His hands are shaking so bad, it's hard to unzip. Feels like he's going to keep going forever. He rinses out his mouth. Then ducks to the faucet to drink and drink. There's a person looking at him from the mirror: a white boy with purple under his eyes and gray sticking out by his ears. Some crazed sicko. "Be careful," the person tells him with a twisty smile. He's relieved to see the guy's got all his teeth.

The smoking room's full of beat-up plastic chairs pushed back against the walls. Public-funding decor. The windows are dark. Daytime when he got here; nighttime now. He manages to get a Camel out, but he can't find his lighter. He gets the cigarette to his lips, but it's still jumping around.

"Here." Ricardo reaches over and gives him a light. *Ricardo N., October 3, 2001.* "You'll get your own matches once you've been here ninety days."

Ninety days. He walks back and forth and smokes. Breathes. Settle down, settle down.

"Some heavy-duty shit, right?" Ricardo says.

He doesn't say anything, just keeps moving. Floor still not quite where he expects it to be. Ricardo sits. He pushes a chair out for him on the other side. One table leg shorter than the others, so when you touch it, it wobbles. That table knows.

Ricardo pulls a can from the bag. "Mountain Dew and a ham sandwich." He can't drink Mountain Dew. All Aaron was living on by then. "Eat. While you eat, I'll fill you in."

He nods and pulls the wrapper from the bread. Wonder Bread.

Brown mustard and limpy lettuce. Not going to be your New Vistas cuisine, but he's got to eat. The bread sticks in his throat; no way he can drink the Mountain Dew.

"Okay," Ricardo says, then he rests his arms on the table. Red petals, blood drops drifting down through his name. "Good news is I'm going to be your Big Brother." Same ho-ho in his voice, then his hand comes across the table. The hand. For a second he reflexes back. A handshake. Ricardo's reaching out to shake his hand. He wipes his palm on his shirt and returns the grip. "So. You lucked out there, Bro." Ricardo laughs. "Going to get the benefit of my experience." Ricardo's got two rows of white teeth and all his fingers. "I've been here six months," Ricardo tells him. "Couple more good months, I'll be going out into a Lazarus apartment."

Ricardo stops. Looks at him to see if he wants to say something. "Well, the thing is, you just got to do what you're told. You know — fake it. You're good at that, right? But it's going to get easier."

He nods. This Ricardo may be okay. Get the static down, subdue the trembles, maybe he could roll into a groove. There are posters with quotes all around the room. Some have suns rising in the corner or trees bursting into bloom. Words. These places are all big on wise sayings. They're not of the Just Say No school of persuasion.

"From here." Ricardo swivels his head a little to pull Mark's attention back to the topic at hand. "From here, I'm going to take you up to your dorm. Your stuff's up there in your locker. Locker with a lock. You'll get another smoke break right before bed. Three other guys in your room. All of them got some time in. They'll be up after Evening Meeting. Give you a chance to settle in. You're supposed to read the orientation manual. Lights out at eleven."

Ricardo pauses again. Mark gives Ricardo another nod. "Lot of rules here. Piss you off at first. But just try to go with it. Later, get some time in, it won't seem like such bullshit." Ricardo's voice is slow and steady. "You do anything out of line, somebody might give you a Pull-Up. You know, point out what you're doing wrong. You just say, Thank you, and go on about your business." Ricardo stops and checks him out. "How you doing?"

He clears his throat, opens his mouth. "I'm coming around," he says. The red glow around Ricardo's head is fading to pink.

"Besides my guidance" — Ricardo grins — "your Caseload meetings with Sydney mornings ought to be your best help. He may seem hard-ass at first, but he knows what's going on. You let him, Sydney will spot-check you when he's sees you sabotaging yourself."

Ricardo leans back in his chair. Looks him up and down. "Got any questions?"

"My wallet?" Spews right out. Fuck.

Ricardo flinches, then he leans across the table and opens both hands, palms up. "You're thinking Go, right?" He doesn't answer, just wraps the plastic around the bread and squeezes it into a gray ball. Ricardo closes his hands. "Your wallet's locked up safe. You want to go, just speak to me or Sydney. Thirty-six hours' notice." He nods. "But don't forget to ask yourself, 'And then what?' You know the answer, right?"

He doesn't say anything.

Ricardo leans toward him again. The light around his head's yellow now. "Jail. Or the nut house. Or the morgue. Hey, maybe even all three."

The room's the size of a big closet. Two metal bunks, a row of gray lockers. A window that only goes up a few inches. Heavy-duty glass that's not glass. Itchy gray army blankets like they used to have at basketball camp. Four hooks for towels. But everything clean-clean. There's a reading light fastened to each of the head rails and, hanging from the foot of each bed, a laundry bag. Lying on his bunk, he can touch the ceiling when he puts up his arm. A copy of the *Lazarus House Orientation Manual* rests on the pillow. It's chewed around the edges like somebody tried to eat it. The name on the inside cover: *Henry J̶o̶h̶n̶s̶o̶n̶,* the cross-off lines pressed into the paper. Looks like Henry tried to cut off a big chunk of his family as well. Maybe what anonymity's really about.

He reads the first sentence:

At Lazarus House you will completely evaluate your life. In order to make this work you need to learn the therapeutic community way of doing things.

The way of doing things. Hey, if his head would stop dividing into little cubes that keep rearranging themselves — cubes with numbers click, click, clicking — maybe he could eat the way of doing things right up. Maybe if he had his new bass, crawl in that and thrum himself quiet.

William T. Carlton S. Jesús V. Their names on the ends of their bunks. His name too. No clues on who they are beyond that. Nothing personal anywhere. If he reaches across the aisle, he can touch the other bunk, Jesús. Tomorrow morning, Jesús is going to be looking right in his face. Being on the top is not good — trapped up high. Nothing he can do about that for now. Signs everywhere here too. ONE DAY AT A TIME right by his pillow. LET GO & LET GOD down by his feet. His legs have stopped twitching, the hum's faded to low. Just do what they tell him to do and be careful. That's enough for now.

Clinical Tools Used by the Family: One-to-Ones, Running Your Story, Pull-Ups, Learning Experiences, Haircuts.

What day is it? He twists his shirt so he can read the name and arrival date on the tag on his chest: *Mark M., March 26, 2002.* Two less than twenty-eight. He's got two days more.

Here they come. His Brothers and Sisters. He swings down and goes to stand by the door. Jesús is first. *January 2, 2002.* Muscled arms and chest under a head meant for a smaller body. Weights. "Yo, Mark," Jesús says. "Going to share our humble. Three hours in the chair about do you?" Jesús motions toward the door. "Meet the other members of our suite: Carlton, our senior fellow."

Carlton shakes his hand. He's maybe six-eight with a stoop and a thin pink scar that runs from the corner of his mouth to his eye. He does a mock dribble in the doorway. "Got a basketball team, the Lazureens. Play the other junkies and psychos vacationing in the nearby communities. You play?"

"A little pickup."

"When you're not picking up, right?" They all laugh. Another man slides into the space.

"And here's your bunky — William." Jesús has crawled up onto his bed to make room, but he's still running things. "Look of him you're bound to be fearful that he may knife you right through the mattress. One scary dude, right?"

And it's true. William's left eye bulges from its socket so far it looks like it might roll out. And the pupil wanders — looking everywhere all at once. Dreadlocks to his shoulders. William laughs. "Only going to knife you if you snore. Last guy in here, Henry, like sleeping in the cockpit of a B-52."

"Yeah, wonder I didn't reach over and McMurphy him one night," Jesús says.

Everybody but him has gotten onto their bunks. No way the four of them could ever be standing in the room simultaneously. Carlton is so tall he has to lean way into the aisle in order to sit down. When William stretches out, his belly humps up like he's about to deliver.

"When's the next smoke?" he asks them.

"Ten minutes. Meanwhile give your fried body some prone, man. Stretch out in the luxury of the Lazarus Hilton."

Jesús zings right through the clicks, looks at him across the aisle. "How many days?"

He eases down flat, watches a spider in the corner above his bed. She's rolling her latest up nice and tight. "Twenty-one," he says. "Twenty-one."

The overhead speaker in the hall booms, "Good night, Family. Sleep tight."

His body's clean, the fear-smell gone. Mattress not too bad, no sag in the middle. He loosens the tight blankets, so he can move, and pulls the sheet up so the scratchy wool doesn't touch his skin. Carlton, William, Jesús all switch off their lights. He follows their cue. Every time William moves the whole bunk shakes and creaks. The window and door are both open, the smell of rain drifts through. Now and then a thud or a voice from out in the hall. Men on this floor, women downstairs.

"Remember about the snoring," William whispers. "This ain't no wolf ticket."

"Wolf ticket?" he asks into the dark. So quiet. Static-interference, zero.

"Threatening violence," someone whispers back. "Get you a Haircut or a Learning Experience for sure."

"A Haircut?"

Jesús raises himself up on his elbow, leans across to keep his voice low. "Say you're late getting to a meeting, somebody on staff calls out real loud, 'This is a Haircut.' You got to assume the Haircut position. They give you a public reprimand. When it's over you got to say thank you."

And before he even asks, Carlton says, "Learning Experience, the most pain-in-the-ass of all. I'm doing one of those myself right now. Got to stand up in the meeting and recite."

"Lay it on him," William says. "You need the practice, Bro."

Laughter. Him too.

"Good evening, Family." Carlton's voice is ghost-story quiet. "My name is Carlton. On March 24th I received a Learning Experience for washing my face beyond personal hygiene time." Creepy steady. "I understand that the rules help reinforce the norm within the community. For four nights in a row, my Learning Experience consists of making this announcement." Suppressed snorts from Jesús. "Due date, March 28th. Thank you, Family."

"You're welcome, Brother Carlton," William says.

Okay, so ask them. "All this . . . all this, hup, hup, hup . . . you think it works?"

Jesús leans over again, sings softly, "Ours not to reason why" — again that voice that's happy about something — "sixty-five days since I been high."

"Ninety-one," William adds.

"One hundred and six," Carlton says. "And still counting."

Then the room is quiet. The only sound, his heart. Every now and then a click, click, click. Cubes going twenty-eight, twenty-seven, twenty-six.

Hard rain. Dark, deep dark, every now and then a flash. Where is he? He can hear breathing. Through the rain he hears him calling, calling, not too far away, the voice watery and getting closer.

Mark ... Mark ... This building is all stone. Stone is dangerous.

Aaron?

Flash. Flash. Boom like the world's blowing up.

Aaron ... remember the lightning that summer. How it would bolt and I'd be whimpering, afraid it would come right down through the plastic roof of the fort. Fiery light and everything would go white. And Mom would yell did we want her to come down and sleep with us, did we want to go up to their tent and sleep with them. And that's what I'd want, but you would holler back, No, we aren't scared. Mark, it's only lightning, you'd say. Chances one in a thousand it would hit here. You were eight. I was ten. But you were wrong. Lightning struck three times. Hit us all.

Hardened egg yolk streaks most of the greasy plates, slicks of yellow tinged with green. But the plates aren't as bad as the bowls gunked with gluey oatmeal. He leans into the rim of the sink to shift his back to a less torturous position, bangs the scrubber against the edge to sling off some of the goo. His first day on the job and the fucking dishwasher is out of order. He is out of order: the clicking is clacking louder than ever. Maybe he should get back on the Zyprexa.

"Better hustle it up there," Watson tells him. Watson, the Kitchen Ramrod. Watson, who must have been absent for the personal space curriculum because he always moves in about three inches too many. "You want your cigarette break before Caseload, you're going to have to pick it up considerable."

He loosens the muscles of his throat, dialing for a reasonable range. "Any chance of getting some hot water?"

Watson reaches over and runs his hand under the lukewarm stream. "Going to have to make it do for these lunch dishes. Manage for now. Cope practice."

Cope practice. Put that sign up by his bed. Something dark is seeping under the doors. Bad news. Buzz, buzz, something's going down. Through the clacking and the banging dishes he listens, but all he hears are bits. Last night . . . a roomie found him . . . at least two days. Stiff. People going and coming look stunned. The Giant's job is to transfer the racks of drying dishes over to the counters. The Giant's name tag is covered by his I AM A BABY sign, a sign that flaps up with his every huffing maneuver. Another man's busy dealing with the trash, bagging and hauling it out to the Dumpsters. Woman with the birthmark, Roxanne, her job is to pull the dishes from the racks and stack them on the shelves. But he's got to stay focused on the oatmeal or he won't have time for a cigarette. Nicotine to get him ready for Sydney. Maybe he'll run into Ricardo or one of his bunkies. Get the story. Somebody's dead.

The hall's a rush of people shifting. Caseload in three minutes. No time for a cigarette. Fucking Watson not willing to cut any slack. He pulls a Camel from his pack just to roll in his fingers while he makes his way against the flow. The hexagon tiles are a problem. Fuck with his brain like some Escher illusion. A lot of people sitting on the benches. Heads down, feet flat. A big blackboard across from the pews lists the current splittees. Six names. Down at the bottom, a name in a neat white box somebody's measured with a ruler: *Henry Johnson.* The man whose bed he just got out of a few hours ago. Henry Johnson is the bad news. Henry Johnson: anonymous no more.

His Caseload room is just beyond the lounge. He sucks in on his way by — catch a little secondhand smoke. As he steps in, Sydney flicks him a look he can't read. He slides into the next-to-last seat. Two beats later and Watson settles into the last place. He surveys the group. Glad to see Roxanne. She gives him a sad smile. Twelve of them in the circle. Young to old, but most of them probably around his age: bottom-out time. Watson, sitting like a rock, his shirt buttoned right up to his neck, spit-and-polish. Six other men. Four women besides Roxanne. All of them look beat: beat-up, beat-down. Most everybody has something missing or scarred. Sydney is right across from him. The woman beside him, *Leora R., December 25, 2001*, hands him a piece of paper: *The Lazarus House Philosophy.*

Sydney says, "We'll begin by reading the philosophy out loud together." This is directed toward him, the newcomer. "Leora, how about starting us off."

" 'We arrived here to share in the understanding that there are no gains without pains, that to manage our lives we must struggle against our worst enemy — that which keeps us closed, alone, and angry.' "

No gain without pain: another Rozmer favorite. Leora turns his way a little, encourages him to catch up, but he's lost the beat. Finally Leora collects his paper, a paper now damp along the edges. Maybe he'll just keep melting until when you look out the window only the two bits of his coal-eyes will be left.

Everybody shifts in their chairs, sits up straighter. He does too. Sydney has a way of leading with his scarred ear. "Mark's first day with us," Sydney says.

"Welcome, Mark," they call out. "How many days?" they say.

"Twenty-two." There it is right in the front part of his brain. Twenty-two. They clap. Then they go around the circle. Each one says how many days they've been clean: ninety-two, fifty-six, one hundred and fifty. Prick Watson, right up there with one hundred and five. After each person, everybody claps. Now Sydney swings his eyes around the circle again. He's a big man, not fat, just broad-chested. His shaved head gleams. He even has a gold tooth that completes the stereotype. Bigger than anyone else in the room.

Sydney says, "You're clean and sober." Everybody cheers. He comes in with a little yeah at the end. "At least for today," Sydney adds. "So here's the story, the Lazarus Way. You aren't the kind who follow the rules. That's what got you here." Sydney stops to see if they're with him. Some are nodding and leaning his way. "So at Lazarus House, you can't act like no junkies no more. 'Cause you don't act like a junkie, you won't use dope. Right?"

He gets the feeling this is a sermon they've all heard many times. Sydney looks at him like he's waiting. The man next to him, Leroy, gives him a little jab. "Right," he tells Sydney. It goes around the circle, each one of them saying, Right.

"You got structure here and rules. Some of you, maybe all of you, are going to bluff your way through." Zap, zap right at him. Then Sydney grins. "I'm an ex-con, an ex-junkie, I know what you're up to." Again Sydney comes to a dead stop, what feels like a full minute. "But listen," he says, "if you follow Lazarus House rules for six months, eight months, most of you will leave knowing how to keep it together."

"What about Henry?" Just a whisper — an older woman sitting right by Sydney.

A man with a big bush of gray hair says, "Yeah, we all thought he was doing so well. Eight months clean. Out in a Lazarus apartment."

Leora's voice tight, low. "Still, there he is, dead. Dead two days before anyone finds him. A needle sticking out of his arm."

Sydney looks around at each of them. "Henry's an exception." Shotgun energy gone. "He was in this Caseload, so we all know partly what went wrong." Taking his time. "Henry was never willing to dump all his garbage here. Shame got him."

People around the circle nod. Some tears. Him too and he didn't even know the guy.

Sydney leans back, his voice is even quieter now. "Henry was too perfect. Laying low. Old days I could've provoked him. We could've run the Game on him. Provoked until he opened up." Sydney looks down. "But the old days are over. Now we got to treat you nice. Don't want to damage your already low self-esteem." Again he looks at each of them. "But I tell you, like Henry, if you don't get it out here, you're going to use again next black time hits you. You hear me?" He looks at Leora.

"I hear you," she says. And again it goes around.

He says, "I hear you," right on the dot.

"There'll be a memorial for Henry next week. Anybody who wants to can be part of that." Sydney settles in, sinks his size down a notch. "All right, who wants to start it off today?"

There's a long silence.

"Remember, if you keep stuffing it, you are going to end picking up. Especially if you're angry. Anger stuffed is the first cause of relapse." Sydney goes quiet then, sits there looking at them one by one.

Finally Roxanne raises her hand a few inches. Roxanne's birthmark stretches all the way down one side of her face, even onto her neck. Could be any age gone wrong. The front of her T-shirt says BELIEVE in letters so faded they almost aren't there. Sydney nods to Roxanne. Her hands tremble so, they won't stay in her lap. "It's because of me . . . my boy's gone." Her voice, the tight of a sob choked back. "James." Just a whisper now. "Me on the street . . ." She sits on those hands to keep them still. "Doing crack." She looks at Sydney. "Dead." Blue-and-red tears. "Nothing's going to change that."

He pushes back in his chair. Sydney flicks him a look. No way. No way is he going to split himself open and bleed out all over this room.

Still no hot water. Grease from the hamburgers gunks the dishwater no matter how many times he changes it, how much detergent he adds. Back and forth, behind him, Watson, checking the dishes in the racks. Roxanne's looking nervous. Even the Giant's making anxious moves, rearranging the racks so they're perfect.

"See this glass," Watson says, pushing it up to his face. "All these glasses . . . they're greasy, spots all over them."

He breathes. "Best I can do with no hot water."

Watson tests the water again. "Well, why didn't you say something? I reported the problem to maintenance this morning. I assumed it was fixed." Watson's voice is heating up. "Why didn't you tell me you still didn't have hot water?" He doesn't say anything, just turns back to scrubbing the plates. "This is a Pull-Up for not communicating." Watson's voice is cool again, businesslike. "Next time you tell me right out what's going on."

"Thank you . . . for the Pull-Up." Voice neutral. Clickety-click. There. There. What are you going to do now, you prick bastard?

Finally Watson turns away. Watson is all part of the dark that's gathering. Watson's breath is still on the back of his neck — watching him wash the pots. The heat is rising in his chest and the hum humming up. Like to spin and wrap Watson's head up tight in the dishrag. Just breathe and scrape. Scrape, scrape. Twenty-eight, twenty-seven . . .

"How about this pot?" He doesn't look at the pot. This Watson is a full-court-press man. "Still got sauce under here." The pot almost in his face. "No reason you can't get the food off even if you don't have hot water." Better back off, Watson. "Got to do it over. Speed it up or you won't be done in time for your break."

Before he knows it, his body's spun out, pot banging down in the sink. Watson doesn't back off an inch. A woman's voice says, "Mark . . ." He looks at Watson. Watson looks at him.

"Here's another Pull-Up for selling wolf tickets. Next time I'm going to support you to staff. Bring you up before a meeting."

His voice just a strangle in his chest. "Thank you for the Pull-Up," he says.

Every move he makes he feels the ridge of irritation around the top of his long johns. Insides of his thighs too. Raw. That's him: in a constant sweat. Only one man on the benches now. Head almost to his knees. The guy's been there all day, every time he's passed through the big hall. No new splittee names on the board. *Henry Johnson* still tucked up tight in the neat box. He turns into the smoking lounge. Empty except for Ricardo. Ricardo has got the bouncety-bounce of a man who knows how to take in the air and hold it. Time for two or three cigarettes.

Ricardo pushes a chair out for him. "Going to be a heavy-duty meeting," he tells him. "Decide if somebody who split and got high is going to be back in or out." Ricardo's looking him over. "You got about-to-detonate written all over you." He's looking real close now. "What's up?"

"Watson," he says.

"Watson — very military. Nam. You got to follow the protocol," Ricardo tells him. "Lucky he's in Sydney's Caseload. Got to confront him right there. Sydney will know how to make it work for both of you."

He doesn't say anything. The thought of bringing it up in group makes his stomach seize.

Ricardo leans back like he's considering his next point. "Mark, you're angry. Deep-down angry. Coming off of you like steam. And it's not just about Watson. You got to bring it all out, man."

He fists his hands so tight his nails bite into his palms. "I can't," he says.

"Look, all you have to do is write your name and Watson's name on a piece of paper and drop it in Sydney's Encounter Box. Sydney will check it out before your next group and he'll know just how to set it up so you can unload." Unload right out of here. "So Watson unloads too. Group will help out. Good for all of you."

He wants to get Ricardo off this. "Maybe," he tells him.

Ricardo shakes his head. "I can smell Go on you from a mile. You just biding your time until you've figured a way, right?"

His shaking knee starts the table wobbling. "I don't know."

"That's horseshit and you know it," Ricardo says. He reaches down and stuffs a wad of paper under the table leg. "Look, I came here totally on the con. They wanted to give me five years. Whole list of felony counts: auto theft, reckless endangerment, assault." The more of Ricardo's story in prime time, the less of his own necessary. "My parole officer recommended a year's time served in Lazarus House. Lazarus House backed me too."

"You're different," he says, partly just to keep the focus on Ricardo and because it's true. Every now and then Ricardo's face becomes Dad. Only happened once before — these face-changes. Time he got committed to Langston Psych. Pepper spray. Stripped his clothes off. Straitjacket. Thorazine. Lock-up ward. Sixty days. Whatever he's going to do, he's got to do it soon before it's too late.

"Different? You know every junkie's the same." Ricardo believes, no question about that. "I used Lazarus to get out of jail. My plan was to run. Drug treatment, the last thing on my mind. But you know what changed all that?" He widens his eyes to keep Ricardo talking. "What changed it was fishing."

Always a warm halo glow around Ricardo's head. But the face blurring in and out.

Ricardo's off on his own now, into his song. "Bunch of us got to go out fishing. Beat-up motorboat down on the river with a Coordinator. Har-har, at first we're doing scenes from the Cuckoo Nest cruise, but once we got out on the river, everybody calms down. Turned the motor off. Quiet. Sun and a little wind coming across the water. Everybody's line out with bait on it."

Ricardo lays his hands out open on the table: nothing to hide. "I mean, for so long I'd gotten my kicks scamming people so I could get high. But here we were out there on that river. Listening to the frogs. And it wasn't hurting anyone."

Ricardo gets up, starts to roam like he understands about giving people plenty of oxygen. "You know I never would have made it out there. I have to stay right here until I get it straight. You hearing me?"

Right now funny business going on up in my attic. "I'm hearing you."

"Mark, roll with it for a while. Put your name and Watson's in the box. Just living here with all these junkies who are working on self-control is powerful." Ricardo stops, puts his arms down like he rests his case. "What's your alternative?"

Got to give Ricardo something. Putting out the good energy. Orange glow now. "Thanks, Ricardo. I appreciate it. It's true — I'm struggling."

Ricardo nods, touches his shoulder. "Got to go into the fear, go through it," Ricardo says. Ricardo and Rozmer making the same

U-turns, reading the same program-approved literature. "Other-wise you know, you know this: you'll be back on the spoon."

All of them, one hundred junkies, start up the long marble stairs, heading toward Lazarus Hall, even some sick guy in hospital pa-jamas. No talking and all eyes down. Up, up, up. Twenty-six, twenty-seven, twenty-eight. Jesús and William up ahead. Rox-anne. He follows Ricardo. Watson — right behind him, slipped in out of nowhere and walking too close. A setup. Somebody's turning up the pressure. Maybe if his head wasn't buzzing. Long line, single file close to the wall, past the pews. Same man, head almost on his knees, sitting all alone.

He follows Ricardo into the big hall, careful not to step inside the black border. Three huge chandeliers light the scene. Build-ing was once a mansion for some railroad baron, then a mon-astery. What it's come to now: junkie reclamation. Chairs three or four deep all around the room in a big circle, with two in the middle: straight back torture chair like they use for the Monad; the other, a padded job, a throne. Seat of authority. Watson sits on his other side. Watson has on a shiny pair of fancy shoes, leather tassels at the ends of the laces.

A counselor he's only seen in the dining room, man named Morris, little guy with huge glasses that owl up his eyes, walks slowly around the circle. The room is silent.

"Listen up," Morris shouts, and all heads rise at once. "This Fam-ily Meeting is to see if this man should come back into the Family. One person at a time, and give Robert a chance to answer." Mor-ris surveys the room to get a nod of agreement from each of them. "Bring him in," Morris tells the two men standing by the door.

Robert is the guy who's been out on the bench all day. Ashy looking, caved in like he's still coming off the dope. They guide him to the hard chair. His jaw muscles are locked, the paper shak-ing as he tries to read the list of his transgressions: "I used drugs. I stole a radio from the community."

A woman directly behind him screams, "Robert, you ain't say-ing what's really in your head." Leora's voice.

A man on the other side of the room, Bernard, the guy who takes care of the kitchen trash, yells, "Start following the rules or stop wasting our time."

Morris comes up close to the crowd. "Let him state his case."

But before Robert can speak, more shouts. Someone way in the back, a large woman with bright red hair, stands. Everything goes quiet. "Did you know Henry?"

Robert shrinks down in his chair like he's been hit. "I was in his work crew."

"Did you know he's dead?"

Robert turns toward Morris. "I'm not to blame."

Another woman rises up slowly. "We're not accusing you, but show some honesty. Why should we take you back?"

Robert fills himself up with a little air. "Because I want to be back in Lazarus. Because I'm done doing drugs."

The Hall becomes a din of whistles and catcalls: "What bullshit." "Get your sorry self a different free ride." "Take your sleaze action somewhere else."

Morris is on his feet again, circling. "Listen up." The room quiets to whispers. "Robert, if the Family votes now, nobody's going to say yes to you returning. You keep ducking responsibility. Making excuses. You've got to stop that or you know what's going to happen to you back out there."

Robert looks at Morris, then he gets up quick out of his chair, knocks it back a little. "I can't make you believe me," he says, and starts for the door.

"Get back in that seat. I'm going to give you three minutes to save your life." Morris turns toward the audience. "Give him time. Let Robert say why he should come back and be a member of this Family."

Robert looks like he's wavering, but then comes back and sits down. For what's got to be two minutes or more, he says nothing, keeps his eyes closed. The room is totally silent. Robert's body begins to shake all over. Finally his voice comes out, not much more than a whisper, "Lazarus House is the only chance I have. I've got no place else to go." Robert is crying so it's hard to hear him.

Mark does not want to listen to Robert. What he wants is to stand up, go down the steps, through the big double doors, out the gate.

"Because I'll die," Robert says. His head is down, his arms wrapped around his legs. "I need you." Robert looks up. He feels like Robert's looking right at him. "You ask me why I'm here? Because I'm an addict."

How can Robert expose himself before this mob? To be beaten on in all this light, how can that help? This is the gentle and kind Sydney talks about? Morris nods and the two who brought Robert in escort him back through the door.

Morris circles the room, his hands behind his back. "Up to you. Robert's past behavior doesn't say much for his chances. Going to take a lot of your energy if you decide to let him come back. Anything you want to say before we take a vote?"

A lot of hands go up: "I say yes to Robert because there but for the grace of God . . ." "I'll help him get his shit together." "Maybe this time he'll see the light."

Morris walks around the front row, gets up close. "Everybody who thinks Robert should be allowed back in Lazarus say aye."

A boom of response.

"Nays?"

Silence.

The door opens and Robert is brought back in to face Morris.

"Robert, do you believe you can change?"

Robert's back to full size, his voice is even cocky. "Of course I do."

"Well, you're lucky because the power's with you today."

Everybody but him swells out of their chairs. They all jam around Robert. "Welcome back, Brother," they shout.

Mark stays on the edge of the swell. This is just a show. Humiliation and rebirth. The sinner will finally say anything to put out the fire.

He's the only one left in the bathroom. The face in the mirror is a death mask. Shifting into Aaron's face. All his teeth ache. Stuff surging up in front of him that he's pretty sure isn't really there. Dad in the pole barn, blood all over. Aaron, drifting down. And always the low hum. On top of the paper towel rack — a book of matches. CLOSE BEFORE STRIKING. Rule: no matches until you're three months clean. No way he's going to sleep tonight. Who's to know if he steps into the john to take a piss and he has a quick smoke. Help him get through a long one.

He looks around and then palms the matches, sticks them in the band of his long johns.

"Good night, Family."

Shit. He's late. Just as he starts for the door: Watson. Watson passes him, checks the towel dispenser. Watson. The matches. Prick set him up.

Watson just puts out his hand.

He can hit him and go out the door or he can suck it in and have time to pull something together. He hands the matches to Watson and turns to go to his room. "Junkie behavior. I'm supporting you to staff. Bring you up before a meeting."

He doesn't say anything, just keeps heading toward the dark door at the end.

The moon's coming through the window. A moon like that night he drove back from Camden, Rozmer conked in the back of Charlie's station wagon. Could use some guidance from Rozmer. No way is he going to go up before the firing squad. He pushes down in the bed. Red and yellow jumping around back of his lids. Legs twitching and he can't make them stop.

What do you think, Aaron? How about if we go out there and yell into the darkness, Yes, we are scared. We are so fucking scared we're going to have to step off, shut it all right down. What you did, buddy. Stepped off and went down, down. Green water. I always think of how cold it must have been.

13 : Almost April

No CHOICE but to keep going until she backs her way to the top. Only about twenty feet more. How had Aaron managed to haul so much stuff up this steep path? Each heave drags the wheelbarrow another few feet. At least there's only the weight of the shovel, the box of trash bags. Then there's the scrabble of Luke behind her, coming down at a dog-gone-wild run. "Stop," she screams. If he bumps her, she'll be upended. He veers off and returns below the barrow, panting. The next trip she'll go the long way, even though that means negotiating a sea of briars.

One last tug and the wheelbarrow bumps over the ridge. The plan is to haul down all the trash and debris: the rotted bags of garbage, the rolls of soggy insulation, the broken windowpanes, even the busted doors, one load at a time. One load at a time, once or twice a week, until the site is clear. Get the guy who picks up her trash to take it all to the dump. Even if she never does anything more beyond clearing away the wreckage, when her mind wanders here, it will feel easier.

True, she may get no further than she did the last three or four springs. The first warm days, she forces herself to go up. She manages to drag down a few bags. Then she doesn't go again. She can never do any of it when Mark's around. But with Mark swaddled in the order of Lazarus House. Twelve more days before he'll even be allowed to call or write.

She pushes the wheelbarrow through the wet leaves, but then

her legs feel so tired she sets it down and straddles a stump. Luke leans his warm side against her leg. In the distance there's the glint of sunlight on Aaron's stovepipe, beyond that she can see a bit of blue almost-April sky. April: more than any other month, the month when people end their lives.

She was living in an apartment in Marwick, renting out the house. It was mid-March and she'd just come back from a month-long artist residency in New Hampshire. Mark and Aaron were living with a bunch of musician-friends in an old house in Danford. Mark was staying with her for a few days because he and his housemates were out of money for oil, heating only one room with a kerosene heater, and Mark was feeling paranoid. She picked him up at the mental health clinic. They stopped at CVS for some different meds. "Going to beaker me up a new trick-or-treat for the red ghoulies," he said.

She was coming up the stairs, Mark ahead of her in the kitchen, when she heard Aaron's voice on the machine. "I'm ready to do the Oprah thing." They played it a few more times, trying to read the sounds of his voice.

"What do you think he means?"

"Finally we're going to talk about Dad. Eighteen years later."

They drove to Danford to get him, all the way speculating on what Aaron was going to say, rehearsing their responses. He was finally going to talk to them. Aaron was twenty-eight years old. He'd been eleven the last time she remembered him being open. A few months after his father died, she found him crying. She sat on his narrow roll-away bed in the house she had rented in town, her arm around his thin boy-shoulders. "Nobody likes me," he said. This had been such a surprise from a child she'd always seen as easy to love, this blond child who was so sunny and patient. "Why, everybody likes you," she told him. He said no more. Later when he retreated into "I'm fine" as his standard answer to all questions about how he was, she regretted her easy response, her not really listening.

When they pulled up to the house, a ramshackle place, sheets hanging over all the windows, Mark went in to get him. She prepared herself for Aaron's appearance. She hadn't seen him since January, the night they'd gone to the movie *Hoop Dreams*. The night she'd asked him to keep an eye on Mark, who'd just gotten a diagnosis of manic-depression. Aaron's response: "I can't."

She saw Aaron coming toward the car: so thin, his tangle of long hair, his stained jeans. The last few years whenever she saw him, always her impulse was to take hold of him, to say up into his thin face, My god, Aaron . . . Instead, she looked away. Right after Lee's death, Aaron had left his notebook lying open next to a panda Lee had won for him at the county fair. Though she would not normally have done such a thing, she read his last entry: "My father didn't want us to be there when it happened. That's why he sent us away." And then, he had carefully crossed out every word. Soon after that, Aaron hung a sign on his door: PRIVATE.

Aaron got in the front seat and gave her a fierce hug. "I do love you, Mom," he said, as though she'd just told him he didn't. "I don't think it's mania," he told Mark. To her he said, "It's just that you were the woman who brought bad news." Not only his father's death, but twice later, the deaths of two friends by suicide. One of the deaths only a few weeks earlier in Lawrence, Massachusetts, where Aaron had gone to high school for a while. He'd just returned from Lawrence, an attempt to reconnect with the whole group who'd been friends with Dan Fitzgerald, the boy, the boy now a man, who'd just died. He was clearly disturbed by this trip. "All the old cycles kept repeating," he told them.

Several times he said, "I keep walking into a trap I've made." By then they were sitting in the living room, the tuna bagel she'd fixed for him uneaten on the end table. "I have trouble getting things down," he said. She offered to make him soup. She said she was always making him the wrong thing. Right after Lee died Aaron had started to have stomachaches and a pediatrician had put him in the hospital for tests. She drove to Marwick to visit him every day after work. He was in a big section all by himself. The nurses only came by now and then to check on him. She hadn't even been there when he'd had to drink glass after glass of barium. "How could I have left you all alone at the hospital like that?" She saw that what she wanted was to have Aaron and Mark, then twenty-eight and thirty, understand why she hadn't been a more loving mother.

What Mark wanted was to be forgiven. "I was terrible to you," Mark said to Aaron. "I was a monster." "Nothing to forgive. We did the best we could" was Aaron's response. They latched on to that.

What Aaron wanted was to talk about his father. "You know he talked to me about it. I was eleven and he discussed with me the moral issues of someone killing himself. We sat up there where he was camping and we talked about how a person had the right to do this if he couldn't find another way. And I agreed with him. The thing is," he said, "I have this fear that someone else is going to die."

Aaron also told them other things: about getting directions, about forces colliding, about wood being safe. Later that evening, after she returned from taking Aaron back to Danford, she and Mark tried to make sense of it: "What did he mean when he said those things about the train?" "I didn't understand the part about the stones." But they were so happy that he'd talked to them, that they'd all forgiven each other for whatever it was they felt they'd done wrong. "We must have missed a transition," they decided. All his life Aaron had convinced them he'd come through.

She remembers that during that drive to Danford she said to Aaron, "You know you could stay at the apartment where it's warm, easier place to get through the winter." "I'm twenty-eight years old" was his answer. When she pulled up in front of his place, he made no move to get out, sat silent for several minutes, then he said, "It was such a sad day." The day she walked toward them from across the street, August 14, 1977, after her in-laws pulled up to the curb and gave her the news. Mark and

Aaron were standing in the yard, watching her come to tell them something terrible. "Yes," she said, "yes, it was." And they sat in the car for a while and cried.

The wheelbarrow moves easily through the leaves and needles. She breathes, readjusts her hold, steels herself for the sight of Aaron's place. From a distance it looks almost all right, the pine-sided loft section rising up to look out across the valley, morning dew steaming off the single slant roof, the doors and windows thrown open to take in as much of this first heat as possible. Two sawhorses stand in the yard, a plank thrown across them as though someone had just left off working. Even daffodils coming up in a bright green clump by the steps.

Luke rushes ahead, begins to nose the matted grass where deer must have bedded down not too long ago. She pushes the wheelbarrow to the steps and looks in. The small downstairs room seems about the same. Only time at work now: the woodstove rusted a deeper shade of brown, with the stovepipe so corroded it has finally come away from the hole, the two-foot planks Aaron had milled to panel the room turning a damp gray. Lots of mouse droppings. She isn't ready to go inside. Instead she pulls a sodden roll of pink insulation from under the steps and sets it in the wheelbarrow.

Aaron had been pleased with this building. That fall he was living back home for a while. He'd started working at a sawmill a couple of years after he decided not to return to music school, that he wasn't interested in the years of disciplined conservatory study, that he just wanted to write music, play on his own, hitch around the country when he'd put together a little savings. This, after trying to make it in Boston, in New York. Doing a lot of busking in the subways, playing his tongue drum, his hat set out for contributions. He must have been twenty-two or twenty-three then. Could he have some of the pines? he'd said. He wanted to build a little shack up on the bluff overlooking the valley.

The next day, she remembers she'd been making chili, when

she looked out the window to see Aaron and his boss coming up the road on a big red tractor, then turn to chug up the hill along the line of pines that grew all the way to the top. All day the chainsaw whined. In the afternoon she looked up to see the tractor laboring back and forth, dragging logs toward the bluff. The next day Aaron and his boss trudged up the hill again, again the whine of the saw, the chug of the tractor, dragging. When Aaron had come down for a jug of water, she'd asked him how it was going. She'd started to believe by then. He told her his boss would be bringing the portable mill the next day, that they'd skidded all the logs he needed, and he'd be milling them all next week. She'd been amazed that someone was going to loan this person with the dozens of mismatched socks all over his bedroom floor an eighteen-thousand-dollar piece of equipment.

The following morning, very early, she'd looked out to see an orange portable mill being winched up their hill. The next evening when she got home from teaching, she'd plodded up the rise to see the mill in operation. There he was, Aaron, his back to the valley below, black trees laced against a lavender sky, putting a big log through, his red wool ski cap pulled down over his ears. She stood in the distance and watched, not wanting to distract his attention from the blades. He looked up and saw her. She waved. He smiled and kept on steering the log along its path.

The loaded garbage bags under the little deck have started to disintegrate. There's no way she can lift them up into the wheelbarrow without them bursting. She will have to slide each one down into a new bag. The wheelbarrow is stacked as high as it will go and still be able to make it down the hill. She sets one last bag on top of the rest, goes up the steps and finally enters. Her eyes look toward the loft. She has never been up there. Afraid of what she might find.

It had been a Wednesday. April 19, 1995. Mark called her at her apartment from the pay phone in Danford. "Come get me," he said. She knew something was terribly wrong. He was waiting on the porch when she drove in. As soon as he got in the car, it came out in a burst. "Aaron's moved back out to the bluff, been there a few days. I hitched out to see him last night. No question he's delusional. Getting messages from Dad. Weird stuff about trains, wearing that striped engineer's cap Grandpa gave him one Christmas. But he's still got the two tracks running. I mean he knows he's getting crazy. And not eating. Nothing but Mountain Dew. He wouldn't come back to town. Just kept saying I should stay there, wood was safe, like he was worried about me. But I'd promised to meet Sammi here. No way to phone her." He'd walked back to town in the dark.

They'd picked up some hot soup and milk and parked at the pole barn, a cold drizzle moving toward snow. Mark had gone up the steep path alone, sure Aaron was more likely to listen to him, to come back down to go to her apartment or the Crisis Center. While she waited, she began to tremble all over, the kind of adrenaline release she used to have when Lee would bang open the door of the apartment in Chittenango in the middle of the night and come raging up the stairs. She heard something and got out of the car, looked up the hill. It was Mark calling: "Aaron. Aaron. Answer me."

The loft-ladder is off in the brush. One good yank and it's free. She drags it into the downstairs, with Luke barking and attacking from the sides, as though the ladder is alive and it's his job to rein it in. "You are not helping," she tells him.

Someone has written the word BEWARE on the crossbeam. After several banging-around attempts, the ladder lands solidly against the loft. She dries her sweating hands on her pants and moves carefully up, stopping on each rung to check to see if it still feels steady, with Luke below, whimpering, pacing around the base. Finally she peers into the loft. Nothing much left. Some burned-down candle stubs, cigarette butts crushed on the floor, a broken beer bottle. The windows smashed and gone, just holes looking up into the blue sky. All the furniture, the mattress, whatever else was up here, long ago flung out onto the ground below. Bare, except over in the corner an old crate, something green shining through the splits in the boards. What she had not wanted to find was a note, because what she had hoped, that whole month before they knew, was that Aaron had walked down to the road, put out his thumb, and hitched a ride out of there.

The next step is the part of climbing that scares her, scrambling from the ladder to the loft floor. She rises and is surprised to see herself, parts of her disheveled, graying self, reflected in a large old mirror that hangs tilted high on the wall across the yawning space. Surely this is the same dresser-mirror that once belonged to Lee's missionary ancestors, the same mirror Lee insisted on loading into the U-Haul their many moves, their many start-overs. More patches of its silver backing flaking away with each transport. Aaron must have unearthed it from a back corner of the pole barn. She pushes her hands toward the mirror, sees them grow larger, her arms foreshorten, this mirror where Aaron saw himself, this mirror that's witnessed so much, that watched the darkness closing in.

She moves to the corner, avoids the shards of broken glass, and lifts the lid of the crate. Right away she knows what it is. Aaron's heavy winter jacket, the one she gave him his last Christmas. She always gave them warm clothing: long underwear, mittens, hats — this jacket — hoping somehow to shelter them from their chaotic lives. She pulls it out and holds it in her arms. She will look through the pockets, but not now. If she had found this jacket when they were searching, well, then she would have known, she would have had to know he hadn't gotten a ride and headed west. He would never have left without his jacket.

Two hundred firemen and volunteers. Two helicopters, several boats. The women's auxiliary set up a relief station down in the big shed that was part of the gravel-bank business: coffee and sandwiches. A couple of county sheriffs and someone from the forestry department were in charge, laying out the grids, keeping track. Mark was determined to search up through the hills, fol-lowing the routes he and Aaron had used to plant marijuana. One of the sheriffs had tried to stop him — having family be part of the search wasn't a good idea — but Richard had said, Let him go, that he'd stay right with him. Two firemen started out with Richard and Mark, but soon dropped behind. Mark's pace was so fierce only Richard could keep up. They went all the way to the end of the ravine, maybe five miles, almost to Carla's, but they found not a sign. She waited in the car. She could not go through the motions of speaking.

About an hour after the first day's search started, Marna came and sat beside her. Richard had called her at work. The only ex-change she remembers: "I know how much you love this child." "Then why didn't I grab hold of him?" "Because he wouldn't let you." They waited. At the end of the third day, the search was called off. Posters went up, missing-person bulletins went into computers. Several times that next month, bits of news made them still hope: an old man and his wife from over on the next road called. They were sure they saw someone of Aaron's description hitching on Baker Brook Road on Thursday, April 20. Someone else said he thought he saw a man who looked just like Aaron in the Utica bus station. Then on May 18, one month later, she was coming back from a life-drawing group at Marna's. There was an Onango County sheriff's car idling in the driveway by her apartment. A man got out. She unlocked the door and had him come upstairs. She went through the apartment and turned on all the lights. The sheriff's deputy stood in the living room and waited. Finally, she sat down on the couch and said, All right. Two fishermen had found a body on the bank of the Onango Creek, the creek right at the foot of their land. Likely someone who had drowned. Did her son have any dental work or broken bones that might help in the identification? Yes, she said. He had broken his left arm when he was eleven. He'd had a double root canal in his right eyetooth, something that ran in the family. She did not tell him that in a way Aaron *had* left a note. Right after he disappeared, she and Mark had found five marijuana plants, all of Aaron's remaining crop, Mark said, spread evenly across Lee's gravestone, the soil still clinging to their roots.

The jacket is warm from the dryer. Its pockets had held nothing but tobacco flakes and the remains of a bus ticket to Lawrence. She takes it into her studio and slides back the screeching closet door to find a needle and thread. She lifts down her mother's sewing basket — her mother, the great seamstress who could make anything on her little featherweight Singer. She moves the chair closer to the window so she can see what she's doing. Luke stretches out beside her, his head between his paws.

Rows of thread arranged by color and here they are: a green spool that's almost a perfect match and a needle with a large enough eye. The cigarette holes will require patching. There's spare material on the inner parts that hold the lining. Snippets can be cut from there to cover the burns, then the raw edges whipped over so they won't ravel. The bottoms of the big pockets have holes. Just a case of restitching those. Then the frays along the cuffs. No buttons missing, which is good because these would have been impossible to match. First, this biggest cigarette burn by the zipper.

She puts her feet up on the stool and rocks a little. Even when he came toward her, looking so not like himself, she saw in his eyes the child who sat in his yellow sleepers on the edge of his bed, reading his Richard Scarry book by the light from the hall, circling with a blue crayon all the words he knew. Years later he said to her, Sometimes I circled a few I didn't know. She still has dreams where she picks up the phone and he says, Mom, it's Aaron.

14 : The Names
of All the Planets

BLACK CLOUDS OF BUS exhaust and the usual destitute, sagging on the benches, smoking, waiting. A New Paltz police car with a fat cop is trolling, surveying the motley. Mark resists the urge to fold in, poked-worm reflex. He's back in a world where being Caucasian's worth Bonus Points. Middle class: his clothes clean, new Pumas, his bass — decked in a shiny gig bag. Gotcha, Fuzz, you don't know I'm a junkie-psycho just escaped over the accordion wire. The slinky guy with the chin whiskers, leaning against the wall, he knows. 'Bout two more minutes, he's going to give a subtle signal: You want; I got.

His exit not dramatic really. He's glad of that. He followed the protocol. Gave the thirty-six hours' notice. Let them lay the whole nine on him. He sat in the reflection chair, read the writing on the wall. Just stayed with the main theme: TC, clearly right for many, but not the appropriate therapy for him at this juncture on his recovery-road. Over and over, minor variations. No way he was going to be up under the lights, do the theater-of-the-absurd thing. Watson story? He didn't get into any of that. The second the thirty-six-hour dong donged, he called the taxi, bye-bye, Brothers and Sisters. Fucking blast of luck, the UPS truck arrives two minutes before take-off: the bass and his Pumas. Split, but he left his mark. *Mark M.* Up there on the big blackboard. But not in a box, not in a box.

He inventories his status: sixty-five dollars, ATM and phone cards. Five packs of Camels, eleven Zyprexa — what was left of his New Vistas medication. Enough trappings of civilized society to keep him from being among the homeless for a day or two. What day is it? He bends to check the date on the newspaper behind the yellowed plastic window: *Wave of pedophile cases casts a dark shadow over all the clergy.* Back in civilized society. March 30. Twenty-five days clean. So — four days until his money shows up in the rep-payee account. Figure access to that later. The trembles are back to moderate and transmissions from outer space reduced to occasional.

The weary are lining up, digging for their tickets. Heads, New York; tails, Marwick. Down to fucking And Then What? time. The pay phone is right next to all the Trailways' roar. He parks his stuff between his legs and leans the bass so it settles against the call box. If he gets Rozmer, some glimmer of understanding for why he had to bail, well, then he'll take the bus for Marwick. If not, well, he'll head for the city, play his bass in the subway, put together enough to get a bike and do the messenger thing. Certainly not going to call his mother until he has to negotiate his money, hear her crash and burn. Ring, ring, ring. Rozmer's machine answers, and even though he may miss the fucking bus to wherever he finds himself going, he's got to catch one last Word for the Day, " 'Man, you aren't going crazy. You're trying to get well. Don't run from these experiences, they could save your life.' " He lets go of the phone. "One way to Marwick," he tells the woman through the glass.

The bus is filling up. He goes all the way to the back — right next to the john, how he likes to do these buscapades. What the fuck, put it out there. See what Rozmer has to say. He'll call him when the bus gets to Delhi, see if Rozmer'll pick him up in Marwick.

*   *   *

Rozmer's truck vroom-vrooms into the Marwick station just as his bus comes to a complete stop — Gabe's face, Rozmer's eight-year-old son, pressed to the glass. Twice-a-month visitation time. Well, that's cool. He likes Gabe. Gabe reminds him of Aaron. Gabe is into the world, the galaxy, where everything is. He needs a cigarette. No smoking in Rozmer's truck or house. Rozmer gives him the I Love You, Man hug. Gabe gives him a high five. He skims his hand over Gabe's blond bristles. "Got a haircut, buddy."

Gabe touches the top of his head and points to his father. "Rozmer," he says, rolling his eyes to the sky. Rozmer's head is likewise buzzed. The two of them have identical bumps in back of their ears.

Rozmer motions for him to throw his backpack into the truck bed. "Got a new gui-tar. Well, well, still got your scamming charm."

Gabe sits between them, a stack of *National Geographics* in his lap.

Rozmer stops before turning out of the parking lot. "Want to catch a meeting?"

"Sure," he says. Ramrod Game running and he's ready. 'Course Rozmer knows.

Rozmer taps Gabe's knee. "You feel up for hanging out at the library for an hour while Mark and I go to a meeting?"

Gabe considers. Raises the magazines up and sets them down. "Yeah, that'll be okay."

Rozmer pulls up by the library drop box. He thumbs through his wallet. "Here's your card. We'll be back about five. I'll come in and find you."

Gabe hands Mark his magazines and gets out Rozmer's side. "Maybe I'll be in the African drum section," he says. "And then are we going to eat?"

"We are," Rozmer tells him, "and you can pick the spot. Any place but fast food."

Rozmer backs all the way to the street, his thick neck straining to stay turned for such a maneuver. No fast food must be Rozmer-in-reform because usually his truck's loaded with Whopper wrappers.

As though Rozmer's been tuned into Mark's head, he says, "Doctor tells me I have to take off seventy-five pounds before I can have this hernia operation." He turns the truck to swing in behind St. Theresa's.

Good it's not a home-group meeting. But there's Charlie's station wagon — the DON'T CROWD ME sticker peeling off its bumper. He's going to have to see people who know he went for treatment. And here he is in two blinks and one nod back at the scene of the crime. My name is Mark and I'm an addict. He is not going to talk, he's only going to listen.

Rozmer turns the truck off, but he doesn't get out. "So what's up?"

"Place was a cult. Made me do what they call a Monad."

"Put you in the ring for the old one-two with God, ehh."

"I don't know about that, but whatever — I started getting crazy: the hums, voices. Too much pressure. Brainwashing."

"Well, you know what Dederich said, the drunk who started the whole therapeutic community movement."

"What?"

"Maybe your brain *needs* washing."

He places the bass carefully on the seat and throws his jacket over it. "You can lock up, right?"

"That side won't lock," Rozmer says. "It'll be okay."

He pulls his jacket and the bass off the seat and closes the door. Have to carry it into the meeting like he thinks he's Mr. Cool. They start in. He's a little ahead, can't really see Rozmer's face when he says, "You pressing me is not what I'm needing right now. It's your Word for the Day, like some just-for-me message, that brought me to your door."

"Hey," Rozmer says, coming up beside him, throwing his arm around his neck. "That message was for me, too. Getting so I have to call myself up to know what's going on. Pressing you? I'm just wanting not to waste time wading through any cockand-bull. You clean?"

"Twenty-five days." Just as they get to the side door, he sees a cement basin full of sand and butts. "Go ahead," he tells Rozmer,

"I'm going to catch a quick smoke." The door shooshes shut. He swallows a Zyprexa and pulls the smoke down, holds it there before letting it go. He hears a blast of laughter down the hall: AA. The cocoon-comfort of staying off the street one more day.

The AA room's fluorescent bright, charged by the smell of strong coffee. Things are just starting, the laughter dying. Must be a men's meeting. Only a dozen or so sitting around a couple of tables. Charlie nods. Rozmer's next to him. A lot of recovery as they say in the AA biz — people who've been sober for a long time. Jerry, Andrew. A couple of young guys looking pale and shaky. He pours himself a cup of coffee, sludge-thick, loads in the sugar and sits beside someone he doesn't know. An old-timer named Kent is reading the opening: "'Alcoholics Anonymous is a fellowship of men and women who share their experience, strength, and hope . . .'"

He has heard these words so often that it's hard to hear meaning. Plus there's a group of redneck purists who think only an alcoholic should enter these hallowed halls. Places where saying, I am an addict, causes the temperature to drop. He settles deeper into the chair and tries not to think Camel.

Kent looks around the table. "Charlie, why don't you start off the Twelve Steps."

Charlie opens his *Daily Reflections* book that he's already got marked with a bright blue ribbon. No question, got to hand it to Charlie: five years clean and sober on top of trying to deal with being schizophrenic. When he asked Charlie once how he did it, Charlie said, When the sign says Stop, I do. "'One. We admitted we were powerless over alcohol . . .'" Charlie's voice is always tight like each word's bound to the next one with wire.

Rozmer's next. "'Two. Came to believe that a power greater than ourselves could restore us to sanity.'"

Coming around his way. Rozmer looks over. He's going to be number eight. Eight is one of the Steps that make him want to stick his fingers in his ears and start yelling. The man, seeing that he doesn't have a book, passes him the paper. "'Made a list of all persons we had harmed...'" He can't hear the remaining Steps. Just the humming and the deep longing to be standing somewhere alone, smoking.

Then Kent's voice again, "Now's the time to share your experience, strength, and hope on a topic of concern. Anyone have an issue they're particularly struggling with?"

Nobody offers anything. Then Rozmer nods. Kent motions Rozmer that he should go on. Shit, Rozmer, don't let this be some grenade you lob across the table at me.

"Would the group be up for the topic of honesty? I'm thinking of it as getting back to being honest with myself. Who I am and who I am not, but you could take it anywhere you want."

The two young guys sit up a little closer to the table. Rozmer doesn't seem to be directly beaming any energy his way. He feels the relief of dropping off the hook.

Kent says, "Go ahead, Rozmer, why don't you start it off."

"Okay. I'm Rozmer and I'm an addict. What's going on is that in the last year I've put on one hundred pounds. What is this about? It's gotten to the place where I have to phone my sponsor every time I pass a Burger King." Rozmer's not using his Rozmer-voice, everything about him set on Low. "Some of you believe what I've been putting out there: Rozmer, the Genius, the guy who can always roll. Well . . . a lot is coming at me right now: my eight-year-old son and his mother are coming back to live with me, I have just started a new job working with troubled adolescents, and I'm moving to a new place tomorrow so Gabe can go to the alternative school here in Marwick. Shaking in my veritable boots — that's me. There, there it is. I appreciate the chance to put this out in the light. Thank you."

Rozmer scared? People's mouths are moving, but he doesn't really hear what they're saying. No time to be asking Rozmer if he can offer him shelter until he gets it together. Then what? Hitch to the city? Tonight, probably he can stay at Rozmer's. Or Charlie's. But tomorrow, tomorrow, he's got to head out for somewhere else. Not treatment. Not his mother's.

The man beside him moves his hand to indicate he's next. People's faces turn his way. "I'm Mark and I'm an addict. Good to be here," the voice says, "but I'm going to pass and just listen. Thanks." Soon after, the standing up, making a ring around the tables. He joins the circle. "'God grant me the serenity to accept the things I cannot change . . .'"

Take-out Chinese is what Gabe opts for. Have to get going on *The Empire Strikes Back* before it's too late, he tells them. Right now his shaved head is bent over a book full of drum pictures and masks.

He can help Rozmer move tomorrow. Some amends. Except for the few last things necessary, everything in the house is packed. Boxes stacked halfway to the ceiling in most of the rooms. No question, Rozmer's got a lot of shit and he's taking it all with him.

Mark dumps the rice in a bowl, the only one not packed apparently. No plastic wrap, so he spreads a paper towel over it and sets the bowl in the middle of the glass tray. He divides the chicken and broccoli up into three coffee cups and arranges these around the rice so they can revolve without banging into the sides. Rozmer will want Gabe to help. "Okay, buddy, how 'bout setting the table." Gabe is gone in the book. He gives Gabe's neck a little wake-up squeeze, his perfect reed of a neck with two elfin ears sticking out. "Earth to Gabe," he says. Gabe looks up and smiles. "How about setting the table?"

Gabe finds a scrap of paper to mark his place and sets the book up on an empty shelf. "Well, we don't need knives," Gabe says. "We don't need spoons." He gets up and starts looking through open boxes. "Dun-ta-dun-ta: forks," he says, and dances three forks over a dozen boxes ready to leap onto the table. "Right or left?" Again his open eyes, all light and good cheer. Gabe's not afraid. "Left or right?" he says again.

"You know what, Gabe, I actually don't know." He closes his eyes and tries to see a table. When he looks, he sees Gabe's got his eyes closed too. "What do you think?" he says.

"You go first," Gabe tells him, holding the forks up above the table, ready to helicopter down on the correct pad.

"All right, in unison, ready, one, two, three . . ." And together they both shout, "Left." Laughing, laughing loud. Rozmer steps into the kitchen with the phone at his ear, gives them a just-checking look. Mark closes the microwave door and presses the Start button.

For a second Gabe rotates his head and whirs like he's in synch with the broccoli. Then he steps up a little closer and gives him a long, serious look. "Mark." His blue eyes home right in. "Mark, now that you're big, what are you going to be?"

15 : Remainder

Betty Dawes straddles a chair, her ample back to them, her large feet rooted to the platform. The flesh of her buttocks pools over the edges. Lynne and Leddy and Marna are already deep into the first life-drawing session. Not to disturb them, Del settles on a stool just inside the door. She wedges the large roll, the study she wants to show them, between her knees, rests her back against the wall. Mark's tucked away at Lazarus for twelve to fourteen months: life is good.

A big board tilted on her lap, Lynne is focusing on the model's turned head, the grizzle of hair. Faces are Lynne's interest. Leddy works at an easel, Betty's form abstracted in washes of brown, black ink edging the shifts in the planes.

Marna wiggles a few of her fingers in greeting, but continues work on a long piece of butcher paper she's taped to the wall — Betty's volume swelling from top to bottom in bold charcoal loops. For years Marna tacked up her canvases in squat apartment living rooms, with Jason ramming his wagon back and forth, or she duct-taped them to the damp cinderblocks of dark garages. What Marna's after has always been wall-size.

What's Del after? Memory: how to go from the day it happened to years later — graphic to lost in the haze. She's been playing around with flaked-mirror reflections, how to make objects surface and recede, how to fade into what remains. With Mark finally gone, she's been tracing the cigarette burns etched along every edge in the loft. Negative strips: the background dark, the burns bled of all color. Evidence. Hieroglyphics.

Of the four of them, Marna is the only one with a real away-from-home space. She still walks around this studio with her arms raised in praise of such vast stretches of emptiness. But the size of Del's studio has never been why she doesn't stay with the work. Unlike her, no matter what's going on with Jason, Marna paints. Still, now that the phone has stopped ringing, she stays in the drawing for hours. No thoughts beyond how to make the amber hue of the kerosene light.

The timer dings. Betty waves and drops her robe over her head, a muumuu, imprinted with the black-and-white faces of Holsteins, globe-eyed and submissive, one of her daughters made for her several decades ago in what used to be called Home Ec. Lynne gets to Del first. She's once again surprised by Lynne's speed, the lightness of her bones. If each of us is allied with an animal spirit, then Lynne is a sparrow and Leddy, a Siamese, all stretch and lanky leap. Lynne takes her hand. "We missed you," she says.

"Yeah." Leddy laughs and gives her a hug. "I thought of you often down there on the Gulf. Especially when I was out raking snow off the roof."

Marna calls from across the room, "Del, we figure this long break, we'll have tea and then take a look at the piece you're working on."

"Betty's going to sit for us for the next three sessions," Lynne tells Del.

At the moment Betty is leaning into the brick wall, stretching her leg muscles. "I wish I *could* sit for the next three weeks. Not get up in between. I am that tired of birthing calves." The Daweses own one of the last dairy farms in the area. Betty is the group's favorite model, all that glorious flesh, though she told them when she started to sit, Don't tell the Baptist Women's Society.

Del stands her drawing against the white cork wall they always use for critiquing. She locates enough pushpins to anchor the large sheet of paper, so she'll be ready. The other women go about the ritual of setting up for the break: the kettle on, the herb teas out, the napkins and spoons. They've been drawing together for many years. Each takes her usual chair at the big round table. All but Betty, who reclines on the couch.

"Del, you look like the cat who got the last of the cream," Betty says.

Del laughs and stirs in a huge dollop of honey.

"It's true," Leddy says, putting a hand on Del's shoulder. "If that's what a month on the Gulf will do . . ."

"I've got a feeling it's more than that," Lynne says. "You're alone and you've been drawing."

Marna looks at Del. "I haven't told them anything."

The tea is hot and sweet. "That's it. Richard's in Vegas. But the big thing is Mark has gone for long-term treatment. A therapeutic community near New Paltz. It may be just what he needs."

"Just what you need, too," Betty says. Betty includes Marna in her look. Marna's son is currently in jail for drug-related shoplifting. They've all granted her first place on the Most Tested Mothers list.

Marna raises her cup. "May the calm continue."

Del scoops out the honey that didn't dissolve and then leans across the table to take them all in. "Here's how I know I'm more okay. My mother put together two big collages of childhood pictures, one for Mark, one for Aaron. You know the kind of stuff I'm talking about: child caught by the camera being so 'who he is.' Well, for years I've had to keep these in the back of my closet, turned to the wall. But yesterday I put them up, side by side in my studio. There they are when I go in, when I go out."

Before Lynne's hand reaches her, Del rises. "Thing is I don't want us to go all weepy, weeping's fine, but right now I want to get your reaction to what I'm trying to do with these drawings."

"Got you," Leddy says.

They put things away. Line up their chairs the right distance from the cork wall.

Del lifts the rolled-up drawing, begins to peel away the plastic wrap. "I don't quite know where I'm going with this, but I'm thinking of a series of memory images, each piece having its own medium, size, and all focusing or fading in on only one section of the whole. The tricky thing is you know me, so hard to judge how it would hit a stranger."

Del unties the string, but doesn't loosen the roll yet. "How close, how far back you are. Okay, enough putting this off." She unrolls the twenty-by-thirty-inch sheet of heavy brown industrial paper and tacks it tight with the pins. For a moment her body hides much of the image. Then she goes and sits with the viewers.

Only the lower left section of a Morris chair: the support for the wooden armrest, a corner of the black-and-brown cushion, the leg with its clawed foot. Darkness, except for this wedge of chair, lit in an amber glow. Suspended in the air, a rifle, blurred by the motion of falling, the barrel pointing up.

Twenty-five years after Lee's mother found Lee in the pole barn that August morning, she said to Del, It was not so terrible as you might think. Only one small wound.

16 : Night Journey 2

Mark takes his phone card from his wallet, along with the three-by-five his mother had laminated for him: hotline numbers, people to call in the night. Hoping he won't call *her*. Well, got to call her now: Guess what, Mom. But the mom-call is less likely to cause meltdown if he presents her with some positive scenario. He shuts his eyes and twirls his finger down. It lands on the number for the Chemical Dependency Clinic. Present his mother with the comfort of appointment dates and times. Possible residential treatment on the horizon. Ask her if she wants to give him a ride to an AA meeting.

He dials CDC. A familiar voice answers. "This is Mark Merrick. Could you get me in to see Joy as soon as possible? . . . Right . . . Yes . . . No, the therapeutic community didn't work out . . . I have a pencil . . . Tomorrow? That soon? . . . No, that's good. April 2nd, nine A.M. Thanks." Going to have to fill out the fucking forms again. Tomorrow. Can still always cancel and go Greyhound. The Mental Health number is busy. So's Social Security. Try Motor V later. Got to do it. No putting it off any longer. He dials the number. His fingers leave wet prints on the phone. Maybe he'll get the machine. Let his machine message get hit by the first volts.

"Hello." His mother's voice so not knowing what's coming.

"Mom, it's me."

* * *

Raining harder now. Darkness always better for confessions. His mom hunched over the wheel, watching for deer, tensed to deflect anything too close to the bone. Give her just enough to understand why leaving Lazarus House was absolutely necessary. And remember to ask how she's doing, remember not to suck up every fucking bit of oxygen on himself.

"Is it the St. Ann's meeting? You think we can make that by eight o'clock?" Her anxiety's right up there. Another night journey.

"Plenty of time. It's only seven thirty. Can't be more than four or five miles from here. You going to the Al-Anon meeting? An Al-Anon meeting you used to go to a lot. You and Marna, right? Okay if I smoke?" He rolls the window down. Last cigarette. Saving it up for the telling of the tale, feeling his way toward a plan she'll go for, turn over his money tomorrow. "What happened was, I started seeing things that were not there. Dad in the barn. Hearing voices. Aaron. The boot-camp stress of Lazarus House was making me sick. It was definitely not the kind of world to go psychotic in. End up in the rubber room."

"What about your meds?"

"No meds. No one thinking about any meds. The whole setup based on 'going to break you open, then put you back together.' Thing is I had no confidence, no trust they knew what the fuck they were up to. You know, all the king's horses, all the king's men . . ."

"But what are you going to do instead?"

There it is. "Like I said, I've got the appointment at CDC tomorrow. See what Joy can help me put together. Then to Mental Health to pick up an emergency prescription to tide me over until I can see Dr. Taylor next week."

"And you're going to stay with Rozmer until you figure out what you're going to do?"

Not the part of the story he wants to turn to next. "Better take the shortcut, a right at the light, go around the lake, come in on the other side of town."

She signals, turns. "Rozmer's going to be able to help you out?"

"Staying with Rozmer isn't an option right now. He's got too much going on with his family coming back. Main thing is not to get high, putting myself in the best situation not to get high. Right?" She doesn't answer. She turns the wipers down a notch. "I'm having trouble sleeping. What I need is some place low stress long enough for me to get my strength back. Go to meetings every day." Of course she knows if she comes in any closer, he's going to grab hold. "Maybe get some dental work done. See what's up with my suspended license. Rozmer says all I've got to do is go to court, pay the fine, that it won't be much."

That's it: every possible come-on he can think of.

She ups the wipers again, slows down. A steep drop through the trees to the lake. No guardrails here. She's gripping the wheel so hard, leaning in so close: magic carpet to another dimension. "What about Charlie? Couldn't you stay with him for a while?"

"Charlie's living in a Catholic Charity room. Can't even have a guest without permission."

They're almost to the turnoff for the church. She sits back a little. Best not to ask for anything out and out. "You have to direct me. I've never come this way," she says.

"Take the next left." Sweat starting to collect in the usual places. She says nothing, drives. He locates the one healthy butt he's got left. Blows the smoke toward the open window. Rainmist cools his face. She pulls up in front of the church. 7:50. People outside smoking, laughing. Still nothing. Not looking good. Now what the fuck is he going to do? He starts to open the door. Throws out his last card. "Or I could just go on to the city. See what I can line up there."

"Wait," she says.

17 : Whom You See Here

THE STREETLIGHT through the car window deepens the hollows of Mark's face. So like Lee in darkness. "If Joy can't come up with a better plan . . ." She takes a deep breath: the thing she said she would never do again, and here she is once more. "You can stay at the house for now. Under these conditions . . ."

He turns her way. "No drugs," he says.

"Mark, if you start using . . . I'll know and that's the day I pay for one night at the Super 8. Drop you at the door."

"No drugs," he says again.

People are starting to go in. No one she recognizes. "What about Rudy?" she says.

"What about him?"

She takes the keys from the ignition. Zips her coat. "He's out of jail and threatening to burn down our barn. Revenge for some wrong you did him. Rudy, Rudy *and* Carla. I don't want them on the land. No phone calls."

"Don't worry. I'm not going to have anything to do with any of them."

"I couldn't bear it," she says. She opens her door and gets out. She laughs. "I'm certainly primed for Al-Anon sharing."

They start up the stairs and step into the long hall. No one in sight now. Just the loud laughter of AA booming up the stairwell. He turns to go down.

"And . . . ," she says. He stops and looks at her straight on, a hard thing for him to do, she knows. "Same money arrangement as before. I stay your rep-payee as long as you're living at the stone house. Three hundred a month to cover your expenses. Plus fifty a month until the drums and computer are paid for."

"Any way you want to do that," he says, and disappears.

Del goes into the big room. Usual sign already out on the table: WHOM YOU SEE HERE, WHAT YOU HEAR HERE, LET IT STAY HERE. Several women arranging the chairs in a circle, a few more setting out the literature, the cups and teabags. No familiar faces. She and Marna used to drive all the way to this meeting almost every week, even in winter. It's been a long time since she's been to any meetings. Years. At first a lot of the slogans — Let go. How important is it? Let it begin with me — seemed simplistic. Give me a break, she used to say to herself. But over time these mantras calmed her enough to hear and then trust a self that watched off to the side. A self that calls out: Not your business. Not about you. Tell him to back off. Over time her "he done me wrong" Lee stories changed. Over time in Al-Anon rooms a lot of the fabricated stories got peeled away. She became willing to turn and let her sorrow be seen. Not that she always follows her wiser self's warnings, but at least she almost always hears them. She almost always knows when she's being crazy. Like now: she's gotten pulled back into rescuing Mark. Fears for him, herself. But he is almost one month clean, she has drawn the lines, and there's a chance orderly surroundings may help him make some gains. She picks a chair near the door.

A tall, thin woman in an expensive beige pantsuit smiles at her, crosses the room. "Welcome," she says. "We're about to get started."

The women begin to take seats. Almost never any men at Al-Anon meetings. Nobody under forty. Several older like her. Certainly it took her years and years, complete desperation, before she came to this room. The willingness to be pitiful out in the light. Only one young woman, still over picking up pamphlets, a black army jacket like Mark's, bursts of dark hair, someone she's seen someplace before. The young woman sits down, a few seats off to Del's left.

"Welcome, everyone. My name's Beth," the woman with the elegant manner says. "Let's begin with a moment of silence and the Serenity Prayer."

Del leans forward and peers down the row through half-closed eyes. No question, absolutely positively for sure, it's Tess, Carla's daughter, Tess. Looking so much like Carla, the young Sophia Loren, that it makes Del's stomach clinch up and stay that way. Tess, no longer safe in Texas. First inclination is to get up, walk out, and wait in the car. She pulls back into her seat, squeezes her eyes shut, as if maybe this way Tess won't know who she is. It's been almost ten years. Then she looks again as Tess opens her eyes and turns. A surprised smile. A small wave. Same wide mouth, same dark eyes: Carla incarnate.

Beth looks at them all and smiles. It's hard not to hold her cool togetherness against her. She raises the Al-Anon guide sheets encased in protective plastic. "'We welcome you to the St. Ann's Al-Anon Family Group . . .'" Beth doesn't need the sheets. Del does not want to hear it. Face it: this is the last place she wants to be. Al-Anon meetings, heading again into living with Mark, him up in that dark loft, window covered with a sheet, casting the whole downstairs into shadow. The sucking perk of coffee in the night, the smell of smoke. A rock weighting her chest every time the goddamned phone rings.

"'We too were frustrated . . .'"

I'll say. Maybe she can live with Richard full time. But how can she leave Mark alone? No car. Mark alone at the stone house: that would make her even more anxious. Richard will not be sympathetic. He thinks she's half the problem: classic case of mothers enabling sons. Still — being at Richard's would give her some distance. Get Mark to find a reliable AA roommate. Maybe Charlie. Charlie's got a car. She could drop by a few days a week to oversee things. Pack up just what she can fit in her car. You're starting to get crazy. Yeah, but it's so comforting.

The woman beside her hands her a book. When the woman sees she hasn't got a clue, she points to the Fourth Step. She's been so busy planning her escape, she's missed the first three. " 'Four. Made a searching and fearless moral inventory of ourselves.' "

Tess gives her a big-eyed stare. Del passes the book on. Del blanks out until she hears Tess's voice, " 'Eight. Made a list of all persons we had harmed, and became willing to make amends to them all.' "

It's the same meeting format Del's used to: the reminder of anonymity; introductions, first names only — Tess says she's Teresa. If only changing what we go by would do the trick. Reports and announcements. Beth puts the plastic sheets down and leans forward. Here it comes: The Topic. Mostly Del wants something that feels irrelevant, either because she's got a good grip on that particular irrational response or because she's got it buried so deep, the topic can't home in. What she wants is a topic that poses no heat-seeking threat. After all, her motivation for being here is skewed: she's Mark's transport to AA.

Beth offers up her name again. "Hello, Beth," they all say.

Beth takes a deep breath. "I wondered if the group would be up for talking about anger. All these years in Al-Anon and here I am again gnashing my teeth. Your experience, strength, and hope when it comes to anger. I'd like to hear what you have to say first and then at the end, if I'm still needing to, maybe you'd let me rant, let off enough rage to keep me from smashing something."

Smashing something. That's a surprise. Del inventories her current level of anger. On a scale of 1 to 5, how pissed is she? Not so much at Mark, but at once again being vulnerable, the possibility of chaos rising up on the periphery. No question she's made some progress. She's gone from "oh, it doesn't bother me" to being able to step out in the yard and scream. B-plus with Richard. C-minus with Mark. Seldom can she risk anger with Mark. His response to her rare bursts is to hurl them back at her with double force.

"Would someone be willing to go first," Beth says. There's that heavy moment of silence. Del shrinks back a little more.

Tess raises both of her hands. A "can you believe it" gesture so like Carla's. She looks around at the group, at Del. "I'm Teresa," she says. "Angry, that's me." Tess locks her fingers and hunkers down. "I've been going to meetings in Texas. And I thought I was getting somewhere. A few weeks ago I decided I needed to come home. My mother has serious health issues. Maybe I could give her some support. Like it says, make amends. But right away, I mean within hours, I'm ready to burst into flames again. Everybody screaming, being nuts. This morning I had to pack up my stuff and get the hell out." Tess throws her hands up again. "I should've known. I've been back a few times, and it's always the same. Last year when my father died" — Tess's voice tightens. She shakes her head. "Even at the wake, he's lying there and my brother . . . my brother's shooting up out in the car."

Tess looks around the room again. "When you said smashing something . . . Well, it's good to be here. The thing is when it blows, I say stuff that can never be forgotten. To my mother, my brother. That terrible man she lives with. Not that I care about him. What I'm wanting to do is learn how to get angry right." Tess laughs. "Luckily I can crash for a few days with a friend who's not a drug addict, but what I've got right here" — she puts both of her hands flat on her chest — "is a hot ball of something." She tugs at her hair. "Over and over in my head. Maybe afterward, there might be somebody in the group who'd be available for an occasional phone call. Till I cool down. Thanks."

"Keep coming back," everyone says. And they all beam her their goodwill. But she definitely will not be offering up her phone number.

Tess — so much younger than Mark and Aaron that she was never part of their scene. She can't help but like Tess. Tess — who the school kept calling ADHD because she wouldn't sit quietly and do the ditto sheets, when surely it was that Tess already knew she had to keep up her guard. Had to get the hell out of there. Bright and talented right from the go.

The woman on Tess's left goes next. A woman with a wonderful face. One look and you feel sure she's years past the "he said this, then I said that" phase. The topic of anger gets handed around, the stick in the relay. They've all been angry. They all struggle with trying to find appropriate ways to get it out. They all know they've got to count to ten or one hundred. The main theme is that slowly they've come to see that what these people in their lives do — that it isn't personal. They're learning to get out of the way. That their best defense is to make sure they're finding time to do what makes them happy. And of course in some cases you just have to pack up and go. No cross talk in meetings. No one gives advice. That's the rule. Who can know what someone else is able to do next? It's a long road. Keep coming back.

Finally it comes to Del and she does pass, says that it's been good to listen. And it has been. Maybe she'll need to come to these rooms again. If chaos threatens, if it all starts going around in *her* head again.

Beth extends her hand. "Thanks. I'm feeling no need to vent. Isn't it amazing that just being here and listening, knowing there are people who understand, hearing how you're dealing with it, helps. I don't mean, Oh, now it's all over, but whatever it was that was squeezing my heart has opened its fist."

Beth reads the closing: " '. . . Talk to each other, reason things out with someone else, but let there be no gossip or criticism of one another. Instead, let the understanding, love and peace of the program grow in you one day at a time.' "

Del lets it wash over her. She catches Tess's eye; Tess shrugs and smiles. She remembers the first meeting she ever went to, a meeting where the topic was humor and she couldn't stop crying long enough even to say her name.

"Will all who care to, join me in a closing prayer."

Like the rest of the women Del folds her chair and carries it over to lean it against the wall. Noise in the hall. The AA meeting is out. Always the AA laughter. She sees that the woman with the wonderful face is giving Tess her phone number. Tess is crying; the woman has put an arm around her shoulder. Good. She turns and goes out. Find Mark and make a run for it. She threads her way through the smokers talking in groups along the sidewalk, oblivious of the rain. No sign of Mark. She looks toward her car, but can't see whether he's in there or not.

Next problem: if Mark goes back to Danford with her, how's he going to get to the Chemical Dependency Clinic, the pharmacy tomorrow? No license, and even if he had one, she wouldn't want to loan him her car. She turns the key in the lock and slides in. She's got a clear view of the doors. Where's Mark? Normally he'd be the first one out to smoke. Why didn't she think to tell him to try to line up a ride for tomorrow, that she's staying at Richard's tonight and going with him early for a consultation at Walter Reed: the slow rise of his PSA count when it should be zero. She is not going to change that plan, but it's critical that Mark see Joy tomorrow. Already you're donning the cape: only you can save him.

The door opens and Tess emerges. She's laughing. Right behind her — Mark. They come down the steps. Mark lights up. He looks toward the car. Del switches on the lights to let him know she's there. Mark raises his index finger: one minute. He and Tess in conference. Tess takes something from her pocket. She writes on it, hands it to Mark. Then she waves toward the car, turns and disappears into the dark.

Mark taps on the glass. She's forgotten to unlock his side. "Hey," he says, and gets in. He rolls the window down, blows his smoke out. He laughs. "Tess Morletti, at your Al-Anon meeting. Not exactly what you had in mind."

"Right," she says, and pulls away from the curb.

"It was a good meeting," he says. "After those crazy Brother and Sister, we are Family, sessions at Lazarus, I wasn't sure I'd ever want to sit in a circle again." He closes the window, switches on the radio, searches. Loud music yawks by. He turns the radio off. "I'm going to stay at Tess's friend's in Marwick tonight. That way I can get to my CDC appointment at nine, pick up the scrip from Mental Health. Then go to the noon NA meeting at St. Theresa's. Probably Rozmer and Charlie will be there."

She turns the wipers up and rolls her neck. The usual vertebra has started to burn.

"Better take I-88," he says. He pulls a paper from his pocket, turns on the overhead light. "486 East Street. Up near the college. Eric. You might even know him. The guy with the dreads who works at the guitar shop." He's thought ahead. Has a positive plan for the day. Be grateful. All right, she is. "Sounds like the usual shit going on at the Morlettis'," he says. "Tess told me she's cut all contact with them. Too crazy." She doesn't respond. They leave the village, just the dark and the rain. "Okay if I smoke?" Mark says. "Guy at the meeting I know let me bum a couple. I'm pretty wound." Again he rolls the window down a little, is careful not to blow the smoke her way.

"I'm going to Washington tomorrow with Richard. He's seeing a specialist. Probably it's nothing, but he wants a second opinion." That's enough information. Let Mark know she's got other things to deal with.

"What are you doing with Luke while you're gone?"

"I left him at Marna's. Richard and I have to leave about four this morning, not get back until really late. You think you can stay with this Eric another night?" Another month? Year?

"Probably not. Eric's roommate's coming back tomorrow. I can't wait to see Luke." Well, that's one good thing. With Mark at the house, the whole hassle with Luke will be over. Mark opens the glove compartment and holds another sheet in the light. "AA area schedule," he says. Well, no question, he's organizing. Thinking. "There's going to be the problem of getting back and forth. I'm going to need to go to at least one meeting a day. Ninety meetings in ninety days. Rozmer's real clear on that. And I'm working on being up for it." He folds the paper and switches off the light. "Looks like there's the choice of both night and day meetings, mostly in Marwick. Be easier once I pay the motor vehicle fine, get the suspension lifted. That is if you're going to be okay to let me borrow your car." He turns her way. "Of course I understand if you aren't."

A reliable housemate with a reliable vehicle. Someone who's got a job. Keep Mark company. She'll set up in her little studio room at Richard's. She can lengthen the umbilical, not have to be every day worrying if Mark's going to make his appointments on time, get to a meeting. She's got to have the distance in order to stay detached. "I'm thinking it might be the best thing for me . . . for you . . . for Richard, but mostly for me, if I move in with Richard for four or five days a week, not just the weekends like now. I'll feel less anxious. Not to be so sitting in the middle of your life. But I'd only feel okay doing this if you could get a good AA-type roommate. Somebody like Charlie." He doesn't say anything, but he's turned completely her way. He has lowered his hood. "Somebody who doesn't use. Who's got a car and is willing to help you out with some rides when I can't take you. Pay a couple hundred a month. Buy his own groceries. We could turn my studio into a bedroom. You and Charlie could have the upper part of the living room to set up your equipment, the amps, your drums. I'd come down maybe Mondays and Tuesdays."

Mark laughs. "Well," he says, "that's a full-scale scenario."

She laughs too. "And oh, so typical. Remember that elaborate transportation schedule I worked out for you to go from the Camden hospital to New Vistas. Every frigging phone number, what you should tip the taxi. Down to the minute. Once I get anxious, no heights I can't climb."

"East Street's coming up." He takes the paper out again and switches on the light.

"You know what this all depends on," she says.

"I do."

She doesn't say any more. She's made the leap. They travel through the silence, only the back and forth of the wipers.

"Next block," he says. "I can see the neon from the deli. There it is." It's your usual college-area rundown converted house. All the windows draped with bedding. A trash barrel overflowing on the porch. Parts of the banister missing.

"You want me to turn into the driveway?"

"No. Park on this side. Just have to get my stuff out of the trunk. I'll run it by Rozmer, Joy. You sure this is something you want to try. You want to move to Richard's?"

"I want to try. See how it goes."

"Well, in the light of day . . . After I talk to Rozmer, I'll see what Charlie says. It would be a great, a great thing for me to be able to set up, record, play every day. Might make all the difference."

That something might make the difference. "What are you going to do about a place to stay tomorrow night?"

He opens the door. "I'll work it out. Could you get to a computer around nine tomorrow? Transfer my share of the money from the rep-payee into my ATM? I'm out of cigarettes. I'll need some money to eat."

The money. Turning the money over to Mark makes her stomach contract. But it is his share. Not her business. "I'll try," she says. "Once Richard gets to the hospital. I'll probably be able to do it then. Two hundred and ninety dollars." Of course she knows to the penny.

He takes his bass and backpack from the trunk. She rolls down the window and opens her hand for the keys.

"Thanks," he says. "Thanks a lot. I'll leave a message on Richard's machine. Let you know how it's going."

"Should I wait? Make sure you get in?"

"No," he says. "It's all set."

All set? Or he might just take his money and get high. She watches him cross the street. His black jacket and pants fade into the night. Mark, who used to gather them around for his magic shows, his eyes wide to catch their surprise when he made the quarter disappear. He turns as he goes up the steps and waves. She puts the car in drive and takes the first right. Richard. She'll have to tell Richard the story: another grand scheme. She already knows what he will say.

18 : Entry

Symptom Checklist-90-R
Name <u>Mark Merrick</u>

Below is a list of problems people sometimes have. Blacken the
circle that best describes HOW MUCH THAT PROBLEM HAS
DISTRESSED YOU DURING THE PAST 7 DAYS.

	Not at all	A little bit	Moderately	Quite a bit	Extremely
1. Shakiness inside	(0)	(1)	(2)	(3)	(4)
2. Disturbed sleep	(0)	(1)	(2)	(3)	(4)
3. Loss of sexual interest	(0)	(1)	(2)	(3)	(4)

And the prize goes to the person with the highest score: private room with your own peephole and padded interior. His own
diagnosis for his current level of extreme distress: (1) no caffeine,
(2) no nicotine, (3) inadequate zzzz's due to inadequate length of
couch, (4) in addition to all the above, going to have to psych
out an alien head because Joy, his usual therapist, has shunted
him off to a new counselor — a small man with the demeanor of
an old hippie.

A king-size mistake not to borrow enough for cigarettes and
coffee from Tess this morning. Tess — up at dawn to go job hunt-
ing. The shame of grubbing under such conditions too great even
for him. Must be he is making *some* progress. April 2: thirty days

clean. Feel like shit now, but today he'll get a one-month token at the NA meeting.

4. Scared for no reason   (0)   (1)   (2)   (3)   (4)

For "no reason"? Point is there is a reason: the CIA has just turned on the transmitter controlling your mind and the zap-zap is naturally causing you quite a bit of anxiety.

Always there is that major decision: How honest does he want to be? Not at all? Moderately? Extremely? Answer: All depends. All depends on whether he's trying to get *in* or *out*. And of course, he has to be consistent. Machine's going to eject you as unreliable if you skid out of the trench too often. Right away he spots his particular modus operandi.

5. Repeated unpleasant thoughts that won't leave your head
7. Feeling that you are watched or talked about by others
10. Hearing voices that others do not hear
19. Seeing things that other people do not see

In the last seven days? All of them extremely. Now that he's out of the Lazarus cooker, he's cooling down. He skims the remaining questions.

90. Thoughts of ending your life

Fill in the (4) on that one and you'll be exchanging your clothes for rear-hanging-out attire.

Ben Jacobs, the new counselor, appears in the doorway. Flannel shirt fraying. Steel-rims. Got the back-to-the-land lean. "How's it coming?" Jacobs says.

"Mostly I've been circling the runway."

Jacobs smiles. He's got a good smile. Quiet. "What's the control tower telling you?"

Mark touches down on the first (4). "Five more minutes," he says and begins dark-marking his way down the page.

First thing he sees, smells, is the coffee. Jacobs follows his gaze and rises, sets about pouring him a cup. Mark sits and places the completed checklist face down on the bare desk. No M. MERRICK folder full of incriminating evidence. No note-taking paraphernalia. No family photos. No framed credentials or inspirational sayings on the walls. No clues.

Jacobs sets a small tray on the desk. "Might need to pull your chair up."

Half-and-half, an almost full sugar dispenser, a spoon. Mark tips the dispenser up and lets the sparkling crystals flow. He drinks. Strong. Hot. Jacobs tilts back in his chair, folds his hands across his chest. No hurry. One thing for sure about this guy: he knows how to get off to a good start. "So," Jacobs says. "Here you are."

"Here I am."

"I haven't looked over your records yet or conferred with your previous counselor. All I know is that you aren't a first-time client, that you're also seeing Dr. Taylor at Mental Health, that you're here on a voluntary basis, not a mandate from the court. If you signed the releases and plan to meet with me regularly, then I'll read through your file, talk to the previous professionals you've worked with."

"All right," Mark says.

"Probably these sessions will be more helpful if you start by saying what's on your mind. Then we can take it from there. Make it a long or a short session this first time."

All the places that sweat, are beginning to. He adds a little more sugar, checks to see if Jacobs notes that. His mind: Does he want to go live or play the usual reruns? He takes the coffee down as fast as he can without burning his throat. The sweet heat hits his empty belly.

"I'm waiting for my disability money to get deposited so I can go buy a pack of cigarettes. I'm wanting to get high. I'm wanting to be saved." He pushes back in the chair, presses his shirt against the padding to stanch the flow.

Again the quiet smile, a little lean his way. "You want to get yourself more coffee."

Moderate tremor on the pour. He fills it to the exact right level so it won't slosh, so he can put in the cream. He settles back into the chair, manages the whole routine without knocking anything over. "I'm thirty days clean."

Jacobs rests his arms on the desk.

"Detox in Camden. Two weeks in psychiatric rehab at New Vistas. And a couple of days at Lazarus House, a therapeutic community downstate."

"A couple of days?" Jacobs knows how to put the queries out there, how not to wake the beast.

"Too confrontational. Stress." The cup's steady. No longer the pulsing in his ears. "I started having symptoms. Not a safe place to lose it."

"What kind of symptoms?"

"Seeing things. Hearing things. Racing thoughts. Insomnia. Stomach pains. It was heavy duty." He flares the corners of the checklist. "A lot of number fours."

"How are you doing right now?"

"I'm calming down."

"How about medication?"

"Zyprexa and Neurontin. None at Lazarus. I'm all set to pick up a new scrip at MH right after I leave here."

"How long since you left Lazarus?"

"Three days."

Jacobs's head dips, a surprised wag of approval, then he fades back a bit, but his eyes still gleam. "What level of treatment are you thinking about at this point?"

As little as I can get away with. Jacobs once again tilts back his chair, turns so he's not head on. Mark cups his sweating hands around his knees. "The level of treatment . . . No more therapeutic communities. I don't think even a halfway. I don't feel like I'm steady enough to be full-time 'out there.' I've done the straitjacket, Thorazine lockdown at Langston Psych and the main thing I learned is I don't wish to do it again."

"Do you have any plan shaping up?"

"I've got a sponsor: twenty years recovery and up for calling me on most of my bullshit. He's pressing me to do the ninety in ninety. My mom's my rep-payee and she's willing to let me live at home temporarily as long as I don't use."

"Anything else?"

"Maybe even line up an AA housemate, with my mom living at her boyfriend's most of the week. Cut down on a lot of the control stuff. Good place for me to work on my music. Give me a chance to take care of old business: the dentist. Get a suspension on my license lifted."

"How about your drug connections?"

"Yeah, no question it's risky business, but it feels like it's all I'm up for."

"Is counseling here at the clinic part of the plan?"

Mark laughs. "Part of my sponsor's plan, my mom's plan. I'm not sure it's totally signed on as part of *my* plan yet. Probably I'm still trying to wiggle out wherever I can. But yeah, I got the voice in my head telling me coming here is part of what I need to do."

Again Jacobs smiles. "Tower giving you any other advice?"

"Yeah, I'd like to be randomly drug-tested."

"What's that about?" Jacobs says.

"Maybe more of my 'making like I mean it,' but also think it might put a little fear into my impulsive tendencies. It might."

"Have any interest in making out a contract? A list of guidelines for yourself. Positive behaviors that are likely to help you avoid slipping into patterns that might lead to relapse. For example: go to meetings at least... However many a week you think will be helpful. Be randomly drug-tested."

A flash of the New Vistas study halls: his assets, his defects. "I'll think about it," Mark says.

"You ever write lyrics? Keep a notebook?"

"Sometimes, but usually only when the mania train's picking up speed."

"Well, think about making that contract list to bring in to look over with me. Even doing some journal entries. Those... just for yourself. You might find it helpful. Even a source for your music." Jacobs reaches in a desk drawer and brings out a sheet, hands it over to Mark. "Some topics that might get you started."

Mark folds the paper without looking at it and pushes it into his pocket. End of session in sight. Get to the ATM, a meeting, talk to Rozmer, Charlie. Maybe Tess can give him a ride to Danford.

"See you next week?" Jacobs says.

"Yeah. I'll make an appointment on my way out. Thanks."

Jacobs rises. He extends his hand. Warm and dry. "I've found it helpful to turn the volume up on the one track, down on the other. When the tower forecasts unfavorable weather, turbulence likely, I listen."

Marna's truck muffler backfires on every hill. Everybody in their circle living the low-budget life. Each time it backfires, Luke and Fritz leap up, bark frantically in his ear. Mark tries reaching around to grab hold of Luke, but that just connects him to a hundred pounds of brown frenzy, jamming his arm into his shoulder socket. He resists yanking on the choke collar. By the time they reach Danford, Mark's head is banging. Charlie's not willing to move in. Doesn't fit his careful guidelines and this *new* idea for a housemate is farfetched. No matter how fast-talking, his mother is never going to go for it. Never. Even if he could wheedle out a provisionary okay from his mother, have to override Rozmer's veto. Shit to pay all around. Warnings of turbulence even with the volume on low. Plus he's about to go back on that land. In that house. All of it haunted.

They pass the school. Marna pumps the brakes as they go down the final hill. The gravel bank comes into view. Aaron's wrecked cabin just visible through the trees up on the ridge.

"You sure you don't want to stay at my place tonight? Wait until your mom gets back?"

Mark unwedges his bass, moves his backpack so his legs are free. "No, I'll be fine. I know where there's a key. Let us off by the mailbox. I want to walk in, give Luke a good run."

If he can just get in, go up to his room and crash. Burrow into the dark. Pull the plug on the phone. Last thing he needs is a call from Rudy or Carla. Though he trusts Tess, that she's not going to tell anybody he's here. Marna turns down into the gravel bank. Luke yelps to be released. Mark opens the door and before he's half out, Luke leaps over the seat and shoves past him. "Jesus Christ, Luke." He tries for a smile. "Thanks, Marna. I appreciate it."

"Call me if you need anything. I mean it," she says. He raises his hand to wave. She swings around and onto the road, the truck rumbling all the way up the hill.

Quiet. Luke, far ahead, looking back from the rise that marks the start of their land. Their road is full of holes, ruts of mud. Winter damage. The kind of work he always told his mother he'd get to, but then never did. If he does end up being able to stay here, maybe he'll do better with all that. Then there it is: the stone house, the grandfather maple, Aaron's cherry tree. The pole barn where they actually lived while they were building the house. Where his father died. Say it: where his father killed himself. Where his father sat down and wrote a note that said, *Dear Loved Ones, Forgive me.* Then, with Coal, the dog they all loved, beside him, lifted the gun he'd taken from his parents' back room and pulled the trigger.

He moves on toward the house. He sets his stuff by the front door and goes around to the little shed in back. Luke is doing his circles of joy, his soggy stuffed monkey dangling from his mouth. "Left your baby out all winter. Now look at it," he says. He reaches his hand down into the watering can where his mother always keeps the spare key. No key. Fuck. He shakes it. Nothing. He feels along the edges of the boards. He goes around to the side door and runs his fingers along the tops of the windows. Now what is he going to do? He and Luke circle the house. No ladders long enough to get in the loft. All the windows locked. And then he sees it: the dog door into the laundry room. He unfastens the gate to the kennel and flips the heavy rubber cover up: a big square of pink insulation, beyond that the sliding metal panel. He stretches out, his back on the ramp Richard built for

Luke when he put in the door. All the while Luke barks and worries at his pants legs. "Shut the fuck up," he tells him, but not too loud, not too mean. He rests his head on the sill and tries to get his fingers under the edge of the cover. It does give an inch, but then it catches on the little release button that's designed to prevent entry. He judges the opening: Could he actually squeeze himself through even if he can jimmy the panel out? He rolls over and presses with both hands, full force. No give. Then he yanks off the ramp and in the mud on his knees lifts up on the door. The release lock breaks. He continues to force the metal cover until it jumps out of the grooves and bangs on the floor inside. Then one shoulder, one arm at a time, births himself until he's all the way through. As soon as he's clear, Luke bursts in as well. "What fun, ehh, Luke?"

The house is cold, but he's not going to build a fire. He snaps both phone cords from their jacks and goes up the ladder to the loft. Luke cries at the bottom. "Got to crash for a while, buddy." The loft is clean, every surface bare, every trace of him folded and tucked away, except for the dozens of black marks along the edges of the sill, the chest, around his bed: cigarette burns. He fastens one of the blankets across the window, pulls off his boots, his pants, and crawls under the down comforter. Cold. Cold and smelling damply clean. He pulls the covers over his head.

Clock says 4:06. He closes down the damper on the stove a little. Only a small fire, but warmth sinks into the places that ache. While the shredded potatoes brown, he breaks eight eggs into a metal bowl, dumps in bits of cheddar, scrambles. Just a couple of hours of sleep, but he's had a solid landing. The thing is the plan he's going to propose does have merit: transportation to meetings and clinic appointments, the support and company of someone who doesn't use, the likelihood that old food will get dumped before mold sets in. Certain valid objections are bound to be raised and must be listened to. He eyes the burning cigarette on the edge of the counter. In the cupboard he finds a chipped saucer. Guideline for his contract: (1) Always use an ashtray.

In fact he needs to start smoking outside only. He squashes the cigarette. One good thing about this last month of institutional living: learning to smoke in the rain without whining. Luke noses the dried food Mark has put in his dish, then backs away. He splits two bagels, butters them, slides them in the toaster oven. He flips the potatoes and pushes them up on the sides of the pan, then pours in the eggs, adds pepper and salt, a dash of garlic, mixes it all together with a fork. The thing about a good omelet is you can't leave it: (2) Stay focused.

He turns the toaster on, pours a giant glass of cranberry juice, lays out his meds and a One-A-Day, even an Omega-3 Fish Oil. He slides the omelet and potatoes onto his plate and sets one of the bagels beside the whole feast. Just as he raises his fork, Luke comes to lean his chin on his knee. "Probably you're right," he says. "Lest greed overtake me." He lifts Luke's bowl to the table and scrapes onto the kibble what he can bring himself to spare.

"Ahhh." There's the sound of both of them chewing. They don't stop until every last bit is gone. Mark sops up the final film of yellow. Then he runs hot water into the frying pan, adds a few drops of detergent and sets it in the sink. He lifts a chair and places it out on the stones. Aaron's walk. He lights up: this and the one with coffee when he first wakes are the best cigarettes of the day. Luke stretches out on the grass, his nose resting on his paws.

Maybe he should sketch out the merit points before he calls. He goes up to the loft and rummages through the trunk: a box of his books, a bag of old cassettes, a folded world map, Aaron's copy of the Bhagavad Gita and what he's looking for — the leather-bound journal Sammi gave him when they were in Austin. Blessedly blank, no seedy fragments scrawled out when he was high. Each page perforated for removal if he changes his mind. Downstairs again, he finds a pencil. A cup of coffee, the portable phone, the ashtray, another chair to set everything on. He arranges it all outside. Should he deliver the core of the proposal first as a machine-message before she and Richard get back tonight or should he wait until she comes down tomorrow? Or only leave enough word to let her know all's well. The thought of her first anxious responses makes him lean toward the easy out of the machine, but if it's presented to her in person, no question he can exert greater pressures of persuasion.

A photo drops from the journal, face down on the walk. His first inclination is to slip it unseen between the back pages, avoid some flash that will knock him out of Proposal Orbit. Instead he flips it over with the end of the pencil: Sammi in a goof on a porn shot — on all fours in a Yoga-cat position, black bra and thong, mascara whiskers. Two bunches of her then-blond hair twisted into pointy ears on top of her head. The spider tattoo on her thigh, the center of the focus. He laughs and lifts it to the fading light. Maybe down the line he'll give Sammi a call, tell her he's doing okay. In his pocket he feels the folded square of paper Jacobs gave him. He opens it. One side is a long list of suggestions for making out a contract: "Take medication as directed." "Sober fun once a day minimum . . ." He turns the sheet over to the *Journal Starters* side. There it is: flashing red, the siren-scream on the way to Emergency:

Choose a person who cares about you and describe how you feel they would respond to your death.

He lights a cigarette and picks up the phone, dials Richard's. At the tone he says, "Mom, I'm home. Marna gave me a ride with Luke. Had a good session at CDC, got my meds, went to a meeting. Charlie says he needs to live in Marwick to finish his classes, but I think I've found someone who'll be a good housemate." He takes a long drag. Exhales. Lets that sink in. "Person has a job . . . doesn't use . . . goes to meetings. We can talk it over when you come down tomorrow." He presses the End button. He smokes and watches the birds dart into the hemlocks, settle for the night.

Part II

JULY

You have reached 456-7631. If this is an emergency, hang up and dial 911. If this is trouble, please call someone else. You cannot count on me; I am not here for you. The news I have is good: you have a place to live; you have been befriended by someone steady. I'm holding on to that. If this is not you, leave a message. I am standing by the phone, praying, an alarm going off in my chest. If it isn't your voice, I'll answer. Whoever it is, that isn't you, be prepared for the gust of relief when I say Hello.

—DEL MERRICK, from the back of a
drawing of a horseshoe crab, June 2002

19 : Night Riders

Better take the Back River Road," Mark says. "Less chance of trouble." Then he braces himself as Tess makes the turn late and wide and going too fast. Luke and Queenie hunker down. One good thing: three months of Tess living at the house, but still no contact from the Morlettis. No more threats from Rudy. Maybe they think Tess went back to Texas, maybe Rudy doesn't even know he's there. Maybe so much shit going down for them, they're too busy to think at all. Mark wedges the Bugler can between his knees and troughs the cigarette paper to catch most of the tobacco. The bump in front of Hoop Dawes's cow yard lifts them both off their seats — truck shocks long gone — and dumps the cigarette-in-progress onto his pants. The Holsteins bug-eye their flash-by.

"Moooo. Morning, girls," Tess calls. "I love those cows. They can stand in muck, let it all hang off their big haunch-bones. I'm thinking I'd like to become a vet tech." She swerves to avoid a squirrel. "Maybe go to Marwick Community in the fall. Get a job milking for the rest of the summer. You know, become a cow. Absorb some of their placidity."

"Stupidity," Mark says. "Shoveling shit. Slow down a little. I'm trying to do brain surgery over here." Tess gives him an indulgent shrug, but she brakes, eases into a steady forty. She's not a smoker and thus is only two steps away from getting on her "killing yourself" soapbox. Plus it stinks. He rolls the cigarette and licks the paper lightly along the edge, pinches off the shreds at the ends. He finds a match and takes the smoke down. Truly nasty this cheap tobacco, but better than nothing. "Keep going slow while I roll a few more."

"You'll be late for the interview."

"Please," he says in a not-please voice. He's got to get a grip. Increasing irritability — not a good sign. If Dr. Taylor would give him a scrip for Xanax so he could have it handy, maybe only five a month, for high-stress times like these. But Taylor's not going for it. Looks like the anti-anxieties haven't worked well for you in the past, he said. Problem is they worked too well. Got himself a superduper dependency a few years back. He places the four cigarettes in a Camel box.

"Look at it this way," Tess says, "yesterday a U.S. two-thousand-pound bomb killed forty members of an Afghani wedding party." Tess often comes up with these little "count your blessings" news clips which he's learned never to acknowledge.

She begins to suck on her teeth, one tooth at a time. She has a terrible fear, she says, of going around with a piece of spinach or something gross stuck on a tooth and she'll walk about and no one will tell her. I'll tell you, I'll tell you, he's said, but it doesn't make her stop. The sucking sound drives him nuts. He breathes, tries to calm down. Dr. Taylor's substitute for Xanax: close your eyes, put yourself in a safe place. Took him a while to imagine himself back in the loft, the covers over his head. Now that he's got his license back, be good if Tess would let him borrow her truck from time to time, safer, but she doesn't offer and he's not asking. He needs a vehicle. Unlikely his mother's going to ever help him get another car. Not after what he did with the Tempo.

When he opens his eyes, they're on Main Street. "It's on Buford, back behind the hospital," he says. But he doesn't want to go that way. Just the mention of it and the cover of darkness is gone and there he is putting a chair through the psych ward window, leaping to his escape because they wouldn't take him out for a smoke. "I don't want to go by the hospital."

"I know that," Tess says.

He told her the whole horror tale back when they were doing that kind of talking, removing the cover-ups, their clothes. Before they freaked, scrammed back to camouflage.

She makes the turn to get to Buford from the other side. Rozmer said red brick, with a parking lot in back. "There," he says, "on the corner. The one with the purple flowers."

"Looks like a regular home. They've got twelve kids in there? You'd think they'd have some sort of sign: Harbor House."

"They don't want to advertise. They had to go through the whole 'not in my backyard' fight. People afraid these kids are going to steal their hubcaps, sell their kids dope."

Tess laughs. "Or worse." She pulls into the driveway. Both dogs rise. Tess takes him right to the front walk, the hole in her muffler announcing his arrival.

He gives the door a good shove. "Sorry I'm so edgy."

She nods. "What time you want me to pick you up?"

The door hinges whine. "What's good for you?"

Of course neither of them's got a watch, but Tess always seems to know. She looks at the sky. "It's about two now," she says.

"Won't be long I think. This interview? More Rozmer wanting me to continue my 'drop and roll' practice."

"The job's only going to be a few hours a week. Might be a good thing."

"Can't think they're going to hire someone with my history to work with kids."

"Your interview's at two, right?" She puts the truck in gear. "I'm going to the library, see what my work schedule is at the store. Want me to pick you up some Golden Seal? Good for bleeding."

Shit. He did not need a mention of his gums right at this ordeal-moment. He shuts the door, tests to make sure it's closed all the way.

Tess cranes her neck to catch his eye. "I'll come back about two forty-five. You want to go to the three o'clock meeting, then do some grocery shopping?"

"I don't know," he says.

He watches her back the rusty pickup straight out of the long driveway, nary a correction of the wheel. She gives him a thumbs up when she makes the turn. He wishes he could back his way into being "just friends" with such ease. What a mistake to jeopardize the whole housemate deal by getting involved with Tess. Why AA advises no new relationships that first year. Plus, well, the fatal attraction is not there. 'Course he never got into that. It's me, not you, he'd said. Her response reassuring: I'm not that into you either. Let that not be just a cover for a hurt that's going to welt up and turn ugly. Rozmer's response to that: dream on. He was a shit and he promptly admits it. He follows the brick walk to the front door. VISITORS PLEASE SPEAK TO A STAFF MEMBER UPON ARRIVAL. He presses the doorbell three times like Rozmer told him. Quick and short: the code for letting staff know you're legit. Foolish really because after one such ring, every delinquent in the place knows exactly what it means and passes it on to the undesirables before nightfall.

The sound of someone coming. Mark adjusts his face, runs his hand over his head, a head shaved so close it reveals his weird hairline and all because Rozmer didn't have a half-inch guard. At least the reflection of his face through the screen looks a little less P.O.W. The added weight? Zyprexa or the hash browns and eggs? Don't wear black, Rozmer told him, as though he needed such a pearl. He's donned his whitest T and a green plaid shirt rolled to the elbows. He looks at his arms: only a few faint needle scars left, the track marks paled to indecipherable. One hundred and thirty days. A boy, maybe fifteen, opens the door, looks at him through the screen. The usual exterior afflictions: acne and a nervous Adam's apple. Plus the doughy paunch of Game-Boy aficionados, anti-psychotic meds. "My name's Mark Merrick. I have an appointment with Ms. Glick at two."

"Wait," the kid says, and leaves him hanging in the sun. The need for a smoke, his fingers beginning their gimme-tingle, and not one of those filterless, loose-ass roll-your-owns of his current life. Why did he let Rozmer pressure him into having this interview? Lot of days lately it's an effort to throw the sheet off, put his feet on the floor. Jacobs says the time between three and six months of recovery is often called the "Fuckits."

From the back he hears voices, then the sound of a vacuum. The boy returns, no efforts at doing anything social with *his* face. He unlocks the screen door. Mark feels the sweat trickle down — his body always so eager to give him away. He follows the boy through a large foyer, a lineup of Macs on either side of the room — state of the art — two girls working at one. They go silent, slide him hostile glances. He feels their eyes on him as he moves away. Troubled teenage girls doing time at Harbor House, always under supervision. Forms of bullshit might be even more inventive than the boys'.

They go down a long hall, doors open onto bedrooms: twin beds, dressers. Neat, everything new. Place just opened up. A Catholic Charity way station for kids coming out of the psych unit but not yet ready to go home or into foster care. Mornings they go to summer school, come back and do homework, have an outing. Place is getting the kinks out, Rozmer says. Already had one slit-wrists rush to Emergency that's upped the reality-amps: twelve fucked-up adolescents bouncing off the walls — no matter how attractive the posters — offers as much calm as the presence of land mines permits. This is why, Rozmer, it ain't a good place for a shell-shock like me. You can play music with them, basketball, Rozmer says. Dream on.

The boy points to a small office at the end of the hall. NAOMI GLICK on the door. Then he disappears into a bedroom, leaves the door ajar. One of the rules. Mark settles in the chair across from the desk. The space is so small he has to cramp up, sit straight to have room for his knees. Naomi Glick's desk is piled with folders; "piled" may be too orderly a word. Geegaws crowd the shelves on the back wall: a collection of what must be doll teacups, a miniature farm: cut-out painted cows, chickens, sheep munching inside a fence backed by a blue silo. Get Tess one of those. The opposite of Ben Jacobs's exterior decor. Lots of clues, but clues to what? No photos though, no smiling family portraits, no line of big-teethed children in front of azure skies with sweet clouds. If Ms. Glick is a large person, things will be close. The air conditioner's on high: frosty. His body's starting to chill along the sweat lanes.

"Hey." Ms. Glick enters, extends her hand. Wiry, short. Knotty little arms. Maybe a few years younger than he is. "Naomi," she says.

He struggles to stand in the awkward space, after a quick brush of his damp fingers on his pants. "Mark Merrick." He's looking down at the top of her head. One thing in common: premature gray.

"Sorry to keep you waiting." She pushes the door to almost closed. "Bill says you're in recovery, out of rehab for three months."

Bill? Bill? Then it comes to him: William Rozmer. "Yes," he says.

She drums her small fingers on the tops of the folders. "Have to go right to the personal in hiring someone to be a per diem aide here. Drugs being one of these kids' main issues as I'm sure you're aware."

Her nails are bitten down, the cuticles raw.

"Actually I'm relieved to have that in the open. Get it over with." And he is.

Her nails, his sweaty tang: their bodies exchanging data.

"Bill says you've made a contract to be randomly drug-tested. I feel that's going to help if you decide you want the job, help clear things with my bosses at Catholic Charities." She takes a sheaf of papers from under the piles, flips through them. "You're a musician, a runner, a basketball player in high school. Still like to play a little pickup?"

"I'm getting back into shape," he says.

She hands him several of the sheets. "An application, releases, references," she says. "We have to run a background check to make sure you have no child abuse offenses. Sooner you get these all back to me the better. If you want the job." She hands him a pamphlet. "Harbor House guidelines. What we give all the kids' parents, their siblings..." Suddenly she leans across the piles, fixes him with her small black eyes. "Bill tells me that both your brother and your father killed themselves, so I'm wondering..."

Something thuds hard against the back wall, the desk vibrates against his knees. Naomi Glick is on her feet and out the door. "Got to go," she says. "Main thing: get everything back to me as soon as you can."

Loud voices, glass breaking. He sits for a few minutes. Down the long hall he sees the front door. He looks at the papers in his wet hands. He can drop them in the trash or leave them on top of the piles. This place is fucked up. He has no business being here.

Tess dances while she shops. Shit Mu-zack, she says, but all we got. He follows her bobbing dreads, gyrating elbows, down the Dinners and Soups aisle, moving their cart to the beat of the music too. His job is to push the cart and to restrain overdoing it on the Family-Size Double Chocolate Brownie mixes. Actually from Tess he's learning to be a good shopper: not so much the price to ounces, but checking the ingredients for poisons and saturated fats, what's good to stock up on, the uses of tofu.

"Heads up," Tess calls from way down the aisle as she underhands him a box of Annie's Shells and Cheese, All Natural. "Pick up a few more if you think those look good," she says and disappears around the corner. Mostly they don't do prepared foods, but every now and then she can't resist a Dirty Rice. He checks over what they have so far: spaghetti sauce, yellow mustard, A.1., whole-wheat wraps, bananas, milk, green tea, a Styrofoam tray of chicken thighs. Be good to give up eating the flesh of others. He places the toilet paper, cat food, detergent, tampons in the child carrier seat. His food stamps cover the edibles until they run out, and Tess buys the rest. Only gets $140 a month so he's got to go light on junk, make the marrow bones for Luke and Queenie an occasional treat. Also he has to chip in on Tess's gas. So far finances not an issue, leaves them the energy to keep their mood swings from knocking one of them down for the count.

He trolls past the bagel and donut cases, Tess bouncing ahead. Tess: cooler than cool. Putting her life back together. Be so good to latch on. Why can't he? But he is glad she talked him into shopping. The forty choices of toothpaste, the babies' grins, swathe Ms. Glick's slash to the heart, the whole Harbor fiasco. How could Rozmer have set him up for so much danger? Serious dip in the Trust and Judgment stocks. Definitely he was not up for a meeting: he is sick of meetings. Give his higher power a little R & R. Plus he doesn't want to see Rozmer right now. Rozmer's own mania streaking up the chart. Phone machine Word for the Day untranslatable. May have to fire Rozmer, rustle up a sponsor who doesn't push him onto the tracks of an oncoming train. He pulls up next to Tess; the fluorescence of the deli counter glints off the rhinestone stud in her nose. "Think we've probably maxed out the benefit card for July."

Tess sets what looks like a silver wheel in the cart. Definitely not edible. He transfers it to the child seat. "Duct tape?" he says.

"For the bats. Three in two days."

"Four." The last two nights he's been startled awake by Tess's screams, her turning on every light, the careen of a bat through the house. Tess's refusal to go back to her room until the two of them have checked every inch, until he promised to place a blanket along the bottom of her door once she sealed herself in. It has been his job to find the bats each morning after their vampire swoops through the dark. Unfortunately two of them today and both of them in Tess's room: one tucked in behind a picture of Queenie, the other actually sitting on Tess's bookcase, its little ears visible against a white mug. He is able to place a towel over their brown stillness and carry them into the woods while they chitter beneath his hand, look up at him once he places them on the rotting stump, their tiny teeth going. "Duct tape?" he says again. "Hang it in strips from the ceiling, catch them like flies in mid-plunge for your hair?"

"Ha, ha. I've decided they're not coming in when we open the door. They're sneaking in somewhere else. Maybe around the edges of that panel in your mom's closet, the one that goes to the storage space under the eaves. I'm going to duct-tape all around that."

"Better clear it with my mother. She's coming down later."

"You going to tell her about Harbor?"

Then they both stop, lean toward the music. "Been a long time since I've heard this one," he says.

"Me, too." They move toward the checkout. Tess begins to sing, "'Well, I've got to run to keep from hiding, and I'm bound to keep on riding . . .'"

The cashier gives them a maternal smile.

Mark swings in behind Tess, hums in his head: "'And I don't own the clothes I'm wearing. And the road goes on forever. But I'm not going to let them catch me, no.'"

Tess rushes down the final hill so fast Mark presses his foot to the floorboards. The B & R Roto-Rooter sign has just emerged from behind the trees. "Want to check the mailbox?" But just as she starts to slow for the turn off the highway, she hits the accelerator again.

The dogs slide to the floor in back as his hands smack the glove compartment to keep from being thrown. "What the hell, Tess?"

"Jesusgod, look who's behind us. Shit, shit, shit. Should I turn in or keep going?"

A green truck coming on full ahead. "Fuck." No question it's Smithy's green truck, Rudy at the wheel. "Turn, turn. But not so fast you turn us over." Tess cuts the corner so wide they almost slide into the ditch. Rudy's coming on too fast to follow. He hits the brakes, skids. Just misses the guardrails. Queenie and Luke leap up. Rudy's head hangs out the passenger window, his face twisted, his mouth at full scream.

Tess hesitates. "Should I drive on through to your road? We'll be trapped. Dead end." There's the scrunch of Rudy grinding the gears to reverse.

"Keep going. At least we'll have a phone. Or I'll beat his head in with your tire iron."

Tess speeds past the Roto-Rooter septic holding tank. Mark keeps his eye on Smithy's truck. Rudy backs up full throttle, barely misses their mailbox. Then he roars down the drive after them. The B & R owner stands in the open door of the big shed, raises his hand in protest. Maybe he'll call the cops. Best scenario. "Step on it," Mark says. The truck bangs up the rise at the beginning of their road. Tess hits every pothole full on. They streak by the pole barn.

"Oh Mark, your mother's already here," Tess yells over the yapping racket.

"Just one good thing after another," he says. "Pull up right behind her car." Tess screeches to a stop. "Take the dogs in. Try to keep it as cool as you can." They all pile out. Queenie and Luke begin a wild chase around the yard. Del opens the front door. Mark hops into the truck bed. "Where's your tire iron? Your jack?"

"I don't have one." Tess is busy grabbing Queenie by the collar, dragging her bulldog reluctance toward the house.

"What's wrong?" Del calls, starting down the walk.

"Tess, bring me the wrecking bar on the other side of my bed. Mom, go back inside. Tess will fill you in." Mark jumps to the ground and unhooks one of the chains that anchors the tailgate. He wraps the steel links around his hand, then turns to face the road.

20 : Echolocation

THROUGH THE WINDOW Del watches Tess run toward Mark, the cordless phone in one hand, the long, heavy bar in the other. Above the scrabble of Queenie's nails, her whines, as she races back and forth between the two doors, Del listens for the rumble of a truck coming. Luke is nowhere in sight. "Queenie," she says, grabbing Tess's dog by the collar, tucking her between her own trembling legs, "it's going to be all right." Del doesn't believe this: "all" and "right" are never paired. She's been expecting some violent contact from Rudy ever since he threatened to burn down their barn, ever since Mark returned, ever since Tess moved in. Every time the phone rings, "This is it" squeezes her stomach hard. Except at Richard's. At Richard's she's able to sink into her drawings, the black of the graphite, the white of the paper.

Mark turns toward the house. He gives her a reassuring wave. She reassures herself with this: Though Mark's still up and down, he seems to be keeping his promise. Tense as it is sometimes between him and Tess when Del comes down from Richard's for her two days of restaking her claim, as irritable as Mark sometimes is with her, he doesn't drop over the edge. He's going to meetings, keeping his appointments. Three months, three months is a long time.

Tess and Mark stand without moving. Del rests her forehead on the glass, unlocks her knees a little on Queenie's pulsing flanks.

Minutes pass. She sees Mark loosen. He leans the bar against the bumper, begins to roll a cigarette. Tess sits on the lowered tailgate. A brown blur streaks around the bend in the road: Luke. He returns at a full run when Mark whistles. She lets go of Queenie, shoves back the bolt on the front door to let Luke in. If Rudy was going to drive up in the truck, he'd be here by now. Possible that he parked in the gravel bank to sneak down over the ridge, but not likely.

The wrecking bar slung over his shoulder, Mark walks toward the barn. The tilt of his dark head, his angular rhythm: always that shock, that second of Lee alive once more, growing smaller and smaller till finally he's gone. Maybe Mark's going to climb the hill, look down over the land to see if Rudy's lurking about, but wouldn't it be better if they all stayed in the house, all possible entries locked. Even the dog panel down. She's going to recommend they put a lock on the kennel gate, start keeping the dog door closed. Rudy's thin enough to slither through.

Tess begins to lift bags from her truck. She should help, but well, she's not quite ready to be out in the open yet. She wishes she was back at Richard's, away from the whole thing. If the phone rings, she's not going to pick it up. She lets Tess in, takes a few of the bags. "Are you thinking Rudy turned around, changed his mind?"

"Probably, but Rudy's crazed on crack, meth, who knows what. That's not the end of it. Once Rudy takes you by the neck . . ."

"Did Mark say what he was up to?" Tess shakes her head. They set the grocery bags on the table. Del watches for Mark from the window. "If he isn't back in five minutes . . ." Well, if he isn't, they'll have to go up the hill, take the dogs and find him. Or she'll call Richard. Tell him to come right away. Del watches Tess, too. While Tess puts the cold stuff in the refrigerator, she stays turned toward the road, always keeps the phone where she can reach it. Even through the bits of hardware, the tangled dreadlocks, the blue chain tattoos, Tess is a beauty, the same larger-than-life energy as Carla.

Tess gives Del a determined look and raises one of her fists. "If

Rudy does show up, I'm calling 911. I know from stuff at my mom's, after you call, it's still a long time before a trooper car gets here. Half an hour, even more."

Another comforting bit of information. Even though Richard questions her judgment in this whole business, she wishes he was here. Richard would know what to do. Though in truth, so far, Mark seems cool-headed. Tess, too. They're all so much braver than she is.

She doesn't want to intrude by helping to unpack Tess and Mark's bags. They're careful not to step into each other's spaces. No rings in the tub, no towels on the floor. Mark always smokes outside. Del busies herself instead with filling the kettle, getting down the herbal teas Tess has brought home from her health store job. She'll know which herb is the most calming.

Here at the sink she must face toward the upper level of the living room where Mark and Tess and Charlie have set up to play and record. She looks at the dozens of cords snaking to mikes, the big black amps looming, the stands and four-track and drums and guitars and cases. Charlie's keyboard. Filling the table, the Mac with its giant monitor. Every single surface jumbled. She's learning to live with it. Each time she passes through, steps over the cords, she tells herself Mark's need to make music is more important than her need for order.

Tess turns as she starts out for more bags, the phone once again in her hand. "I'm sorry. My being here is going to further complicate things. Not just Rudy, but now my mother's bound to come here. I want no contact with them. Best thing I can do is find another place to live."

"Wait," Del says. She keeps herself from clutching Tess, Oh god, don't leave me. "Wait and see how it all goes." What will she do if Mark doesn't have a reliable housemate? She cannot live with him again, but it would be too lonely for Mark with no one here. She follows Tess to her truck. They watch Mark come down the hill from the direction of Aaron's cabin, the wrecking bar still resting on his shoulder. He looks lighter. Not the bearer of dangerous news.

"I walked from the gravel bank up over the ridge and back down," he says when he reaches them. He takes the phone from Tess. "No sign of Rudy, no sign of Smithy's truck."

They start for the house. "Did Rudy tear past the Roto-Rooter shed?" Mark's ahead of her. If he answers, she doesn't hear him. "Was the B & R owner there? Did he see the truck race by?" Mark disappears into the house. She looks at Tess. Tess nods yes. Shit, now she's going to have to deal with that. Have to listen to Roberts threaten to close off her right-of-way.

The kettle is whistling when they go in. A rank odor hits her, the wet smell of something decaying in the dark.

Mark has started up the steps to the loft. "I've got to chill for a while," he says.

"Don't you want a cup of tea?"

"I want to smoke."

She takes a saucer from the drainer and places it on the highest step she can reach. "Here's an ashtray." She never wants to have another burn mark anywhere in this house. She hears the window open, his fan go on at top speed, the clank of the bar being placed on the floor. All right, he has to chill; they all need to chill. Del sniffs, sniffs, tries to follow her nose, but she can't quite pin it down. Possibly a dead mouse between the wallboard and the insulation. "Do you smell anything?" Tess doesn't answer. She's unloading the bags, a faraway look in her eye.

Del smiles at her. She wants company, commiseration. "Tess? How about a cup of tea? Which one's the most soothing?"

Tess looks over the boxes on the table. "Chamomile, but it's a lot like drinking hot yellow water. Or worse. No tea for me. Too hot."

"Of course it's too hot. What was I thinking? But let's not open the windows for a while." She switches on the ceiling fan, then takes cubes from the freezer, makes a pitcher of ice water, squeezes in lemon. She pours them each a glass. Then she sits at the table, slides one of the ice cubes up and down her wrist. Such sensible purchases, all lined up in the cupboard.

Tess sets the chicken thighs on the cutting board, trims away the extra flaps of skin and fat. "Fry these up for the animals," she says.

There are important things Del wants to discuss with Mark. But she should wait until she sees what's going to happen with the Morlettis, what Tess decides to do. Still, if Mark's going to start working part time, he'll need a car. Maybe she'll ask Richard if she can use his winter-beater for a while, so she can loan Mark her car, keep it down here. After all it's old, closing in on 200,000 miles. But keep it in her name this time, under her insurance; not make the Tempo mistake again. Also Mark's gums. If he doesn't have the surgery, his teeth might start to fall out. The main thing though is the car: to go to work, the periodontist, meetings. He *is* doing well. She and Tess can't keep chauffeuring him around.

Tess sits at the end of the table so both of them still have a clear view of the road. She holds her glass to her cheek, fans herself with the *Pennysaver*. Luke and Queenie lie on the hearth, the only cool place in the house. "Here's another thing," Tess says, her voice lowered to a whisper.

"Another thing?"

"The last few nights, we've had bats in the house."

Del lowers her voice as well. "Bats? How many bats?"

"Four. Too many to be coming in the door. We've been keeping that closed when it starts to get dark. I'm thinking that sliding panel in your closet may be where they're getting in. That's what I got this tape for." She pushes the roll back and forth between her hands.

"Mom." From the loft, Mark's disembodied, weary voice. Del goes to the foot of the steps. "I'm going to try to sleep. Be better if we don't answer the phone. Even unplug it. Give it all time to cool down."

The phone off? The phone on? Which will make her the most anxious? They don't want to be fumbling around if they need to call 911. Anyway, isn't it better to know what the Morlettis are up to? "I'll turn down the machine," she says, "but I have to leave the phones on."

"I'm not going to talk to anyone," Mark says. "I'm not here."

Tess joins in with a "Me either."

Bats. Rudy. Carla. Tess, maybe moving out. Something rotting in an undisclosed location. What fun. "Okay. What I'm going to do is plug the machine into the phone in Tess's room, then I'm going to close the hall door. Tess, let's go up to my room. That way you can tell me about the bats. Bring the tape and the scissors and the dogs."

A scan with the flashlight of the entire length of the storage space under the eaves does not reveal any hanging bunches. If there are any bats in there, if they're coming in the two vents at the ends, sealing the space around the panel should keep them out. If bats don't gnaw. Bats are okay fluttering high in the sky, eating bugs, but bats diving around in a dark bedroom, making ultrasonic bleeps are not. Tess and Del agree on this. It's not a fear of rabies so much as the kamikaze swoops that cause both of them to run around screaming. Creeps me out big time, Tess's closing summary.

"Ready," Del says, extending another long strip of duct tape toward Tess's raised hand.

Tess sticks it along the final side. "I can't help it; whenever a bat flies at me, I think he's going to sink a fang into my neck." Now every single edge is double-taped, even the groove along the floor. Tess scoots out of the closet on her rear.

"Well, if any more come in, I'll call up the bat guy. I've seen his van parked in front of the P.O. Wild Life Control, pictures of bats on the sides. Get him to come over and deal with it." The phone. Del's heart seizes up. "Damn." Luke and Queenie rush to the window, bark. She hurries down to Tess's room, to be ready to pick up. Depending. Tess stands on the landing, shushes the dogs. Ring, ring, ring. One more and the machine will come on. Del waits with her hand on the receiver.

"Tess?" It's Carla. "Tess, are you there? Pick up. Rudy said you're there. Jesus, pick up. It's about Rudy. Del? Mark? Somebody pick up."

"I'm not here," Tess whispers from the hall.

And as though Carla has heard, she says, "Tess, I know you're there. I need to tell you what Rudy's up to. He's gone berserk. I've already called the troopers."

With that, Del lifts the receiver. "Carla, Mark and Tess aren't here."

"Oh, thank god you answered. I'm out of my mind. Rudy just called, making all kinds of crazy threats about Mark, how he's going to . . . , well, terrible things."

"How long ago?"

"Two minutes. He said he saw Tess's truck going up your road, Tess and Mark. Where are they?"

There's a soft click, the hollow sound of someone else on the line. Probably Mark. Or it could even be Rudy. Carla and Rudy in cahoots? "Carla, you say you already called the police?"

"Yes, but I don't know where Rudy is, where he was when he called. He can't be too far because the tank was almost empty and I don't think he has any money." Carla coughs, a long ragged cigarette hack. "He came up here, tried to steal my medication — then he takes off in Smithy's truck. Steals the truck. Smithy's not here. He's in treatment." Tess now stands in the doorway flashing her hands back and forth: she is still not here. Carla's voice ups a few notches. "I think you should call the troopers· too. Direct. Not 911. Their number's . . . got a pencil? . . . Their number's 731-6000." Del writes that down. "Get them to have a car keep an eye on your road. Where's Tess? Is Tess living with you? I thought Tess had gone back to Texas."

Del sits down on the bed. "I have to think about what I want to do. I'm going to hang up. Call me again if you hear that the troopers have arrested Rudy. I'm going to hang up now."

"Del . . ."

Del puts down the phone. Tess comes in and sits on the bed beside her. Ghost-pale. "Rudy just called your mother and he's making threats to come here. He stole Smithy's truck. Your mother's already called the state police."

Mark opens the hall door and comes in, the cordless in his hand, his Bugler can under his arm. "I heard most of it," he says. The three of them sit, look back and forth at each other. "Grokking it," Mark says. He takes the papers from the can and begins to roll himself a cigarette. "Okay if I smoke, stink up the room? In lieu of other tranquilization?"

They nod. Breathe. Mark licks the paper, sticks the loose shreds in his pocket. Then he unlocks the window and cranks it open. Del wishes he wouldn't. Maybe what they need is a moat. Tess takes a saucer from beneath one of her African violets and sets it on the desk. For the first time Del takes a quick scan of Tess's setup. Both big windows lined with pots: jade, spider plants, cactus. One whole window blooming violets, deep pinks and purples, blues. Clearly well fed. The bookshelves stacked with paperbacks, an old set of *Britannica*s. A poster of three Jersey cows, their mouths caught in mid-chew. *Jitterbug Perfume* lies open on the floor. Aaron's room transformed: no moldy glasses, no upturned Chinese checkerboard brimming with butts, and she assumes no marijuana under grow-lights in the closet.

The phone rings again. Tess puts her hands on her ears. Again the dogs rise. "Down," Mark tells them, and they both sink back onto the rug. Mark lights his cigarette and watches the machine.

"Pick up the phone, Mark. Pick it up or I'm going to come over there with a Molotov cocktail and waste you, waste the whole fucking scene. Tess, I'm warning you, you better get the fuck out of there."

Mark lifts the receiver, exhales. "Rudy," he says as he turns the machine down, lets it continue to record. "I'm listening." Even with the phone to Mark's ear, they can both hear the blasts of Rudy's rage. Mark listens and listens.

Tess begins to rock back and forth. Del reaches out and squeezes her hand. At least for the moment, they know Rudy is somewhere else, not about to jump through the window. Rudy, Aaron's friend. She used to give the two of them rides mornings when they worked at the sawmill. Rudy, sitting in the back, a red bandanna wrapped around his head, inventorying what his girl-friend had packed him for lunch. How he'd sing "Truckin'," beat out the rhythm on the seat, when it was his favorite: peanut but-ter and marshmallow fluff.

Mark swivels in the chair. "Yeah, I can see why it might look like that to you." Tess goes into the hall, walks up and down. "Tess isn't here." More listening. No longer can she hear scream-ing. Mark extends the cordless phone toward her, toward Tess. You want to listen in? Both of them decline like it's a fiery coal. "Nothing between Tess and me . . . I ran into her in Marwick. She dropped me off. Said she's heading back to Texas with some guy in the morning. Did Smithy *loan* you his truck? . . . Rudy, that doesn't sound promising . . . Sounds like you could be in a shitload of trouble . . . Hey, I thought we were past the Molotov threats . . . You need money? . . . You strung out? . . . Sounds to me like the best thing you could do is turn yourself in. Get your-self into some treatment . . . No, nada, I've got nada . . . No Xanax . . . I swear . . . You need money? Where are you? . . . Shit, Rudy, I'm telling you, it's going to go best if you turn yourself in . . . Go off for a little R & R, get straight . . . Is that your final answer . . . your final threat? Are you saying you want me to loan you enough money to get to the city, get yourself really fucked up? That you won't come over here and kill me if I do? . . . All right, all right, no more threats . . . Stay there. I'm going to do right by you." Mark hangs up the phone and pushes the blink-ing machine away from the edge. "Don't erase that message," he says. Then he leans toward them. Tess is bent over on the bed, her arms around her stomach. "Okay. Seems like we have to do what we have to do." They both look at him. "And by the looks of it, I'm the one who's going to have to do it, right?"

They both nod. Mark lifts the receiver. "I'm going to tell the troopers exactly where Rudy is." Del hands him the number.

Tess uncurls. "Then I'll call my mother. Jesusgod, here we go again."

Mark dials. "Best for all of us," he says.

Not how Rudy's going to translate it. Another betrayal. Del's hand goes to her mouth, her fingers zip her lips.

Something wakes her. She doesn't move. She listens. Someone is there in the dark. Then she sees the sweep of movement above her head. She gropes for the lamp, but stops: lights will make it worse. She ducks low, gets her bearings, then goes down the steps, holding on to the wall. She looks back up the stairwell: no sounds, nothing diving through the dark. How best to deal with this without waking Tess and Mark? It's already been such a hard day: Rudy's arrest, Carla's calls every five minutes. Mark's sad interview, his loss of trust in Rozmer.

Again Del leans onto the stairs and listens. Maybe she imagined the flutter of black above the bed. Hard as the day was, at least it looks as if Tess isn't going to bolt, and Mark's spirits have been lifted by the offer of her car once he gets a part-time job.

She goes back up the stairs to the landing and looks toward her ceiling. Nothing is flying about, no squeaks. She feels around the wall for the switch and flicks it on. Ohgod. Back in darkness, she trips, almost falls, as she runs into the bathroom. Their bright eyes watching her, wings moving: three bats clinging to her ceiling light. She pushes a towel tight along the bottom of the door. But she doesn't scream, she doesn't scream and wake the whole house.

She lowers the toilet seat and sits; the nightlight casts an orange glow over her toes. Okay, the hall door's closed and Tess has a blanket blocking her room, so at least the bats are confined. Not too long until dawn. Then they'll flatten themselves, try to hide until another day falls into night. She's not afraid of them during their torpor-time. Tomorrow, if they're still in her room, Mark can carry them out. Her plan: to be up and gone early, back to her drawings, the order of her life at Richard's.

She pulls a comforter and a sheet from the closet and makes a bed on the laundry room floor. Several rolled towels will do for a pillow. She cranks the window open: safe now that Rudy's locked up. Rain's coming, the sweet smell of summer grass going wet, that rustle of wind through the leaves. She settles on the floor. Maybe she'll sleep. At least all this stealing about in the night didn't rouse Queenie and Luke from their slumber in Tess's room. She looks up at the ceiling. Above, in her room, maybe the three bats are wheeling about in the dark, diving into the hall, desperately searching for an exit, feeling just as trapped as she does.

She turns on her side, the floor hard under her hip. If they didn't come in by gnawing, how the hell did they get in? Could they have already been in the room before Tess taped the storage door? First thing in the morning, before she goes, she'll check the tape. Then she'll call the Wild Life Control man from Richard's, have him come and get rid of the bats for good.

She turns to the other hip and begins to rehearse the words she'll use to tell him about her new plan: Mark's going to be starting a part-time job soon, so I've decided to let him use my car until he can afford to buy himself a vehicle. Too obviously prepared for the press. No matter how she composes her text, she knows his response will be some variation of "Hope springs eternal." Translation: Will you never learn?

She pulls one of the towels from under her head and slides it beneath her hip. Definitely she wants to be gone before the drama of Tess's reunion with Carla tomorrow. The possible danger this reconnection will pose for Mark. The darkness is graying. The first bird sings: this tree belongs to me. In her little room at Richard's she'll let her pencil drop on the right place to begin. Like dowsing for water.

21 : Struts

FUCKING PHONE. Just when he sinks into the nothingness, they drag him back with their machine-words: Rozmer. Charlie. His mom. Mark presses both pillows against his ears.

"Mark, just want to make sure you saw my note . . ." Even with the pillowcase stuffed halfway to his brain, every word in stereo. "The Wild Life Control man probably won't get there until tomorrow, but he says he can definitely fix it so no more bats . . ." He heaves the pillow over the railing full force. The machine crashes to the floor. "I'll drop the car off early tomorrow so you can get to the periodontist . . ." He goes down two steps at a time. "Well . . ."

He mutes the machine, turns off the ringer. Days and days since he's really slept. Meds not doing their thing: red ghoulies hanging out on the edges. He opens the hall door, then Tess's door a crack. No Tess, no dogs. He looks out the window. Tess's truck is parked right where they left it. Then he sees her sitting on the picnic table, Queenie and Luke underneath.

A full sheet of paper stuck to the coffee can. His mom's message. Perfect black marker block print, second draft. He sets the paper aside and loads the coffeemaker: high-test. Rolls a cigarette. He is not going out to smoke. He doesn't want to talk to Tess. He doesn't want to talk to anyone. No meetings. No check-ins with his sponsor. He loads his coffee with sugar and starts up the stairs, then he backs down again and wads the message into a ball, sticks it in his shorts pocket. Maybe he'll read it later; maybe he won't.

He removes the towel he's tacked over the window, but there's no air out there, only a heavy blanket of swamp-heat. He turns the fan on full, turns it on his sweating chest. He lies so his head is at the bottom of the bed, so the sun doesn't blind him. Everything sticks. He smokes, drinks his coffee. Maybe he's going to make it through this; maybe he isn't. He needs something, something to make it semi-bearable. He could get something, somewhere. Nothing heavy duty. Just a toke of hope. Not through any of the Morletti connections. Somebody else. Who? Get something going with his music again. Weeks since he's written any songs, really played. Everything turns to shit. At least there's this: Rudy's ass is in jail and he is going to have access to a car. He unwads the ball of paper, smoothes out some wrinkles, then holds it up to the sun.

> Bats flying around in my bedroom woke me up about 4:30. I turned on the light: three of them were hanging from the overhead globe in my ceiling. The sliding door in my closet is still completely sealed, so I have no idea how they're getting in. I think they must have already been in the room when we duct-taped. Would you please locate them and put them out? You and Tess should close yourselves off again tonight. I left a message for the Wild Life person. Car's by the barn, so you can get to the periodontist. Call me when you get up and going. Mom.

Barking, hullabaloo, the dogs roar up: their "someone's coming" frenzy. The noise trails off down the drive. Mark puts his head out the window. Smithy's truck. Carla. He ducks back. Tess is directly below, still sitting on the table.

He hasn't seen Carla since the night before he went to detox — four-plus months ago. He watches her cross the yard. Shit warmed over: bony, all the jolt gone. Her eyes two dark pools you could fall into. And wearing long sleeves on the hottest day of the year. The prosecution rests its case. No hugs. Tess sits on one side of the table; Carla sits on the other. She stretches both hands toward Tess, flops her palms open, her wrist braces a reminder of her pain. Meek: how she's going to play it. "Oh Tess. I was hoping you were back in Texas. Away from all this." Carla's words loud and clear. He might as well be sitting at the table. She takes out her cigarettes. Too bad he can't swoop down and bum a couple. "Del around?" Tess shrugs. Carla edges forward a little more. "You know I never meant for you to get messed up in this." Tears in the throat. Not even a shrug this time. Carla reaches out. Tess fades back: no touching. "But, well, it's good to see you . . . see you looking so . . . healthy."

Tess pushes up from the table. "*Not* getting messed up. That's what I'm working on. I'm applying to Marwick Community for the fall." Her voice is so soft, he has to risk moving closer to the window. "Like I told you on the phone: I'm going to see about a regular job in a few minutes, so I don't have much time."

"Smithy's . . ."

Tess smacks her hands over her ears. "I'm paying rent and being careful not to cause Del any worry. It's not going to work if you start coming here, keep calling. And you know why."

"Tess . . ."

"You know why."

Carla squashes out her cigarette and lights another. "I know why. Such a good thing you're going to go to college. What courses are you taking?"

Tess stops pacing. She gives Carla a long look. Then she sits down, hesitates. "I'm going to take the vet tech course."

"Vet tech?"

"Veterinary technician. In two years I can have an AS degree: give shots, dress wounds, do follow-up exams."

"You mean you might have to get in a stall with a horse? Sounds dangerous." Compared to the safety and security of her current life.

Now Tess is doing the leaning forward. "You know what I'd really like to do?"

Carla smiles. "What?"

"Work in a zoo."

Carla throws up her hands and laughs. Her old guffaw, the old Carla. "Zoo? Why, baby, you don't even have to leave home to do that."

When Mark comes out of the bathroom, both trucks are gone. Tess off to see about shoveling shit for Hoop Dawes. Already she's trying to line him up as her helper: earn a few bucks, get his ass out of bed. Six A.M. He's going to have to score some under-the-table cash if he wants to score some under-the-table bliss. "Dog day afternoon," he says to Luke and Queenie, who lie stretched on the hearth. Mark brings the fan down from the loft and sets it so it rotates slowly back and forth across the dogs' heaving sides. He picks the machine up off the floor, erases his mother's message and presses the Play button again: "Mark, I don't know what happened at Harbor exactly, but I know you're pissed. And I know you're up there in the rack, on the rack, with the covers over your third eye. It's important you call me and get yourself to a meeting. If you're having trouble getting a ride . . ." He deletes Rozmer. "This is Charlie. I'm not going to be able to jam with you and Tess tonight. Maybe I'll see you at the noon meeting." Third time Charlie's canceled. Finally they've got this great space to practice and record, but Charlie and Tess always got places to go, people to see. Screw it: whatever he wants to do, going to have to do it on his own.

Nooley. Might be able to wangle something there. Not that he's exactly got an open invitation to Nooley's, but maybe if he left his bass with him as a guarantee that when his money comes . . . He checks the calendar: July 24. Ten days until he gets his part of his SSD. Way too early for harvest, but maybe Nooley's got some summer stash. And what are you going to say when one of *them* asks, Mark, where's your bass?

The first bat was easy: a pouch of brown stuck to the closet door. Usual semi-somnolent protest as he carried it out to the woods: squeak, squeak. He slides the closet door back again, shines the flashlight along the floorboards below the clothes. A heap of something dark. He catches it with the hook of a hanger and drags it into the light. A crumple of fur, two stiff feet splayed underneath. He doubles the dish towel and scoops it up. Bat number two: DOA.

The woods are cooler than inside. The bat's ears are folded forward, the eyes closed. So small now. Maybe not even full grown. He turns the bat over and slowly pulls the wing open: a thumb and four long ridges, covered by a thin membrane that webs between them and connects to its body. Four bony fingers. The bat's hands are its wings. Mark raises his arm, spreads his fingers, does a drum-roll flutter through the air: lift off and glide away. He folds the wing back against the bat's body. Then he scuffs out a place under a log and places the bat in the hole, pushes the earth in, presses it down. "R.I.P., buddy, R.I.P."

The dogs' muffled barks come from the house. He sprints to the side door and locks it behind him. The bolt's already on in front. The dogs up the volume. Mark climbs the stairs to his mom's room, steps to the edge of her big window so he can see, but not be seen. A rattle-trap panel truck appears over the crest, turns at the barn and then slowly backs toward the house.

Wild Life Control
Experienced Licensed Agent
Zephyr P. Dixon
433-6622
Humane 24-Hour Emergency Service

Life-sized silhouettes of creatures creep about beneath the letters: a raccoon, a fox, a skunk. Several bats float above. Zephyr. Five bucks says his hippie parents had just downed a tab when they came up with that one. Zephyr's short legs show up first as they jut from the truck, camouflage fatigues, black army boots. The rest of him follows: a small person with a humping gait who pauses every few steps as though he's sniffing the air.

Mark waits. Queenie emits indignant yelps. Luke's barks have turned to savage snarls. There's a hard knock. The dogs quiet down. Another knock. Then the man appears at the side door directly below. He raps on the glass. "Wild Life Control. Anybody home?"

Bugger off, Bat Man. No Longer Speaking's indisposed. The man takes something from his pocket and sticks it in the door. Then he slowly begins to walk along the edge of the house, staring up at where roof and stone wall meet. He vanishes around the corner and appears in back, all the while looking up at the wall and pacing off the length of the house. If it's holes he's after, ground-level inspection is not likely to yield diddly. From time to time the man draws a paper and pencil from his pocket and jots down notes. Then he returns to his truck.

Now that he's turned away the expert, he's going to have to rise to the occasion. He's already been inch by inch through the bedroom and the hall. The big thing is how they're getting in. He stretches out on the braided rug at the foot of his mom's bed and stares up at the high ceiling. His mom said she woke up and there were three bats clinging to that globe. He shifts over a few feet and turns his head to the side, squints to bring into focus the thin dark ridge around the top of the silver bracket that holds the globe. An open space, not much more than a quarter of an inch wide. Impossible, but indeed that's possibly it.

On the top shelf of the closet in the laundry room he finds what he's looking for: the tube of silicone caulking they used to seal around the bathtub. Back in the bedroom he pushes a trunk directly below the light, then he places the stool on top of that. He rests one hand on the ceiling for balance. Carefully he squeezes the caulking along the narrow opening on one side, then presses the bulge flat with his thumb. He steps down onto the trunk and then back up on the stool, facing the other way. He caulks the space on that side, careful to make sure the opening is completely sealed. Small dark bits, scatterings, shadow the bottom of the translucent glass of the globe. He laughs. Bat shit. Guano calling cards. Proof this is their fucking entry. The world outside is taking on that glow, that golden-pink of the sun going, dusk coming on. The third bat is somewhere close, getting ready.

There's the sound of the key in the lock. No barks. The dogs know it's Tess. Quietly he steps down onto the floor. There are muffled sounds of her calling up her news to the loft. Got to hand it to Tess. In the up-and-going category she gets the blue ribbon. Fucked-up family not going to back her down. But for now let her think he's up in his bed, brooding, buried in the wet sheets.

The last light's going. Nighttime: his time. One by one he removes the screens from the windows. Then he sits on the stool in the corner, the cordless phone in his lap. No hurry. He leans his head against the wall. Finally cooling down. A skitter of sound and there it is: swooping, fluttering, around and around. Mark doesn't move, just keeps his eyes wide. He wants to see the moment of exit, the flash into the night. Maybe he blinks, maybe he looks toward the wrong window, but suddenly the air is empty.

He listens down the stairs. There's the sound of dishes. He lifts the phone. Nooley's number? Been a while, but then, there it is. He dials. He's got the song all ready. The phone rings, rings. He watches the sky, the evening star. Soon he'll be up there. Far. Far away.

22 : Roost

WHAT DEL WANTS is for her pencil to find the flash of light, the glitter of eyes. Instead, night is what she keeps coming up with, the graphite grinding blacker and blacker until there's no tooth left on the paper. The only way she can find anything in that blackness is by squashing the kneaded eraser hard against the surface, then lifting the lead away one tedious layer at a time. The heel of her hand is sooty, and she knows if she looks in the mirror, the smears will be all over her face.

The screen door opens. She hears Richard in the kitchen, probably going through his mail. She knows he will be giving the Harbor Freight catalog and new offers of interest-free credit cards his full attention, that when she enters he will not even mention his appointment with the urologist, his rising PSA count that theoretically should read zero since the prostate was removed eight years ago.

The phone. That immediate contraction in her chest. Did Mark make it to the periodontist this morning? It's worrisome he didn't respond to her note or her call yesterday, but maybe it's only Tess with a bat report. She rushes into the bedroom to pick up. Richard always lets the machine answer. The machine does get there first with Richard's concise-as-a-knife message that she now has to yell over to be heard.

"Wild Life Control here," the voice says, "Zephyr P. Dixon."

For a second she's at a loss. "Oh, yes, about the bats."

"No one home when I went by your place last night, but I was able to do a careful external assessment."

One problem at least about to be solved. "How are the bats getting in?"

"You've probably got a hole, maybe even holes, in the screening behind your vents. You've got six vents, four main ones and two small. Could be going in any one or all of those. Screening rots out."

"But those vents don't lead into my bedroom. How are they getting in there? We've had at least seven bats in two days. Maybe more."

"Bats can get through a space not much bigger than a crack. What you've probably got are the babies just starting to fly. They feel a current of air and that's where they go."

"Babies? I want you to get rid of all the bats and close up the holes so they can't ever get in again."

"I can seal up where they're getting in your bedroom. But I can't do anything about the bats that may be up in the airspace above your ceiling until the fall, say early October?"

"October? Why not now?"

"Got to wait until they all can fly. Trap them up there and you'll have to smell a bunch of dead bats right over your head. In October I'll get the bats out of the airspaces, put new screening in your vents, and caulk all the holes between the stone walls and the roof. That's the main thing, caulking all those holes, and you've got plenty of them."

"Oh, I don't think bats are in the stone house section. You're sure there are holes above the wall?"

"Yep, and if I shut the bats out of their current entries, when they come back in the spring they'll find a way in. They just need one tiny hole, and they'll all take up residence above one of your ceilings."

"Spring? They're coming back in the spring?"

"Absolutely, April or May, they'll be back."

"How many bats are you talking about?"

"Hard to say. Depends on how many years they've been living in your house. You want a rough idea . . ." There's a long pause. "Sunset's at 8:57 tonight. Get enough people so you can see all six vents at once. Watch until it's almost dark. Don't blink. A bat is fast — a little flash and then it's gone."

"Let me get this straight, you'll come now and find where they're getting into my room and we won't have any more bats in the house. Guaranteed."

"Right. Then I come back in the fall, get all the bats out of the airspaces, and bat-proof your house so they can't get back in."

"That's great." A gust of relief. "About how much will the whole thing cost?" Richard has come to stand in the doorway. He's wearing his "Beware, it's a jungle out there" frown.

"Better if I come to your place and go over the estimate — time and materials — with you."

Richard's silence is gaining in volume. "Well, just give me an overall estimate for now," she says in her most in-charge tone. She pulls a pencil and a pad from the bedside drawer.

There's a pause, a rustle of papers by Zephyr's phone. A clicking sound. "Whole thing's going to take a few days, plus all the sealant and screening. I should be able to do it for about seventeen hundred."

She sits down on the bed. "One thousand seven hundred dollars?" Richard takes the pencil from her and writes on the pad: *There's a solid sill between your roof and the stone wall.*

She stands up and waves for Richard to let her deal with this. "I can't afford seventeen hundred dollars. What will you charge just to come and seal the bedroom . . . and then to come back in the fall to get rid of the bats and change the screening on just those vents?"

Zephyr P. Dixon clears his throat — not a good sign. "I make it a policy to only do complete bat-proofing. If I do a partial, well, the bats come back, people see my truck parked in front of your house again and again like my work is ineffective. It's bad for my reputation."

"Mr. Dixon, my house is on a private road. No one is going to see anything." Richard's hand reaches out and tugs at the waistband of her shorts, pulls her down to sit on the edge of the bed and hands her the pad once again. *I'll get rid of the bats. Guaranteed.*

Again that weird clicking. "Sorry, that's my policy. Full bat-proofing or nothing."

She sets the pad on Richard's chest, thumps it lightly. "Thank you for your time." Slowly she replaces the receiver. Richard moves over and she settles on her back beside him. They listen to the whir of the fan, stare at the ceiling. "What did the urologist say?"

"Same thing the Walter Reed doctor said three months ago. As long as the count's low, rising so gradually, it's best to wait. Get another test in six months."

"And how do you feel about that?"

He reaches over and brushes his thumb across her cheek. "Carbon," he says.

She threads her fingers though his, presses the callused pad of his palm. "Richard?"

He taps a button on the fan: oscillation. Summer swings back and forth over their bodies. "What'll be, will be."

Del places the two camp chairs and the binoculars on the back seat of Richard's truck; one of them can sit on the picnic table and they can bring out the stool for the fourth person. Main thing is to have each of them located in a spot where they can see all the vents at once so they'll know where the holes are. How many bats are there anyway? Fifteen, forty? No doubt the seven Mark returned to the woods got right up and flew back in. One thing she's learned: little brown bats are what they've got. *Chioptera.* She found what may be a helpful site: *batcontrol.com*.

She checks the sky: the edges of the clouds glow pink. 8:10. Best if she and Richard arrive not too long before the sun sets. Say 8:50 — such a wonder that every day the sun, the earth are so right on time. It should only take a few minutes to rally Mark and Tess and get the four of them in position. Make the whole count quick to keep Mark from wandering off.

Del grabs the handhold above the door and pulls herself up into the truck. Either the trucks Richard buys are getting higher or she's getting older. At least she hopes Mark is going to be a part of this. Tess was mostly full of her new milking job that starts tomorrow, the news that Hoop might be willing to take Mark on for chores a few evenings a week. Tess sounded inconclusive about what was up with Mark, if she'd even be able to talk him into being part of the . . . bat watch. But even if Mark is reluctant, nothing can take away the fact that he's the one who accomplished the most important part of the job: figuring out that the bats were coming in around her light and caulking that up. Not a single bat since.

Richard's getting something from his shed, but he wouldn't say what. 8:13. It's right this minute she'd like to be leaving, but she's learned to trust Richard on timing. She watches him move down the hill with a length of PVC pipe, at least fifteen feet long with a row of holes. He's got it in perfect balance, held at just the right spot so he doesn't have to break his stride. Richard's backlit by the sun as well, his lean arms, his green-as-the-trees work shirt. Richard, the tightrope walker, and he *will* figure out how to get those bats out of there.

He bungees the pipe into the bed of the truck and sets a big, rattling bag on the back seat. Then they're off. Maybe now that he's got no catalogs, now that he's stuck in space going forty miles an hour, is a good time to try to pin him down a little more. What are the best treatments available if the count starts to spike? She glances at Richard's straight-ahead profile, his sure hands on the wheel. "What's in the bag?"

"Naphthalene. Right after sunset tomorrow, when I'll have a better idea what's up with the bats, I'll slide that pipe, full of mothballs, in above your ceiling. Any lingerers will clear out; then I'll replace the screening. Leave the mothballs for a few weeks: the bats will not be back."

"What about the smell in my room?"

"Once the pipe's out, it'll dissipate. Meanwhile you can stay with me: be my love full time." He squeezes the back of her neck. "Got to check the sill on your stone wall too. I felt around in there when I put up your new gutters, but I want to make one hundred percent sure."

Richard pulls in by the barn so he can stow the mothballs and pipe. Her car's there, so Mark must be around, and Tess's truck is at the end of the drive, but the front door is closed and everything's still. She hauls out the camp chairs and binoculars. As she turns toward the back of the house to line up one of the chairs with her bedroom vent on that side, she gives Mark's loft window a quick glance: instant foreboding — closed up tight in this heat, the light-blocking towel gone. Nothing visible beyond the dark of the glass.

She places the second chair almost against the dog kennel so her other bedroom vent will be easy to watch without cricking her neck. This is going to be her spot. She's almost positive this is the bats' main entry. Mark? She's going to have him sit on the stool at this end of the stone section, and Richard and Tess can decide who'll take the chair, who'll take the picnic table on the other end. 8:40. In fifteen minutes they all need to be sitting, unblinking, at their posts.

She hesitates at the front door. Even though she still lives here two days a week, her initial reentries always feel intrusive. She gives a warning rap before she walks in. "Hello," she calls. "Mark, Tess? We're almost ready to begin watching for the bats." She aims this cheer at the loft even though already she can feel Mark isn't up there. In fact, her voice echoes in a new kind of silence. That sudden knowing the space has changed the way one feels the first big snow. She turns and there it is or there it isn't. The center of the living room is empty: Mark's drum set is gone. She scans the rest of the surfaces. Everything of Mark's has been removed. All the rest of the equipment is lined up and dusted off.

Surely Tess's contribution. The answering machine flashes: four red signals as if it's about to detonate.

8:45. Richard is on his way from the barn, balancing the ladder this time. Someone's in the bathroom. There's the flush of the toilet. The sound of the washing machine. This is reassuring. Things cannot be too dire if someone is doing laundry. The door opens. Tess appears, looking like herself. Del tries for a calm tone. "What's going on? Where's Mark?"

Tess gives her a squint. "Where's all his stuff? His drums?"

Tess steps a little closer, checks the peripheries. "Moved it all down to his drum-room. I came back from learning how to run the milk machines and he was hauling the last loads in the wheelbarrow. He said . . . he had to get the fuck out of this house."

Del turns back into the living room. Out the window, she sees Richard has already settled on the picnic table. Should they try to go on with the bat watch? Del points to the phone.

"I was here, but I figured it was better to let the machine pick up. I do not want to talk to my mother."

"Any messages for me?"

"Maybe one I didn't hear. But the rest are for Mark: Charlie, Rozmer, Ben Jacobs from the clinic. All giving 'here for you' respiration."

8:50. Sunset in seven minutes. Del starts up the loft-ladder. "Do you still feel like doing the bats?"

"Sure."

"Be good if you'd sit in the chair that's already set up in back." She points toward where she means. "And not just where they're coming out, but could you keep a good count too?" At the top of the ladder, she leans into the loft. "My god, Tess, he took his mattress, all his bedding."

"Yep. Everything. I'm going to quick go get my glasses."

"I'll go around by the kennel as soon as I see if I can rouse Mark." As she starts toward the barn, she waves to Richard sitting on the table, the binoculars by his side. He motions toward his watch. "I know. Only a few more minutes." She calls to Tess, "Where's Luke?"

"Down there, too." Tess disappears around the corner.

No sounds of drums coming from the barn. Luke there. That's a comfort. Del goes through the garage, leans her ear against the drum-room door. Nothing. "Mark, we're about to watch to see where the bats are going out." Silence. No light above the sill. She knocks. She could try the knob. Pound and wail. Instead she steps out into the falling light. She hurries toward the house, her eyes on the back section above the kennel. No flutters of wings circling, only a few darting birds heading for their night roosts. Probably Mark and Luke have gone for a walk. Otherwise, surely Luke would have beat his tail, whined hello. Surely? Nothing is sure. Before they go if Mark hasn't appeared, if he doesn't answer when they call, she, Tess, Richard, one of them is going to have to turn that knob, unlock that door and go into the dark.

9:00. Soon it will be too dark to see anything. And no matter how hard she tries, she can't help blinking. Her eyes are starting to cross, the slats of the vent to blur.

"Del." Richard's voice flies over the roof, caught by the hill to echo back. "See anything yet?"

"No." Best not to be making noise. The bats might decide to skip their dinner. The little bit of the article she had time to read said each bat eats up to three thousand insects a night. But not when it rains. Motion. A flick of something in the left corner of the vent. Then a quiver of dark drops, is gone. Jesus, that's all it's going to be. That's one. She dares to glance up. No question, a bat now high above the roof. No way of knowing if it's one of her bats. Flick. The same corner. Flash away into the trees this time. That's definitely two. Unless she missed one earlier. So much quicker, less fanfare than expected. Flick. Three. She wants to scream out. Watch. But she doesn't: four, five, two right together. Don't let them come out any faster than that or she won't be able to keep track. Six, seven, eight. Let it not get so dark she can't see.

"Del." Tess's voice. "Five, Del, so far five." That vent too. That makes thirteen. Silence from Richard's direction. Nine. Another swoop. Ten. Coming so fast. Eleven.

Down the road, the creak of the big barn door closing. Luke's bark. Thirteen. Fourteen. The glow of a light. Probably Mark going into the drum-room. Fifteen, sixteen. The sound of drums. Seventeen. Other mothers complained of the amps turned up, the scream of guitars, but she was always happy to know where they were, playing together.

Completely dark now. Only the headlights of the truck jetting across the rock pile, shining on the thickets of Queen Anne's lace. She's so glad Mark is there, that he's got enough up-energy to be drumming. Maybe she can come back tomorrow, connect with him, without seeming as if she's bearing down. Tell him how much she appreciates him caulking the light. The periodontist? She not going to think about that. She slides over a little closer to Richard, puts her hand on his knee. "One hundred and seventy-five bats out my vent. One hundred and seventy-five, plus Tess's thirteen. One hundred and eighty-eight. Amazing. They've been living up above me all this time and I didn't even know they were there. And not a bat out the vent above the loft. Just like you said. No bats getting in the stone section."

Richard makes the turn toward Back River Road. Back River Road: she's always loved the sound of that name. Won't be long, if she watches carefully, before she'll see Richard's outside light glowing way up on the hill, glowing through the trees.

www.batcontrol.com. She scrolls past the title "A Single Bat in the House," the picture of a man placing a saucer over a hanging daytime bat, scrolls past "Identifying Entrances." They are way beyond all that. Her eyes stop on "House Bat Maternity Colonies ... these 'house bats' situate their roosts in hot attics, which act as incubators for the growing pups . . ." My god, what she has is a maternity colony.

> The best time for bat-proofing is in the fall, after the bats have left. If bat-proofing must be done while bats are inhabiting a building, it should be done by installing a one-way door after the pups are able to fly. Otherwise the flightless bats will be trapped inside and the mothers will frantically attempt to reenter to rejoin their young.

Not just 188 bats. There are a bunch of babies in there too. Why, Zephyr P. Dixon, aren't you ashamed talking as if you had a big job getting bats out that had already migrated? Have to tell Richard no mothballs. We have to wait till all the bat babies go.

23 : Whistling

BEFORE HE UNLOCKS the drum-room door, Mark checks to see that the scrap of brown paper he always tucks in at the bottom is still exactly as he left it, ripped side out, small black dot in front. All those years of reading Hardy Boys were not for naught. He stows the paper; his T-shirt, smelling heavily of cannabis; and his dandy little pipe in a plastic bag which he then stuffs in a box, under a jumble of old cassettes his mother would never discard or mess with. Too bad he can't burn incense, but trusting as she is, even his mother would have to wake up on that one. This skulking behind a tree up on the hill to sneak a toke, all this subterfuge ridiculous, but what else can he do?

Dark inside: the windows curtained with towels. He finds his way through the mayhem to stretch out on his mattress. No question Nooley's weed is of an excellent quality. Dear friends, I want you to know I plan to take this lying down. He lights a candle and pulls his notebook from beneath his pillow. Plenty of time to wig out for a few hours before he has to go do barn chores with Tess.

He thumbs through the notebook until he comes to a blank page. So good to be off the meds, the plod, plod of them, his tongue sticking to his teeth. So good to have his mind back, the grid up and running again. In only a few weeks since his return to the land of the living, he's laid down about ten new bass lines. Doobie do, doobie da. A lot of it just playing around with words, lists of words that launch him into a phrase he can then lay out in chords. He leans the notebook toward the candle and lets his pen write whatever flows out: *subterfuge.* Bad enough he has to do all his imbibing on the sly, give his clothes the smell-test before he goes up to the house. Tess is already giving him the sniffs. No doubt she knows, no doubt she doesn't approve, but she will not tell. Another thing he likes about Tess.

Trick scheme evasion dodge. Lot of writing went on in this barn. His bed almost exactly where his dad sat in his black-and-brown chair, scrawling on his yellow pads. Fucked up on grass too. Mark fishes two vials from beneath his piles of clothes and a tube of glue from his backpack. Do a little cave mosaic with his meds. He's got six hundred dollars' worth of meds at his disposal. He uncaps the black Magic Marker. Along the wall, about a foot above the bed, he draws a straight black line as far as he can reach without rising. Along the line, several inches apart, he draws a series of jagged saucer-size circles. He contemplates the empty circles: little vats where faces are developing. One remains blank: the barefaced liar who's going to go to a meeting and receive his six months Clean and Sober medal soon.

When he stretches out his leg, his foot hits a cymbal stand. Number-two problem: the extreme crowded conditions — wall-to-wall drums, mattress, weight bench, computer, four-track, and the innards of a piano, with one narrow path to the door. He studies the first circle, then he lifts the marker and draws a large eye in the center, an eye that reaches across and touches the outer edges. On a scrap of cardboard he squeezes a blob of glue. Using his handy roach clip he dips in one side of a Neurontin tablet. Then he presses it below the eye and holds. When he's sure the tab's secure, he pastes another below that, and then another.

Outside Luke barks. Luke, his sentry. Mark scoops the pills into their vial and pushpins a towel so it drapes over his mosaic-in-progress. He gives himself a quick smell-check. Camels and sweat, mildew, no hint of dope. He lifts the edge of the towel covering the window that looks out on the road. Charlie's car dusting along up the drive. Too late, Charlie, I've up and gone solo.

Mark puts on his baseball hat — some cover. High pretty much gone. He steps out, locks the door. Got to whistle a happy tune past the graveyard. Uh-oh, Charlie's brung backup. Mark speeds his amble. The passenger door opens. Rozmer's big leg swings out. Fee Fi Fo Fum. All they need now would be Ben Jacobs and they could have an intervention party.

Rozmer steps forward, bows. He's slimming down, making it past the Burger King drive-throughs. Rozmer gives him the complete once-over. Red alert on because his sponsee isn't doing his daily check-ins. No question what impression Mark's got to bring out for this one: Howdy do. Careful Charlie's looking a little schizy. Luke does his happiness run. Round and round, swerving just as he's about to hit them head on. Diversionary havoc welcome.

Rozmer doesn't give him a hug. The distance is there and he respects it. "Sorry not to hear from you in the last few days, buddy."

"Yeah," Mark says. Don't offer up any shit-excuses Rozmer will make you eat. "I'm struggling. Got the Fuckits, but I'm working on it. I'll give you a call tomorrow after my appointment with Jacobs." An appointment he was previously planning on canceling. "Get myself to the twelve o'clock." Solid plan presented.

"Sounds good," Rozmer says, smiles.

And of course he's going to have to keep his word. Got to go through more of the motions. But he's going to take what he likes and leave the rest.

Rozmer squeezes Charlie's arm. "We're on our way to a meeting in Bayville. Speaker's meeting. Charlie's home group. His anniversary. He's going to tell his story."

"Five years, right, Charlie?" Mark says, and shakes his hand. "Got to be a good feeling. I'd like to be there, but I have to load the manure spreader this evening." Bulletproof Reason.

"How many evenings are you working now?" Charlie says.

"Three. And it's going okay." Now what would be best would be if they'd re-board and tootle-loo down the lane, but it's clear he's going to have to offer full hospitality. Just as soon not take them into the emptiness of the living room, the death of their big Jam Together fantasy. 'Course Charlie knows he's moved all his stuff to the barn, but Mark hasn't fully outlined that for Rozmer and he knows Charlie has said very little. Charlie's good that way, like Tess. "Such a hot night, how about if we sit out here?"

"Yeah, we've got lots of time," Rozmer says.

He leads them toward the picnic table. He sees Tess moving around in the kitchen. Be good if she came out. More welcome diversion. The more talkety-talk he has to do, the riskier it is. He's been keeping the lies simple, but make no mistake about this: Rozmer's always got the scam-o-meter running. They settle and as a real feat of control, he doesn't light up. He knows Rozmer will notice that and maybe be impressed with his lack of compulsion. Or Rozmer's so sharp, he knows just what he's up to by not sucking away. So fuck it, might as well smoke. No, keep his twitchy fingers from groping for his pack.

"Not long before you'll be coming up for being six months clean. What day exactly?"

Dangerous topic #1. Sweat breaking out. But a sign of just how devious he is, he's got the date pre-stamped right in his frontal lobes. "September 3rd," he says.

"I hope you're planning on telling your story at a Speaker's meeting that day," Rozmer says.

He would rather walk over a bed of hot coals. "I'm thinking about it."

Rozmer sniffs, sniffs. Wiggles his nose in the direction of the house. "You smell that?" Rozmer rises and goes toward the open window. "Pie. Blueberry pie. Don't you think we'd better give Tess a hello before we go?"

Charlie laughs. Without further encouragement, Rozmer heads for the front. Blueberries and sugar. Tess, at the stove. How sweet it is. Oh, Tess, hon-you-babe, as his dad used to say.

"Blueberries. I picked them up on the hill this morning," she tells them. "Crust needs two more minutes. Have a seat."

Three blips on the machine. He knows what they are already. His mom: Don't forget to take the car for inspection. Jacobs about

his appointment tomorrow. Gum torture reminder. Smell of promise — feeling so good, he may be up for all three, go for gold stars
right across the deportment chart. Tess sets a plate in front of
each of them, hands them forks. Rozmer licks his lips.

Relapse Inquiry adjourned.

Mark slows for the turn on. He drives the three evenings a week
he works. Even this far away he's always able to check out the
Dawes farm up on the ridge: who's there, who isn't. Figure how
much ventriloquy he's going to have to do. He usually gets high
before he goes. Drift through the chores this way. Hoop's herd,
black-and-white movement, already starting toward the gate.
Cows may be dumb, but they've got the routine memorized.
Chew, chew, no mood-zonkers for them. Only the hired man's
truck is by the barn. Budd, who's got to be at least eighty, and
as close to mute as they come. No other vehicles in the drive.
"Where are the Daweses?"

Tess shifts the pie in her lap and leans forward to check things
out too. There's a whiff of cow manure from her hair. Dreadlocks and barn work not compatible. "Hoop and Betty are judg-
ing 4-H at the Onango Fair. Just me, you, and Budd. They said
we're doing such a good job, they can leave us on our own. Who
knows — Angel's about to freshen. You might have to help me
birth a calf."

"Count me out," he says. "You've already got me scraping yuck
into the gutters against my will. Maternity assistant I am not."

"Oh, she's such an old hand mama, probably she won't need
any assistance."

He heads up Dawes Road. Road named after them means
Hoop's family's been shoveling shit, getting up to milk in the dark,
seven days a week, four or five generations. He pulls to the left
to avoid a washout. Road's all gullies and drop-offs, going to be
a bitch in the winter. Not his problem. Surely he'll be long gone
by then.

"Park by Budd's truck. We'll most likely be done before they
get back."

Not going to have to do one "Howdy." Not one "Yeah, it sure is wet for August."

At the far end of the barn, Budd is already loading the wagon with grain. He nods in their direction. About all they're going to get out of Budd. Tess is always trying to jolly him into some dialogue, but Budd never falls for it. Budd broke his leg bad some years back. He can load, but he can no longer push the cart. Mark's first job after they get the cows in is to grain them, dump the feed into the mangers. Twenty-pound scoops. Better than lifting weights. Tess and Budd do all the milking: teat dip, stripping each quarter to get the milk going, putting on the cups. Plus doing the fall back when a cow slams out with a hoof. The entire trip. Amazing really. Maybe when he gets a little more seasoned, he'll give it a try. He pulls his coveralls from the hook, dons his rubber barn boots. Even wears a cap. Trick is to take as little barn muck home with you as possible.

Tess trots across the road. He follows. She's loving this whole venture, she keeps telling him, practically dances with the cows. Mark trudges up the road to set out a couple of orange cones just around the blind curve while Tess opens the big gate. Almost no traffic on this road, and they've got a cow crossing sign, but still it's a worry that some idiot may come tearing around the corner. Below he hears Tess calling the few cows who are still lingering up on the hill. "Boss. Boss." A bunch have already started to amble across by the time he gets there. Cows: who can believe their architecture, that so much loose weight can hang off of all that scaffolding? That they've got these huge bags bumping back and forth between their legs every move they make doesn't seem to faze them. Defies physics that any form that top-heavy can continue to move without toppling. Getgo and Mooney are now dawdling off to the side. He heads them back into the main stream by a shoo, shoo with his hands. The Dawes cows aren't just milk machines. Most of them have names, get treated like ladies. No prods, no kicks to their rears. A small herd — only about eighty milkers. If you treat them nice, Hoop says, they let their milk down faster. Cows don't like the unexpected.

"Mark, I don't see Angel. I'm afraid she might have calved up in the pasture. You call the rest of the cows, keep moving them along. I'm going to go look."

"*You* better get the cows in. They'll go all over the place if I do it. Chaos for sure. Give Budd a call. I'll find Angel."

"But what if she won't come along for you? What if she's already gone into labor?"

Mark is halfway up the hill. He calls back over his shoulder, "Angel knows me. I'll come get you if she doesn't follow right along, if it's something I can't handle." Should have brought a pipe, he and Angel could have had a couple of hits. At first he doesn't see her. Then there she is close to the fence. She's got her head turned, sniffing at her rear. "Angel. What's up?" He moves slowly toward her. Something's out of kilter and he doesn't want to end up chasing her halfway around the pasture. He looks down the hill toward the barn. No sign of Tess, but he can hear the sound of music coming from the radio. A crow caws a warning that he's invaded their territory.

Angel doesn't move off. Just gives him one wet-eyed look, then returns to smelling her bottom. He steps closer. Jesus and no wonder: something that looks like a broken balloon poking out, fluid and blood running down. Giving birth — no question. He cups his hands and yells, "Tess." The name bounces back at him. No one appears at the barn door. He calls again, even louder this time. Still no sign of anyone. Suddenly Angel lies down with a big whomp.

"Okay, Mama, but you're on your own 'cause I haven't got a clue. Not a clue."

Angel turns on her side. Something poking out: hooves, feet first. Is that the way this goes? Mark moves back. "I'm telling you again, you get in trouble, you are on your own."

Angel's sides heave up and down. A couple of big grunts. Pushing, pushing. A head. Then one, two, the shoulders. Whoosh, a big mess of wet and the whole calf slides out. Once again he turns and yells down the hill. "Calf. Calf."

Angel lumbers up. "No, Angel, I suggest you keep doing this

lying down. Seems definitely the best way to go." But Angel pays him absolutely no mind. Big sack of stuff hanging from her rear. The afterbirth probably. Meanwhile Angel is licking, licking the calf, licking away all the gunk. The calf is shaking its head now, still a big mess of dark wet. Now it's slapping its ears back and forth. Up with its head, kicking its feet a little. Well, baby's alive, looking all there. He hoists himself up on the fence. Just going to bear witness to the world while Charlie's off telling his story. Can't believe Tess has gone and forgotten about them. Or maybe she figures he can deal.

He lights a cigarette. Looks out across the valley. Creeks high, twisting, brown and shining, the sun going low now. From here he can see Sawyer's Bridge where he and Aaron and Dad used to put the canoe in. Had to portage three or four places before they got to their land: big trees down and blocking the way. He always scooted around it, clinging to the bank while Aaron and Dad pulled the canoe over the blockage. Aaron, the daredevil. Who knows, maybe it *was* an accident. That's what the death certificate says. Went walking in the dark up on the ridge above the creek, buzzed and delusional, and he fell in. "Death still a mystery," the paper said. A mystery. An accident: give anything to believe that.

The calf is all clean now. Looking around. Fluffy, a curly ball with legs. Silent, no waaa, waaa. He slides down off the fence, but stays back. "You done good, Angel." The calf squirms, rocks, heaves like it's trying to rise up. "Oh, I can't think that's a good idea." Angel gives the calf an encouraging butt and up the calf comes. Then bang, back down, all four hooves splay out. "Tess," he calls again with everything he's got. And finally, finally Tess appears and starts toward them up the hill. Tess, running now, awkward in her barn boots.

One more heave and the calf is up, somehow makes it to Angel's big bag, latches on. Angel all the while licking, going nudge, nudge. No more than a half hour old and this calf is already up and going. Got it all over humans for sure.

Part III

OCTOBER

If I'd been thinking right, I would have recognized your voice, but I wasn't on account of the dark days of winter . . .

—AARON MERRICK,
blue notebook, April 1995

24 : Interior Construction

Del holds the diagram for installing a one-way door at the ready even though it's unlikely Richard will need her assistance. Once he's done here, he'll finish building the bat house, using the full set of plans she downloaded from *batcontrol.com,* the tricky part being the routing of the grooves for the quarter-inch interior baffles — the "roosting chambers" — a row of partitions three hundred bats can cling to, and the whole house about the size of . . . well, a double bread box. Like her, Richard's done a complete reversal on these little winged mamas.

"You've got something else you have to do, go on," Richard tells her as he places the tall ladder solidly below the vent. "Good time to do your last mow."

"I want to watch," she says. She doesn't tell him the real reason for not mowing. She's trying to keep things quiet. After days of insomnia, Mark's breathing in the loft sounds like sleep. Still in bed at noon: No wonder he's depressed, Richard's silent shrug would say.

Halfheartedly she begins to pull away weeds that are growing against the board and battens so the wood won't rot, but what she's really doing is following Richard's body as he climbs. She likes to watch the flow of his hips, the hard muscles of his calves against the backs of his jeans as up he goes. No hesitation, no awkward adjustments that would be her style on such a venture.

"Mow, so I can get your mower ready for winter before you leave for Owl Lake."

Owl Lake: a month of uninterrupted work on the memory series. The joy of that. But can she really leave when Mark's so down, so clearly not taking care of business? At least Tess will be around to keep an eye on things, though between school and milking not around much. Such a shame Mark quit helping with the barn chores.

"Mow, because by the time you get back in November, we could have a foot of snow."

The sound of the phone. Even through the stone wall. Her stomach contracts. Always the barometer of her anxiety level. The phone stops on the second ring. Mark must have picked up, a total break of pattern. Unless he's waiting for a call. And what call could he be waiting for? Not from Rozmer or Charlie or Ben Jacobs: Mark never picks up for them these days. She can't help collecting the clues even when she doesn't want to know. And another thing, she's pretty sure Mark's off his meds, been off them for a long time. Through the glass she watches for any sign of movement in the loft. But all is still. She's glad he's moved all his stuff back to the loft at least, that his drums are again in the living room, especially now that he's so depressed.

Richard's replaced the screening on all the vents but this one. He had to do that before setting up this one-way door, so that the few mother bats or adolescents who haven't migrated — they're down to eleven her last count — can go out to feed tonight, but then when they return at first light, they won't be able to find their way back in. The instructions say that bats go by smell rather than vision. They'll smell their entrance and land on the mesh by their hole and then they'll stay focused there rather than moving to the opening at the bottom of the wire to gain entry.

With his weight leaned into the ladder, Richard crimps the edges of the screening. Then he carefully staples the top of the mesh so it rounds out a few inches above the hole in the vent.

Richard looks so healthy, so vigorous, the maples and poplars, a brilliant red and yellow, forming the rest of the picture, that she simply can never believe that anything sinister can be traveling toward his lymph nodes, setting up shop in his bones. Three more months until his next PSA check. Mostly that date seldom blinks red on her periphery. Richard doesn't refer to it either.

Staple, staple, staple, down each side of the mesh Richard shapes an open mound. Tomorrow morning those bats are going to get a big surprise. Richard descends. He rolls the jagged wire scraps and sets them aside. "Couple of days I'll come back down and replace this last screen."

"Can we be sure they're all out by then?"

No answer. Richard doesn't answer certain kinds of questions. "Get the bat house up before I leave for Colorado. That way it'll be weathered, smell less suspicious when they come back in the spring."

Richard is off to hunt elk. She's off to a place where she'll be very hard to reach by phone. She folds the diagram and pushes it down in her pocket. Maybe she'll work the bats into the memory series: these mothers, waiting for the right moment to let go.

"If you can come up with some guano," Richard says, "you're supposed to make a slurry and drip it on the house. Got to be their guano."

"You're kidding." Then she does see movement inside. Mark is by the refrigerator.

"How about a beer?" Richard says as he heads for the side door.

She'd just as soon not take Richard in until Mark retreats into the dark of the loft again. Plus the place stinks since Mark has reneged on his agreement not to smoke in the house. A thing she hasn't mentioned to Richard. Plus she does not have any beer, never keeps any alcohol around. Another thing Richard doesn't know. It's rare that he ever comes to the stone house.

Mark has his back to them. He's busy pouring sugar in a mug. He does not turn or in any way acknowledge that they are there. Richard sits at the table and is likewise silent. This is often how it is when Mark stops by Richard's.

"Hey," she says. "The screening's just about done, so the bats won't be able to get back in tomorrow morning." This, though Mark has no interest in the bats one way or the other. Mark side-steps around her to get the half-and-half from the fridge. "Maybe you can help me come up with some bat droppings from the space above the light since you were so good with figuring that out." Beyond all this blather, she needs to warn Mark about the noise. "Richard's going to be doing some work out on the picnic table. Building a bat house. That way the bats will have a home when they come back next year."

Mark heads for the loft-ladder. No contact. He leaves the half-and-half out, the empty coffeemaker on, the old filter full of grounds on the cutting board.

She opens the refrigerator. "No beer," she says. "There's apple juice. Water."

Richard rises. "Be good if you'd bring the tar paper up from the barn." And he's gone. In a minute there's the sound of the power saw.

Heavy steps in the loft. Mark's legs coming down.

"Mark," she says. He keeps right on going. She watches him get into the car, her car, watches him back at full speed down the drive, turn at the barn. Disappear. She could punch up the last call on caller ID, but she doesn't.

Del manages to get the tall stepladder open directly below her ceiling light, jockeys it until it feels firmly planted into the braided rug. Mark should be helping with this, but no, she'll have to break her neck instead. Even before she gets halfway up she sees several dark blotches in the center of the frosted light fixture, shadowy specks the size of confetti. Spots she'd always assumed were dead bugs when she considered them from her bed. Chances are good it's guano. But certainly not a cupful as called for in the slurry recipe.

Should she pour the slurry down so it drips over the roof and exterior or should she drizzle the walls of the roosting chambers?

The instructions don't say and since she was only able to come up with half as many droppings as called for, she's got to be strategic with this little pitcher of guano goop. She turns the bat house upside down on the edge of the picnic table.

Luke emerges from beneath. He growls. Someone is coming, but nothing in sight yet. It's not Mark in her car or Luke would be wagging and surging forward with joy. A torpedo of a car appears over the ridge, approaches slowly. Luke holds his ground. Del sets the pitcher down and gets ready. The car pulls up to the walk. For a minute no one gets out. Then the door opens. A man. A gray beard, a thinning ponytail. A gaunt, gray man, lean like the guys who used to run the Ferris wheel. He advances a few steps. "Mark around," he says.

Luke's tail begins to wag, the man extends his fingers for Luke to smell. Maybe Luke knows him and maybe he doesn't. "Wayne Smith." Smithy. "He was supposed to stop by my place."

Smithy. One day a car comes up the road. And there it is. "Mark isn't here. Luke." She takes hold of Luke's collar and turns him toward the house. Once they're inside, she pushes the bolt hard into its socket. Smithy is still standing at the end of the walk. She goes to the side door, locks it, then places the phone on the counter.

This not going to meetings, not keeping his appointments, going off in the car full speed: of course she suspected what this probably meant. But now she knows. If it's Smithy, this isn't about marijuana. And now she has to do something. She has to confront Mark. Smithy gets in the car, but instead of backing to the barn, he turns on the lawn and as he does he rolls his window down. He looks at the house. His look is full on, appraising. It seems to say, I'll be back.

Money. That's what this is about: money. Mark owes Smithy money. A lot of money. It was that kind of look. She checks the numbers she's listed in the emergency page of the phone book. Smithy's car slows at the barn and stops. The brake lights glow in the dusk.

She lifts the phone. Her hand is shaking. She dials Rozmer's number. By the fourth ring she knows Rozmer is not there. She can hang up, try him at Harbor House. Mark may be back any minute now. She does not want to be in the middle of this and have him walk in. The machine clicks on and she knows what's coming: Rozmer's Word for the Day. "An old master-at-arms had advice for sinking sailors: 'Be grateful you're not burning.'"

She wishes she could come up with a laugh of irony, have it last past the beep for her message, but she can't. "Rozmer, this is Del, Del Merrick. Wayne Smith was just here looking for Mark. I feel certain Mark is using again . . . Please help me."

25 : Reap

GOING TO HAVE to sell it all: everything. Pay Smithy and get on the bus. Before the car comes to the crest, he turns off the headlights, slows down to a crawl. Best scenario: she's at Richard's. Get the car loaded without an inquisition. Without having to say, If I don't come up with the money, the dealer's going to break my arms. Or worse. Not chicken-shit local Smithy, the low man on the pole; no, a guy from the city. All business. Steering wheel's greasy. Sweat, jitters coming on. One thing: got enough in reserve to ward off being sick midway through the drama.

The house is dark. Only one vehicle hunched at the end of the drive. He cuts the engine, coasts. Just ahead: Tess's truck. *Only* Tess's truck. Bad as he is, karma-gods letting him off a little longer. Tess? He owes her money too. She's going to trail him, saying shit he does not want to hear, but he can deal with her. Main thing: his mother is at Richard's, he's not going to have to head into her stricken look when he starts loading his drums.

No cigarettes. He extracts a handful of butts from the ashtray, rips a few apart, then sifts the bits of tobacco down the center of an E-Z Wider. Nasty. Just like old times. He leaves the car door ajar. Cold. Couldn't pass the "what day is it?" test tonight, but winter's definitely coming on. First things first: get his works from the barn. So dark that for a few seconds there's nothing but black where the barn ought to be. As long as he's got gravel under his feet, he's okay. Finally the barn rises up square and solid right where it's supposed to be. Have to fuck around finding the right key by feel. The gods extracting payment one drop of blood at a time. He tries the knob and the shop door opens. Someone's been here. Drum-room's locked, but he can't feel if his spy-detector paper is still there. Been so fogged in lately, maybe he didn't remember to stick it in place last time he was here.

Best not risk the lights. Hard to know what alert-level Tess is on. He pats along the window ledge until he finds the candle, the box of matches. His shadow rises up huge and menacing on the wall. He slides his fingers down behind the piano strings, careful not to set them thrumming. Relief: the bag is still where he left it. Through the cloth, he can feel it's all there: the bulge of syringes, his cooker, a Bic, and even a vial of Clorox. But going to have to dumpster it all before he gets on the bus. He doesn't lock either door. Fuck it. No evidence left and all the tools with resale value long gone. His bass, all his CDs gone as well.

Without even a click, he leans into the car, stows the works far back under the front seat. The house is still dark, silent. Where are the dogs? All hell's bound to erupt soon. He unlocks the trunk, surveys the space; that, and the back seat, and half the front. Going to be a major squeeze to get it all in. Trick will be not to look too strung out when he negotiates the sales. The computer? Where to take that? Someplace where they'll believe it's his. The computer. Shit, really crossing the line on that one.

With his thumb pressed down on the handle, he pushes into the front door. The bolt's in place. Of course. Have to go around to the side. Queenie's got to be in with Tess and Luke must have gone with his mom to Richard's. A bad sign that some shit has already gone down because Richard would only be up for that due to extreme conditions. Chances are good Smithy's been calling, even been here pumping out scary vibes: his mother finally putting it all together.

He eases the side door open and steps into the hall. Not a sound from Tess's room. He closes the door between the big room and the hall, lets the handle down to soften the sound. Answering machine's a steady blink of red. No one in the world he wants to talk to. Do the bass drum first. Then, there it is: The Note. Taped to Mr. Coffee. Taped shut. M-A-R-K. He unfolds it under the light, scans for the one word he hopes is not there:

> Wayne Smith was here today. This, along with a whole series of other things this last month or so, can only mean one thing. You and I had an agreement. As you said, if you broke that, the whole world would change for all of us. I called Rozmer . . .

Rozmer. He crushes the paper into a tight ball. One thirty. Too late to try to do any damage control. Main thing: have to take care of this business. Load up, park somewhere until morning, sell the stuff, pay Smithy, leave the car where she can pick it up, get on a bus.

Back and forth. Back and forth. The back seat's packed to the ceiling, the trunk's jammed. Only the computer left. Each time he steps into the living room, he expects Tess to be standing there, ready to go at it. Each time it's a relief when she isn't. Especially now that he's about to heist the computer. Yeah, heist. He begins to unhook all the connections. A thousand cords to untangle. All the "original packing" is under the table. Be worth more if he used that, but no way would it go in the car then. Monitor box wouldn't even fit through the passenger door. He slides one of the plastic bags from the boxes down over the monitor. Put that in first. Just as he starts for the door, he hears something. He freezes and waits. Waits. Heart at full volume. The hall door does not open. No headlights appear on the road. He stands there feeling caught even when he hasn't been, feels the full weight of the monitor. He sets it back on the table. Not the fucking computer. May mean he can't get any farther than Albany, but stealing the computer, no, he's not going to do that.

He throws his backpack in front, shoves the rear door hard to get it to close on the amplifier. That's it. His jaw muscles have gone into clinch, the bones in his hips ache. Sure signs. He takes the bag from under the seat: wrap himself in a little warmth before he finds a pull-in to wait for things to open up in the morning. But he's got to take it easy, ration out the last of his supply. His supply not quite as much as he hoped. He goes back up the stone walk: Aaron's walk. Only the glow of the stove light. Why hasn't Tess burst out of her room onto the scene? No way is she in there snug in her bed, sleeping. Not her usual in-your-face M.O. Maybe she's going to sit this one out.

A glass of water, the bag tucked under his arm, he turns off the light and makes his way up the loft-ladder. He sets up by the window, then pulls his frayed army belt out of the loops of his pants and retrieves the baggie through the hole in his pocket. Definitely less heroin left than he imagined. He twists off the needle cap and examines his left arm — right one's done for, several hard red lumps heating up to abscess. Have the thrill of lancing them in a lurching bus toilet in the back of a speeding Greyhound. Junkie entertainment. He finds a vein, ties off, places one end of the belt in his teeth. He pours a little water in the spoon. His hand is shaking. He sifts in enough to get him there, watches the brown granules dissolve, then the spoon over the candle. Such a fucking ritual. Last rites.

The hall door opens. Steady, you mother, steady.

"Mark . . ." Tess and Queenie move through the darkness below. The big ceiling light goes on. No way she can see him this far back in the loft unless she climbs the ladder.

He sinks the needle in, depresses the pump, feels the cold enter the vein, retracts a little blood, then pumps that back.

"Mark, answer me."

In a few more seconds it's going to hit him, wrap him up and take him there.

"Mark, I know you're here." Her feet on the ladder.

"Don't come up."

She stops. Only Queenie's pant.

He closes the baggie, presses it through the hole in his jacket pocket, unties his belt, scoops the works into the bag. Heat rushes through him. Saliva gone.

"Mark, what's going on?" Her voice blooms blue from below. "Your mother called me at Hoop's, said Smithy'd been here looking for you. Smithy, Jesus Christ, that scumbag. Are you completely crazy or what?"

His skin's hot. He's going to be able to do it all. He slides the works, his belt into his pocket and goes to the top of the ladder.

Tess watches him descend. He laughs. "Shit, you're high." She turns. "Where is everything? Your drums? Jesus, Mark, you owe those evil people money."

He goes down. There's the car. Get in the car, turn the key, back out. He hears her behind him. He closes the car door, but there she is in the lights, her mouth still going. He stuffs the works under the seat, puts the car in reverse. The rear window's blocked with crap. He turns on the lawn. Tess disappears. The cherry tree, the barn, the sound of the brook, Aaron's cabin up on the hill: it all disappears. He turns onto the highway. Follow the yellow lines until he gets to where he has to go next.

Who is he going to miss? Luke. And that is fucking all.

A thud slams him against the steering wheel, the screech of metal. Breaking glass. Trees upside down. He turns over and over, held by the belt. The car skids on its side, smashes against something, wedges him between the door and the amp. Stops. The windows gone. The smell of gas. He releases the belt. His hand is bleeding. He pulls himself through the opening, rolls onto the road, crawls, runs. Hissing, then a boom. Another boom. Flames light the sky. Flames as high as the trees. Gone. Everything gone.

He went on the nod. That's what happened: he went on the nod.

Sirens, the flash of red lights heading his way. He wipes his hand on his sweatshirt and pulls the baggie out, sifts what's left along the shoulder, rips the plastic, gives the tatters to the hot wind.

26 : Fugue This

THE ROOM IS BLACK dark. Del feels her way to the bed. She listens to Richard gargling in the bathroom, the ping of the raised seat against the back of the toilet. She pulls her nightgown off and crawls in between the sheets. She'd rather stay clothed, shielded from it all. But . . . but there's no sense in adding to the tension. Her body's one big knot already: no response from Mark about her note, no word from Rozmer. And Richard? Instead of being a comfort, his silence is just one more goddamned thing.

The bathroom door opens. She moves a little closer to the edge and works on breathing that sounds like sleep. Richard slides in, pushes his legs over to her side, brushes her ankle with his foot. Even though he doesn't move, she can feel him getting closer. Warmer, warmer, and any second he's going to send out an exploratory tentacle. In and out, she keeps her breath slumberous. In all their years together, though she's feigned sleep occasionally and he's not intruded, she has never rebuffed an outright paw on her hip. He turns and nuzzles her neck. Make it better or make it worse. She presses her shoulder against his chest. His arm crosses over, his hand caresses her belly. And really could it not end with this tender contact? To just lie nested into each other? But no: there's the throb of him against her rear. His hand cups her breast. She turns toward him, cradles the warm sack of his balls in her palm.

*   *   *

Richard is rationing out their vitamins. The raisins, just the right number, are plumping up in the boiling water. She dumps in a cup of old-fashioned oatmeal and lowers the heat to medium. If she can just keep going through the motions, maybe she won't lose her mind. Let the phone ring. Let it be Rozmer. Her stomach is fisted: dread, fear, anger. Richard smiles at her standing there at the stove, stirring. Well, at least there's that. Thank you for that. Plus here's Luke, settled on his mat, no complaints from Richard. Thank you for that as well.

After breakfast she is going to go in there and put her underwear in her suitcase, her pencils in her pencil box, the journals and photos in a duffel, the memory studies in her portfolio — though truly this memory project she's planned is the last thing she wants to do now. What she wants is to draw a blank, slip her mind, write it off. An Amnesiac series. She plops the oatmeal into two bowls and sets one in front of Richard. He pats her bottom as she passes.

"Much obliged," he says, and smiles at her again.

She sits across from him. He does not read the paper. "You know what?" she says.

"What?"

"I'm going."

"Good. Best thing you could do all around — for yourself and ultimately for Mark. Get out of the way."

She's going to pack everything and march it to the car. No matter what, no matter how crazy it gets, day after tomorrow, she's going to Owl Lake for one month and she is not giving any of them her number. Except for Richard and even him only the emergency number. Anyway he'll be in the wilds of Colorado, an elk in *his* crosshairs. And then? Well, then, if she has to, in order to never have to live with Mark again, she can rent out the house to some orderly retired couple. A long, long lease. She can move in with Richard. Do not, do not mention this until you see how it all unfolds.

The phone. "Oh, Jesus," she says, "here it is." Her stomach hurts. She goes into the bedroom, closes the door, breathes and picks up the receiver.

"I got home too late to return your call last night."

Rozmer. "I'm glad it's you. Have you heard from Mark? I know he's going to be very angry that I called you."

"I think you should sit down. Mark's okay, but he totaled your car sometime about four this morning. No one was hurt. No property damage. No tickets issued."

"My god. What happened?"

"He told the troopers a deer ran in front of him and he over-reacted. On the way to buy cigarettes. Rolled the car a few times."

She does sit down.

"They gave him a breathalyzer. No alcohol. But no question he was high. All the signs. Tess says he drove off high. First he called her to come and get him; then she called me. By the time I got there, a wrecker from over in Stanton had picked up the car. I said, You're high. He denied it." She's going to have to hear it all. "He wouldn't let me look at his arms." Close-ups, the sound track running. The whole movie. A movie she'd never go see. "I suggested he take a piss test today according to his contract. He said, Fuck the contract." She sees she's drawn a black dot in the center of the telephone pad and it's getting bigger and bigger, blacker and blacker. "I said, What about your mother's rules? His response: I don't care about *her* rules."

She brings each corner of the sheet to the center and flattens it, careful not to get any carbon on her hands. "I'm telling you this to help you do what you have to do."

What *does* she have to do? She's got to get out of the loop: follow through on the terms of the agreement, stop being his rep-payee.

"Consequences," Rozmer says.

"I know. I know I have to tell him to move, but where will he go? I feel I have to give him a little time to find a place to stay."

"I'd give him no time at all. 'You have to leave today and if you don't, I'll call the sheriff.'"

"I don't know if I can do that."

"Do you want me to go with you?"

*   *   *

Rozmer will meet her at the gravel bank at one. Tess is staying with the Daweses for now, until she finds out if she can go on living at the stone house. Rozmer said he'll see if Tess wants to go along, get some of her stuff. After all, Tess cares about Mark too. She rehearses what she's supposed to say. It doesn't feel like anything she would ever say. Not a part she would get if she had to audition. Maybe that's the key: where Mark's concerned, she should do the opposite of what feels right.

Richard passes by the window carrying a propane tank for his travel trailer. She's going to have to tell him about the car. His response: Never should have loaned it in the first place. Just set Mark up for trouble. Or silence.

1. Get Richard's advice on the insurance.
2. Wrecker: plates & registration.
3. S.S. ofc. Stop rep-payee.
4. Leave notes for Dr. Taylor and Ben Jacobs. No details.
5. Call sheriff's dept. to get procedure.

9:00. Four hours to get as much of this accomplished as possible. Present Mark with "already done," otherwise she'll be easy prey for his manipulation. She runs water in the oatmeal pot and puts on her jacket. Luke leaps with joy. "You aren't going," she tells him.

Richard is under the trailer, only his boots sticking out. She bends down a little. "I have to talk to you for a minute."

"Go ahead," he says. "I can hear you."

She moves closer to where his ear might be, bends down farther, but sees only his midsection stretched out on one of those padded boards on wheels. "Mark wasn't hurt, but he totaled the car last night. No tickets issued. A wrecker took it away. What's the best way to handle it with Allstate?"

A long pause. "Tell Allstate you're taking the car off the road." He rolls out and looks up at her. He taps her shoe with the index finger that's not greasy. "Only that and nothing more. Drop the plates off at Motor V. Cost you a dollar." Again he disappears. There's the ratchet, ratchet of a wrench.

*   *   *

Just as Del crests the hill on Cobb's Road, the orange flash of their grandfather maple, still in full leaf, far below across the field, the brook, and then the blue-gray of the stone house roof. She slows. Lots of smoke coming from the chimney. Mark must be there and up and about enough to be stoking a good fire.

12:45. She's made the calls, written the notes, signed off as payee. Too late to stop the October payment, but she can return that to Social Security as soon as it gets deposited in the representative-payee account tomorrow. Only Motor V left once she picks up the license plates and registration at Stanton Wrecking. The sheriff's department does not come and remove wayward children unless they're holed up with a gun, doing something considered a harm to themselves or others. She has to go to the town justice — Hoop Dawes — if she wants to evict Mark, and it's a long involved process. But this doesn't mean she can't use the sheriff as a threat in her speech if Rozmer thinks it's needed.

She passes the Cobb farmhouse, rented out since Lee's mother's death. Two years ago this October. Then there's the left onto the highway and a quick turn into the gravel bank. No one around at B & R Roto-Rooter & Excavating. She pulls the car behind the huge pile of gravel that cascades onto her right-of-way. She makes herself look up the hill. Just one corner of Aaron's cabin is visible through the hemlocks. Aaron. Eight years in April. Maybe in the calm of Owl Lake, Mark behind her, she can finally turn toward that. Read his blue notebook, the words he wrote only a few days before he died.

Again she rehearses her speech. Two points only: no longer his rep-payee, move out today. Tess's truck pulls in behind Del. She and Queenie slide out. Del motions them to get in front, but they push into the back instead.

"Let Rozmer ride shotgun," Tess says. Tess's dreadlocks are twisted under a black bandanna and all the hardware is gone from her face. She looks exhausted.

"I am not looking forward to this," Del says.

Tess laughs. "It's good Rozmer's going with us." Tess hugs

Queenie. "And of course Queenie, who always keeps things in perspective." Queenie pants on Del's shoulder, licks her.

"I'm going to keep it brief," Del says.

"All depends if he's high or hungry."

"He's got a good fire going. Lots of smoke coming from the chimney."

"Then he's high. Going to be black irony and 'don't give a fuck.' If he didn't have a fix, the fire would be out and he'd be shivering up in his bed."

"Oh, dear. Well, I hope it's going to work out for you to go on living at the house, at least until I return from Owl Lake, that Luke can stay with you this month. All depends on Mark's attitude, his moving out, and if you think you can stand up to keeping him from moving back in. But then once I get back from the residency, I think I'm going to have to rent the house out."

"I'm not afraid of Mark, but here's the thing: Mark's into it deep with Wayne Smith, my mom's lovely companion, Smithy and his higher-ups, Mark's drums, everything..." Tess stops. "Well, look, don't worry about us. I can find a place for me and Queenie to stay. Maybe even Luke too, if Mark turns out to be... more than pain-in-the-ass nasty."

Rozmer's truck turns off the highway, heads straight for them.

She drives them slowly toward the house. Rozmer knocks on the door. Rozmer's like a big wall standing there. Thank the gods for Rozmer. The three of them step back and wait. Rozmer knocks again. There's the scrape of furniture across the floor, the sound of steps. The clank of the bolt. Mark opens the door, an empty coffeepot in his hand. Unshaven. Bright eyes peer out at them from his hooded sweatshirt. Thin, thin like those famine victims, the worst she's ever seen him. He gives them a tilted smile.

"Well, well... lookee... who's here." He turns away and goes to the sink.

They step inside. Rozmer signals "go" with his eyebrows. "We need to talk," Del says.

Mark doesn't respond. He squint-eyes the slow trickle from the faucet into the carafe as though an exact measure is critical. "Talk?" he says.

"Yes."

Mark sets the carafe down on the edge of the microwave, pats the pockets of his sweatshirt, checks the fluid in his lighter. "We'll . . . hold our little . . . talk . . . outside . . ." His words lurch, bump into each other. ". . . once I make some . . . coffee." All the while that same small smile. ". . . so I can sm . . . oke."

This in deference to Rozmer. Any kind of deference at all offers some hope. The three of them watch his slow trek around the kitchen: the pouring of the water, the placing of the filter, the tapping of the bottom of the can to get the last grains out. They sit down. Only the gurgle of liquid streaming into the carafe, the clink of the spoon against the mug as he loads in sugar. With the cup held away from his body as though it is pulling him along, he starts for the door. They rise. He stumbles against the counter, a splash of coffee hits the floor.

Del's hand goes out as if to keep herself from falling. "Mark, you're high right now."

He looks at her for the first time. "What are they" — he sweeps his arm toward Rozmer and Tess — "doing here?" And then he is out the door.

On the back of the counter: a wrist brace, its fraying Velcro straps undone. Tess picks the brace up. "My mother's," she says. "Doing an 'angel of mercy' before we got here."

Rozmer motions for her to go first. By the time they get seated, she and Tess across from him, Rozmer off to the side — maybe this means she's on her own — Mark is stripping out shreds of tobacco from the pile of butts in front of him. He rolls a cigarette, lights it, blows the smoke off in another direction.

"Now," he says, and laughs.

"Mark . . ."

"I want . . . my money. I'm . . . leaving . . . the area." He keeps his eyes on a distant point like he's waiting for a train.

"Today," Rozmer says. "Your mother wants you to leave the house today."

"You her translator?"

Silence. Her cue for sure. She opens her mouth, trusts something will come out. "You and I had an agreement. I'd like you to move out today."

Mark turns his body, looks toward Rozmer for the first time. "This woman . . . thirty-seven years ago . . . note the rapport." Then he swings his legs from under the table and sits with his back to all three of them. All she can see is the ragged edge of his hood, the slump of his shoulders. "Is she," he says, his voice low and reasoned, as he flourishes with his arm to take it all in: the brook, the thorn apples, the hill where Aaron and Lee's ashes are buried, "I ask you, is she . . . responsible . . . for any of this?"

She is not going to cry. She is going to tell him the rest of what she has to say. "Leave today," she says again. "We can make arrangements to bring you your drums, all your . . ."

Mark laughs, a boom of sound. "My drums?" he says. All of it a source of much amusement. "I am not . . . going to treatment. I was delusional . . . when I signed that contract."

"Nobody's going to force you into treatment," Rozmer says. He rises and walks to where he can face Mark, but he keeps some distance, puts his hands in his pockets. "You have all sorts of options."

"Options?"

"Between 'nowhere to go' and long-term treatment. Go to a meeting, go to a shelter . . . The main thing is to focus on what you need to do today."

"Anybody comes here and tries to force me into treatment . . ."

"Today," Rozmer says again. "What are you going to do today?"

"I'm leaving. I need my October money." All his words are steady now.

Del breathes in and says it: "I'm no longer your rep-payee. The money is between you and Social Security."

"That money gets deposited tomorrow. No way you could have stopped that. That money is between you and me." Silence. "Look, there's something I have to take care of."

What she needs to say is No. Instead she says nothing.

Mark scoops up the butts and stuffs them in his pocket. "Fine," he says, "fine. I can go on being the . . . family martyr." He rises, does not look at her. "My mother wants me out of the house, why, I'll get out of the house. If Tess is going to stay here, be good if I can get some transport from her. Maybe the Morlettis will take me in." He starts to move away, but stops after a few steps. "If," he says and then turns and looks at her head on, "if I had the October money, I'd have a chance."

She looks toward Rozmer, but he gives her no clues. "I don't know," she finally says.

"You don't know?" His voice is full of contempt. Again he turns.

A red leaf spirals past, lands by her hand. What chance does he have? "I'll think about it," she says, so low maybe he didn't hear her.

He disappears around the side of the house, Queenie at his heels.

Just beyond the Stanton limits, Del turns right at Bellow's Corners, one of those enclaves of rusted trailers with added-on plywood rooms and teetering porches, three-sided sheds of scrap lumber, yards full of old cars and derelict machinery. Stacks of tires and random piles of exotic objects. Once a social worker had explained to the faculty at her school that this was not junk. These were heaps of spare parts and salvage to be bartered, traded, or modified to get something going. But worthy goods or not, this much chaos would finish her off for sure.

Two miles to Dry Brook. She sets the trip odometer to zero. Pay the two hundred dollars — two hundred dollars — for transporting her totaled car, take the goddamned plates to Motor V and then tomorrow morning early she's out of here. Weird the car, the accident, never even mentioned. The October money.

Maybe she *should* turn that over to him. Give him a more positive option than the Morlettis'.

No, she is not, she is not going to let him pull her back into this. She's going to pack up and go to Owl Lake. Maybe take only Aaron's box. Leave the rest of them behind. Tess is going to stay in the house and take care of Luke, and if Mark hasn't moved out by the time she gets back, well, she's going to go to Hoop and begin eviction proceedings, put an ad in the *Sun:* "House for Rent," but for the next month she's going to draw and go for walks and read and not think about Mark.

The leaves are heading for peak, as they say, and the hills are bursting orange and red and yellow, and if she had a semi-normal life, she could just drive merrily on and enjoy the brilliance. Is she responsible for some of this? Well, yes, yes, yes. All of them stumbling through Lee's dark silence all those years, the food so heavy during a lot of those dinners it was hard to lift the fork, her throat so locked she couldn't swallow. Aaron's death. Yes, she should have grabbed hold of him, said, My god, Aaron, you look terrible, what is the matter? Instead of looking away, always looking away. All of her energy diverted toward rescuing Mark. But, Jesus, Mark, this is now, now, it's time to get up in the morning, do the dishes after meals, and watch where you're going. Watch where you're going.

Dry Brook Road. She brakes and turns right. No question she's found it, for far off in the distance, scattered across the hill, piles and piles of wrecked vehicles, giving off beams of chrome-light in the sun. The office is in a trailer similar to the ones she's just passed. She imagines the owner will have a belly that rolls down over his belt and very few teeth. She knocks and is told to come on in. A man is sitting at a computer. He is lean, wearing clean navy coveralls similar to Richard's, and when he smiles, none of his teeth are missing.

"I spoke to you earlier on the phone. Del Merrick. You picked up my wrecked car, a 1995 Escort, on Route 8 near the Hesse Station."

"An Escort," he says. "That's what it was."

"Yes." She opens her pocketbook. The man pushes a bill he's already prepared across the desk. She counts out the money. He marks the bill paid and gives her the yellow copy.

"I'd like the plates to take into Motor V and I'd like to get my registration out of the glove compartment."

The man looks her over in a friendly way. "Your registration?" he says. "Your plates? Well, just follow me and I'll let you take a look. It's not far."

He takes her out the back door and down a wide aisle, stack after stack of hubcaps, a stake with a printed number marking off each row. "I've got almost the entire inventory on the computer," he says. "That way, you come in, needing a wheel for a 1995 Ford truck, I can rustle it up in a jiffy. Plus of course I can send a buyer to the right spot who wants to remove a clutch or pull out some bucket seats. Just down this way," he says.

They stop in an open area by the road. "There she is," he tells her.

The black, twisted structure before her looks more like the carcass of a huge volcanic-blasted insect. Nothing is left but the shell. It rests on black wheels, a few melted globs of rubber. All of the glass is gone. There are no seats. The glove compartment is a dark hole.

"Oh," she says. "I didn't know."

The man steps aside, lets her pass. "The driver was one lucky guy," he says.

"Yes," she says. "Yes, lucky. Lucky."

27 : Gone

THE LOFT'S DARK. He must have been asleep for hours. He gropes along the edge of the bed for his sweatshirt and turns the pocket inside-out to dump the few remaining butts, all the loose shreds of tobacco, on the stool. Two cigarette papers left and stomach cramps coming on.

Mark stuffs Carla's wrist brace in his sweatshirt pocket. Chances are good he'll get his October money tomorrow: six hundred and seventy plus. She's going to see it's the right thing to do. If Tess is around, get her to give him a ride to the Morlettis'. Get Carla to give him a few doses to tide him through. Promise Smithy enough of the money to tamp the situation down. Go Greyhound. Going to be sick on the bus. Sick on the Styx, title for his next song.

There's a rustle of life from below. He leans over the rail. Thump, thump. Luke has returned. Must be Tess is still going to caretake while his mom's away. Mark goes down. Only light: the green glow of time passing 7:00, 7:01 and the red flash of the answering machine.

Luke rolls onto his back, presents his belly. Mark obliges, feels Luke's heat against his aching thigh. "Hey, buddy, maybe I'll get myself a white cane, take you along as my seeing-eye."

There's the soft fuzz of the radio coming from Tess's room. Back early from milking. Knockety-knock. The radio fades. "What?"

"Be good if I could talk to you."

"Talk," she says.

"Face to face."

Queenie sniffs at the crack on the other side, a small whine of apology. Luke slumps against the frame and looks at him: you humans, always fucking it up.

"Be good for both of us. Sooner I get things settled, sooner I'll be gone." Unlocking of door. He steps back. Give her plenty of room. The door opens.

Tess: *pissed.* "What?"

"I'm planning on leaving tomorrow when I get my money, but tonight I need to talk to Smithy in person, assure him he's going to get some of that money in payment of my debt, that I'll make good on the rest once I get it together."

She starts to shut the door. "I am not giving you a ride to my mother's. I am *not* going to be part of this shit."

"I don't suppose you'd let me borrow your truck? Half an hour?" Her eyes widen. "Just kidding," he says. Re-morse. "Tess, my drums are gone. Everything's gone. I need to get out of here. Get myself straight. But the way to do that is to settle things with Smithy the best I can. Best for my mother, best for all of us. I don't want any of those maniacs, your brother, coming down here causing trouble, threatening to break in, burn the place down." She's listening. "Best chance is for me to go up there and do what I can to take the pressure off. You can park up the road. They don't even need to know you're there. Half an hour."

"No," she says. She closes the door and locks it again. From the other side, loud and clear, "And if you do anything threatening, I'll call the troopers."

He turns away, lifts his jacket from the hook. He and Luke step into the night. He'd like to slam the door so hard the glass breaks, but he does not. He pulls it closed and then they both begin to run. Three miles to Carla's.

Moon's rising. He jumps the rocks to cross the brook, scrambles up the bank. Weeds waist-high in the field and wet. He climbs the fence, steps onto Cobb's Road. Uphill all the way now.

Night sky clouding, but enough light to keep to the center. Stones sharp under his sneakers. Luke takes the lead. Now and again, the glint of eyes checking back to gauge his progress. His progress? Spiking down so sharp it's off the chart. The pump of adrenaline is bringing the dope-sickness on. No works of his own. Going to have to risk one of Carla's needles. And clean it in Clorox: everybody's got hep C in that house. At last the abandoned sawmill looms up on the left. Halfway there. At the top of the hill he stops, loosens the cramps in his legs. When he gets too far behind, Luke waits.

One vehicle pulled up in the yard. He whistles low for Luke and slows down, works on his breathing. Smithy's old car. There's a light in the kitchen, the rest of the house, dark. He edges around the side to look in the back windows. Probably Rudy not here. At least there's that. Rudy, Smithy, Carla all at one time, more than his dope-sick self can negotiate.

He goes up the back steps, semi-crouches behind a cord of firewood. Only Carla at the kitchen table, Carla, looking off the chart as well, sunk down and grim around the mouth. Pack of cigarettes by her hand, so all is not lost. No sign of Smithy. Clock over Carla's head says eight. Score something if he can, talk to Smithy if he must, and then back down to call his mother to see about getting the money tomorrow.

He flicks his lighter, holds it so Carla will see it's him when he taps the glass. She starts, then comes and unlocks the door. No smile of welcome. "This isn't a good time," she whispers.

"Smithy around?"

"He's sleeping. And you do not want to wake him. You are number one on his shit list." She does not budge from the door, keeps her knee out so Luke can't bolt by. "I told him about the accident. How everything you'd planned to sell burned up."

"And?"

"That kept him from going down to the stone house with reinforcements to drag you out tonight."

He hands her the wrist brace. "Well, tell him I plan to give him four hundred tomorrow when my money comes."

"Promises aren't going to do much. If Smithy doesn't see the money tomorrow, they're going to come after you." Carla steps back, begins to close the door. "No shit, Mark, they are."

The door locks. Luke has already gone down the steps. Not even a couple of Camels for the road.

Tess's light is out. Both the doors locked. His keys? Maybe still soldered to the ignition. No spare hidden in the shed. Out of Rudy-fear, even the dog-entry's barred shut. He leans into the side door: his whole body shaking, waves of nausea bringing on the sweat. Got to keep it together until he brings his mother around. And have to make that call *now* before the ring becomes an alarm in the night. He gives a firm, but friendly, knock. He waits. He waits. He goes around to the back and taps on Tess's window: a nonthreatening tap. "Tess, I don't have a key." He wipes his nose on his sleeve, the steady stream of mucus, and returns to the side. He moves back, aims, runs, turns his body, hits the door with all his rage. The frame cracks, gives. He runs again, all his weight behind his screaming shoulder. The door crashes back. Pain, hot pain. A moment of blackout. He heads for the flashing light and dials the number. He breathes, breathes, lets his body down into the chair.

"Hello." Fear.

"It's me. I'm packing up to leave tomorrow. I'm thinking of going to Key West, get a dishwashing job, a cheap room for the winter, get myself straightened out."

"All right."

"But I need my money in the morning. I need to pay Wayne Smith four hundred for a drug debt. I need the rest for a bus ticket."

"Mark . . ." His stomach seizes up: Bad News coming. The phone, a slick of snot and sweat. "Mark, I already mailed a check returning the money to Social Security this afternoon."

Bursts of fire explode down his arm across his chest. "You can stop payment."

"As soon as you find a new rep-payee or get a psychiatrist to say you don't need one, Social Security will deposit all the money . . ."

His scream lifts him, locks his fingers on the phone. "You've done it now."

"Mark, it's not good for you to be so dependent on me."

He kicks the chair over. Luke jumps out of the way, disappears. "Listen . . . you listen to me: Anything you ever gave me, I got by scamming you. You never gave me what I need. You . . . you're the one, the one most responsible . . . for what happened to my brother."

"Mark, I'm going to hang up now."

"Don't you hang up." He pulls the drainer off the counter. There's a crash of dishes, the breaking of glass. "Don't you dare hang up." He throws the door open. "I am not leaving."

Cold rain. He grips the wet stones. "This is my land, my house more than yours. My father built it. My father's blood . . ."

A dial tone. Rain pounds his face. She's gone.

28 : Aaron Merrick,
1967–1995

SHE TURNS THE NOTEBOOK over, inspects it: 120 sheets, wide ruled. Two torn shreds of paper bunch inside the spirals: the remains of two sheets that have been removed. On the back cover, a number: 994-7755. "Keep this," Mark said when he handed it to her the day after the memorial service. "Found it by his bed in town." Aaron's last words. Page after page of unsent letters to his old Lawrence high school friends, written only days before he moved back to his cabin that April. This worn spiral neither of them has ever read. She begins where she left off the last time she tried this. Finally she has gone up into the loft of his cabin, now she is going to go here:

April 7, 1995

Hey, Cuz, thanks for letting me know about Fitz. Very sorry to hear it. He was one of the few and first real artists I've ever known. Fitz was an affront to the sensibilities of many of the white suburbanites' offspring that attended Lawrence High. He was a **freak** and would clearly never be the perfect consumer, therefore automatically ineligible for instant happiness. He wasn't weak, so it must have been a big ass bus that ran him over.

She is the one who delivered the message about the death of Aaron's friend Dan Fitzgerald. It was the third suicide message she delivered to Aaron: his father; Justin, another friend from the same high school crowd a few years earlier; and Dan. Soon after, Aaron called her the woman who brought bad news.

Below her room, the murmur of the other seven Owl Lake residents' after-dinner talk, their chairs pulled up close to the fire. She is glad to begin reading these letters where if she needs to, she can drift down to join them: a poet, a fiction writer, a journalist, a composer, a printmaker, a photographer, a sculptor. Four men and four women, including herself. The youngest, perhaps thirty, the oldest, maybe in his late seventies. Talk has been mostly about what they're all working on. This is the space she would like to stay in, the comfort of almost-strangers, none of whom seems inclined to ask, And do you have children?

> Me, I just can't get enough of my beloved hometown, located at the end of the path of least resistance. My only struggles here are with boredom, but I have a secret appreciation for stability. At the same time I am completely unattached, so I can freebird it outta here when monotony overwhelms.

Her studio is in the boathouse. Twenty by thirty feet of floating space, with a huge sliding door at one end that opens directly onto the lake. Skylights, several high, long tables, so she's able to spread out her preliminary drawings, to let images float around in her mind's periphery: the Morris chair, Aaron's jacket. But not the studies of Mark: the cigarette burns, the blasted Escort skeleton. They're in the trunk. After all, Mark hardly qualifies as a "memory." He's right there banging away in the front part of her brain much of the time. If he hasn't moved when she returns home at the end of the month, she'll have to begin eviction proceedings. Then get the house ready to rent and make her escape to Richard's. She has only given Tess and Richard the emergency office number. Her main fear, when she goes back to her room each evening, is that she will find a "Please call" note attached to her door. Always there is that rush of relief when nothing is there.

April 9
Hey Ken

Here's some buds. I recommend ½ dosage. Wow — it was great to see you guys again. With Lana it was a lot like walking into a trap that I had set for myself way back when. I hope she knows I have no intention of complicating her life.

Lana. Aaron's first love when he was seventeen. A girl five or six years older. Ken's sister.

But Lana was immediately brought to mind when my mother handed me a sealed envelope and told me a friend had died. Lana is the girl who introduced me to love, sex, and high-stakes mind games, and she took me to see Hotel New Hampshire 6 times. It is my nature to spend the second half of my life correcting the mistakes of the first half, which I think is better as opposed to continuing to make the same ones over and over. Starting to wander here, so I'll sign off.

These last letters all about those days, what went wrong with Lana years ago. His trip back to Lawrence after Dan's death. Not what she expected, feared. What did she expect? Not Aaron so alone. Aaron, who as a child had seemed so out the door without a care.

Each morning she sits in the boathouse doorway and watches the mist rise off the water, watches the sun light the trees across the lake. A Prussian blue mountain in the distance. The smell of water, black soil, pines. When she wants to wake herself up, she reaches down and lifts a handful of cold water to her face. Her lunch is delivered in a basket. One of the staff hangs it from the boathouse door. When she realizes she's hungry, there it is: lentil soup, homemade oatmeal cookies. While she eats, sitting with her feet almost touching the water, the open pages of master drawings in her lap, she follows the lines of Dürer, Ingres, Watteau with the same excitement she used to feel when she was twelve and tying her shoe skates to get out on the roller-rink floor, to leg over leg make the turns to the swell of the organ, those notes that held on and on. Finally, hours pass when she does not think of Mark at all.

She places Lee's grandmother's mirror, the one from Aaron's cabin, on the back of her drawing table. Even more of the silver backing has flaked away. She enlarges some of Aaron's cartoon figures, some of the phrases from his songs. *Take my words home to your point of view and watch them change.* She arranges these and some of his belongings so that they're reflected in the mirror: Aaron's Chinese checkerboard full of non-filter Camel cigarette butts, his wire-rimmed glasses with the duct tape holding the frame to the stem. She decides which parts of the objects she wants to be missing.

> So here's the trap: the more I focus on connecting in any way, the more she will feel I'm seeking special treatment, causing resentment. It is most definitely not in my nature to ignore something like that, but I can't have her thinking I've been brooding over her these many years can I? What signals must I send to express the fact that I do have a life, yet without seeming defensive and therefore perceived as bitter?

Draft after draft about Lana, but now not addressed to anyone. Each a fresh start, but all of them containing the word "trap." Always that underlying longing to stop feeling the pain of Lana's past and recent rejection. Her cruelty. And all of them reminding her of how she had often felt about Lee beginning in high school and lasting until several years after his death. Lee, I do have a life.

All morning she draws the great coil of rope Aaron used when they were taking down trees. As she draws, the boathouse gently rocks, the lap of the water amniotic. Rendering the heavy twists of rope from every angle, on torn sheets from a lovely Lavis Fidelis roll. So far she works with graphite only, some erasing away, but mostly using the white of the paper to catch the light on the loops. This rope she was relieved to finally find, hanging from a hook behind a door in their barn, that first week after Aaron disappeared — at least one terrible vision cut from the possibilities.

> I usually just expect people to know that I'm not capable of *completely* losing my mind, but I see now that anyone who knew me then (and Justin and Fitz too) would have no reason to assume that I was automatically OK.

We did believe he was okay. That he would be okay. How are you doing? she'd say. "I'm fine." She knew he wasn't fine, but she always thought he'd come through: freebird it outta all that family darkness. The coroner whispered to her that they had written "accidental drowning" as the cause of death as though somehow this would make it easier. But knowing that he had taken his own life never led her to "Why?" From the moment the sheriff told her a body had been found, her sorrow took her to this: Aaron was gone and they would never be able to get him back.

She blurs the drawing of the leather harness Aaron used when he climbed trees. Smudges the lines. Images seen through water. Images surface.

Coal is in the creek, just his big black head visible; Mark grips Coal's collar, to be pulled to the bank on the other side. She is sitting on the grass reading. Aaron is off somewhere, probably damming up one of the springs that flows into the creek. Often he absents himself to get away from Mark's insults and directives. The water must be cold, late May or early June, because the three of them are still living in the pole barn, Lee staying up on the pine bluff in a tent, working on the stone house alone while they're all in school — Mark in seventh grade, Aaron in fifth. If Lee walked to the edge of the bluff, beyond the stand of hemlocks, he would be able to see them. She knows Aaron and Mark climb the hill to visit him; not together, each goes on his own. They do not tell her about this. They do not talk of him at all. They do not say his eyes are strange.

"Don't look now, Mom," Mark says, pointing toward the bridge that crosses the creek downstream.

Aaron is up on the top girder of the bridge, his arms out like a coasting gull, each step steady and without pause. Something catches the light, streaks down each time he lifts his foot. Both sneakers are untied.

> When it comes to suicide, well, I want you to know, I would never, ever do that and I suspect most people who have lost a father "that way" (I can say it, but only once to a page) would not be able to do that, no matter how badly they want to. Even if this isn't true, I feel that it is in my case, and my brother's as well. And the less said about "mental health" the better . . . I would not know how to begin to explain to someone that I am not crazy . . .

> When it comes to suicide . . .

The letters are not what she feared. They are not about them. They are not about the silent dinners, the time she stayed out all night and forgot he needed a ride to the All-County band try-outs. So far only one mention of his brother, his father . . . Beyond bringing bad news, he does not seem to blame her. Or is it that he can't say any of that even once on the page?

She doesn't know where she's going to start or what image she's going to start with, but she fastens a long roll of paper, six feet wide and horizontal, on the boathouse wall, pins down tight eight feet of it, where the morning light seems best. She pulls a small table close and spreads out her pencils and pens, charcoal, the watercolors, erasers, brushes, India inks, glasses of water, clean rags. Tomorrow, she's going to leap into the empty space, drop down and down, try to make it to the other side.

> If I'd been thinking right, I would have recognized your voice, but I wasn't on account of the dark days of winter . . .

Early one morning — it must have been 1992, '93, she was still living in the apartment in Marwick, renting out the stone house

— there's a steady knock on the downstairs door. Her body gets ready to flee or lift a car off a child. From the top of the stairs, she cannot see who it is. She goes down, peeks out. It's Aaron. When she opens the door, the strong smell of beer hits her. He says he and Mark went to Albany last night because someone's drummer had an accident and they wanted Mark to fill in. In the end the injured drummer showed up and played anyway and it was all a bust. They got back at three; he's only had a couple of hours of sleep and he wants to hitch a ride to Stanton so he can get to work at the sawmill.

She finishes dressing for school, six classes and a study hall today. Aaron sits in the rocker in the living room. "Want some breakfast?" she says.

"Not this early. Unless you have a Mountain Dew."

She only looks at Aaron a little at a time. Finally she fully takes him in. Beneath the matted hair, the duct-taped glasses, the greasy jeans, he's in there. She sits on the couch and eats her cereal, Aaron across from her. Once Aaron told of seeing the sunrise from the window of his cabin, but soon after, the town began building a central school in the adjacent fields, and every day the bulldozers rumbled by from the gravel bank to the site. Aaron has moved to an old camping trailer near the mill. His explanation for moving: one day fields of flowers and the sounds of birds, the next day dust and the roar of machines.

Aaron sits and rocks, his eyes closed. She drinks coffee. The squeak of the chair, the sound of her swallowing. She bets if they did a study of families where there has been a suicide, they would find there had been half as many words as the average the years before the death and one-quarter as many after. Finally she says, "It was a hard winter, wasn't it?"

"I wouldn't do it again."

"Do you ever think of going back to school?"

He laughs. "I've been in school."

"The school of life you mean?"

"The school of life. Yes, sometimes I think of going back, but I don't have any credit to get a loan."

Aaron had bought a truck on time. She had refused to co-sign. Then he moved to California and didn't make the payments. When the bank called her, her bank too, she said she didn't know where he was; which was true; she didn't. Don't call me again, she said. It's too painful.

"If you ever decide going to school is what you want to do, there's probably a way. That's what I've found if I really want to do something. I could help."

"I'll see," he says.

April 14

Four days before Aaron disappeared.

I'm still here and doing fine. Feeling sad about old friends and broken connections from the old "glory days" at Lawrence. As I am unable to correctly express myself in a letter, this dotted half note will have to do until we meet again. I have your number and will be in the neighborhood sometime this month, so don't be surprised when I call you. If I don't, that means I have crawled back under the rock, and am completely undeserving of your correspondence. Thanks for thinking of me and I hope to see you again soon.

Love, Aaron

And then, on the last page of the notebook, Aaron's final entry.

Near life experience almost touched the ground
Midway deliverance was found
but now I'm lost, could drown
just beneath the surface. Hard to breathe
just beneath the surface. Don't know what to think
How to act
How to sink
swim

For weeks, after the fishermen found Aaron's body, the investigator from the Onango County sheriff's department kept calling her. I have a few final effects. The things that were in your son's pockets. I need to return them to you in order to close the case. No. Not yet, she kept telling him. When she opened the door, the investigator was standing there with a small plastic bag. She had to take it. Fourteen stiff one-dollar bills, a Bic lighter, and eight pennies, the copper turned green. She still has the investigator's card in her wallet — *Martin J. Murphy 446-9175* — as if one day the question she'd wanted to ask him may come to her.

She unpins the long roll of paper from the boathouse wall. Using a stepladder she anchors the paper lengthwise this time, as high as it will go where the ceiling and the wall meet. She pins it down to finally touch at the level of the floor. Up on the ladder again, she splashes ink from five bottles onto the center of the emptiness. Quick strokes with a thick brush and the image begins to emerge. The locomotive engine, its great steel force, fills the entire space, rams off all the edges.

The night Mark visited Aaron up in his cabin, the night she and Mark feel certain was Aaron's last night, Aaron stood on the ridge high above the gravel bank, and said he knew the train was coming, that his father was telling him he better get on that train.

The engine lights are so bright, you can't see if a hand's on the throttle. The rest of the image is huge, black, black, head on: no room to leap away.

Mark, he kept saying, can't you feel the vibrations of it coming down the track?

29 : small

Ben Jacobs sets a cup of coffee in front of him. Ahhh, Mark's body says, whooshes it out: gratitude. He wraps both hands around the heat of the mug. Airlift from the icy waters. One look and Jacobs knew pouring his own not an option. Lucky if he can get the cup up and back without a major slosh. He takes it slow. Plenty of cream and a ton of sugar. They've been out of coffee for weeks. Dog food the only thing Tess still supplying.

Jacobs takes a seat behind his desk, his usual no-hurry position: chair back, hands across his flannel chest, a look away out the window. Nothing but bare trees now. Like they left off talking minutes ago, when it's been months since he sat here. Two, three? "I'm ready," he says.

"Ready?" Jacobs leans his way, gives him the full check. Jacobs doesn't bore in like Rozmer, but he's always got the BS meter running.

"Ready to give it another shot. Rehab. Halfway. And like I said on the phone, preferably on another planet."

"They've got a bed for you at Onango Valley in Tremont — small unit, only ten people — and if all goes well, they think a halfway up near Buffalo. Dual-diagnosis house." Hep, hep coming up. Slogging to the Twelve-Step shuffle. "You've got a ride? Your stuff with you?"

Tess so glad to see him go she actually did his laundry, packed him up a little bag. "Getaway car idling at the curb as we speak."

"Have you got your meds? Hospital wants you only to bring your vials with the prescriptions on them."

"No meds. No meds again ever."

"Why's that?"

"Land of the Living Dead. Plus have you been reading lately what the long-range side effects are?"

"What about the manic episodes, the psychosis?"

He makes himself meet Jacobs's eyes straight on. "Going to have to ride that train if it comes, try to make it through the tunnel."

Jacobs leans toward him, places his open hands in the space between them. "You think not taking the medication is a wise decision?"

"How I'm going to do it."

Jacobs lets that sit there. "The rehab unit says you're going to have to do some detox. They'll check your urine first thing."

"Whatever. But it's been weeks. Since . . . what month do we find ourselves in?"

"October 29th, 2002."

"Since early October. My abstinence — not on the basis of turning over a new leaf. No money. Nothing left to sell. Plus my main supplier OD'ed. Dead on arrival."

"So — did that give you pause?"

Pause? Smithy's death from a heroin overdose certainly gave *him* pause, ultimate end of the line. "I've been too sick, too out of cigarettes, too oh, poor me, for any long-term pausing." Beyond this: rehab, halfway, better than a refrigerator box under a bridge. Not going to mention that his disability money is in limbo, that there's an eviction situation looming, that he and his mother are incommunicado. Possible she's even sent Jacobs a carefully revised epistle: how for the good of them both, she's dropping out of the drama.

"What's up with your NA sponsor in all this?"

"He leaves messages I don't return. He knocks; I don't answer."

"And Twelve Step? How are you feeling about that?"

"My story? Double pass."

"Well, that's why I think this new rehab may be a good thing for you. Onango Valley uses a nontraditional approach to treatment. In other words it doesn't use Twelve Step."

"Place allow cigarette breaks?" Not that he's got any cigarettes.

"Yes," Jacobs says. Jacobs lifts a yellow paperback and a few loose sheets from his desk drawer. He pushes them across the divide.

the small book: A Revolutionary Alternative for Overcoming Alcohol and Drug Dependence

Jacobs relaxes back in his chair, his "up to you" position. "Onango Valley uses Rational-Emotive Behavioral Therapy. REBT. I thought you might want to look it over while you're on your own in detox. See what you think."

He does not even glance at any of the words on the sheets. Instead he folds the papers and places them, with the book, in his jacket pocket. "Well," he says.

"You know how to get there?"

"Get there?"

Jacobs smiles. "Where the hospital is." He nods. "I'll tell them you're on your way."

Jacobs rises. He does too. He places the mug over by the coffeemaker. His hands have calmed down. When he turns back, Ben Jacobs is writing something on a note card. "My cell phone," he says. "For the tunnel or just to give me a report on the snow in Buffalo."

He sees Tess's truck below in the parking lot, but she can't see him. He pulls his hood back onto his head, tugs on the edges. Then he uses the corner of the yellow book to sift through the second layer of butts in the bucket by the door. Sand has already been picked over by some other lost soul. He dusts off the one healthy remain. Filter doesn't look too nasty. He lights up and leans against the rail, watches Luke's brown nose sniffing from one window, Queenie's pug face out the other. There's a white flash of something through the windshield. He takes a few steps down and leans over the rail. Carla's in the front seat, her leg cast across Tess's lap. She must have just picked her mother up at the hospital. Tess up half the night taking her mother to Emergency to get her leg set after her fall down the stairs. Must be Carla blasted her way to a quick discharge even though Tess hoped they'd hold her for a day or two so she wouldn't have to deal with both of them at once. Going to be a long crowded ride to Tremont.

He grinds out the butt and drops it, along with a handful of sandy stubs, into the folds of the papers Jacobs gave him. Going to be rolling his own from these leavings before long even if he can scrounge a pack or two from Carla. Maybe Tess will lift her smoking ban. Sympathy for her mother's accident, her mother's forlorn state since Smithy's death. Tess's relief at finally having Smithy, and now him, gone. He heads for the truck, the possibility that Carla may lay some Camels on him. He hasn't seen Carla since the night he banged on her back door and came away with nothing. One thing about Smithy's death, which soon followed, chaos so extreme up on the hill, his drug debt seems to have disappeared from the ledger.

He steps over the Burger King bag in the gutter, resists the urge to check it out in hope of a few fries. His stomach is so empty, it feels like it's caved in on his spine. Been so long since he's had anything but frozen hotdogs, he's actually looking forward to rehab cuisine. And going to be singing a new song. What was it Jacobs called it? Rational something. The Rational Rehab Rag.

As soon as Tess sees him, she starts the truck. He knocks on the glass where Carla's gray head is pressed. "Carla," he calls, "I'm going to open your door for a second."

Tess takes hold of her mother's hand and pulls her forward enough so Carla doesn't fall backwards. He releases the catch on the back door and squeezes himself and his bag onto the seat between the two dogs, and then leans over the front and Carla, neither of them smelling their best, and wrestles the door shut. "Clowns in a phone booth," he says.

"Clowns," Tess says. "You've got that right." But she isn't laughing. Tess not at her best either. They all look like candidates for a meth lab lineup.

"I've got a bed at Onango Valley in Tremont. Maybe an hour's drive. Sounds like it's better than that place in Utica." He catches Tess's eye in the rearview. "I owe you big time."

"My pleasure," she tells the mirror.

Carla has not spoken. Her head is back against the window, her eyes closed. She's the color of someone laid out on the embalming table, her hands across her chest, both wrists wrapped in her Velcro braces. Her cast goes halfway up her thigh. Her toes jutting out in front of the steering wheel look swollen and a little blue, but flawlessly painted a subtle shade of red.

"God," she moans and shifts a little.

"Pain?" he says.

"Pain."

"Are they giving you anything?"

"Tylenol."

"Extra Strength?"

He and Carla laugh. "I'm off everything," Carla says. "Everything. On my own."

He hopes she doesn't mean nicotine too. He checks to see if the ashtray is a little pulled out. Not looking good. "How long do you have to be in the cast?"

Tess flashes him a rearview. Her BS meter always running as well. Knows his small talk has a motive.

Carla opens her eyes and looks at him for the first time. "Six weeks," she says. "Lucky it wasn't my right leg. No way you could have jammed me in then."

Tess pats her mother's cast. "There, there," she says.

They are all quiet now, just the breathing of the dogs. The world racing by is gray, the air full of winter coming on. Queenie collapses against his shoulder, his legs numb from the weight of Luke asleep across his lap. Trying to write a letter under these all-of-the-above conditions may force him to blow his human-decency cover. No way he can do it on the top of Luke's head. And it has got to be done in a letter, not on the phone. He knows what he wants to say, the words scrawling his mind for days. Simple and brief. He strokes Luke's ears. Nothing silkier than Lab ears. He pulls on his collar to rouse him. Luke turns and gives him the total treatment, the full plead of his liquid brown eyes. "Sorry, buddy, but you've got to get up." Luke rises, manages to turn his hundred-plus pounds, and applies his nose to the few inches of open window. Queenie accommodates him and gathers air on the other side.

He breaks the spine on the yellow paperback to form a flat surface. Turns the bright blue title upside down so it doesn't stare up at him from his lap. He pulls out the papers Jacobs gave him, careful not to dump the butts when he peels away the bottom sheet, then smoothes the page out, with the blank side up. Good that the back says "Onango Valley Hospital — Rational-Emotive Behavioral Therapy" on the top, a kind of certification that he is where he says he is, proof that he's stepping into the rehab river what must be at least his fifth time. That, in itself, will offer some assurance. "Either of you have a pen or a pencil? Actually a pencil would be better."

"In the glove compartment," Tess says.

Carla reaches in, locates a pencil, and passes it back. A pencil with a sharp point and an eraser. But he cannot write this letter without the accompanying support of a cigarette. "I want to write a letter for you to give to my mom, but I need a nicotine jolt to crash the barrier." Tess's rearview eyes say he's registered a ten on the con. Tess looks at *her* mother.

"Fine by me," Carla says and pulls out a pack of Juicy Fruit from her pocket.

"Smoke 'em if you've got 'em," Tess tells him.

When he doesn't immediately light up, Carla pushes a stick of gum over the seat. "No thanks," he says.

"Gave up the cigarettes too," Carla announces, "but with Juicy Fruit at the ready, I don't miss it at all." She bursts into her old Carla laugh.

"Would you be willing to close your window for a minute while I roll a few of my own?" Tess hesitates for a second, then obliges without comment. He reaches over and puts up Luke and Queenie's windows to all but a life-saving crack. He retrieves the folded paper and begins to rip apart the butts, pushing each spill of tobacco into a little mound. Carla and Tess covertly eye his operation. He scoops up the bits of trash and gives these to the wind out the crack in Luke's window, then sets the second piece of paper on his bag in case he wants to make a kind of envelope. Next he retrieves a small leather Bible from his other pocket; the gold leaf of its edges gives off a flash.

Carla's eyes widen. "Mark?" she says.

He's sure he's got Tess's attention. He could say, Now for my first miracle, but better to proceed as though this is business as usual. He opens to Revelation, a section he's already used, and folds one of the tissue-thin pages back tight against the center binding, creases it with his fingernail, then oh so carefully tears it away straight down the fold. He repeats the process until there are four perfect sheets. He folds these sheets in half, runs his nail over the crease, and again tears along that edge. Then he places the Bible back in his pocket, ready when needed: a dandy source of papers or . . . irrational therapy.

For his benefit, Tess has slowed down to forty. He sprinkles the right amount of tobacco down the center of all those warnings, rolls a cigarette and dampens the edge with a flick of his tongue, pinches off the few shreds. Whole phrases run up the sides of the cylinder: *turned to see the voice that spoke to me; His eyes were like a flame of fire; the time is near.* Maybe this dude John is off his meds. He rolls three more cigarettes and wraps them in the remaining Bible pages, places the small packet solidly in one corner of his sweatshirt pocket. Get him through a few hours of the first day of his life. Again. He cranks the dogs' windows open enough for them to get their noses out. And just as Tess does the same, a rush of air sails the sheet sitting on his bag into the front to rest on Carla's chest.

Her eyes open. "Airmail," she says.

"A little bedside reading from the clinic. Tells about the rehab program at Onango Valley."

"Okay if I check it out?" she says. She pulls her reading glasses from her bag. "You never know."

"Be my guest." He places the point of his pencil on the paper and, without too much jiggle, writes *10/29/02* — more reassurance; then he lights up. The final words of *I have the keys of Death and of Hades* flare up, turn to ash. He takes the smoke down and down.

WELCOME TO TREMONT

He reads the letter over. Half a page. Everything he's able to say now. He signs his name. No love. She won't be up for that yet after his accusations on the phone. Then he goes back and adds *Your son* right before his signature.

Blue hospital signs. Tess takes the turn wide and a little too fast. The dogs lean into him. Only have to keep whistling a happy tune for a few more blocks, get through the bon voyage. The goodbye to Luke.

Carla scooches herself up. "Listen to this," she says.

"Maybe not, Mamo." Tess shoots him an appraising look. Last few seconds before good riddance and she doesn't want anything to jeopardize the departure.

"Hit me," he says.

"'One. You are responsible for your own emotions and actions.'"

He reaches down, pulls his bag free and places it on his lap.

"'Two. Your harmful emotions and dysfunctional behaviors are the product of your irrational thinking.'"

Tess makes a left at the next sign. He sees the hospital, small, red brick, looking down over the town.

"'Three. You can learn more realistic views and, with practice, make them part of you.'"

He'll go inside and then, when the truck makes the turn, he'll step back out and have a last smoke.

"'Four.' Now listen, this is the last one. 'You'll experience a deeper acceptance of yourself and greater satisfactions in life by developing a reality-based perspective.'" Carla passes the sheet back.

"My gift to you," he says and begins to lift his body for the jump. Geronimo.

"Humm," Carla says, and tucks the paper in her pocket. "I'm taking all the help I can get." Tess pulls up to the Emergency entrance. "Want me to hobble out on my crutches and pretend I'm your mother? Build immediate sympathy for your plight."

"I need to make this quick," he says. "Hit the ground running. But, good for you, Carla, looks like you're getting there and I'm wishing you well."

"Thanks. You too," she says.

He hands Tess the letter. "Can you give this to my mother?"

Tess takes it and tucks it under the truck visor. "I haven't talked to her all month, but she's supposed to be back tomorrow."

Hit the ground running. "Likely I'm going to go to a halfway up near Buffalo in a few weeks. They'll become my payee and then I'll send you some of what I owe you."

"Good. Here." She hands him a carton of cigarettes from under her seat.

He laughs, feels his mouth beaming. "How I appreciate this," he says.

"Yep." Tess takes Carla's hand and pulls her forward. He leans over and opens Carla's door.

"You have to stay, Luke." He hauls himself out and turns, holds Luke against him for a minute. "I'll be back to get you, buddy." He closes the doors and sets off at a run up the walk. He knows Luke is watching him get smaller, smaller, small. Watching him disappear.

Part IV

FEBRUARY

10/29/02

I don't think anyone will understand what happened that night in Aaron's cabin, but I do know this: I left him there even though he begged me to stay. It's taken me this long to accept that and begin to forgive myself. I can't do it alone. There's a lot more to Aaron's story than you'll ever know. Unless you get to know me, you'll die without ever knowing your children.

Once I prove I can stay clean, I'm asking you to at least give me a section of the land to build on. I am no longer interested in going out into the world. My brother and my father completely let me down. All I can say now is Fuck 'em. This thing can be turned around and I know how to do it. I'll be back. You're going to have to take a risk.

Your son MARK

30 : Gulf

Richard leans against the condo railing, swats at a no-see-um. She feels the heaviness descending. Though he almost never opens the topic for discussion, he's been weighing his treatment options for months. She readies herself: "bringing it up" is about to happen.

"The thing is," he says, "it's a total crapshoot."

She reaches over and cups her hand around his warm calf. Waits for him to go on, to finally make the decision, here in the strange dark of the Gulf of Mexico, twelve hundred miles from their more familiar territory, the daily routines they've chiseled out over the years. Gotten the friction down to occasional. Especially these last four months with no rescue calls from Mark. No calls at all.

Richard shifts his leg, turns a little her way. "Those doctors at Hillside don't know any more than I do what's the best alternative." She traces the bony ridges of his knee. Waits for him to go on.

Night on the water. She listens to the swash of the tide, the soft slap of it against the flood wall below the condo deck. Takes in the gusts of briny sea air. Far across the water, the red and green beacons blink in the channel almost in line with the closest island. And off to the left, twenty miles away, the white glow of two towers, the nuclear plant at Dawson River. People in Crystal Key sometimes speculate on how long fallout from an accident would take to reach here.

Richard walks to the end of the deck. Not even his shirt is visible now. There's only his voice. "Every alternative couched in disclaimers: 'sometimes,' 'may,' 'research studies are in progress,' some doctors recommend this, some recommend the other. Or combining all of the therapies. Therapies." Nothing new here. Almost the exact same words she's heard before. Only now accompanied by the sound of his hand slapping against his skin. "'In the end,' they actually say that, 'in the end the decision will lie with the patient.' All bullshit."

"And you didn't have any more confidence in what they recommended at Walter Reed?"

"Fucking bugs," he says, and goes back inside.

Movement wakes her. Richard's arms and legs in mid-flail. She reaches across and takes hold of his hand, squeezes: you will choose; you are going to be okay. He *will* soon choose, but the okay part is full of disclaimers as well. To avoid being caught by a left in the night, she once again curls as far away as possible without herself dropping over. There's the roar of wind, the smack of palms brushing the walls, the whole condo gives a little: built not to resist. Below, the heavy metal table scrapes inch by inch across the deck, backs up against the rail. A flash of lightning and minutes later, thunder. A big storm's coming.

A ringing in the dark. For a second she doesn't know what it is. The wind still blowing, the rain hard against the balcony windows. "Oh god," she says. The phone and she knows who it is. How could he have gotten the number? She gropes toward the little red light of the cordless and even as she lifts it to press Talk, she makes her way down the stairs, heads for the half-bathroom. Eleven o'clock. Not the middle of the night. Maybe it isn't dire.

"It's me," he says.

She closes the door, lowers the lid on the toilet and sits.

"I hope you weren't sleeping."

"Yes." Yes, what? The only information she really wants is to learn that he's still three thousand miles away from "I'll be back."

"This isn't a trouble call. I'm doing okay. I just wanted to get the number for the dentist. Thought I'd better get my teeth cleaned. I don't want to go through that gum torture again."

"You aren't in Portland, staying with your cousin Kerry?"

"I'm in Marwick, staying with Rozmer. Clean for four months."

She breathes, comes up with a calm tone. "Good for you," she says. "That's a long time." What she wants is to get off as quickly as possible, taking this unqualified good news with her. "It's the Walton Dental Clinic. It's in the yellow pages. They've got a big ad."

"Rozmer's my rep-payee now. No smoking allowed. Haven't had a cigarette in fifteen days. Except a few puffs now and then when I can dig a butt out of the bucket by the library. Off the meds too. Forever."

No counsel. Don't open any doors. "Good . . . that you have a place to stay."

"I got your number from those people you've let live in our house. They seem a little wacked. You left the desktop computer there. That was not a smart thing to do. Where's Luke?"

He must have actually gone to the house. She'll have to call the tenants tomorrow. "He's with Marna."

"The place down there doesn't allow dogs?"

"They're allowed, but it seemed like a better idea to leave him with Marna."

"I'd like to go see him."

Go see Luke? Involve Marna in this?

There's a screeching sound, something opening, closing. "I'm going to see if I can get visitation rights. Going to give Marna a call. Don't worry; not tonight. Tomorrow."

"Okay." Marna's good at saying no if she needs to. Beyond Mark's voice, there's the sound of traffic, trucks passing. He must be calling from a pay phone near a highway. He's together enough to have a phone card, but why isn't he calling from Rozmer's?

"Rozmer's wife would never allow Luke to stay with me. Not even a visit. Too bad because Gabe loves Luke."

She does not want to hear bad things about Rozmer's wife.

Mark drums on something metal close to the receiver. "And you know what else, Wolfie died. Wolfie died and Sammi got married. She actually sent me a wedding invitation in Portland. P.S. Wolfie died. Sammi married and Wolfie dead all in one envelope."

"Oh, Mark . . ."

"Have you seen my Rumi book, my *Portable Jung*? They're not in the barn, not on the bookshelves in the living room. You left a lot of books with the tenants. Not a good idea either to let them see the titles."

"They invited you in the house?" She does not ask the real question. Were the tenants there? He doesn't answer, but she's almost positive Tess would not have given him a key. Maybe she'll have to call Tess at Carla's as well. The return to the need to jam her fist in the dike.

"Well, I just wanted to let you know I'm back and doing okay."

"I'm glad to hear that," she says. "I'll have the Rumi and Jung sent to you from Amazon Used Books. Are there any other books you need? Because it isn't a good idea for you to go to the house. The tenants have a long-term lease and it says we won't come on the property without a prior phone call."

"Got to go," he says. "The pay phone's eating up my minutes."

"All right." She stands, prepares to press End. More drumming.

"The only really bad thing about living in Marwick is the crows."

"The crows?"

"They're always watching me."

She makes her way back through the dark. She'll call Marna tomorrow, leave her a heads-up message on her machine if she's already gone to work. Marna cares about Mark. It might even be a good thing. Have to warn her about the crows, have to do that live over the phone. That he's reading: not a good sign either. Always a sign of mania coming on these days. She slips onto her side with as little movement as possible, but she can tell Richard is awake. "Mark's staying with Rozmer. Says he's doing okay. He just wanted the name of the dentist." She doesn't wait for a response. She already knows Richard is not going to say anything. The wind has died back some, the palms no longer brush the windows, the building has stopped moving. The shoe has dropped. They both lie awake for a long time.

The place next to her is empty. Richard's already up. It's late. She'd like to go on sleeping. She sits, pulls on her nightgown. Her body feels as if it's been caught in a bus door and dragged down the road. A month of yoga stretches will be required to release her from the lock of one phone call. The storm is over. The sun is bright. There's the fishy odor of something dead in the mud flat, the smell of hot, dusty carpet. From the balcony windows she sees that the tide is so far out, there's a spit of sand that extends almost to the island. Portly senior citizens are wandering barefoot out there, carrying buckets. The gulls wheel about, scream. They all rise up from the condo dock and then resettle. A few minutes later they do it again. No apparent cause.

She listens. Richard is making strange noises below. Going in and out, up and down the outside stairs. Something's up. Something presses on her chest. She pulls on the clothes she wore yesterday and brushes her teeth. Downstairs she watches Richard moving about below. His truck is backed out of the garage, the tailgate is down. He has disassembled his bike and is now maneuvering the frame in. She scans the room. His book is gone from the little table by the La-Z-Boy, his rolls of quarters from the shelf, his sweatshirt and raincoat from the hooks. She sits down. Waits. When she hears him on the stairs, she opens the door. "What?" she says.

He passes her, goes to the closet and drops his mud sneakers into a plastic bag. "I'm going back to Danford."

"You're going back to Danford? What do you mean you're going back to Danford?"

"I called Hillside this morning. I'm going to start radiation Monday." All the while he is opening drawers, rifling through.

"You're going to start treatments Monday?" He doesn't answer. He's looking under things, the couch, his chair. Down in the cushions. "Did you lose something?" Again he doesn't respond. "You're going back to start radiation treatments. Well, then, of course I'm going with you. You have to give me time to get my stuff packed."

He opens the door again, starts toward the stairs. "You're not going with me. I'll come back down to get you next month, end of March." She starts to follow. He signals for her to go back. "Get yourself some breakfast. I only have a few more things to put in the car and then we'll talk."

Richard sits across from her, a folder marked MEDICAL RECORDS 1993–2003 in front of him. He does not look tired. In fact, tanned and trim from his bike rides, long walks, he is, as they say, the picture of health. The handsome older man, his loving gaze turned her way, like on those cruise ship ads. "The treatments are going to take five weeks. I'm going to get up every morning, drive to the hospital. Each treatment only takes a couple of minutes. Hillside has the latest, best equipment to beam in on specific areas of the prostate to minimize tissue damage, any side effects. I've thoroughly researched that. Everything."

"But I thought you said they don't know for sure that the recurrence is even in the prostate area."

"That's the crapshoot part. But from everything I've read, what the urologist says, this is the best number to bet on. So far the only signs are showing up in the PSA. The number's still small, but doubling, and even though there's no detectable tumor, it seems likely, for a shoot in the dark, the prostate's the best place to aim."

"God, Richard."

"Yep, why I've had such a time deciding."

"I want to go with you. Be available to drive you if you don't feel up to it."

"I'm going to feel up to it." He takes her hand. "It's going to be better for me to know you're here painting, walking the beach. We've already paid the rent for this place. I am not going to be good company. The best way for me to deal with this is to get involved in a big project, come back from the hospital and go at it. If the weather's not good, I'm going to finally tile the basement floor, but if it's a warm, sunny March . . ."

"Be real," she says.

"If it is, I've got outside jobs I'm looking forward to. Either way fall into bed at night, tired, my mind clear."

The phone. "Oh, god," she says. "I'm not going to answer it." It rings and rings. Richard takes the folder, closes the door decisively. From the window she sees him raise the hood, pull out the oil stick. She goes down, the phone still ringing behind her.

"And that's the other thing," he says. He is not looking at her, is turned away to get a wrench from his tool box. "Whether you're here or in Danford, he's going to call. He's going to call and it's all going to start up again. I don't need that right now."

"I know."

"Chances are he'll even end up down here."

"That is not happening."

He does look at her now. "If he wants to come down, he's going to chip away at you. And if I'm here, you're going to chip away at me to say it's okay."

Richard is wrong: Mark is not going to call and call. She has changed the phone number, made it unlisted. Even the tenants will have to go through Marna. And now she must let Mark know.

Mark, the Rumi Collection and *Portable Jung* should come to Rozmer's P.O. Box in a week or so. It's good to know that you have a secure place to live and that you have had such a long time of not using. Of course, after a continued long period of recovery, if you are able to do some part-time work and to save money toward us having a place built on the other side of the brook, I will help you with that.

For now I am painting and working on becoming less anxious. To help with that, I won't be available by phone. If you need to reach me, Rozmer has my email address or you can write to me at P.O. Box 271, Crystal Key, FL 32455.

Love, Mom

The other letters attempting to tell Mark not to call are crumpled on her drawing board. It never feels okay not to try to help. When Mark first told her how Aaron begged him to stay that night, about his terrible guilt for leaving, for a moment she wished she could have been the last one in the cabin, the one who left Aaron there alone, wished she could lift Mark's burden onto herself, but right away, something in her drew back from that wish: no, no, how could she live with that?

"It's fine with me if Mark wants to come and visit Luke," Marna says. She must be in her studio. There's the echo of all that space. "Luke will be thrilled. He's been a little down in the mouth. Tearing after Sheba the only game in town."

"And the business with the crows?"

"Doesn't sound good. But the fact that he's not drugging —and likely that's the truth or Rozmer wouldn't be giving him shelter — that's such a positive. I'm sure Rozmer's got his eye on him."

"He says no more meds ever."

"Here's the thing, Del, trust that Rozmer and I are up for it, that we'll give it our considerable best. We love Mark, but we've got some distance. So I'm not going to call to fill you in. How's the egg tempera feeling? I haven't worked that carefully since grad school."

"It's lovely. The illumination. You can do 'looking down through water' at pebbles, fish, that kind of clarity. I'm excited to start on the horseshoe crabs once they return. I think of you painting Hoop."

"I've got him with his head leaning into the side of a mostly black Holstein, biggest bag I've ever seen. Fastened my drawing paper right to the barn wall, cow shit and all. And Richard?"

"He begins his treatments Monday."

For the first time she punches up "prostate cancer recurrence" on the internet. Until this moment, the few facts she has have always been filtered through Richard. Pages and pages of sites flash up. Richard was right, it's full of "mays." A lot of "ifs" as well. But there's so much specific information she's never known about Richard's original diagnosis and treatment in 1994, she can't figure out which "if" fits Richard: Was Richard's original Gleason grade below 7, the PSA before surgery less than 10? Were the margins clear when they completed the operation? Without that knowledge, she doesn't know which set of "maybes" to drop into. She does know that when the residents who'd assisted the surgeon emerged from the operating room after five hours, they looked as if they'd been run over. As they huddled together waiting for the elevator, one said to the others that he'd never seen so much blood. They didn't realize that the woman who sat waiting on the bench was listening.

All of the sites talk about hormonal therapy. "However, there is data available that the early addition of hormonal therapy to whatever local therapy is given may significantly increase life expectancy." Why hadn't Richard chosen to have hormonal therapy once his PSA began to indicate a possible recurrence? Why not now? She knows Richard is already aware of all this, but has decided not to go that route. She knows he would not welcome a call urging him to reconsider. She reads on. When she comes to the words "impending spinal collapse," she hits Close. She gets on her bike and rides out to the airstrip, the shining Gulf on her left all the way.

Though she often hears their raucous caws in the distance, crows never come to the deck. Not even when she strings hunks of bread along the railing. These, gone in minutes, swooped up by the gulls and boat-tailed grackles. Not even when she lays out the fat she's trimmed from the chicken thighs after the great white egret wings in, does his daily mindful tai chi stalk back and forth until she brings him something raw and wet. This egret, who will follow her into the living room if she doesn't remember to slide the screen door shut. She's not had much interest in the crows up until now.

She's been working in egg tempera all month, the egret's trailing white wedding plumage, his long yellow beak's bright green streak much more compelling than the sooty crow, an ink-and-pencil bird. But this morning, here one is, only a few feet from her, alone on the railing, facing toward the foggy sea, one leg slightly twisted, perhaps from an injury or a birth defect. She moves softly to the open window and as she lifts her pad and pencil, one black eye turns her way.

The phone does not ring. She draws. She's getting some work ready for a group show in Crystal Key along with six other artists in a critique group she's been part of all the years they've been coming down here. She's had a few of the memory pieces matted and framed.

She and Richard seldom talk. She emails him daily, humorous, upbeat messages: the return of the white pelicans who sit in rows out on the flats, all facing in the same direction; how the two horned owlets peer down at her from an old osprey nest each time she rides her bike through the cemetery; that three dolphin cruise by daily, beating the water as they form a circle to herd the mullet. Always the doings of the egret. Richard's emails are brief and to the point: ten treatments into the total twenty-five and he feels no negative effects. These first days of March have been sunny and in the high sixties: perfect outdoor project weather. He's rented a big bulldozer and is doing major excavations, the definitive solution to all the drainage problems.

Then, the emails begin:

> I hate to risk using the internet because I feel certain those people at the house have hacked into our system and that it will be all used as evidence against me. But sending mail takes too long and probably is no safer. The thing is, the shadow has the most disturbing influence. To become conscious of the shadow involves recognizing the dark aspects of the personality as present and real.

Jung. Must be he's gotten the books. Evidence of what?

I have warned both Marna and Rozmer that they are not to give out any information. No point in saying anything to Rozmer's wife since I already know she's part of it. Yesterday she placed a black frame by the door where I'd left my basketball. A frame. Do you get it?

Dear Mark, in order to lessen my anxiety, I have joined a Zen monastery where there is no contact with the outside world. She leaves a message on Marna's machine: "Marna, if Mark is starting to call you, starting to come by your house uninvited, give him my number. I just received a very disturbing email: extreme paranoia. There's no reason why you should be pulled into this further. I'll call you tonight."

Rozmer will be working at this hour and she doesn't really want to call him anyway since Mark might answer the phone. And she doesn't want to email Rozmer either. Mark might have Rozmer's ID number. Speaking of paranoia. And the tenants? She doesn't want to frighten them. They must already wonder what's going on from her last vague call about changing her phone number, that they should contact Marna if they needed to get in touch. And now these emails are going to pour down the wire into her machine, into her mind. Really just as threatening in their own way. Maybe more so. The cool of words composed more daring than words spoken. And of course she must answer in a way that doesn't escalate the situation. From previous experience she knows (1) not to suggest he go to the hospital and get on meds, and (2) not to suggest that the delusions are delusions.

Mark, it sounds as if things are difficult for you right now, a frightening time. I think Rozmer often has a good understanding of you and what's going on. I hope you are able to trust his perspective, that you will let him be a help to you. Love, Mom

Immediately a return message:

Rozmer is away at a week-long training. My presence in this house is unwelcome. Today I found two crow feathers and a red mitten planted beneath the basketball net. Red and black. My arrest is imminent.

Then before she can consider a response — and what the hell response might there be to such a message? — another email:

Flies will gather around the wound. The wound is your own dark hole. I have to relocate immediately. I'm going to ask Marna if I can stay with her until the danger passes.

If Mark were using drugs, calling her for money, she'd have the right to go into the monastery, wouldn't she? But now he is sick, sick and clean, heading toward the beyond, and it's looking as if this long time of calm is over. He is her son, not Marna's. She clicks on Reply:

My number is (546) 342-6721. Call collect if you need to. Do not call Marna. Love, Mom

She takes the phone out on the deck. Two o'clock: Marna will be at work, but she can leave a message on her machine. "Give Mark my number if he calls. I'm going to try to get him to go to the hospital. I'll call you around six." The phone doesn't ring. She waits. The phone doesn't ring. The gulls scream and settle. Scream and settle.

Finally at 5:45, the ring comes. "I'm at the Quickway on Main. I can't talk long because they're tracing my calls. I've moved out of Rozmer's. I've got all my stuff. Could you work it out with Marna for me to stay at her house for a few days? Maybe they won't find me there."

"Mark, I think the best thing is for you to come down here where you'll be safe, where you can walk on the beach and get some quiet rest. Richard is not here. He's undergoing treatments for the prostate cancer and he won't be back until the end of the month."

There's a long silence, except for the sound of traffic. "Mark?"

"I'm thinking," he says. "Six red cars just went by. Listen, surely nobody believes this WMD horseshit? Oil, this is about oil. And kicking Saddam's ass. Eight red cars in five minutes. Proof enough for me."

"Mark, I think this is a good place for you to be. You'll be away from all that."

"Nobody's ever going to be away from all that ever again. But, yes," he says, "Crystal Key. Maybe for now they won't know I'm there."

"But Mark, I am only going to arrange the bus ticket, the taxi ride from Gainesville, if you're willing to let Marna take you to the Crisis Center to be admitted for a week or two until the world becomes less dangerous, until it will be less frightening on the bus." There's a banging right next to her ear. "Mark?"

"I am not going to the hospital. I am not going to go back on meds. Zombie out and get fat and diabetic and lose all my teeth like those people in the halfway house — why I left there to go stay with Kerry in Portland in the first place. They'll commit me, zap me full of Thorazine, ship me off to Langston Psych."

"I think Crystal Key is a safe, quiet place for you. Your room has its own deck and bathroom, its own entry with locks on both the doors. The Gulf is only a few feet away."

"What about the crows?"

"A beautiful white egret comes to beg food every day."

Another long silence. "All right."

"You will let Marna take you to Crisis for an evaluation? You'll let them admit you if they think it will help you feel more safe?"

"Yes."

"Then just before you're discharged, I'll arrange the bus ticket to Gainesville, the taxi ride here. I'm going to call Marna now. Don't go anywhere. Call me back in fifteen minutes."

"I need a cigarette."

"I'll arrange for Marna to buy you a carton." She dials Marna. Having Mark come to Crystal Key for a few weeks is better than her going home. Mark could not stay at Richard's when he's discharged. Probably he wouldn't even go to Crisis without the lure of the Gulf.

Marna answers. Of course she's willing to pick him up and

take him to Hillside. She'll bring Luke along for moral support. She'll buy a carton of the right kind of cigarettes at the cheap smoke shop. Once he's been admitted, she'll call. Not to worry, Marna tells her, sometimes you have to wait for hours before the Crisis people even get to you, but of course she knows all that. "Yes," Marna says, "this seems like a good plan. He's not drugging. That's the main thing."

At 6:45 the phone rings. "Marna's here. She's going to take me to Hillside. She said to tell you she'll call you later. Could you email Rozmer at his workshop and arrange to get my March money? Tell him to come visit me when he gets back. I know what you're going to do now, Mom. Luke says hello."

GREYHOUND TICKET CENTER:
MARWICK, NY, TO GAINESVILLE, FL

Departs	Arrives	Duration	Transfers	Carrier Schedule
06:05 am	10:45 am	1d, 4h, 40m	2	PHK0705
07:55 am	08:55 pm	1d, 13h, 0m	2	ADT0107
12:50 pm	09:15 pm	1d, 8h, 25m	3	ADT0136

Yellow Cab: 775-2460, $75.00 from Gainesville to Crystal Key

The "transport loom," as Mark calls it, calms her. Now she knows there's a way for him to get here that's manageable. Next she clicks on "Musician's Friend" and orders the same inexpensive acoustic bass and practice amp Mark has had her order several times before. The same drum pad and sticks. A Spalding leather basketball. Express delivery. So important for Mark to have something to do that he cares about. And, what the heck, she orders Pumas too. No doubt he'll arrive down and out. She is going to have to tell Richard, but not until Mark actually steps out of that taxi, since of course he may not arrive at all. But if he does, no matter what Richard says or even if he makes no response, the message will be, He calls; you jump.

She keeps the phone in her pocket as she gets the room she's been using as her studio ready for Mark. She brings down a chaise lounge and opens it out on what will be Mark's deck. She sits in it and sees what Mark will see: the ibises' ribbon of flight going out to the island for the night, the last sun flashing off their white wings. What she wants to hear more than anything else is Marna's voice saying, He's been admitted. By nine o'clock she's transferred all her materials and paintings out to the garage. Surely Marna will call any minute. She arranges clean blue towels on the rack behind the toilet and pulls the shower curtain so the magnets grip along all the edges, then checks the room again to make sure there's nothing red and nothing black. No weird numbers like 666 on any of the decor.

Dark now. Back in the balcony, she doesn't think she'll be able to sleep, but she stretches out on the bed anyway, the phone right by her ear. She moves her hand over to Richard's side; his warm, sweet body is not there.

The phone. Ten o'clock. It takes her a few seconds to find it under the pillow.

"Del? Mark is here at my house. He's sleeping. He's doing okay. Hillside would not admit him."

"They wouldn't admit him?"

"They said he did not appear to be a danger to himself or others. They did not have any beds and they didn't think it warranted transporting him to Albany. Of course they wouldn't let me go in for the evaluation and they wouldn't tell me much, but from what I've gathered from spending the last few hours with him, he's able to completely veil the psychotic symptoms. No weird images whatsoever to me. Other than being incredibly thin, he seems normal. Still handsome. Maybe a bit piercing, the look in his eyes, but he seldom looks at me straight on. I don't remember him ever doing a lot of that."

"No," she says. "And what does he say about Florida?"

"He says if you'll let him, he wants to take the bus. Tomorrow, if you can put it together. He says he thinks it will be the best thing for him to do. And Del, when I asked him about the drugging, he did look at me and he says he has not used for four months. I believe him."

She breathes and presses her hand against her head. "There's a bus at twelve fifty tomorrow. Thirty-two hours and three transfers. One of them in New York. What do you think?"

"It breaks my heart to look at him. So thin and lost. Harder for me to be tough with Mark than it is with my own son. Maybe that's because I know I'm not going to wake up in the morning with my TV set gone."

"Let me think for a minute," she says. She gets up. The Gulf sky is full of stars, the Milky Way, a streak of light. "Can you put him on the bus tomorrow at twelve fifty? I'll call in the morning once I get it arranged. How's Luke?"

She sits on the deck all morning once everything is set. She's too jumpy to do anything but watch the tide going out. 1:05. The phone rings. "I just put him on the bus," Marna says.

Her shoulders let down. "In about thirty-five hours he'll be here. If he doesn't do some kind of drug deal in New York with the hundred dollars of food money."

"I'm pretty sure he's not going to do that." Marna laughs. "Because he's got a guardian angel with him. Are you ready for this, Del?"

"No." No, she is not.

"He comes out of the bus station looking jubilant. He puts his duffel underneath. He comes and gives me a hug. Then he takes Luke's leash. 'I've got a pass to take Luke on the bus. American Disability Act. Richard's not at the condo and I'm sure my mom won't mind. Think of it, Luke and I playing take-away along the beaches of the Gulf. Thanks for everything,' he says, and he gets on the bus, with Luke, his service dog, heeling all the way. Waves to me until the bus turns the corner and disappears. What an artist."

Del stands on Mark's deck, leans over the rail. Low tide. The sand spit reaches the closest island. She can almost see them: Luke leaping for the orange Frisbee sailing through the last glow.

31 : Chant

THERE IT IS AGAIN: watching him. Same exact spot on the railing by his door every morning. The crow with the fucked-up leg. If he even blinks, that crow knows. Its black eye always turned toward the slit between the curtains. He could pin that slit closed, but then the crow would know even more. Of course they would pick a crow with a crippled leg to be their envoy: their black agent of doom. We know where you are.

Slowly, not to make a sound, she slides the screen to the deck open. A black bird whirs by, startles her. Both of them caught spying, Mark would say. It disappears into the palm trees. Please not that same crow again or she'll have to hear a thousand non-stop words about the goddamned thing the next time Mark permits contact. Without meds, what if he never comes out of this; what if the delusions go on and on? Another week and she'll be as bonkers as he is.

With the bird no longer watching, Mark opens the leather notebook again. Black. Of course black.

Christmas 1977

Dear Mark,
    Because this is the first Christmas since your father left us, we'd like to give you and Aaron some thoughts to remember about him — some nice, amusing, and happy things . . .

Left us. You bet. His grandparents gave Aaron a notebook exactly like this, except of course, his was maroon. Black and red. This notebook that he was sure was lost, but there it was right on top of a box in the barn when he was searching for Aaron's map. Right there on top of the box where they'd put it. Where they knew he couldn't miss it when he came back.

She leans forward just enough to peer down through the top deck's floorboards for Mark's dark head sticking out like a turtle. The sparkling Gulf fifteen feet away and the only time he opens his door is for a cigarette and then click, clack, both locks lock and he disappears back into that dark room. All night long too, that clicking and clacking. But at least he isn't smoking inside. The condo owners were steely about that.

He pushes the notebook behind the TV. Then he steps over Luke, moves away from his wheezing snores, and goes into the closet. Turns out it's the best place to hear what's going on upstairs. His mother was definitely walking around in the living room, but he can't hear her now. So much less chance of having to talk if he can time his cigarettes for when she's inside or out in the garage painting. Those are the best times because even if she doesn't actually creep down from her deck through the narrow opening, backwards, step by step on the steep stairs, to try to cheer him up or get him to eat a banana, he can always feel her *concern* tensing his air.

He checks the phone: tone sounds normal, but have to be careful because it's probably bugged. He checks the door: both locks are set. Too bad no smoking inside, but his mother is dug in on that one. If she smells smoke, well, it wouldn't be worth it. He pulls the curtain enough to make a quick check both ways down the beach. Empty, tides splashing the flood wall. Every time he has to lean out into the world, he risks being seen. Those two guys by the water tower last night, chances are good they're the same men from the bus station.

*   *   *

From the far end of the deck she sees Mark and Luke jogging in the distance, running in and out of the water. High tide. She gets the phone and brings it out to the deck so she can keep track of them. No Frisbee, but Luke is tearing around, bounding into the waves and then the brown dash of him returns. Two weeks since Mark arrived and virtually disappeared from view, but maybe, maybe, maybe this venture out in the light of day means something.

She gets Richard's machine, his "be brief" message. Richard's machine is set up so that if you aren't brief, it cuts you off. "I'm doing okay. Painting and riding my bike. Looks like it's warm and sunny in Danford too. Have you heard the geese yet? I'll call back tonight." Richard has made no reference to Mark since she emailed him two weeks ago explaining her reasons for having Mark come to Florida after all.

"Here's the big question for you, Luke: Why is everyone trying desperately to hang on to his own twisted concept of reality?" Luke looks back at him, his ears raised, his head cocked to the side. "That's why you're the best — you know to just let me talk. It's stressful when she puts up resistance. Even if she doesn't say anything, her eyes get that 'I don't believe you' glaze."

Mark wades into the water. "Got to thank her for the beach sandals though, ehh. Am I cool or what?" He scoops up a handful of water and drizzles it over Luke's head. "Okay, here's the other question: Why is everyone trying so desperately to grasp hold of someone else's twisted concept of reality?"

This time Luke keeps right on going. "Yeah, you're right. Enough of this bullshit."

At that Luke picks up a long stick of driftwood and carries it high, his tail a proud flag all the way to the condo.

"Okay, I'm going to do what you say, Luke, and give Rozmer a call."

Mark bends down a little so he can unlock the door without taking the shoelace-keyholder from around his neck. Little trick he learned from Careful Charlie and he hasn't locked himself out once since he got to Crystal Key.

Luke hangs by the garage: Let's go play some more.

"Yeah, we are going back. Take your moms for the surprise in a minute, but something we have to do first." He pulls the leather notebook from its hiding place and sticks it and the phone in the pocket of his shorts. He and Luke go out on the deck. He unfolds the canvas chair, another cool gift. Sits in it for the first time and puts his feet up on the rail. "Getting it together," he tells Luke, who settles in the shade behind the open door.

He flips the notebook to the right page, lights a cigarette, and dials Rozmer's number. If he gets Rozmer's wife, well, probably he'll hang up. If he gets his machine, well, maybe he'll go ahead and read this to him anyway and then call again later. He hears his mother's steps overhead.

She leans on the rail, watches Mark's feet beating out some tune against the boards below, feet that have been beating since he was a little boy. How I learned to drum, he's told her, every night in bed, I moved my feet.

"Hey," he calls up. "I'm just trying to get Rozmer. Stick around. Might be of interest to you as well," he says. "Then Luke and I have something we want to show you down by that abandoned houseboat."

Stick around? Definitely a new one. Now he's quiet. Probably listening to Rozmer's Word for the Day.

Rozmer's machine picks up. Mark leans in close. "'The presentation of one's story is a magic ritual that keeps the beast within under control, kind of an incantation that affords protection from evil.' Hey, buddy, if this is you and you don't want to leave a message, keep calling, I'm bound to pick up sooner than later."

"Rozmer. Something I want to read to you. It's from a notebook my grandparents gave me and Aaron in 1977, the Christmas after our father died. Introduction says they wanted to leave us with some happy memories. I've been reading it for the first time. Took me twenty-five years to get to it. Ready?

> When your father was about 10 months old, he was very imitative of sounds of every sort. He would laugh or cough exaggeratedly when anyone else did, and make a throaty noise to copy any motor sound, even the vacuum cleaner or the water pump. He was something of a clown, too. Before he could walk, he often raised up on all fours, legs stiff and head on the floor, looking back between his legs, sometimes picking up toys and playing with them in his hands with his head and feet as his 3-point anchor.

"More to follow. Grist for the incantation as you say. I'm not quite ready to give out the number here and since it's unlisted it won't be on your ID. But I'll be in touch. The noise in the tunnel's only coming through one speaker now. Haven't seen the crow in a couple of days. Earth to Gabe. How are you doing, buddy?"

The tide is so high they have to go by the road part of the way.

"Don't worry," Mark says, "it's something that'll make you happy."

Luke is in and out of the water. Every now and then checking back to make sure they're still with him.

Hot. Pelicans glide by high over their heads, for a moment blot out the sun. Here and there they detour around patches of gooey tar. No cars. Only a few people stretched on deck chairs by the Gulf Motel pool. Two men fish off the bridge, one with a baby in a carrier on his back. A great blue heron sits on the rocks, watches the fishing lines as they reel them in. The roof of the ravaged houseboat comes into view just below the sea wall.

"We're almost there," Mark says. "What do you think it is?"

"I have no idea. Not a dead shark or dolphin. Not a beached whale in these shallow waters. Something for me to draw."

Mark helps her climb down off the wall. Luke appears on the other side.

"There." He points. "What you've been waiting for."

"Oh," she says and goes up close. "Horseshoe crabs. Spawning."

Dozens of large females laying their eggs: many are almost completely dug in, moving mounds of sand all along the water's edge. Often three or four males waiting to fertilize the hundreds of eggs in each hole. Many more females are crawling forward out of the tide, with the much smaller males clasped to their backs.

"You know they're not really crabs at all," she says. "More related to spiders. Been at it for millions of years."

"Got the basics down," Mark says.

They walk along the beach. Luke stays well back from the horseshoes, regards them with suspicion. One of the largest females has tipped onto her back, her legs waving in the air, her tail switching back and forth leaving a fan of effort in the sand.

"Aaron should be here," Mark says. "He would have appreciated all the metaphorical possibilities. Especially all these puny males."

Mark reaches down, takes hold of the rim of the overturned female's helmet of a shell, slowly lifts her, and sets her right side up.

"You remember the time Dad picked up the hummingbird that had knocked itself out against the pole barn window? He had it cupped in his closed palm, sure it was dead. Trying to keep it from Coal's curious nose. Then he opened his hands to show us its red throat . . ."

"And it flew away."

Mark opens his hand and raises it to the blue sky so they can see the bird's ruby iridescence flash up again.

"You know what we ought to do?" he says. "We ought to write a book together. For god's sake, let's do something."

Epilogue : June

FIRST LIGHT. The surrounding hilltops are hidden by morning mist. The brook is silent now; only a few pools stand still beneath the sycamore roots. Across the brook, the meadow, locusts bloom all along the abandoned log road just beyond the old Cobb barn. The grandfather maple beside the stone house shades the loft and the kitchen below in summer-green light and spread out on the front lawn, dozens of spider-web handkerchiefs, their drops of dew ready to be jeweled by the first rays. Bursts of lavender phlox bank the path up to the gravestones. The hemlock woods beyond is dark.

If she still lived in this house, she'd hear the faint scratching, the muffled chittering and muted cries. She'd rise from her bed in her upstairs room to watch through the long landing window, the flutter of hundreds of dark wings wheeling about, their desperation and confusion at not being able to gain entry. She'd watch for many long minutes the air, full of the flying commotion of all those pregnant mothers with their now pregnant children, and then, just as the sun rises orange over the trees, she'd see them vanish.

Acknowledgments

I wish to express my thanks to my first mentors, Charlotte Zoë Walker and Russell Banks. Always I am grateful for the comments of my West Kortright Centre and Cedar Key groups. My thanks also for the gifts of time without interruption granted to me by Blue Mountain Center, Hedgebrook, Ucross, and the Saltonstall Foundation. Thanks also to my agent, Alice Tasman, for her availability and enthusiasm, and to my editor, Ann Patty, for her invaluable help. Finally, much appreciation goes to the other writers who have critiqued the work along the way: Mermer Blakeslee, Robbin Thompson, Sue Spivack, Forrest Bachner, Bertha Rogers, Wayne Somers, Stephanie Dickinson, and Alice Lichtenstein.